WHEEL OF FATE

INHERITANCE, BOOK TEN

AK FAULKNER

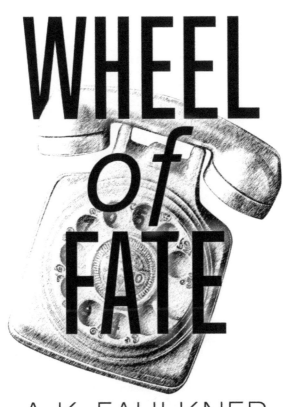

WHEEL of FATE

A.K. FAULKNER

Wheel of Fate © AK Faulkner 2024.
Cover design by Dominic Forbes.

All rights reserved. No part of this story may be used, reproduced or transmitted in any form or by any means without written permission of the copyright holder, except in the case of brief quotations embodied within critical reviews and articles.

This book is a work of fiction. The names, characters, places, and incidents are products of the writer's imagination or have been used fictitiously and are not to be construed as real. Any resemblance to persons, living or dead, actual events, locales or organizations is entirely coincidental.

The right of AK Faulkner to be identified as author of this work has been asserted by them in accordance with the Copyright, Designs and Patents Act, 1988.

First publication: May 2024.

discoverinheritance.com

Wheel of Fate is set in the USA, and as such uses American English throughout.

CONTENTS

Prologue	1
1. Laurence	5
2. Quentin	11
3. Laurence	17
4. Laurence	24
5. Laurence	31
6. Laurence	39
7. Quentin	46
8. Laurence	52
9. Quentin	59
10. Laurence	67
11. Quentin	73
12. Laurence	80
13. Laurence	87
14. Quentin	93
15. Laurence	101
16. Myriam	107
17. Soraya	115
18. Myriam	123
19. Laurence	129
20. Laurence	136
21. Myriam	141
22. Laurence	148
23. Myriam	155
24. Laurence	162
25. Myriam	169
26. Laurence	176
27. Laurence	183
28. Quentin	189
29. Laurence	195
30. Myriam	203
31. Frederick	210

32. Quentin	217
33. Laurence	225
34. Quentin	231
35. Laurence	237
36. Quentin	243
37. Laurence	249
38. Quentin	255
39. Laurence	260
40. Laurence	265
41. Quentin	271
42. Laurence	277
43. Quentin	283
44. Laurence	289
45. Quentin	295
46. Laurence	303
47. Soraya	309
48. Quentin	317
49. Laurence	323
50. Quentin	328
51. Laurence	334
52. Quentin	339
53. Laurence	344
54. Laurence	350
55. Laurence	358
56. Quentin	364
57. Laurence	371
58. Laurence	377
59. Quentin	384
Epilogue	391
Acknowledgments	395
About the author	397
Inheritance	399

PROLOGUE

24 YEARS AGO

"I didn't even know you were pregnant!"

Amy clasped her hands together in her lap and did her best not to wring them as she watched Paula and Todd coo over the newborn in Paula's arms. They were both besotted with him, and who could blame them? He was breathtaking, with his bright blue eyes and wisps of ginger hair.

So much like his mother.

Amy smiled tightly. "I can hide a lot behind an apron, but in the last month... Well. He's here now. That's what matters."

Paula was nodding, but Amy could tell she wasn't really listening. The baby had his pudgy little fingers coiled tightly around one of hers, and Paula let out a small laugh.

"What's his name?" Todd managed to tear his gaze off the baby.

Amy licked her lips. This was about to get weird, because her plan was audacious as hell, and the most important part of it wasn't avoidable anymore.

"He doesn't have one," she breathed.

That finally got Paula's full attention. She blinked and stared at Amy, her brow creased in confusion. "But... I don't understand?"

Amy shuffled forward to the edge of the couch, and met Paula's eye. "What would *you* call him? If he was yours?"

Paula's gasp was pained, and tears sprang to her eyes in a flash. "Amy, how... How can you ask me that. You know I..." But she ran out of words. All she could do was shake her head.

"You *know* how hard we've been looking for something — anything — that can help us," Todd cut in, his tone quiet, but sharp. "This isn't funny."

"It's not meant to be," she blurted. Her hands finally began to wring themselves together as she watched her child, the baby she had carried for nine months and given birth to less than a week ago, safely cradled in Paula's arms. "I've got nothing, Paula. Do you understand? His father told me to get an abortion, and now he's gone, and I live in a trailer in Encinitas. A *trailer*. You have a *home*." Amy gestured to the living room around them, bigger than her whole trailer, with its fresh décor and its new furniture. There wasn't any peeling wallpaper here, no collapsed couch or broken HVAC. "You can give *him* a home."

Pain twisted in her gut at the thought of walking out of here without her baby. When she'd come up with this idea, it was all so neat, so sensible, and so obvious. It fixed everyone's problems, and they all got what they wanted out of it. But now that she was in the moment, faced with letting go of this piece of herself she had carried for so long, it hurt so badly.

It's too late, she told herself. *The time to fix all this was nine months ago.*

Except she hadn't. Vincent told her that he loved her, and like a fool she'd believed him, but Vincent didn't want her, and he sure didn't want his own child. So even though Amy had refused to get the abortion that Vincent had demanded of her, the fact was that she was poor as dirt, and Paula and Todd Grant weren't.

"You can give him a *safe* home," Amy finished, her voice suddenly weak. "You can afford to feed him, send him to a good school, give him everything I can't. I'm just a potter, and I got pregnant. You've got a home and good jobs and all you ever wanted was a family to share it all with. Please." She pressed her lips together and tried not to sob. "Please, give him a future."

"But his name—" Todd began.

"Nobody knows I've had him," Amy insisted. "I gave birth in my own home. He doesn't have a birth certificate. All you have to do is register him. He's *yours*... If you want him." She wiped her eyes like she could stop more tears coming if she was quick enough, even though it never worked that way.

It didn't now, either.

"We can't..." Todd's own voice broke. "Amy... He's got red hair. Nobody's going to believe he's ours."

"Nobody will care. And even if they do, you can protect him from that, too."

Silence fell between them. She knew damn well what she was suggesting, and they were both smart. They knew it, too.

Every adult in this room was a skilled witch. Creating a charm to disguise a baby's hair was well within their power.

"And can he..." Todd hesitated, and he turned to watch the child, with his whole posture melting like he was already admitting defeat. "Will he have magic, d'you think?"

"I have," Amy said. "And so does his father. The chances are good, but these things aren't ever certain, are they?"

She watched Paula and Todd exchange a shielded, guilty look, so charged with yearning that she knew she'd succeeded before either of them said a word. The irony was that her success would lead to the greatest loss she'd ever endured in her life, but what could she do? Raise a child on her own, with a precariously unsteady income, in a trailer park? Half the time she could barely afford to feed herself. How was she going to give her son the nutrition he needed, never mind the education?

How can I protect him from Vincent?

The thought turned the pain to fire in her belly.

Vincent had soured the moment she told him she was pregnant, and abandoned her soon after, but what if he changed his mind some day? What if he walked back into her life and demanded she give him his son?

Paula was the best planar engineer in the USA. She could do more than just ward the baby. She could raise him outside of the mortal world completely, keep him safe until he was old enough to make his own decisions and use his own magic. Amy didn't doubt that Paula could turn this this whole fancy house of theirs into a sanctum if she really wanted to, and maybe one day Amy could suggest it if Paula didn't think of it herself.

"Rufus," Paula finally sighed. "I would call him Rufus."

Amy felt like something inside her got crushed to death, and she nodded slowly to wait for the sickening feeling to pass.

"Rufus," she echoed.

Just like that, the decision was made. Amy would leave this piece of her heart behind and never look back, and Rufus would never know that Paula and Todd weren't his birth parents.

And may the Goddess watch over them all.

1

LAURENCE

"You look like feeling numb is a distant memory," Pauline Hammond stated with a smile the moment Laurence stepped into her office. "How was your week?"

Laurence laughed briefly. There was nothing funny about her question, but his response flew out of him like he'd been popped, and when it was over he lingered next to the chair he usually sat in. "It's been... A week," he eventually said. He offered a small smile to show it wasn't as bad as his words might have sounded, but rather than settle into his chair, he crossed to the windows instead.

He stared out of them. The view wasn't the greatest. Pauline's office didn't overlook Coronado Island or anything. Instead it faced into the East Village it was a part of, so all he could see was construction work, the trolley as it meandered along three stories below, bare branches from deciduous trees that had already lost their foliage, and the splashes of green from palm leaves and cacti that lined the streets. As the fall stretched out towards winter, days grew a little cooler and a lot shorter, and the flora always knew when that change was coming.

Change was definitely coming. Laurence felt it in his bones. He was standing on a ledge, about to dive off it into a whole new life, and it wasn't anywhere near as terrifying as it had seemed a year ago. With Samhain around the corner, it felt like now was the right time, too.

"All right," Pauline said. She turned in her chair to face him, and immediately adopted her professional, patient demeanor. "From the top?

He wasn't ready to talk, but he wasn't *unready* either. He hadn't looked ahead, hadn't spared the time it would take, but the past week had crammed so much shit into his life that he absolutely had to push on through if Pauline was going to be his therapist for much longer. The thought of finding a new one made his skin itch.

Oh. Yeah. That isn't good.

Laurence rubbed at his left elbow to try and make it stop before a full-blown craving could erupt, and he blurted out a command before he could change his mind.

"Ask me if I can trust you not to betray me."

Pauline blinked slowly. As surprised reactions went it was a pretty good one, and did a great job of hiding how startled she might really be. "All right," she murmured. "Can you trust me not to betray you?"

"Yes," Laurence said, without hesitation.

Goddess, he still wasn't used to that. And how could he be? They'd only just discovered this new side effect of overindulging in Mnemosyne's waters, and it didn't seem to work if Laurence thought the question, or even spoke it out loud himself, but the moment someone came at him with a request for future knowledge it was just *there*, coming out of his mouth without context or other knowledge, like a…

He straightened his shoulders when his brain supplied the answer.

Like a prophecy.

Pauline smiled faintly. "Can I ask what that was about?"

"Well, there's a whole lot of stuff I haven't told you, and if I'm gonna talk about the past week I can't avoid it anymore, which means I have to know you aren't going to out me to anyone. Ever."

Her quizzical look was totally fair. She already knew he was bisexual. He'd covered that way back when he'd first started seeing her.

"I'm a demigod," Laurence began. "I've got gifts most people don't, and I can use magic. You're gonna want a demonstration, which is totally fair after someone drops a claim like that in your lap, so—" He ran his thumb across the surface of one of his rings, and breathed, "Les vignes."

The pause as the universe waited for him to trigger his spell was brief, over almost as soon as it had begun, and as time snapped back into place the magic stored within the ring flared into life and deposited a small heartleaf philodendron into the palm of his hand, complete with the hemp pot Laurence had transferred it into. It was only a baby, barely ten leaves and five inches wide, but one just like it had been more than enough to contain Nicola Strickland after he'd applied his gifts to it, and it was plenty for what he needed right now.

He pushed his life out into it, nudging it into growing vines and leaves out as fast as it possibly could. The roots broke the fragile hemp pot apart. Dirt rained down onto the carpet, and within moments the roots and vines followed it. For a little added flair, Laurence spread his arms wide, and directed the vines to circle the outer edges of the office until ropes of fresh, vibrant greenery met together along the far wall.

Then he stopped, and finally made his way to his chair. He sat slowly and wiped the remaining dirt from his hands onto his pants.

"Shitting dicknipples," Pauline gasped. Then she coughed into her hand, and added, "Sorry, that was unprofessional. What I meant was... that was not at all how I could have anticipated this session might go."

"Nice recovery." Laurence smiled warmly. He sympathized with how she must be feeling, he really did, but now that he'd finally got the truth out he wanted way bigger things off his chest. "You good?"

Pauline nodded, scribbling frantically in her notepad. "Carry on."

"From the top, then," he answered. He scratched at his jaw,

fingers pushing through stubble, and decided to just leap in with both feet and let everything unfold from there. "Met some demigods, they were total Nazis, we got into a fight, nearly lost one of the kids, Quen got badly injured and airlifted to hospital, then I proposed and he said yes."

He said yes.

A grin crept up on him as warmth flushed through his chest, and he dropped his hand away from his jaw to brush a speck of dirt off the knee of his pants.

Pauline paused her scribbling. She raised her head and eyed him. "That sounds like a lot."

"Yeah." He licked his lips, then gnawed on them. "Yeah, it was. But you know what? It feels so right. I gotta stop holding myself back, 'cause there's a whole world out there that already wants to do it, and it doesn't need my help."

She jotted something down. "We'll circle back to that another time. First, talk to me about these demigods."

Laurence nodded. "Okay, so, this kinda all started back when Neil offered to take Quen out into the desert for some practice…"

THE REST of his session was spent filling Pauline in on as much as he could, and Laurence was impressed at how she kept on writing, but otherwise didn't butt in or insist anything was impossible. In one way it almost felt like starting over with a new therapist, when the early sessions were pure infodumping about his life so that there was context once they really got into it, but Pauline already knew half of everything. All Laurence did now was give her the other half.

She seemed to be taking it well, but he figured the real test would be whether she texted him before his next appointment to cancel it.

"I think that's as good a place as any to leave it for this week," Pauline murmured, though she eyed the overgrown philodendron that circled her office. "Do you agree?"

"Yeah. Yeah, I think that's about as much as we've got time for anyway, right?" Laurence stood up and walked over to the leafy vines nearest to him. "I guess you don't want me to leave this here."

"I think it'll get in the way of opening the door," she agreed dryly.

He scratched the back of his head while he contemplated exactly what he was supposed to do about all this. Summoning the plant should've been plenty, but he'd wanted to make sure there was no way she could tell herself it had been some kind of sleight of hand. And maybe he'd relished the opportunity to flex, too, since his gifts usually weren't as demonstrable as Quen's.

What he wouldn't give for a bag of holding to stuff the evidence into, but if Ru had one of those, he was totally holding out on Laurence about it.

"All right," he sighed, and reached toward the vines. He splayed his fingers and pulled on the philodendron's energy — which, he figured, was really just his own — to draw the vines back from the walls and into as tight a bundle as he could manage. It was still the size of a beach ball, but at least now he could pick it up. "I don't suppose you've got a garbage bag I could use?"

Pauline laughed. "Probably. Let's go look under the sink. We must have them somewhere."

"Great." He followed her out of the office, leaving a trail of earth on her carpet in his wake. "I'm gonna get charged extra for this, aren't I?"

She didn't answer with anything other than a smile, which absolutely meant this bag was gonna cost him — well, Quen — at least ten bucks.

"Money *is* magic," he murmured, half to himself, as she found a bag in the kitchenette and held it open for him to drop the philodendron into.

"It transforms into food and shelter," Pauline agreed. "And maybe also a wedding venue, and a tux, and flowers, and a ring..."

He let out a strangled sound at the reminder — whether or not she'd meant it as one — that he hadn't had time to look into any of that stuff yet, and drew the bag against his chest like a shield. "Yeah, and on that note, I better get going. Same time next week?"

"You're on," she said. "It's lovely to see you smile, Laurence. I'm really proud of you. Take care, yes?"

"I..." Words failed him, and he followed her as she led him down the hallway and past the waiting room. "Thanks. You too."

He hurried out of her office and made his way down the stairs, and felt strangely excited that — for the first time in his whole life — a therapist was *proud* of him. That had to be some kind of achievement, something that ought to come with a certificate or plaque, and he stepped on out into the early winter sunshine with a whole new spring in his step.

2

QUENTIN

Violeta's eyes widened the moment Quentin entered the self-storage unit, but she waited until he had closed the doors before she asked, "Are you okay? What happened?"

He couldn't even be facetious and pretend he didn't know what she referred to. The sling which immobilized his right arm and shoulder was hardly subtle. Even though it was beneath his jacket, the excessive quantity of Velcro-backed straps seemed designed to draw attention to themselves, and he wasn't able to fasten any buttons over the extra bulk. It forced him to telekinetically hold the jacket in place whenever there was the slightest gust of wind, and he could hardly wait to be rid of it in a couple of weeks' time.

"It's quite a long story," he finally said. He walked to his cushion on the floor, crossed his legs at the ankles, then slowly sank down onto it with his left arm held out for balance. Once settled, he met Violeta's gaze. "I cannot conceive of a way to say this which does not waste our time, and so I shall do my utmost to keep it simple. We came under attack from a group endowed with powerful gifts, and barely survived. My shoulder was broken during the altercation."

She assessed him for a few seconds, jotted some notes, then said, "What medications are you on right now?"

Quentin smiled, though it felt somewhat hazy. "Something called Vicodin. It feels quite like codeine in many ways. I am in no less pain; I simply seem not to care about it too terribly much at present. Isn't that peculiar, for something which claims to *kill* pain?"

Violeta's brows creased a little. "Quentin, if you're on Vicodin, you shouldn't be here. You should be at home, resting."

"I had an appointment," he said.

"Cancellation is an option," she replied.

"That would be rude. And unnecessary."

"You are more likely to say things you might not want to," Violeta said. "Opioids can dampen our inhibitions. I don't mind cancelling, and we can try again next week, once you are no longer—"

"I need to see you." Quentin cut in, doing his best to keep his tone measured but firm. "Now. It cannot wait. I thought this through before I came, fully aware of the side effects of medications like this one, and I..." He paused for a breath. "I decided to take advantage of it, actually, lest I avoid the subject if I leave it too long. A man named Nathan Anderson did this to me, and I killed him."

He pushed the words out before Violeta could stop him — before he could even think to stop himself — because if she knew the cause of the urgency she would understand the nature of his problem, surely?

Or because he was taking full advantage of the Vicodin to say what he might not be able to once his full faculties were restored.

Violeta blinked slowly, but then she set her notepad and pen to one side, and folded her hands together in her lap. "You have my undivided attention," she said gently. 'Tell me more."

Doing so would hurt. But as with his shoulder, the Vicodin would make this pain tolerable too, and Quentin was not about to waste this opportunity to lay everything out with all the calm efficiency the medication afforded him.

"Very well," he said. "Recall my intention to travel with Neil for the purpose of testing the extent of my gifts?"

"I do." Violeta nodded.

"Mmm. Well, we were followed."

Quentin relayed as much as he could, in as linear a fashion as he was able to manage. Time slid by with him barely aware of it, although occasionally he was somewhat conscious of words tumbling from his lips in a manner which seemed rambling yet which he was not capable of stopping or corralling into more coherent form. Still, the work was getting done, and Violeta did not interrupt him. Best of all, as he had hoped, his gifts did not manifest themselves at any point. The medication left him so level-headed that he was not at risk of losing control, and as he finished his story he felt rather satisfied with how it had gone.

"Is it awful, do you think?" He asked the question before he really grasped what he was getting at, so he let himself continue. "To have intentionally killed another person?"

Violeta's lips pursed together while her dark eyes met his. "Out of context? I think so, yes. But you are asking within the context of the death of Nathan Anderson specifically, aren't you?"

Quentin tilted his head while he tried to nail down the problem with her question. "If we begin to draw lines which delineate acceptable and unacceptable circumstances for the taking of a life, do we not run the risk of moving the goalposts so as to allow for the justification of our own actions?"

"You're trying to find a way in which what you did was bad," she countered. "What purpose does that serve?"

"To keep me from repeating the error?"

"Was it an error?"

Her gaze seemed soft, but he could readily determine the steel hidden beneath her gentle exterior.

Or he was absolutely off his head on this Vicodin stuff.

"No," he mused. "It was not."

"Let me explain something," she said. "You are experiencing what we call a moral injury. When a person is placed in a situation which leads to them acting in opposition to their own ethics, it can be deeply traumatic. What is most important for you to know right now is that I'm not judging you. And I can understand why you chose to come to your appointment today and push ahead with what you needed to say. You made a sound decision, and a brave one." Violeta tipped her head ever so faintly as she watched him. "Most importantly, you make no attempt to dehumanize Mr. Anderson. You accept and continue to believe that he was a person even though you know that he didn't afford you, your fiancé, or your friends the same status. Your choice was born from love, Quentin. His was forged in hatred. And because of this, it's absolutely natural for you to feel guilt, even though you know that he felt none at all."

Like so many other times, Violeta's words seemed both logical and false at the same time, and Quentin rolled them around alongside his own thoughts, trying to see how they could fit together. It was difficult, largely because his brain was floating along on a cloud which he had experienced all too often in his youth. Ultimately, the best he could come up with, was, "Why do people do this?"

"Hate?"

He nodded. "Yes."

"That's a subject which straddles the line between psychology and philosophy, I'm afraid." Violeta let out a faint sigh. "We still don't know. In many cases, hatred comes from a place of hurt, or fear. In some, it is founded on disgust. The problem is that it's a difficult area to study, since it's ethically unsound to induce hatred in even voluntary subjects in order to study it."

Quentin felt the urge to lace his fingers together, but with one hand strapped tightly against his chest, it wasn't an option. He resorted instead to gripping his knee with his left hand and giving it a tight squeeze.

"Then what is it for?" He raised his head in a challenge, as though he could somehow fight something so abstract as a concept if only it would come out of the shadows and face him.

"Most negative emotions help us deal with a perceived threat," she said. "Disgust makes us back away from the threat, which is useful for avoiding disease. Anger makes us confront the threat, most often with the goal of making the threat back down or change its behavior towards us." Violeta hesitated, and even glanced away for a second before she continued. "The goal of hate is to eradicate the perceived threat."

Quentin frowned as he attempted to overlay this theory onto his memories of Anderson, but it left him with nothing but confusion. "Anderson perceived Laurence's... 'queerness' to be a threat. But that's no threat at all. To anyone."

Violeta nodded. "You're right. It isn't. But that doesn't stop some people *seeing* us as threats, just for who or what we are. Rather than spend your therapy dollars on a Bigotry 101 class, why don't I email you a few links, and you can do a little research in your own time? Then when we see each other again next week we can talk about this with a more complete set of tools at our disposal?" She plastered a thin smile across her lips, and added, "And you'll be off the Vicodin by then, won't you?"

"I will, yes." Even if it meant setting fire to any unused tablets, Quentin would make sure that he was done with this nasty opioid before it became habit-forming. He had been down that road before, and it was *not* one he wished to walk ever again.

"Great. Then consider that your homework. Hopefully it'll keep you out of trouble until next week. And once you're no longer medicated, we can run through an autism assessment questionnaire to see whether your young friend is secretly a psychologist." She carefully eased herself to her feet, one hand against the floor and the other holding her skirt in place until she was upright, then she gently straightened her blouse and hair before she held out her hand to him. "Would you like any help?"

His natural inclination was to decline the offer of assistance, but help was the exact thing that he came to her for, and there would be absolutely no benefit to him falling on his arse if he lost his balance, so he took her hand and allowed her to steady him as he stood. "Thank you. I take it that we are out of time?"

"I'm afraid so." She smiled at him, sympathy tilting her eyebrows up a touch as she let go of his hand. "Rest, focus on allowing your shoulder to heal, and remember that you are not a bad person, Quentin. The world we live in is complex and difficult, and sometimes we are placed in terrible situations through no fault of our own."

Quentin nodded slowly. "A Kobayashi Maru," he mused.

She blinked in surprise, and her smile widened. "A Kobayashi Maru," she agreed.

"That's all very well and good, but what *is* a Kobayashi Maru?"

Violeta laughed gently and crouched down to pick up her notebook and pen, then she escorted him to the doors. "So in addition to some reading, I'll also send over a list of Star Trek episodes for you to watch. It's a television program," she added before he could ask. "I think you might enjoy it."

He very much doubted that he would, but he said nothing, and followed her down to the lobby so that he could wait for Laurence to come and collect him.

After that, he could perhaps sleep for three days, which was incredibly appealing right now — especially if it meant delaying any of Violeta's homework until he had the mental capacity to engage with it.

3

LAURENCE

LAURENCE PULLED OFF HOTEL CIRCLE SOUTH AND FOUND A SPACE to park in out front of the beige and sand colored rectangle Quen had his therapy in. Back when he'd started coming here it had seemed kind of shady, but Laurence was used to it now, and nothing weird had gone down. No weirder than therapy in a storage unit, anyway.

Quen would be in the lobby, a little service area that stocked boxes, tape, and whatever else people who used self-storage might need at the eleventh hour, but it also had a couple of desks people could work at, and Quen usually perched himself at one of those if he was waiting for Laurence to collect him — on the days when he hadn't decided to walk the almost two miles to the Fashion Valley mall. Laurence checked his phone to make sure Quen hadn't had a last-minute change of location, because the thought of him walking all that way while hopped up on meds didn't fill Laurence with joy, but thankfully there weren't any disastrous messages, so he got out of the truck and strode to the lobby doors.

The sight that greeted him once he stepped into the shade was kind of adorable, but also — if he was being totally honest with himself — slightly frustrating. Quen was half asleep at the desk, his good shoulder leaning against the wall and his eyes heavily lidded, and Laurence didn't want to think of what might happen if he dozed off completely. He hurried over and settled fingertips against Quen's spine. "Hey, baby," he breathed. "I'm here. How're you feeling?"

Quen groaned faintly. "Starting to wear off."

"Yeah," Laurence agreed. "C'mon, let's go home. Slowly," he added. He'd seen way too many users pass out from standing up too fast. "Take your time. I've got you."

He hadn't really. Quen was almost jammed up against the wall, and there was no way for Laurence to get to his uninjured side. All he could do was stand there and offer a hand once Quen was upright, which Quen took with a slight smile before he leaned in for a kiss.

"Uh huh," Laurence said dryly against Quen's lips. "All this was just a play, huh? Man, the lengths you'll go to. You know all you gotta do is ask, right?"

Quentin grinned up at him. "I do," he said. Then he grabbed Laurence by the shoulder to steady himself, and sucked in a breath. "All right, I think that's quite enough upright for me today. Would you be so kind as to take me home, Mr. Riley?"

"Sure thing, Mr. Riley." Laurence returned the grin and looped Quen's good arm over his shoulder before Quentin had time to process what Laurence had just said. He waited for it, though, as he slowly steered Quen out to the truck and helped him up into the passenger seat.

It wasn't until Laurence started the engine that Quentin said, "Ooooh," in a tone that seemed to suggest he'd just worked out something scandalous, and Laurence laughed as he reversed out of the parking space.

There wasn't another peep out of Quen until they got home, and it didn't take long for Laurence to notice that it was because he'd finally fallen asleep.

"I DO NOT WISH to go to bed."

"Cool story, babe." Laurence locked the truck. "I can help you, or I can carry you, which do you want?"

There was a strain to Quen's eyes, a patchiness to the coloration of his cheeks, that stood out like a lighthouse to Laurence's senses and made it obvious that the Vicodin was wearing off. They both had weird super-metabolisms that practically halved the staying power of any drugs they took, so Laurence wasn't at all surprised that Quen was already flagging, but he really didn't want Quen to push himself too hard. There were so many problems that might lead to, not least of which was that Laurence hated having that shit in the house to begin with.

Goddess, he realized. *No wonder I was itching in Pauline's office.*

Quentin was giving him an imperious look that would've been sexy under literally any other circumstances, but right now came off like a toddler about to throw a tantrum, so Laurence decided to head it off at the pass and put on his best Bambi eyes.

"You know I'm right," he said.

Quen took a couple more seconds to back down, but at least he did it, letting out a little sigh as the rigidity left him. "You are," he agreed. "I would appreciate your assistance, if you do not mind?"

"I don't mind," Laurence assured him. "C'mon, let's get up those stairs, then I'll bring you some tea, and Win can tell you all about his morning."

"Oh? What on Earth has he been up to?"

Laurence shook his head and held up his pointer finger. "Spoilers!"

THE HOUSE FELT like a well-oiled machine. Martin had tea ready by the time Laurence went back downstairs for it, and dinner prep was well underway. Soraya, Kim, and Mel had taken the dogs out for a late afternoon walk along the beach, of their own initiative. Clifton and Felipe were swimming in the pool together, while Lisa and Estelita did their homework under a parasol, and

Mia did squats on the patio overlooking the ocean while she acted like she wasn't really out there to be the boys' lifeguard.

The only cog that didn't fit right just yet was Alex, and Laurence couldn't blame them. They'd chosen to stay, at least, but the house was reaching capacity and that meant Alex had to use a shared bathroom up on the top floor, even if he was the only one who needed it so far. While he figured that was the least of Alex's troubles right now, it made Laurence feel like a bad host, and the house had only recently been renovated; doing it again to put en suites into the remaining bedrooms wasn't feasible.

Dinnertime came and went. Alex finally emerged from their room to eat. Laurence touched base on how many of the teens had found a therapist they liked the look of, then tasked Martin with making bookings and organizing the calendar. Mia agreed to drive anyone who couldn't drive themselves. Once everything was settled, Laurence took water and a light meal up to Quen, and petted Win while gently bullying Quen into eating all of it.

Tomorrow he could start looking into wedding venues, the license, and whatever else needed to be done, but for tonight all he had to do was take care of the man he loved and make sure Quen got as much rest as possible.

Wake time!

Laurence groaned and rolled over in bed in the vain hope that he could bury his face in pillows and make Windsor go away, but the bird was in his thoughts, and smug as hell.

Wake time! Win repeated.

Okay. I'm up.

Is a lie! Win's whole vibe was pleased *and* chiding with that statement, both emotions vibrating along their connection like it was a guitar string.

Yeah, he agreed. *It's a lie. Give me a minute.*

Okay! Good bird!

Good bird, Laurence assured him.

There was no point reaching for his phone. It was in the

kitchen, with Windsor's whole body covering it like he was trying to make it hatch. The idea was that Laurence's alarm wouldn't wake Quen, and Win could get Laurence's ass up first thing in the morning without having to make a sound, but Laurence had regrets now, and his pillow was really inviting.

Bad! Windsor chittered.

Laurence cursed under his breath and focused his attention on the sounds around him. It was relatively easy to pick out the soft, shallow rhythm of Quentin's breathing that indicated he was still fast asleep. More breathing from beyond the end of the bed made it clear that the dogs were sleeping, too. He picked out the slightest noise from the stairs, but he and Quen hadn't gotten up to anything since the hospital, so his senses were beginning to lose their edge.

Finally, he forced his eyes open.

Quen was where he should be, propped up on his own side of the bed by an enormous, wedge-shaped foam cushion so he could sleep sitting up like the surgeons wanted him to, and Laurence gazed at him for a while.

How many more times would he do this? Over how many years? There wasn't ever gonna come a time when all the evil pricks of the world woke up and decided to turn over a new leaf — not even Freddy could make *that* happen — so this was potentially unending, right?

Until we *end*, he thought, and while the thought wasn't wholly bitter, he'd be lying if he pretended there wasn't some sadness attached to it, because he *liked* this life. He *loved* it — when they weren't getting attacked by witch hunters, Neo-Nazi demigods, or crazed warlocks, anyway. The part where he was Bambi Laurence Riley, and lived with, loved, and had amazing sex with Quentin Ichabod d'Arcy, though? Yeah, he wasn't ready to let go of any of that. Not now, and maybe not ever. He didn't want that eternity in Annwn while they worked through shit so their souls could be recycled, he wanted it *now*, while they were alive.

He'd just started being able to accept himself, to *like* himself, and by the Goddess he deserved to enjoy that for a while. So did

Quen. After everything he'd been through, he was due some time where he could just *be*.

So, if bad guys weren't going to pack up and go home, it was in Laurence's best interests to start pulling his own weight. This past year had shown him super clearly that no matter how much he might yearn for a life he'd originally thought of as 'normal,' no such thing really existed for anyone, and as much as Quen had figured out that his pacifism was being enabled by everyone around him, Laurence had begun to see that his vision of normalcy was a pipe dream.

Clinging to it was going to get people killed.

He'd relied on instinct whenever he picked up a blade, but he would have to pair it with skill sooner or later. Sure, he wasn't going to kick ass the way Quen could, but Quen's way led to life flights and Vicodin and metal plates in his shoulder.

The other problem was that there were only so many hours in the day, which left Laurence facing the fact he'd spent so long avoiding: He didn't have time to study magic, practice his gifts, learn how to fight, *and* hold down a job. He was already a liability to his mom's business, absent for way more weeks in the year than any other employee could get away with. It didn't matter that she wasn't paying him when he wasn't there. What counted was that the shop still had work to be done, and Myriam was left carrying the can on short notice way too often.

It wasn't what he wanted, but there were things he needed, and maybe this was what it was like to grow the fuck up.

What if adulthood was all about letting go of smaller dreams so that he could fully inhabit much bigger ones?

When he looked at it *that* way it didn't seem like a terrible thing. His life was a partnership now, so once Quen was feeling better, Laurence would talk it over with him, and they could figure it out together.

It is alive!

Laurence blinked as Windsor cut in on his introspection, and he tried to work out what the fuck his familiar was talking about. The only way to do it was to reach across the distance between them and look out through Windsor's eyes, which made it clear almost immediately.

The phone Win was snuggled down over was ringing as it vibrated under his chest, and Windsor cackled in glee as it tickled him.

It's ringing, Laurence told him. *Can you stand up and look at it?*

Windsor was reluctant, far more interested in enjoying the way the device shook his entire body with every pulse, but after a *Please?* from Laurence he waddled off it and tipped his head.

Rufus Grant, the screen read.

Laurence tried so hard not to sigh, but if Ru was calling him it was urgent, because the witch had to stand outside his sanctum to get any signal and he *hated* being outside.

Good bird. I'll be down in a minute.

He returned to his body, eased out of bed without making a single sound, and grabbed a pair of briefs and yesterday's t-shirt off the floor so he could go get his phone without exposing himself to Martin.

Whatever Ru wanted to talk to him about at six o'clock in the morning had better be worth it.

4

LAURENCE

The phone had stopped ringing by the time Laurence made it to the kitchen, but there weren't any notifications about voicemail, so Laurence helped himself to an apple and shared it with Windsor while he waited for Rufus to call back.

Sure enough, once he had a mouthful, the phone vibrated with the incoming call, and Laurence tapped it with his thumb. "Ru," he greeted.

"I need a ride," Rufus grunted.

Ru hadn't given him anywhere near enough time to swallow, so Laurence prompted, "Huh?" while he tried to hurry it up.

"To Encinitas," Ru said.

That didn't really help, so Laurence swallowed a huge lump of fruit to get it out of the way, and grunted in discomfort as he felt it sluggishly shove its way down his throat.

"It's six in the morning, Ru," he finally complained.

"And if you leave now we can be in Encinitas by seven."

"I'm not dressed. I haven't even showered yet." Laurence offered a piece of apple to Win, who gobbled it down like he hadn't eaten in days. "What's this about?"

"Amy isn't here."

Ru sounded off. Strained, even. It wasn't something Laurence had heard from him before, and it took a second to realize it was *worry*.

He straightened up slowly. Ran a hand through his hair and tried to focus. "I take it she's supposed to be, and you've tried calling her already, and she's not answering, so you want to go to her home and check it out?"

"Correct," Ru said.

"Got it. Well. Uh…" He puffed out his cheeks, then shook his head slowly. "If there's a problem, we lose an hour your way. Why don't you wait a sec and I'll try to see if she's okay?"

He heard a distant grunt from Ru. "I guess that makes sense."

"Yeah. Hold on, this won't take long."

Laurence put the phone down next to his apple, then placed his hands either side of both, on the cool marble kitchen countertop. He spread his feet slightly until he was sure he was stable, and closed his eyes, trying to figure out how to bait this hook.

Amy Jenkins. Supposed to be at Ru's house by now. So she would've maybe got up around five to give herself time to shower, get dressed, and drive to Carlsbad…

Very little drifted by as he tried to immerse himself in the stream, and nothing was taking the bait, but there *were* visions. His gift was working.

It had to be the bait that was wrong.

He was used to thinking through what to ask of tarot cards before a spread got laid, so he turned the problem over and tackled it from different angles until it started to take shape.

Didn't get up at five? How about four? Did she get up? Did she go to bed? Okay, Amy Jenkins, at her home in Encinitas, the last time she left it…

Finally, a vision snatched his attention, and he reached for it in response.

Amy Jenkins, in her own home, with another woman Laurence didn't recognize. They walked to the front door, the stranger in the lead and Amy following. Nothing was said, so Laurence tailed them as they went out into the bright afternoon sun, and they got into a dusty older car that had a third woman behind the wheel and a baby seat in the back.

Nobody spoke.

Laurence came closer, in time to see a look of horror on Amy's face as she turned to face the baby seat, but the car pulled away and Laurence was too dumbfounded to follow it. He could come back to this vision later if he had to, but right now he needed to know when this had happened, and nothing in a car full of people who weren't speaking would give him that, so he ran back into the house, through the closed door, and searched for the slightest clue — a newspaper, an abandoned cellphone, a calendar, anything at all.

He found what he needed in the kitchen: a calendar on the front of the refrigerator with days neatly crossed through. It suggested that Amy kept up to date with it, so hopefully it was correct.

The last date crossed out was October 26th, and that was a couple of days ago.

Laurence cursed and debated going back to the car, but Ru was waiting, so he withdrew from the vision and picked up his phone. "Still with me, Ru?"

"Of course."

"Amy left the house with a couple of women I didn't recognize," Laurence said, trying to get the information across succinctly. "On or after the 26th, depending on what time of day she crosses off dates on her calendar. The light looked like it was mid-afternoon, so I'd hazard a guess that it was the day before yesterday. There's no point going to her house. She's not there."

Ru snarled. "Then where *is* she?"

"I don't know. I'll need more time to work that out, but I know you don't wanna be standing around outside while I do it. Why don't you go back indoors, I'll head on over, then we can look into it more once I get there, okay?" It was the best solution Laurence could think of right now, especially since Ru had no way of coming here to the mansion without a ride, so Laurence would have to do all the driving no matter what got decided.

He waited while the other witch probably went through the exact same list of options, then Ru grunted. "Fine. I'll wait for you here."

"I'm on my wa—"

Ru hung up on him before he could finish his sentence.

LAURENCE MANAGED to sneak back into the bedroom without waking Quen, but taking a shower turned out to be the tipping point, and by the time he came out of the bathroom Quen's eyes were open and settled on him while the bottle of Vicodin at his side was opening itself and tipping a pill out into his outstretched palm.

"Sorry," Laurence whispered. He offered Quen a small smile and gestured to the walk-in. "Something came up. I've gotta run. You going to be okay for a while?"

The bottle capped itself, and Quentin popped the tablet into his mouth then grabbed the glass of water that floated into his hand, and sipped from it. Only once he'd put the glass down again did he answer.

"Trouble?"

Laurence winced. "Maybe. Amy seems like she might've gone missing. Ru's Amy," he added, in case Quen thought Neil Storm's sister Ames had vanished. "I'm gonna go up there and see if I can find out where she is."

Quentin frowned slightly. "Do you think she is in danger?"

"I... don't know," he said. He hurried to the closet and toweled himself off aggressively once he was out of sight so that Quen wouldn't feel compelled to tell him to be more careful with his skin. "She left with some people I don't recognize, but they could just be friends..."

Laurence tailed off as he remembered the total horror on Amy's face.

Yeah, there's no way they're friends, he thought.

What could possibly be in a child's car seat to make her pull *that* kind of expression, anyway?

He'd have to find out later, once he was at Ru's. For now he needed to get dressed, so he grabbed fresh boxer shorts and socks, and hurried into them.

"I see. Then I had best accompany you."

Laurence heard sheets move and footsteps fall. The dogs' breathing shifted, and their tails thumped lazily against the bedroom carpet.

He snatched a fresh shirt and pulled it on over his damp hair. "I'll be fine, baby. I'm just going to Ru's and we can figure it out from there."

"And when you do, you will proceed directly to her whereabouts," Quentin replied. "I will join you."

Quen's frame loomed in the doorway, and Laurence's head popped free of his shirt just in time to catch sight of him swaying ever so slightly on his feet.

"Baby," Laurence let out a soft breath as he tugged fresh pants on. "You have to rest."

"Once the painkillers take effect I shall be quite all right," Quen insisted.

"You nearly fell asleep in the storage company's front office yesterday," Laurence countered.

"I just need a shower before we go," Quen said.

Laurence flexed his jaw. He didn't like to argue at the best of times, but Quentin was injured, in a hell of a lot of pain, and taking fucking *opiates* to cope with it all. This was worse than when Jack had sliced him open like a can of beans. This time Quen had broken bones and needed surgical intervention, and he was still pretending he could go out and fight the world only days later. If that shoulder was ever going to heal, Laurence would have to make sure Quen stayed put, and for that to happen he'd have to draw the line super firmly.

Assertiveness wasn't his strongest skill, but he could fake it if he had to, so he straightened up and puffed out his chest.

"Anderson fucked up your collarbone and shoulder so badly that you got helicoptered to a specialist surgical team, and they had to put metal plates in your body to hold you together while you heal, hon. Plus you had two migraines in one week through pushing yourself too hard, and you've never had one before in your entire life. I can't stand by and let you give yourself a fucking aneurism or something just 'cause you refuse to lay in bed for a few days." Laurence fastened his fly, then planted a fist on his hip and raised a finger to point directly at Quen's nose, doing his best to look as stern as he possibly could. "I am *not* backing down on this. You're gonna get back into that bed and you are going to *rest*. You are going to let me handle this, and *if* we need you I will call you. Got it?"

Quen's lips parted. His cheeks flushed, stark against his pale, clammy skin. Grey eyes grew wide, but lacked the edge that suggested he was at all alert enough to really object to being bossed around like this.

If he wasn't so obviously in pain right now, Laurence might find it cute. Instead he found it worrying, and he gently took Quen's uninjured arm so he could steer his fiancé back to bed.

"No bathing on your own while I'm gone, either," Laurence murmured. "I'll ask Martin to bring breakfast up to you and take care of the girls. Go back to sleep. I'll come home once we've figured out what's going on, I promise."

Quen grimaced as he lowered himself onto the mattress, and let out a faint grunt while Laurence helped him get his legs back under the covers. All his brainpower was obviously being consumed by agony and exhaustion, and he was in no fit state to face stepping out of reality and into Ru's extremely magical sanctum. He didn't even have the strength to argue with Laurence or to exert his usually immense willpower, so Laurence tucked him up in the sheets before he could go off.

Once the Vicodin kicked in, Quentin might be more capable of thought or will, but Laurence had no intention of giving him enough time to get there. He leaned in and kissed Quen's forehead, then whispered, "How about I ask Mom to come over so you can hash out some wedding ideas, huh?"

It was a dirty trick, and Laurence didn't feel the slightest bit guilty for using it.

"Ooh," Quen breathed.

"Uh-huh." Laurence offered him a slight smile and brushed fingers across his cheek. "I love you, baby. Go back to sleep."

"I love you, darling," Quen whispered. His eyes were already losing the fight to stay open.

Laurence stole another kiss, then he hurried out before Quen could gather his wits, and didn't look back.

All he had to do was get to Ru, solve this weird shit with Amy, and come home in one piece before Quen decided to intervene, but he had the unnerving feeling that today wasn't going to work out like that at all.

5

LAURENCE

There was more life in the kitchen the second time Laurence made it downstairs. Martin had arrived, and was already halfway through breakfast preparations, as well as having set out a bowl of fruit and seeds for Windsor. The dogs sauntered past Laurence as though he didn't exist anymore, and went to harass Martin for breakfast. Alex was at the table, fidgeting with a spoon like they weren't sure if they were supposed to do anything else, and still wearing the body they'd had when Laurence met them less than a week ago. Estelita sat opposite Alex with a grim pout on her face.

"You want us to keep an eye on him?" She asked the moment she laid eyes on Laurence.

Laurence sighed. She must've heard everything. Whether she'd woken Alex for this or they'd already been up wasn't clear, but Laurence didn't want the teens caught up in anything bad, and giving them a job to take their minds off worrying might keep them out of trouble, too.

"Would you mind?" He grabbed the keys to his truck from a hook by the door and stuffed them into his pocket. "I'm gonna ask Mom to stop by, too, but she's got a store to run, and if it's busy there she might not be able to get away."

Estelita nodded. Her hair was tied back in a messy ponytail

surrounded by loose, flyaway strands, and she was wearing yesterday's t-shirt. She must've rushed downstairs the moment she was awake enough.

"I'll let the others know, once they're up," she said. "He ain't going nowhere."

"You think you can stop him?" Alex put the spoon down and frowned at Estelita.

She just smiled sweetly. "Easy. If he wants to be a responsible dad he'll do what we say."

Laurence snorted, but she had a point. If she could leverage Quen's protectiveness somehow, he'd absolutely stay here for the day to take care of them all. "Worth a shot," he agreed. "Martin, can you take breakfast up when it's done and walk the dogs? I gotta go out."

"Of course," Martin said with a soft smile. "Consider it done."

"Thanks. Okay, everyone stay out of trouble." Laurence nodded to Estelita. "I'm leaving you in charge. Think you can handle it?"

"Totally!" She grinned, and the mischief in her eyes was matched only by the worry in Alex's.

It'd have to do.

"Great!" Laurence offered Windsor his arm, then swept out of the kitchen and hurried for the garage before he could change his mind.

HE WAITED until he was on the 5 before calling his mom, and when she answered, he could tell from the lack of background noise that she hadn't left the farm yet.

"Bright blessings, Bambi!" She sounded cheerful. "This is early!"

"Hey, Mom! Blessed be!" Laurence smiled to himself, despite the situation he was in. "It's nothing urgent, I hope. I need to ask you for a favor."

"Of course, dear," Myriam said. "How can I help?"

Laurence drummed his fingers on the steering wheel, but he

figured dancing around the question was totally unnecessary. His mom always cut to the heart of things anyway, so why not do it himself and save her the trouble?

"Is there any way you can spare some time to visit Quen today? I've got to go see Ru, and Quen's already itching to get out of bed, but I figure if you talk wedding arrangements with him he'll behave himself for longer."

Myriam chuckled. "Leave it to me, Bambi. I'll do what I can. What do *you* want?"

"Uh…" Laurence blinked. "I want him to stay in bed and not totally fuck his shoulder's recovery?"

"For the ceremony," she said dryly.

He felt his face grow warm with embarrassment and was glad she couldn't see it. "Oh. Duh. I guess… Just a regular handfasting, you know?"

Laurence hadn't attended many of them, especially not as an adult, and he was kind of hazy on the details. Mostly what he remembered was the food, dancing, and falling asleep in his mom's arms in the RV after, but he was sure that was true of any kind of wedding.

"I'll talk it over with Quentin," Myriam said with a laugh. "Be careful today, dear."

He frowned, and took a second to check all the truck's mirrors. "What? Have you seen something?"

"No. I just have a feeling." Myriam's tone was suddenly sober. "Perhaps I should close the store."

Great. Now I have a feeling, too, and it's getting worse by the second.

"Uh… If you think that's wise?" Laurence tried to keep the worry out of his tone. Windsor's concerned cooing sounds from the passenger seat didn't help much.

"I do." She sighed faintly. "All right, then, that's settled. I will get the keys to Maria, and they can take care of today's deliveries without trying to keep the store open, too. That way I can head directly to La Jolla once it's done, and wait for you there."

Laurence opened his mouth at her phrasing, then clamped it shut again. It wasn't intentional, but her words *did* have meaning, and they heavily implied that he'd be going home again after he was done with Ru, so at least he was going to make it through whatever the fuck was going to happen within the next hour.

"Okay," he said. "Thanks, mom. Merry part."

"So mote it be," she replied, and ended the call.

Laurence stared at the road ahead with grim determination. His mom was willing their next meeting into existence with those words, and as he continued north, the sick feeling in his gut only worsened.

This was going to be bad, and he couldn't pretend otherwise.

Ru YANKED the front door open the second Laurence closed the gate, and strode across the gravel drive toward him. Every step crunched loudly, and his scowl was worse than usual.

Laurence hurried to meet him halfway, but Ru spoke before he could get a word in.

"What do you need?" Ru asked. "I've made a fresh pot of coffee, but you prefer tea, and I don't have milk. I have herbal teas, though. Will one of those do? Did you have breakfast? I'm out of fruit, but I have..." He tailed off. "I don't know what I've got. I might have bread in the freezer?"

Laurence blinked at him.

Was Ru... *babbling*?

He still looked sour as a lemon, but he was definitely talking way more than usual, and with far less forethought. He had to be worried sick *and* working his ass off to not alienate Laurence, so Laurence figured it was best not to feed into Ru's anxiety. Instead, he gestured to the house.

"Let's go inside," he said gently. "It'll be better if I don't eat or drink before I do this. I'll just get straight to it, then we can figure things out from there, okay?"

Ru grunted, but he turned and led the way, only to dither once he made it to the vast hallway.

Laurence eased around him and headed for the living room. He nodded to a chair, and Win took the hint, hopping off his shoulder and gliding across the room to hunker down on the chair back instead so that Laurence could sit on a couch alone.

Ru hovered in the doorway. "So... No coffee?"

"I'm just gonna get started, if that's okay with you?" Laurence clasped his hands together and leaned back. "You've got to be worried. I don't want to keep either you *or* Amy waiting any longer than we had to."

"Okay." Ru clenched his hands, then added, "Thanks," and moved closer so he could sit down facing Laurence.

Laurence nodded, and didn't say anything else. He was already really *not* looking forward to this, but if Amy was in trouble she needed them, and whatever Laurence was about to see was the price he'd have to pay to get to her.

He drew a deep breath and closed his eyes as he released it. He already knew what he was looking for, since he'd already seen some of it, so baiting his visions came way easier this time around, and by the time he took his next breath he'd already caught one.

The car pulled up outside Amy's home. Laurence had been there a few times, and he recognized it immediately: the sprawling, white-walled place in Encinitas, with the garage to one side that she used for her pottery studio, now made cozy with fall decorations: orange and red leaf garlands, a matching wreath on the door, and small pumpkins on the porch. The strangers' dusty little Honda didn't look out of place, and Laurence took in as much about the occupants as he could.

There was the driver, a white woman in her late thirties or early forties, whose dark hair was kept in a neat, glossy bob. She wore a navy suit jacket and an eggshell blue shirt, and her skin carried no trace of a tan. Her passenger was in the back seat, where Amy would be later, and Laurence didn't get a good look at her until she left the vehicle: another white woman, but much younger, somewhere around Laurence's age. She wore a frumpy sweater and baggy sweatpants, as well as a sneer that could curdle milk. Her mid-brown hair was clean, but not brushed or styled in any way, so it hung down her back in messy locks with strands floating from the static of the sweater.

She grinned when she looked up at Amy's house, all teeth and malice, and sliced her hand through the air with a spoken word in a language

Laurence didn't recognize before she pressed her palm to the front door and said another.

Laurence heard the clicking of locks and latches, and the door swung inwards.

He gasped in shock and hurried after the woman as she stepped into Amy's home and yelled, "Face me!"

What was this? Some kind of feud? Was Amy mixed up in something with another witch? Laurence wracked his brains to try and marry this woman's face up against all the local pagans he'd been talking to back while he was trying to make contact with Amy last year, but came up totally blank.

Footsteps pre-empted Amy's arrival, and when she stepped into the living room she still had dust on her coveralls, and a pinkish stain from clay on her hands. She looked utterly shocked as she stopped and stared at the woman.

"Who are you? What are you doing in my home?" Amy's fingers curled slightly, but she was otherwise still.

"Amy Jenkins," the stranger said, looking Amy over slowly. The sneer had returned. "Allow me to extend an invitation. I want you to come home with me, and I promise you that it's in your best interests to do so without a fight." But then the sneer transformed back into that haunting, malicious grin again, like she hoped Amy would refuse.

"I'm not going anywhere. Get out of my house." Amy began to move, slowly, and Laurence tried to guess at where she might be going, but the only thing in her path was her bookshelf. Maybe she kept a weapon there, or a protective spell she could trigger in an emergency.

The other woman leapt into action. She lunged at Amy and thrust her hand against Amy's chest — though not, it seemed, to do any harm. After that she maintained eye contact as she dug a tiny item out of the pocket of Amy's overalls and tossed it aside as she took a step back. Laurence's gaze followed it as it bounced on the carpet. It looked like a vintage phone made out of silver. There was a little loop on top like it was meant for a charm bracelet, but Laurence figured it had to be holding an imbued spell for this woman to bother taking it away.

He didn't have time to think it over. Amy screamed, and when he looked back to her she'd made a break for the shelves, grabbing wildly at them while she stared at the intruder, who closed the distance and *pressed right up against her. She grabbed Amy's wrists, and finally managed to pin them against the shelves.*

"It's me!" She showed the first hint of annoyance Laurence had seen in her since this started. "Pay attention. You didn't spend all those years keeping him from me without knowing that your actions would catch up with you in the end."

Amy struggled, then bucked her whole body, using her weight advantage to toss the smaller woman right off of her, and the stranger stumbled back until she hit a couch. Amy's features were slowly twisting into confusion, and then understanding.

"It can't be," she breathed. "Vincent? What is this?" She gestured to the stranger. "Is it a disguise? Or is she a real person? One of your coven? Are you possessing *her?"*

The other woman snorted disdainfully. "Riley's boy is out of town for a few days," was all she said to that. "Did you know he had magic? Yes, I suppose you did, or you wouldn't have taken him to Grant, would you?"

Laurence's blood ran cold as pieces rearranged themselves right in front of his eyes. Whoever this woman was, she also wasn't. Somehow, instead, she was Vincent Harrow. Angela's father.

The warlock.

And he knew Laurence had been away.

Before Laurence could even begin to speculate just how much Harrow knew about his comings and goings, Amy balled her hands into fists and scowled.

"You need to leave."

"I have waited*," Vincent snarled, "for so long. But I am done waiting. If he won't come out for his own student, he'll* have *to come out for you. The woman who birthed him. The woman who lied to him. The woman who took him from his father." He took a step towards her and raised his hand. "You thought you could get away with taking* my *son and giving him to Paula and Todd Grant like he was* nothing*?"*

"Fuck." Laurence blurted. The word was punched out of him like he'd been body slammed by a pro wrestler, and it left him breathless.

Was this why Amy stepped in to raise Ru after the accident? Because she was his birth mom? Did Ru even know?

Worse, did he have any idea that his biological father was a fucking warlock?

Laurence's head was spinning, and he hadn't even left the vision yet.

"You never wanted him!" Amy screamed at him. "You wanted me to have an abortion!"

"Maybe you should have," he snarled. "Then we wouldn't be here. But now you reap what you sowed." Vincent spat out another word Laurence didn't understand, then switched back to English. "Now shut up, and come with me."

Vincent straightened up off the back of the couch and took a moment to tug his — or his host's — unflattering clothes back into some semblance of shape and place, and then he walked through the house to the front door, and Amy followed him, saying nothing. Laurence drifted after them, dimly aware that his body was shaking, that Ru was yelling into his ear, but he had to try and find out where Amy got taken. He had to ignore the present even though the past threatened to overwhelm him.

Amy got into the back seat of the car, and this time Laurence leaned in closer. Any clue, any sign, anything that would lead him to finding her was important, no matter how small.

But finally, he saw what Amy did, and he understood her horror.

There was a baby in the infant's car seat, no more than a handful of months old, wearing a light blue romper with a matching sun hat.

It was still. Silent. Unmistakably dead. The skin was so pale that it was almost the same color as the clothes, and all that held the little body in place was the seat that was meant to protect it.

The vehicle pulled away, and Laurence retched violently as it left him behind.

"Laurence! What are you seeing? Tell me!"

Everything in his gut came up all at once. Laurence was dimly aware that Ru was right in front of him, but by the time he put two and two together it was too late, and for a split second all he could think about was how glad he was that he'd refused the coffee.

Then everything in the vision slammed back into him, and he started retching all over again.

6

LAURENCE

It was all too much. Laurence was trapped on the couch by Ru kneeling in front of him. They were both covered in vomit and reeked of stomach acid, and every time he blinked tears out of his eyes all he saw was a baby's corpse. He writhed in place, trying to break free of Ru's grip on his arms, to at least lean aside and throw up onto the floor instead, but when he finally made it, all he had left was bile and spit.

At least Ru had stopped shaking him.

Laurence sagged over the arm of the couch as he waited to be sure he was finally done puking. Occasionally a bit more saliva came up, and he spat it out on autopilot, because his head was busy blending everything in his vision together into one huge, horrible smoothie, and he didn't know what to focus on first.

"What did you see?" Ru stood up and took a step back.

So much. So fucking much, man.

"She's been taken." Laurence felt the wetness where puke soaked through his shirt, and was overcome with a distracting need to get it off his skin. "Vincent went to her house. He took her. Alive."

"Where is she now?"

Laurence couldn't stand it anymore. He peeled the shirt off over his head and tried not to heave again as it drew most of his sick right past his face. He bundled it up as wel as he could, but that left him with a horrible package he couldn't let go of.

Truck? Windsor offered.

Laurence just grunted and shook his head, both for Win and for Ru. "I'd have to go back in to find out." He stood, sidestepping Ru. "Man, I've gotta go shower. I'm sorry."

"Then go back in." Ru planted a hand firmly against Laurence's chest and stood right in his way, and it was only then that Laurence really looked at him and saw just how much of him had been caught in the mess.

It was a *lot*.

Laurence grimaced. "You could use one too. I'm sorry," he repeated. "Look, there's a lot of information, and I promise you I'll tell you what it is, but not like this. Trust me. You don't want it to be like this."

He waited. Ru's hand against his skin was warm, firm, and Laurence happily used it to help himself stay steady as a wave of dizziness passed through him.

Ru's jaw flexed, then he pulled back with an annoyed grunt. "If this delay costs us…"

Windsor spread his wings, then flapped them while he gripped onto the chair back. The movement sent a gust of cool air across the room, momentarily pushing the stench away. He didn't say anything, but his smugness radiated through his link with Laurence: he was very pleased with himself.

Ru hesitated, then huffed. "Fine. Have it your way."

Laurence dipped his head. "I won't take long, I promise."

Ru didn't answer, so Laurence hurried around him and made his way upstairs.

He rinsed his mouth out before he stripped, and once he was in the shower enclosure, Laurence washed his t-shirt as quickly as he could, and tried to clean himself just as fast. His pants were mostly okay; he could take care of those in the sink.

The enclosure's glass walls fogged with condensation and let him pretend that he was in a safe little cocoon, shut off from the rest of the world.

Well, more so than being in a sanctum, he thought. *We're already shut off.*

Goddess, this was rough. He wanted to call his mom so badly, talk this over with her, seek some support or insight, but he couldn't. Not without leaving the boundary of the sanctum and returning to the real world, where cellphones worked.

And he wanted to know just how much Vincent knew about him. He couldn't only be getting his information from Angela, right? She was being extremely careful with what she fed back to her adoptive father, trying to limit the damage and create some space for Laurence to keep a surprise or two up his sleeve.

Her adoptive father.

Laurence huffed and rested his hands against the wall as the hot water ran over him. He let his eyes drift closed while he picked apart all the strands of thought that were tying themselves into knots.

Did Vincent encourage Angela to befriend Ru when they were children so that he could keep tabs on his son? But if he'd told Amy to get an abortion, why did he even care? And why, once Ru was a teenager, did he kill Ru's parents but not step in to take Ru himself?

Then there was the fact that the murder was eleven years ago now. If Vincent wanted Ru back *then*, why had he waited until *now* to try and force things? Why didn't he step in back when Amy had? Vincent told Amy he'd waited, but something must've changed for him to not want to wait any longer.

If he won't come out for his own student...

Laurence gasped and opened his eyes.

Had Vincent made the black dog take Quen to see if Laurence would call on Ru's help?

Did he find Cameron Delaney and put the kid on Quen's tail to force Laurence to take action that might pull Ru out of hiding?

Was he the one who'd sent Mel's Instagram details to Derek Brooks, leading to Nate Anderson tracking them all down in the desert, just in case Laurence finally managed to coax Ru out of his house long enough for whatever Vincent wanted?

Laurence gritted his teeth and growled through them, then shut the shower off and grabbed his shirt to squeeze as much water out of it as he could. He coiled it up and gripped it tight, crushing it as his growl became a snarl. Then he took a breath and stepped out of the enclosure, back into the enormous white-tiled bathroom, where cooler air helped him get a hold of himself.

Ru had left his sanctum a couple of months back, while they were trying to track down the spell that trapped Lethe in a cycle of memory erasure. Had Vincent missed that, or was it not for long enough?

What Laurence wouldn't give for Quen's tactical brain right now, but if he tried to talk to Quen about this it wouldn't end well. Either Quen would have a problem with all the magic, or he'd want to rush over here and help out, and *then* have a problem with all the magic. Nope. Laurence was on his own for now.

He dried himself off with a towel that had definitely seen better days, then wrapped it around his waist while he scoured the gross bits off his pants, using hand soap and a nail brush to scrub at them until they were as clean as he could make them.

Why was Vincent driving around with a dead baby in the car, anyway?

No. No, no, no no no, he did *not* want to find out the answer to *that* one. He rolled his pants in another towel and squeezed to get them as dry as possible, but he couldn't walk around the house in only his boxers, even if Ru thought wearing nothing but his birthday suit was acceptable. He'd have to make do with damp pants and hope they dried out — or he got accustomed to them — soon enough, so he got dressed in everything but his t-shirt, and carried that out of the bathroom in one hand.

Ru was already there, waiting for him. His curls were so wet that they were the color of blood, and he'd changed into fresh clothes. He looked about ready to say something, then faltered while his gaze flicked across Laurence's chest.

Laurence's fingers tightened faintly on the shirt in his hand.

Something made the hairs raise on the back of his neck, and a couple of seconds later he figured out what it was.

Ru's pupils had dilated. His cheeks had flushed the faintest pink. His breath had paused, for a brief moment.

He's not just looking. He's checking me out.

Laurence snorted. He didn't have time to deal with Ru finally noticing how hot his student was.

Unless he's always known, and that's why he's naked so often.

Fuck, was he trying to flirt with me all this time? Is this why he hates Quen so much? Is he fucking jealous?

"Uh," Laurence mumbled. "My eyes are up here?"

Ru's lip curled, and he turned away, marching through to the library without another word and forcing Laurence to chase after him. "Now tell me what you saw."

Laurence sat in a chair that faced the long, wooden desk in the center of the room, and he dumped his soggy shirt on the polished surface. "Vincent looked like a woman. Amy didn't recognize him at first, then she wanted to know whether it was a disguise, or whether Vincent was possessing someone. He didn't tell her which it was." He turned to face the door just as Windsor stomped into the library, and held an arm out for him to come perch on, then he faced Ru once Windsor took him up on the offer. "He told Amy to leave with him, and she did. I don't think she had a choice. I'm pretty sure there was magic involved."

Ru sank into a chair across the table and faced him, sapphire eyes bright with anger. "Pretty sure?"

"Yeah. I can't always see magic in my visions, even with the talismans. My phone doesn't translate anything in them for me, either. I can only see what my own eyes would've seen if I was there. But he was definitely saying things I didn't understand, like he was triggering spells he'd already prepared." Laurence licked his lips hesitantly, but Windsor let out a soft rumble of encouragement, so he decided to push on. "They argued first, though — before he made her go with him."

"About what?"

"About you." Laurence took a deep breath and sat up straight, holding his head high so he could look Ru right in the eye. If Ru was about to explode in murderous rage, Laurence wanted to be alert to every single possible clue. "They're your biological parents, Ru."

Rufus blinked slowly, like Laurence had just told a joke he didn't get. "No they aren't."

"Yeah. They are. Amy got pregnant and Vincent wanted her to have an abortion, but she refused. She gave you to Paula and Todd, to raise you. I don't know why, but I think it might've been to protect you from Vincent. That's what he thinks, too. He seemed convinced that she'd been hiding you from him for years — maybe your whole life. But he's been keeping an eye on her, *and* on me. He knows Amy brought me to you, and he knew I was out of town when he came to get her. He's done it because he thinks you'll come out of hiding to find her..." Laurence let his words trail off, because he wasn't sure Ru was still paying attention. The other witch was staring down at the table with furrowed brows, and it looked like his thoughts were somewhere else, which was understandable. Laurence would totally be having a crisis if he'd just been told his whole life was a lie.

"You're lying," Ru finally breathed.

Anger flushed Laurence's cheeks. Of all the shit he'd just watched, to be accused of making it up was a straight up slap in the face.

"I am not," he ground out between clenched teeth.

Ru's eyes flitted up to meet his, and Ru at least seemed to consider, before he said, "*They're* lying."

"I don't think they are, man," Laurence said, more levelly. "I'm so sorry. I know this is huge. I can't imagine what you're feeling right now, but I've gotta find out where they are so we can put a stop to whatever Vincent's got planned—"

"No." Ru shoved his chair back and stood, then turned his back on Laurence and went to look out the window with his fists clenched at his sides. "Forget it."

Laurence eyed Ru while he pushed his own feelings back down so that he could think more clearly. The anger wasn't necessary, the moment had passed, and Ru had given the closest Laurence was going to get to an apology, so he forced himself to let it go. Once he was steady, more sure of himself, he breathed, "I'm not gonna do that. But if it stops you rushing out of here to go after her I'm on board with you taking a breather. Vincent's obviously trying to provoke you, so just… Stay here. I'll look into it, and then once we know everything we can come up with a plan, okay?"

"I don't want to know. She *lied* to me. My whole life, she lied! I don't…" Ru sucked in a breath, and only then did Laurence realize he was crying. "Fine. Sure. Find her. If she leads us to him, we get to kill the bastard that murdered my parents." He paused. "My real parents. The ones who bothered to raise me."

Laurence didn't know whether to try and console Ru, or to do as he was asked, but self-preservation was a powerful instinct and he didn't feel like getting roasted alive by a furious witch, so he nodded to himself and leaned back in his chair.

"Okay," he said with a soft sigh. "Let's see what I can find."

Then he dove into the river, and prayed that it wasn't about to drown him.

7
―――――――

QUENTIN

"And that's why I think you should stay in bed today," Estelita finished, sounding very pleased with herself.

Quentin found it very difficult to pick at his toast with only one hand. Instead he had to hold an entire half a slice and nibble away at it, which was tiresome and off-putting. But nibble he did, since it allowed him the space with which to avoid responding to Estelita's long and winding speech — most of which he had already forgotten.

"Well?" Alex whispered, glancing at her.

Estelita shrugged. "I think that means he knows we're right," she said.

Quentin's nose crinkled, and he set down the remaining piece of toast. Martin had purchased a tray with a bean bag attached to the underside so that Quentin could eat in bed, and his plate and teacup were balanced on it very comfortably, but it did mean that simply exiting the conversation through the traditional means of walking away was not an option.

"You *are* right," he finally sighed, wiping his fingertips on the napkin tucked alongside his plate. "Although it would at least be nice to rest in the garden instead, for a little fresh air, and the view…"

"Bed," Estelita said, as though she were presenting a

counteroffer. "Remember, if you don't get better, you can't look after us, so it's actually in our best interests for you to stay here."

"It's incredibly tedious—"

"I'll bring you some of Kim's books." Estelita pointed to his toast. "Finish that, I'll be right back." Then she whirled on her heel and swung her finger towards Alex. "Keep an eye on him."

"Um," Alex said.

Estelita was gone in a flash, and Quentin eyed the remainder of his toast.

"I do apologize for not being in a position to help you settle in," he said, and raised his gaze to Alex. The poor bugger's world was in utter disarray, and all Quentin could do about it was sit in bed, high as a kite, when he should be on his feet. "Or to find a place of your own, if that is what you would prefer," he added.

Alex shrugged and drifted around the room until they reached the windows, and they stared out of them with hands clasped together behind their back. "I don't know what I want," they said.

Quentin forced himself to chew on another piece of the cold toast, and he washed it down with some tea before he spoke again. "Quite understandable. Would it help to talk, do you think?"

"To you?" Alex's platinum eyebrows lifted, though they didn't turn to face him.

"To anyone. To the dogs. To the sea. I find that sometimes the process of sifting my thoughts into words helps me to narrow them down and understand them better, though of course that doesn't mean it will work for you too. But it might?"

He waited patiently, occasionally sipping his tea while Alex grappled with whatever thoughts were plaguing them. The urge to fill the void with words was not terribly strong just yet, so the Vicodin hadn't completely settled in, but it had already begun to diminish the amount of space in his thoughts entirely occupied by pain. All he had to do was use this delicate time wisely by keeping his mouth shut.

Alex turned slightly and sat in one of the chairs by the window. They laced their long fingers together in their lap, and tapped thumbs together. "This isn't how I look," they murmured.

Quentin neatly placed his empty cup down in the center of its saucer and folded his arm into the gap between tray and lap. "It is within your power to change your appearance, if you wish to?" He turned it into a question with a simple shift in tone, so as not to give the impression that it was a command.

"Would you? If you could?"

"I don't know." Quentin let out a faint snort of amusement. "If you had asked me that a year ago, the answer would have undoubtedly been 'yes,' but now I am more... Accepting of this body, and its flaws. But there are still days, or moments within days, where I wish that it could be..." He tried to find the right word, but it was eluding him, chased away by pain and opiates and the discomfort of toast working its way down to his stomach.

"Normal?" Alex suggested.

"Is there really any such thing?"

"No. Normality is an illusion, a lie that only exists to reinforce the kyriarchy."

Quentin blinked slowly. "The what?"

Estelita hurried back into the bedroom, this time with Kim and Soraya.

Soraya carried a stack of books in her hands which she promptly dumped on a side table. "Oh, I have *got* to be here for this."

"Where's Mel?" Kim pulled out her phone and started tapping at it. "She'd love it."

Quentin huffed at the interruption. "This is not a stage production."

"Popcorn *would* be great right about now," Estelita said with a grin. Then she gestured to Alex. "Don't stop, or he'll zone out."

Alex looked unsure about whether or not they really should keep talking, but Estelita nodded at them and waved her hands impatiently, so they wriggled in their chair and closed their posture in more tightly. "There are many overlapping and intersecting systems of oppression in most societies. In ours, the kyriarchy is what keeps all those systems in place and enforced."

Quentin's brows tugged together slowly as he tried to follow Alex's explanation. "Systems of oppression?"

"Sexism, racism, classism, ableism, homophobia, ageism, fatphobia," Kim mumbled. "They're not only ways to hate people who are different from you."

"Right," Soraya agreed. "They're also used to explain why people different from you should be treated differently. Worse access to education, healthcare, housing, jobs, all that shit." She paused, then narrowed her eyes. "Do you know what segregation is?"

"Er…" Quentin took a breath while his brain dredged up the definition of the word. "The act of separating…" *Items, or people.* The thought completed itself, though the words didn't pass his lips, and little flickers of memory popped up at random — though the more of them which arrived, the more they seemed to form a tapestry. Lessons from school, which seemed so abstract at the time, yet which now combined horribly neatly with many of his experiences in the past couple of years.

Concentration camps. Holocaust. Brixton riots. Nate Anderson. Hillsides alight with burning livestock. School bullies. Laurence's distrust of police. Apartheid. First-class check-in and security. All boys' schools.

"I… do, yes," he concluded quietly.

"Systems of oppression," Soraya said.

Quentin nodded with care so as not to move his shoulder at the same time. "I see. Upholding a platonic ideal of normalcy allows for the easy separation of those who fall outside the template?"

"And once you've identified the abnormal, you can push it aside and justify treating it differently. You can oppress it," Alex said.

"Which forces those with abnormalities to hide them so as to conform and remain within the bounds of accepted normalcy," Quentin concluded. "It's about control."

Estelita snapped her fingers. "You got it!"

"Doing pretty good for a rich white cis guy," Soraya agreed.

"Queerness and neurodivergence put him outside the boundaries of normality," Kim mumbled. "Probably makes it a bit easier to see where the privilege ends."

Quentin's thoughts were starting to slide around as the Vicodin finally settled in and smothered them all in goo, as though his brain were about to undergo an ultrasound. That goo must have a name, surely, but he didn't know what it was. Jelly? Lubricant? Gloop? He'd never asked. Though in defense of his lack of curiosity at the time, he *was* in rather a lot of pain from the damage done to him yet again by his father.

His mood soured, and he suddenly despised everything that was in physical contact with him. He tried to push his tray away, but the bean bag didn't allow for it, so he moved it telekinetically instead and almost dropped the teacup.

Soraya grabbed it in time, and carried the tray away altogether, putting it down next to the books. "Hold up," she said.

"I have to—"

"You don't gotta do shit except stay the fuck in bed and rest." She came back to the bed and planted her fists on her hips as she glowered down at him.

His skin crawled. He wanted the sling off, the bandages off, the pajamas off, the sheets off, the sweat off. He wanted a shower, he wanted clean sheets, he wanted peace and quiet and absolutely nothing *touching him*—

"What's happening?" Alex said.

"Oh, it's just the zoning out thing," Estelita replied. "Quentin? It's okay, just count down from ten. You're okay."

It didn't *feel* like zoning out, and he bristled at being told what to do.

"Ten, nine, eight," Estelita said calmly. "You got this."

Seven. Six. Five. His brain took up the count automatically, as though conditioned to it.

Calm down. You are surrounded by people who care about you, and who you care for a great deal. Just calm down.

Four. Three. Two.

"One," he whispered.

The room was quiet but for the breathing of all within it. Quentin still hated the sensations and the contact, but it was less overwhelming now, and he was exhausted.

"Still with us?" Soraya asked.

"I am," he murmured.

"Nice. Okay. Everyone else out. I'll stay, make sure he doesn't get into trouble, but Laurence is gonna kill us if we break him. Shoo." Soraya's voice moved from one end of the room to the other, and feet shuffled over carpet with it.

Quentin sucked in air and struggled to focus himself, to pay attention to what was happening, and to grasp the last strand of his tapestry of thought before it could unravel completely. He caught sight of Alex about to leave the room, and managed to say something.

"If it was to become myself," he said, "I would." Then he suspected that those words didn't make sense to anyone but himself, so he added, "Change. My appearance. If I could, if it would achieve..." He felt himself floundering, and flexed his working fingers. "I am not normal," he concluded. "And I have no desire to conform to some sort of mass delusion."

Alex stopped in the doorway. They turned slowly, and met his gaze with their features set into a grimace, but then they sighed and raised their head. "Yeah," they said. "Fuck the kyriarchy."

And then they underwent the most breathtaking transformation that Quentin had ever had the honor of witnessing.

8

LAURENCE

AMY SAT IN THE BACK OF THE CAR, UNABLE TO LOOK ANYWHERE BUT THE child seat, and unable to speak. But Laurence saw the tears as they ran rivers down her cheeks, and he watched while they fell onto her apron and turned it darker than any clay could.

What he couldn't do was face the same direction as her.

He told himself he paid attention to the world outside the car so that he could find out where they'd taken Amy, and it was true.

He also knew he did it because he couldn't do what Amy had the strength to.

Encinitas wasn't an area he was intimately familiar with. He knew the streets around Amy's house and pottery studio, in passing, and once the driver got them onto the 5 he knew they were going north, but so much of this time wasn't useful for much other than to try and be the comfort Amy didn't have back when this had happened to her.

Really, he was only comforting himself.

Laurence couldn't change the past, and he couldn't even be present for the people he watched there. But he could absorb every little detail possible, because anything could become relevant later.

So he stayed.

They took the turn for Carlsbad, and for a moment Laurence wondered whether Vincent lived near Rufus all this time, but the car kept heading east until Carlsbad wasn't even in the rear-view mirror *anymore. The road wound through towns in a valley right up until the car pulled into an In'N'Out parking lot, but the engine kept running.*

Vincent turned to look at Amy in the back seat, with no reaction at all to the distress she was obviously in, and all he said was, "You're going to stay quiet, and go with Marcella. Do everything she says. I'll catch up."

For a wild second, Laurence thought Vincent was going to get a fucking snack right in the middle of all this. The driver — Marcella — got out of the car, and Amy followed her, shooting Vincent one final, loathing-filled glare before both women got into the unremarkable SUV they were parked next to, but all Vincent did was get out of the passenger seat and walk around the car to slip into the driver's seat Marcella had just vacated.

They were splitting up.

Laurence gritted his teeth. He needed to follow Amy, but he really wanted to know what the hell Vincent was up to, too.

I can do both.

He clenched his jaw as he made his decision. He'd stick with Vincent for now, then come back to this moment and follow Amy to wherever Marcella was taking her.

Vincent pulled out of the parking lot and smirked at the rear-view mirror. "Enjoy the ride," he said. "It'll be over soon, don't worry."

Laurence's heart clamored in his chest.

Vincent couldn't see him, could he? It was impossible! Laurence was never here!

"Uh," he said. "Wait. What?"

Vincent didn't answer. He went back to paying attention to the road, a satisfied little smirk on his face, and Laurence's heart was still trying to break out of his ribcage while sweat prickled his scalp.

Did Vincent see him?

Laurence gnawed on his lip, then lunged forward and held his hand in front of Vincent's eyes, but Vincent didn't react. He didn't flinch, and he sure as hell didn't crash the car, or even lift his foot off the gas.

So who had he been talking to? Himself?

The thud of his heart blossomed into sickness in his gut.

No. He was talking to the woman in the driver's seat. Amy was right. Vincent was possessing someone. Someone completely innocent.

Laurence finally turned to stare down at the dead baby by his side.

Someone who was being forced to drive her dead child around in her own fucking car.

He lost track of where they were. Lost too much time trying not to throw up. He'd already done it once; his stomach had nothing left to give, but it sure was going for it anyway, and he had to spit out bile and saliva and not worry about where it landed. By the time he was able to focus on the car's surroundings again he was totally lost.

Well, not totally. The ocean was on his right, which meant they were traveling south.

Laurence scrutinized the world as Vincent hummed to himself. They weren't using the interstate, and so many of the roads around home looked alike...

Around home.

This was La Jolla.

Vincent drove casually around the winding bends and tree-lined streets, and he was so close to the beach Laurence half expected to look out and see Quen jogging along it with the dogs. When he turned down Camino de la Costa, Laurence felt sick all over again.

Vincent had driven past their home. *Right past it! He even grinned as he passed the mansion's wall, and his humming turned jaunty.*

Motherfucker knows where I live. He's doing this deliberately! *Laurence's jaw tightened, and he watched the house disappear behind them, then returned to looking ahead, through the windshield.*

This had to end soon, right? He couldn't still be driving around California two days later?

The car went on. It felt like forever, but Laurence knew it wasn't, because Sunset Cliffs wasn't forever away. It was barely twenty minutes, at best, but as the car stuck to Sunset Cliffs Boulevard the ocean disappeared for a few minutes, then reappeared when it met up with the cliffs on its way toward Point Loma.

"Here we go," Vincent chuckled. "Still in one piece. And such a beautiful view, too! Can't be beat, can it?"

His foot slammed down on the gas, and the car lunged forward. The view was *stunning, and Vincent was charging at it at* — *Laurence stared at the speedometer in horror* — *fifty... fifty-five...*

Sixty miles per hour, and the car horns around them blared while Vincent wove around slower traffic.

"Come on," Vincent snarled. "This hunk of junk can go faster, right?"

"Watch out!" *Laurence blurted, even though there was no point. This was already done. Whatever Vincent's game was, it was already over. Laurence was just watching the replay.*

The cliffs by the road were so close, barely a strip of sandy path between asphalt and certain death, and then even the strip of sand was gone, replaced only by a flimsy wooden fence that already had wilted flowers tied to it to mourn someone else's death.

Vincent yanked the wheel and gave the gas one last push as he aimed directly at the dead bouquet.

The car smashed through the useless fence, and sailed out into fresh, salt-laden air like it could learn to fly.

"Bon voyage," Vincent said.

There was a horrible stillness, for a split second, but then the driver seemed to come to her senses, and she screamed as the car plunged down to the choppy waters at the base of the cliffs.

Laurence jerked back at the impact. He felt like he'd been thrown bodily out of the vision, and the only thing that kept him upright was the solidity of the library chair's arms around his sides, and the desk in front of him that kept him from falling out of it. He grabbed the arms while vertigo made his head swim, and clung on until the sense of motion began to pass.

"Well?" Ru growled.

"I'm not done," Laurence gasped.

"But what did you—"

"I'm *not done!*"

Ru actually stopped talking, so Laurence went back. Back to the In'N'Out parking lot. Back to Amy and Marcella as they switched cars.

Back to watching things he couldn't change.

THAT VISION WAS FAR LESS eventful, thank the Goddess. Marcella drove the SUV up into the mountains north of Los Angeles, along switchbacks that sometimes made Laurence wonder whether she too was going to nosedive the car off a road and toss Amy down a mountain like a rag doll, but instead all that happened was the vision cut out, and no amount of trying could pick it up again.

It was way less disconcerting than it once was, now that Laurence knew what might cause it. Either they'd driven straight into Otherworld — which he ruled out as unlikely — or into an area where powers were shut off — way more plausible, and also terrifying. He doubted anyone like the Marlowes were involved in this, but it strongly suggested that Vincent or Marcella had the knowledge to interfere with gifts, and that meant they knew gifts existed *and* how to fuck with them.

Bad enough that Vincent was a warlock who had been spying on Laurence for months, if not a whole year. Worse that he had the magical knowledge to protect himself from more than just other people's magic.

This was bad. It was bad, and Laurence wasn't prepared. He'd thought he could take on Quen's father, and he'd almost died. The duke was an abusive piece of shit, but he seemed to mostly keep to himself when he wasn't trying to ruin his own children's lives.

Vincent was actively out in the world, doing whatever the fuck he wanted, and killing with impunity. Worse, he knew almost everything about Laurence *and* Rufus, and he knew what buttons to push. That was why he'd taken Amy: to force Ru's hand. And Laurence had to assume it was why he'd chosen to drive right by Laurence's home, too: to rub salt in the wound and provoke a reaction.

Which meant Vincent knew Laurence could see through time.

"Shit," he breathed. Did Angela sell him out on that one, or had Vincent found out some other way?

"Now?" Ru grunted at him.

Laurence shook his head and ran hands into his curls so he could tug on them and sharpen his focus. He drew a breath and held it for a couple of seconds, then puffed it all out and pulled himself upright in the chair.

A glint of light caught his eye, and he looked at the drying spit on the desk in front of him.

You should wipe that up. You can't let another witch get hold of it.

He hated how he knew it, and he hated that he felt like he couldn't trust Ru with something so simple as saliva anymore, but he grabbed the still-damp t-shirt from beside it and used it to wipe away at the mark until there was none left.

"They took Amy up north of LA," Laurence said. If he skipped all the horrible parts this might go easier. "Then I lost them. I figure they drove into a warded area, or a sanctum; somewhere I can't see into. I don't know the area too well, but, uh..." He pushed his chair back and turned away, searching the library with a quick look until he found what he wanted, then hurried along the shelves to pluck an atlas down. He flipped through the pages until he found California, and scoured the map, but it wasn't granular enough. Still, he took it back to the table and put it down in front of Ru, then pointed to roughly where he'd lost sight of Amy. "Here."

Ru leaned in to examine the area. "Well, that's a lot of finger, but it's a start. Angeles National Forest. How long does it take to get there?"

"No idea, man," Laurence sighed. "LA traffic is wild. Could take two hours, could take five." He went back to his original side of the table to grab the damp shirt. "What made you call me at six in the morning, anyway?"

Rufus snorted at him like Laurence was an idiot. "I told you. She didn't show up."

"No, I meant..." Laurence waved his hand to try and encompass what he was trying to put into words, but it was a futile gesture. "She was due here that early?"

"Of course." Ru got up, and took the atlas back to where it belonged. "We go grocery shopping every week before the store gets crowded."

Laurence stared at the back of Ru's head.

Amy left her home before sunrise every single week, just so she could take Rufus to the store to buy all the food he needed before it got too busy for Ru's comfort, and all that time she'd done it because she *knew* he was her son.

Laurence's fingers flexed. His grip on the damp shirt

tightened. His gaze swept across the library like he could somehow land on the one book or artifact that would help him know way, *way* more than he did so that he was even half-equipped to go square up against a warlock, but all he found were the small collection of books Rufus had once told him were for healing.

He moved toward them slowly, and ran a fingertip along their spines.

"Hey," he breathed. "Is there anything in here for broken bones?"

Of all the bad ideas he'd ever had this could easily be somewhere near the top of the list, but he could sense a hunt looming on the horizon, and he wasn't a hundred percent sure he was the hunter this time.

Vincent knew where Laurence lived; Laurence had to do everything he could to protect the most precious person in his life.

Even if Quen hated him for it.

9

QUENTIN

Alex's transformation was subtle and yet so very beautiful at the same time. Certainly there were aspects of their physical appearance which changed, but it was not that which took Quentin's breath away.

It was the way Alex's misery sloughed away, replaced by radiant, comfortable joy.

Their hair withdrew until it was much shorter, barely brushing against their shoulder blades, and it remained platinum blond. They lost a good three or four inches of height, and their bulk rearranged itself to soften harder edges and round out cheeks and jawline. Initially Quentin found himself tempted to apply the word *feminine*, but he was no longer certain that *feminine* was a word which bore any meaning whatsoever. As the shift took place, Alex had to grab hold of their trousers to keep them from falling, and their shirt sagged as it became oversized.

But oh how their head was held high, and a sparkle shone from their eyes, as though they had returned home after being lost for so long.

Quentin blinked slowly, and became concerned that he might be staring, so he turned his attention to the ill-fitting clothes and latched onto the opportunity they presented.

"If you all wish to go shopping, you may take my wallet," he offered. "I would come along, but, ah…" He used his functional hand to gesture to Soraya.

She nodded firmly. "That's right," she agreed. "You're going nowhere."

Alex's delicate brows lowered. "You're just going to let us spend your money on whatever we want?"

Even their voice sounded slightly softer, and had lost a tension to it which Quentin had foolishly attributed to anything and everything other than Alex's discomfort with their previous form.

"You need clothes which fit you," Quentin reasoned. "I'm afraid the only way we can achieve that in short order is to purchase them."

"It's fine," Estelita added. "We promise not to buy a car."

"We could buy a car!" Soraya gasped, and pumped her fist into the air. "Yeah, I'm coming with you. You stay here," she added, pointing to Quentin as she moved away from the bed. "Where's your wallet?"

"It's here," Kimberly said before Quentin could answer. She pointed to where it rested, on a side table, along with Quentin's phone and keys.

"Great! I'm driving. Catch you later," Soraya called as she ushered everyone else out the door. She grabbed the tray as she went, though, which would save Quentin from being interrupted by Martin later. "Stay in bed!"

Quentin snorted as they all filed out, but they closed the door after, and he was finally able to sink into the hazy comfort the Vicodin offered.

WHEN CONSCIOUSNESS RETURNED, it was accompanied by the strong sense that he wasn't alone. Nobody was in physical contact with him, but if Quentin didn't open his eyes he wouldn't be able to work out who it was.

Did he *want* to know, or would he rather go back to sleep?

Someone is in your room.

Reluctantly, but now trying to stifle a tiny alarm bell, he

allowed his eyes to drift open. As much as he might prefer not to be troubled by whatever may have invaded his life now, it was best not to let it murder him in his sleep, so he blinked away the blurriness and scanned his surroundings.

Then he found the source of the sensation, and relaxed once more. Myriam sat in a chair by the window, reading one of the books that Estelita had left for Quentin, but she raised her head from it the moment he found her and smiled broadly at him.

"There you are," she said. She closed the book and set it on the table. "How are you feeling?"

"Absolutely terrible," he replied, perhaps a little too honestly, "but it's quite all right. They have me on some medication which makes that immaterial so that I am able to rest."

Myriam regarded him as her hands settled together in her lap. "Do they now," she mused.

"Vicodin. Some sort of opiate, but with paracetamol added. Acetaminophen," Quentin clarified as he remembered the drug's American name. "It's all right I suppose, but it does very little to combat the pain itself. Although perhaps it's working extremely well and I would be in considerably more discomfort without it. The only way to find out is to stop taking it, but the surgeon would like it to continue until at least tomorrow."

He felt his mouth charge ahead without any input from his brain, filling the space between them with words as though he'd lost all ability to stem the tide, which meant that the medication hadn't worn off in his sleep. And *that* meant that it was still morning.

"Vicodin," Myriam echoed. "I see. And have you had opiates before?"

Quentin raised his chin faintly. "I have. Morphine, and occasionally codeine, though realistically that metabolizes to morphine in the body, so effectively I suppose that was simply more morphine." He laughed faintly, though the laugh ran away with him a little. "I've had problems with it in the past. It can be a little too tantalizing, you know? If one were able to simply keep taking it, perhaps the pain might never return... Or, at least, the capacity to care about it would remain absent. There's no dealing with pain, is there? Not fully."

Myriam nodded slowly to herself and eased to her feet. She approached the bed and stopped next to Quentin's elbow, then picked up the Vicodin bottle from his bedside table. She peered at the label, unscrewed the lid, looked inside, and closed it again. "All right," she said. "I'm going to take this away from you. Do you object?"

Take it away? Do you not trust me?
Yes. Yes, please. Take it. Dispose of it.
No, you need it!
I do not—

"Take it," he gasped. "Yes. Please. Get rid of it, would you?" Quentin ground his teeth slowly and shifted his weight against the cushion to try and redirect the nervous energy which had flared in him at the thought of the Vicodin leaving this room. That wasn't a good sign. He was all too familiar with how bad a sign it was, in fact, and having the bottle in here was upsetting Laurence, too. "Thank you," he added, in case he'd come off as rude in any way.

"Five minutes," Myriam assured him. "I'll be right back, dear, don't worry."

She left him alone, and the bottle was gone with her before he could try and persuade her to leave it behind, so he summoned his phone to his hand from across the room and checked that he hadn't missed any messages from Laurence.

He had texts from Neil, Ames, and Freddy, but nothing from Laurence, so he read and replied to those from the Storm siblings — checking in on him, asking if they could bring anything over or pay him a visit — before he stopped on Freddy's message.

It had to be two in the morning in London. Was Freddy awake late, up early, or not in London?

None of those seemed good, but especially not any option which placed Freddy in Quentin's timezone, because Quentin was reasonably sure he was still capable of hauling himself out of bed and kicking Freddy's arse from here to New York if his brother so much as tried to place a single foot inside this house.

Only opening the message would furnish Quentin with an answer, though. Delaying that would not solve anything.

He sighed and tapped it.

Icky. I understand there was an accident. Are you well?

Quentin scoffed. Freddy's internet observations must still be in full swing, and Quentin's name had likely cropped up in a news article somewhere about Neil's helicopter crash. Quentin certainly hadn't told him, and he doubted that Laurence had, either.

He typed out a reply without thinking too hard.

Yes, thank you. I shall need Nicky's address, please.

While he was wondering whether perhaps he could have thought a *little* harder, Freddy's reply came in, which at least confirmed that Freddy was awake this very moment.

Of course. I shall find it for you. May I ask why?

So that I may send him an invitation to the wedding, Quentin sent. Then he huffed and tossed the phone aside, irritated with himself for telling Freddy anything at all.

Unsurprisingly, the phone began to ring. Quentin groaned at it. He debated ignoring it, but Freddy would doubtless call back right away, and Quentin couldn't avoid him forever, so he snatched the device up and answered it.

"Go to bed," he muttered.

"*What* wedding?" Freddy countered.

"Mine," Quentin said.

Freddy was quiet a moment, and Myriam slipped back into the room. She had a small bottle of medicine with her which she placed beside Quentin's glass of water, and she raised her eyebrows at the phone.

Quentin put his thumb over the microphone, and whispered, "Freddy."

Myriam nodded thoughtfully. "Shall I leave?"

"No, it's quite all right."

Myriam busied herself bringing the chair closer so that she could sit by Quentin's side, and Freddy began speaking again.

"Good for you. When's the happy day?"

"I don't know. We haven't decided." Quentin laid his head back against the cushion and let his eyes fall closed. "He told me what you did, Fred."

"What *did* I do?" Freddy asked. He sounded quite cagey.

"You know full well," Quentin snapped. "And you had best not be anywhere near here, or I will find you, and give you a bloody good hiding. How *dare* you come to our home, talk to him as though everything were normal, foist a butler off on us, and not *once* admit to me what you did to Laurence. I swear to you, Frederick, that if I catch sight of you within a hundred miles of him I will pull your sodding arms off and let you bleed out in the middle of the desert. Is that clear?"

"Perfectly," Freddy said slowly.

"Good. And what's the situation with Martin? Is he reporting back to you? Spying on us for you? Why did you choose him? What's your angle there? You may as well tell me, I'll have to bloody fire him."

"Icky, no—"

"Why not?" Quentin's jaw felt like it might lock into place, and he forced himself to open his eyes, to try and calm down before something got broken.

"He's nothing of the sort. I promise you. I am not in contact with him, and it's not right that he should lose his job. It's me you're angry at, and rightfully so." Freddy's voice was terse, his words clipped. "You may not trust me, but you can trust Martin."

"Why?"

He heard Freddy's huff, then a faint grunt.

"Because he encountered something supernatural. When he was a child. He has no idea what it was, and nor do I, but it almost killed him. He has no gifts, no magic, and an abiding love for comic books." Freddy paused. "The boy wants absolutely nothing more than to be able to support the kinds of people who *can* stand up to monsters, and that's you, Icky. You, and Laurence, and everyone else in that house. Let him help you. He needs it, and so do you. What drugs are you on?"

"Vicodin," Quentin said before he realized that Freddy had crept that question up on him. He scowled. "Myriam has disposed of them for me. I shall be taking paracetamol from here on out."

"Good. You don't need that muck. You were injured in the crash?"

"Goodbye, Freddy," Quentin snapped. He hung up and threw the phone down onto the sheets before he could give away even more information he didn't wish to, and rubbed his face with his palm. "Bugger," he sighed.

Myriam's hand rested over his forearm and squeezed slightly. "You handled that well," she said.

She didn't *sound* as though she were being sarcastic, and when Quentin dropped his hand so he could look at her, there was nothing but sympathy in her warm brown eyes.

"I handled it awfully," he groused.

"I think you got the important parts across to him pretty clearly." Myriam offered him a small smile and withdrew her hand. "He's not welcome here unless you say so. It's healthy to have boundaries, and you've set yours." Then her smile widened and those eyes of hers sparkled playfully. "And I'm debating whether or not I would like to see you tear his arms off."

"It was... A figure of speech?" He winced as he said it, quite certain that it wasn't at all convincing.

"Uh huh. Well, you can talk that over with your therapist before you go dismembering anyone, just to make sure." Myriam withdrew her phone from her handbag and unlocked it. "Now, Bambi asked me to talk to you about the wedding," she said, changing the subject with ease. "I'd like to get a feel for what you want for the ceremony, how many guests you'd invite, whether they're people with limited availability we need to coordinate around, and whether you're taking my son away on a honeymoon that I need to schedule coverage for at the store."

Quentin struggled to release his anger at Freddy so that he could stick with Myriam's list, and it was easy once he understood what she was saying and how huge an undertaking planning a wedding might actually be. He'd never done such a thing, of course, but he had attended a few, and thinking back on them now, they all had guests, and food, and décor, and a venue, and it suddenly all seemed so incomprehensibly massive.

"Oh," he breathed. "Um. I don't... I don't know."

"Don't worry. That's why I'm here. I've organized so many weddings that I've lost count." Myriam chuckled and patted the back of his hand. "Bambi was thinking of a handfasting. Does that suit you, or would you like something more familiar to you?"

Quentin envisioned vast cathedrals with hundreds of guests, a pompous cleric of some sort, and the interminable boredom of sermons and hymns. None of that filled him with excitement, and he could only imagine it to be a hundred times more awful for Laurence, who would likely feel incredibly out of place at such events.

It was not reasonable to ask Laurence to put up with all that nonsense, especially when Quentin himself cared not one iota for any of it, so he took Myriam's hand in his own and squeezed lightly.

"Explain this handfasting to me?" he asked.

She nodded and curled her warm fingers around his, then began to talk.

All he had to do was try to take it all in.

10

LAURENCE

"What's the connection?" Rufus glanced at the books Laurence had indicated, then he jolted into action and almost ran to them. His fingers spread across their spines as he began to search the shelves. "Amy's injured," he concluded.

Laurence opened his mouth, but stopped himself from answering. If Ru thought the spell was for Amy, he'd dig it up right away.

No. He's too smart. He'll figure out in no time that I have no way of knowing whether or not she's been hurt since she was taken.

"I don't know," he sighed. Better to tell the truth now than have it bite him in the ass later. "But Quentin is."

Ru's hands stopped immediately. Of course they did. He seemed to really hate Quen.

And he's got the hots for you.

Laurence kept his groan as internal as he could manage. Was Ru's snippy attitude toward Quen nothing more than petty jealousy? Goddess, this was a mess, and there wasn't any time to untangle it. It'd have to wait until they'd rescued Amy and put a stop to Vincent's bullshit — whatever that was.

"We're not going to La Jolla," Rufus grunted. "We need to go north, and you want to add two hours for nothing?"

"Hear me out." Laurence draped the t-shirt over his left arm, then invited Windsor to use it as a perch. He continued speaking to Ru while his familiar leapt up and made himself comfortable. "We need to talk to Angela. She knows where Vincent lives. She might even know what his wards are like, whether he's got traps set up in his sanctum, and how we can get in there and rescue Amy without dying horribly. You were the one who told me some sanctums are just straight up going to kill any unknown magic user without hesitation, right?" He petted Windsor's head. "Vincent's a warlock. What kind of shit has he got in there we don't know about?"

"You can call her," Rufus grunted. He still wasn't digging out any bone-fixing spells, or doing much of anything at all.

"And what if she wants to meet up with us? Walk us through how to get in and out in one piece? Give us something that could help?" Laurence bit the tip of his tongue for a second, to force himself to stay calm, to stick with an appeal to logic instead of yell at Ru that his gut was all but screaming at him that this was the right thing to do, and he couldn't allow Ru's distaste for Laurence's instincts to get in the way.

"She can meet us en route," Ru said.

Laurence puffed out his cheeks and paced away from the table, away from Rufus, hugging Windsor to his chest while he tried to work out how to put a pin in Ru's rashness — an impatience that only showed itself when his need for revenge reared its head, because he sure had all the patience in the world when it came to teaching Laurence magic as slowly as possible.

That's it. He paused at the door and turned on his heel, letting himself tease at the thought a while longer. *Vincent's been stalking us. He knows Ru wants revenge.*

"He's playing us," he breathed when his gaze settled on Ru again. "Pushing your buttons. He took Amy to make you move because he knows you've got no chill when it comes to vengeance. You'll put the brakes on and read books for every other situation, but revenge makes you lose all perspective and throw caution out the window." He hesitated, then let out a soft huff. "If this wasn't Amy, if it was Quen who'd been taken, what would you do?"

Ru pulled away from the books at last and flexed his fingers in a way that didn't make Laurence feel entirely at ease. "But it's not."

"C'mon, man," Laurence wheedled. "You didn't even come to London when Freddy took me. You stayed here and you sent Quen the spell he'd need, but you knew he couldn't cast it. You weren't going to be drawn out of your sanctum for me, and that's okay." He raised his hand before Rufus could argue. "You don't owe me shit. And Amy's…" He sucked in fresh air. "She's your mom. Even if you're angry about that, even if she's not the person you think of when you think *Mom*, she raised you after Vincent killed your parents, and you care about her. But if you run right into whatever his trap is, how does that help her?"

There was a hair-raising pause where Rufus looked ready to boil the flesh off Laurence's bones just to get past him.

"Think," Laurence hissed, clutching Win a bit tighter to his chest. "That thing you keep telling me I need to do."

Ru let out a frustrated sound like an angry tomcat. He whirled back to the shelves, snatched a book up, and stormed to the table, where he slapped it down and flicked through pages until he found the one he wanted. He pointed at it and scowled at Laurence. "Here. It'll accelerate bone healing. It's not instant, but it'll put a break back together in half the time and reduce the risk of infection."

It wasn't ideal, but Laurence would take it. Maybe if it would stack with Quen's already-fast healing it'd knock a couple of extra weeks off, so he approached the table and took photos of the page. "Thanks," he said. "There's nothing faster?"

"Probably, but I'd have to go looking for it. It's not a section I have much cause to read." Ru had the grace to look vaguely apologetic, though it was possible he was just embarrassed about the gap in the index system that only existed inside his head. "What if Angela doesn't answer? Are you going to her house?"

Laurence sighed and gestured to his own bare chest, then wished he hadn't. "I've got to go home and get fresh clothes. I can swing by hers on the way if she doesn't pick up, but if she's not there I'll have to come up with something else." He stuffed the phone into his pocket. "You wanna come with me? We can figure out more options as we go, and if we need to come back here to hit up the books on the way to Vincent's we can."

He half hoped that Rufus would say no and stay here, but he also suspected that could lead to Ru charging off to try and track down Vincent on his own, which he also didn't want. Nothing good could come of that, especially since it seemed to be exactly what Vincent wanted, so he turned on his Bambi eyes.

The hardness in Ru's features melted slightly, and his shoulders dipped a few millimeters. "That would be the smart thing to do," he grumbled.

"And you *are* smart." Laurence gave him a thumbs up, and headed for the door. "Let's go. The sooner we figure this shit out, the faster we get Amy back."

Windsor cooed softly against his skin as he hurried down the stairs, expressing his concern without using any words.

"Yeah," Laurence breathed. "You and me both, Win."

The sense of dread he'd come here with hadn't eased off any.

LAURENCE FORCED himself to put the damp t-shirt on before he got into the truck, and hoped his body heat would dry it off before too long. He waited for Ru to settle in the passenger seat, and Windsor to get comfortable in Ru's lap, before he tapped at the dashboard to call Angela. Once it was ringing, he checked his mirrors, and pulled out into the street.

"Laurence," Angela said. Then she added, "You're driving?"

"Yeah, and Ru's with me. Look, we gotta talk. Can we meet up some place?"

"Rufus," Angela said, either in greeting or acknowledgment. Reading her in person was hard enough; over a phone call was just straight up impossible. "What is this in regard to?"

"Your dad's made his move," Rufus grunted. "He's taken Amy Jenkins."

"Jenkins," Angela echoed. "Ah, yes. From Encinitas. Interesting. Is there a ransom?"

Laurence risked a quick glance across to Rufus, but had to turn his eyes back to the road. "No," he said. "None we've seen, that is. Feels like he's decided to knock over the apple cart and watch what happens."

"No," she said. "There is always a larger plan." She paused. "Very well. Where do you want to meet?"

"I can be home in an hour. Meet us there?" Laurence ignored Ru's scowl, even though he only caught it out of the corner of his eye.

"Easily," she replied, and ended the call before Laurence could even say goodbye.

"She'll betray us, you know," Ru muttered.

Windsor made a variety of rude noises, disagreeing vehemently through the medium of blowing raspberries, and Ru shushed him.

"She won't," Laurence said automatically, and he frowned at himself. Was that his own belief, an instinct, or was it accidental prophecy? "Why do you think she will?"

"She's already told him all about you. Worse, we *know* she's doing it, and we're still letting her teach you."

Laurence huffed and stopped talking for a while so he could concentrate on joining the interstate. "She's withholding as much as she can from him," he argued. "Ask me whether she's going to betray us."

"What, you're going to look into the future while you're driving?" Ru squirmed in his seat, pulling his knees up and tightening his hold on Win. "Yeah, no thanks."

"No, I'm not. Just ask me, okay?"

They'd gone a whole mile before Rufus finally gave in. "Is she going to betray us?"

"No," Laurence said. And this time it *was* prophecy, without a doubt. It came out of him like a bullet from a gun, and his shoulders drooped slightly once it was done. "Okay," he breathed. "Good. That's—"

"Are *you* going to betray *me*?" Ru cut in.

"No," Laurence blurted, as certain as his last answer had been. He blinked and tried not to turn to stare at Rufus for even *thinking* of asking him that, but the 5 was busy, and the last thing they needed was to wind up as street pizza.

Besides, maybe Rufus had a right to ask. Laurence was standing between Ru and the vengeance Ru had been craving for more than a decade already. Even now, after finding out who his birth parents were and that his whole life wasn't what he thought it was, Ru was still a hundred percent fixated on making Vincent pay for his parents' deaths, yet here Laurence was driving him away from his goal *and* insisting they meet up with the woman who'd almost succeeded in making sure they never even made it *this* far.

Laurence sighed softly and shook his head. "I'm so sorry. This has to be hard for you on so many levels. I'm…" He hesitated and tried to figure out whether what he wanted to say could be misread or misconstrued, but he needed to say it anyway, so he pushed on. "I'm here for you, man. I said I'd find the truth for you, and that I wouldn't stop until we got it, and I keep my word. You're not going to face this alone. You might not be used to having or needing or even wanting help, but you've got it anyway. We're going to get Amy back, and we're gonna make him pay for everything he's done, and we're doing it *together*. Okay?"

Rufus was silent a whole ten miles this time, but Laurence didn't push. He was used to Quen taking time to figure out what he wanted to say, and Quen was a social butterfly compared to Rufus, so he just paid attention to driving and figured Ru would get back to him if he wanted to.

Eventually, all Ru said was, "Okay."

Laurence nodded, but didn't add anything more. Instead, he began to chew over the problem he already knew he didn't have the answers to.

How the hell were they supposed to rescue Amy from a warlock who'd been pulling Ru's strings his whole life?

11

QUENTIN

Quentin drifted awake, largely provoked into doing so by the increasing pressure from his bladder, and he was almost ready to throw his bedsheets off when the rest of his morning caught up with him and he thought to check his surroundings first.

It was just as well, as Myriam sat in a chair by the window, reading.

"Oh, um." Quentin cleared his throat softly, then winced. "I am so sorry. Did we manage to, um… Finish the conversation before I nodded off?"

Myriam peered over the top of the book before lowering it to her lap, and she cast a warm smile to him. "The important parts, yes," she assured him. "But I thought it best to let you rest, dear."

"You are most kind." He tried to corral his thoughts — perhaps convince them to allow him to string a sentence together — but they were being most disobedient. The best that he could manage was, "I must, um…" with an apologetic glance to the bathroom.

"Of course." Myriam looked as though she intended to return to the book, then her eyebrows raised. "Oh. Why don't I step outside so you can have some privacy? You can call me if you need me."

"Thank you." Quentin exhaled softly and watched Myriam gather up her handbag and head out of the room, and once the door clicked closed he tossed the sheets off and began the laborious process of shifting his center of balance so that he could get up without undue strain.

It was not that he was undressed. Far from it. He wore pajama bottoms and one of Laurence's t-shirts, which hung off him like a sheet of tarpaulin. But he preferred that Laurence's mother not see him in sleepwear if it were avoidable — particularly not if she was to officiate at his wedding. He did not wish to spend the event distracted by the knowledge that the person performing their ceremony had seen him in any inappropriate situation.

The trek to the bathroom was not laborious once he was on his feet, and thankfully his gifts made it far easier to remove clothing or maintain cleanliness than he might otherwise find things with his right arm thoroughly immobilized. Still, as much as he keenly desired a shower, he was not so foolish as to try that without Laurence's aid. He made do with a wet facecloth, then shaved cursorily, and brushed his teeth. When he regarded his reflection, he was satisfied that he was presentable enough to remain well within the confines of his own home, which was the best he could ask for at this juncture.

He took the time to moisturize what he could reach, resolved to ask Laurence to help with his back later on, then made his way out of the bathroom and into the walk-in wardrobe.

Long-sleeved shirts were out of the question. He hadn't the patience to try and wrangle one on, and he'd have even less patience to remove it later, so he plucked another of Laurence's t-shirts from a drawer and focused all his attention on the delicate series of maneuvers to unfasten Velcro straps, thread the shirt up his right arm, pull it over his head and slip his left arm through it, and then re-fasten all the Velcro around his chest until the sling was firm once more.

It was exhausting. He had to pause, to stand still and do nothing but breathe, until the queasiness of the pain passed and he was no longer light-headed. But once he was done, underpants, socks, trousers, and slippers were all well within his power.

He'd had quite enough time in bed. For a change of scenery, he would go downstairs and pass out there instead.

"You are supposed to be resting," Myriam said the moment he opened the bedroom door.

"It's boring," Quentin said, not caring in the slightest that he felt like a whining toddler.

"It is," Myriam agreed, not unkindly. Then she offered him her arm. "You'll use the elevator, and we can sit in the garden. It's a beautiful day, and the fresh air will do you some good."

He took her arm and allowed her to steer him along the corridor while he debated demanding he be allowed to use the stairs in his own home. The lift was tiny, and very rarely of any use to anyone, to the point where Quentin largely forgot that it existed, but it was functional, and would give Myriam peace of mind for him to use it.

She prodded the button for the lift, and Quentin pursed his lips as he finally caught on to her canny negotiation technique.

"All right," he said, relenting quietly. "I shall meet you downstairs."

Myriam smiled and patted his arm, but she also waited until he was in the lift and the doors were closed, watching him like a hawk.

Quentin sighed faintly and tapped the ground floor button. As the lift moved slowly downwards, he had a momentary flash of being elsewhere: hot, dark, on his back, a towering brute of a man standing on his breastbone and leering as the agony from a shattered shoulder soaked through Quentin's body—

But he was shaken out of it with a soft *ding*, and light flooded into his world when the door slid open.

Myriam took his arm before he'd even managed a single step, and she frowned up at him. "It's all right," she murmured. "If this is too much, we can go back upstairs?"

"No," Quentin croaked. He leaned against her for support as

he steadied himself, then allowed her to steer him out of the lift. "I would rather like to see the ocean."

Myriam nodded, her lips pressed tightly together, and she waited for him to right himself before she guided him through the kitchen and out into the garden.

THEY SETTLED ONCE MORE, into recliners which faced the sea, beneath the shade of a brightly colored canopy. Myriam fetched a pitcher of water and a couple of glasses, as well as something for Quentin to read, and then they simply relaxed. Perhaps Quentin dozed; he wasn't certain, and didn't care, because Myriam was right: the fresh air *was* doing him good. The slosh of the choppy ocean crashing against the rocks on the far side of the wall at the end of the garden was accompanied by a cool breeze which carried the fresh taste of salt inland. A handful of little grey and white birds with yellow patches on them were lined up on top of the wall, eyeing the pool and the humans while they debated whether all that water was truly fresh, and Quentin smiled faintly as he watched them think it over.

He was only now starting to familiarize himself with the local wildlife, and while he recognized the yellow-rumped warblers, he wasn't sure which sub-species they were. They likely came down from colder climes at this time of the year to see through the winter months in San Diego's more temperate environment, and the gardens of La Jolla contained a feast of insects and berries to keep the little birds well-fed.

As one, though, the birds took to the air and flocked together, scurrying south. Quentin didn't have to wonder for terribly long what had startled them: the dogs trundled into the garden, Grace with her nose almost to Pepper's tail as they ambled towards him with all the eager enthusiasm of having spent their morning running quite enough already, and he laughed softly.

Myriam put her book down and reached out to pet the dogs as they passed her by, but they were much more interested in receiving attention from Quentin, and settled by his side once they had it.

"This must mean Martin's back," Myriam said. "Sit tight, dear, and I'll let him know you're out here so he doesn't worry himself that you're not in bed."

Quentin petted the top of Pepper's head, since she was easier for him to reach. "Thank you."

"No getting into trouble." Myriam wagged a finger at him as she stood, and then she straightened out her pastel yellow dress with a few pats before she made her way to the house.

"Would I?" he asked of Pepper.

Pepper grinned and thudded her tail against the flagstones. She evidently had little opinion on the matter, and no interest in forming one, which Quentin was completely willing to accept as her prerogative.

"Quite right," he murmured to her. "See? I can be a good patient."

She slobbered on his hand, then laid down on the stones and sprawled onto her side, bumping up against Grace, who didn't move out of the way. They rested together, eyes closed, until Quentin was sure they'd fallen asleep in scant seconds, and he considered following suit.

It was a consideration which did not last very long.

Myriam emerged from behind the hedgerow which separated the back patio from the rest of the garden, but she was not alone. By her side, quite placid and unhurried, was Angela.

Quentin frowned faintly and moved to stand, and while Myriam sped up and gestured with open palms to the ground to try and prevent him, he made it to his feet just in time for her to arrive at the table, so she huffed at him.

"Is something the matter?" He looked to Myriam, and then to Angela.

Angela eyed his sling, and her eyebrow lifted a fraction. "Of the two of us, I would suggest that you are the one in need of aid."

Quentin scoffed faintly and offered his left hand to her, along with a warm smile. "Aid has already been given, I assure you. I'm afraid that Laurence isn't here at the moment."

"So I've been told," she intoned. "But he is on his way. Do you mind if I join you?" She seemed unfazed by the left-handed handshake, and eased her fingers around his to squeeze briefly.

Quentin glanced to Myriam, whose features were creased with faint traces of concern, and he took that to be a sign of something perhaps a little more serious than either of them wished to bring to his attention, so he gestured to a third recliner and summoned it closer with care. He settled it down within Angela's reach. "Please," he murmured. "Would you like some water?"

"I'll get you a glass," Myriam said without waiting for Angela's response.

Angela blinked slowly as Myriam hurried back to the house, then she adjusted the chair and settled into it. "I suppose I'm having water," she said dryly. "Thank you."

Quentin adjusted his own chair so that it was upright before he, too, sat, and then he regarded the sorcerer across the table and did his best not to catastrophize. Angela was a smart individual, and incredibly logical from what little he had seen of her, even if her logic *had* led to Laurence almost being eaten by a shark.

She was a child, he reminded himself. *She could not possibly have foreseen the outcome of her choices all those years ago.*

He couldn't help but think of how difficult it must have been for her as a teen: raised by a warlock, all but alone in this world, and manipulated by her father into doing whatever it took to save Rufus' life from the crash which claimed both of his parents — only to realize far too late that she had been a party to their murder. Of course she had done the only thing she thought would protect both Rufus and herself, even if that meant losing him and isolating herself even further, potentially without ever finding out she'd done it.

Her situation was not so dissimilar from Quentin's own in some regards, and he found himself unable to hold her remotely responsible for Laurence's close call with nature.

"Quentin?"

He took a breath and forced his attention back to her in time to see Myriam return with a fresh glass, and pour water for Angela before she retook her own seat.

"I apologize," he murmured. "It's the medication. Is everything all right?"

Angela nodded gratefully to Myriam and drank half her water before she looked Quentin in the eye. "Laurence asked me to meet him here, but I have evidently arrived before him. It's nothing to worry about."

He wanted to believe her. Truly, he did. But she had returned to her blank mien, and another look at Myriam revealed that the concern on *her* face had only deepened.

"All right," he said. "I appreciate that it may well be none of my business. At least allow me to ask instead whether Laurence is in any danger?"

Angela drained the rest of her glass, set it down on the table, and then raised her head. "That depends on what he chooses to do next. But I suspect that the answer will become 'yes.'"

Quentin straightened up in his seat as his pulse began to race. His head swam, and while he took a deep breath to steady it, all that did was add more oxygen, and he grew light-headed in an instant. "What's happening?"

"It's my father," Angela said. "He's taken Amy Jenkins. I've come to see whether I can talk Laurence out of taking foolhardy action, and I suspect I'm going to need your help for that."

"Of course," he said without thinking.

Then he thought about it, and wasn't certain that he'd said the right thing at all.

12

LAURENCE

Laurence parked the truck in the garage, and Windsor leapt into his lap the moment the engine shut off.

"Nice try," he said to the bird, and tucked him under one arm. "We're not gonna sit here all day, though."

Windsor clacked his beak and made discontented rumbles, but he knew he'd been busted — the reluctant acceptance of his failure thrummed along their bond and revealed his complaints to be a good-humored admission of guilt.

Laurence got out of the truck and helped Win up to his shoulder while he glanced across the empty space where the SUV should've been. A faint sniff of the air gave him a jumble of scents that implied at least four of the kids had been through here, as well as Martin and the dogs more recently.

Teens are out, Martin's home, not sure about Mia.

Hopefully that meant Quen was still in bed, and Mom was making sure he didn't get up to anything he shouldn't.

"This way," Laurence said as he hurried past Rufus before Ru could invade the house, and he led the way through to the corridor, where he almost collided with Martin.

"Laurence," Martin said, greeting him politely and not even flinching as Laurence barely missed him. "Your guest has arrived and is in the back garden with Lord Banbury and Mrs.

Riley." He stepped smoothly aside. "Would you care for refreshments?"

"I feel like this is a coffee kinda day," Laurence confessed.

Rufus didn't bother answering. He just barged right on past them both as his long legs chewed up the distance between him and the kitchen, and Laurence spared Martin an apologetic glance, but Martin only smiled.

"I'll bring a fresh pot," he murmured.

"Thanks, man." Laurence hurried after Ru and did his best not to worry about whether today was the day Rufus was going to try to kill Angela again, or how he'd get Quen back into bed, or even whether coffee was a great idea on an empty stomach. Those were Future Laurence problems, even if he was only two minutes away.

With only a fleeting apology to Future Laurence, he caught up to Rufus as he rounded the hedge, and matched pace with the witch on his approach to the parasol that Quen, Myriam, and Angela sat under. The dogs were at Quentin's feet as usual, though they wagged tails at Laurence's arrival.

"Hey," Laurence said, in case Rufus tried to kick things off with less tact. "Hope you weren't waiting long?"

Angela shook her head. "Barely five minutes."

"Great. Hi, Mom. Thanks for coming over. Morning, baby." Laurence circled the table and stepped in behind Quen so that he could lean over and kiss the top of his head. "Needed a better view, huh?"

"Alas," Quentin murmured.

"So long as you're still resting." And he was: Laurence could pick out the scents of toothpaste and soap, but Quentin's hair hadn't been washed, so at least he'd behaved and stayed out of the shower. "I've got to borrow Angela, though. Nothing for you to worry about, just... you know... Magic talk."

"You can stay," Quentin said.

Laurence eyed him, but couldn't read his expression from the back of Quentin's head, so he glanced at his mom instead.

Myriam sighed gently. "Vincent has taken Amy, hasn't he?"

Laurence tried hard not to shrivel up and die on the inside.

Angela had told them. Goddess, she'd been here all of five minutes, and she'd already told them what was going on. How the hell was he supposed to keep Quen away from all this now?

"Yeah," Rufus grunted. He grabbed another chair and brought it to the table, and slouched in it like a teen who'd just been sent to his room to do his homework. "And instead of going to get her, we're all here." He glowered up at Laurence.

"Because we need a plan," Laurence said. He moved away to collect a chair for himself, and took the opportunity for a deep, calming breath. Maybe Quen's tactical brain could help them with the plan, and then he could stay right here while Laurence rescued Amy.

Yeah, like that'll work...

He felt a muscle in his jaw twitch, but he couldn't stop it, so he picked up the chair and put it down next to Quentin. "And the first step is that we need to know where Vincent is, which I'm hoping you do." He had his hands on the chair still as he faced Angela across the table, and felt no inclination to sit down.

"Where he always is," Angela said. "He leaves his sanctum even less than Rufus does. That's where he'll be holding Jenkins, too."

"So it's a trap," Quentin stated, no hint of a question in his tone.

"Yeah. He wants Rufus." Laurence hesitated, unsure of whether he should tell anyone the rest, and he looked at Ru. "You want to tell them, or should I do it?"

Ru scowled at him, but Martin arrived bearing a tray loaded with coffee, mugs, milk, and sugar, and Rufus pressed his lips together as he watched the butler offload everything onto the table. Whether that meant Ru didn't want Martin to know or was delaying the inevitable wasn't clear, but Laurence was willing to wait a minute to find out.

His grip on the back of the chair tightened.

So did a knot in his gut.

The hairs on his forearms lifted, and Windsor cawed a wordless question in his ear, but before Laurence could say anything, time slowed down as the universe began to take a breath.

Everything happened at once, yet time was like molasses. Laurence saw it all: Rufus' head whipped toward the pool; Angela reached into her purse; Quentin's eyes widened as he assessed everyone at the table before he, too, turned his attention in the direction of the pool; Myriam's expression of resignation, as though whatever she had worried about this morning was finally here.

And he saw black threads of magic drip like oil into the space between table and pool. They coalesced until they were so thick that he could see stars glinting in the void they created, watching him as if they yearned to consume him. The blackness took form between one blink and the next, and though the afterimage of the void clung to the depths of the shadows in its suit, squirming like maggots in rotting meat, the stars were no longer watching.

Time snapped back into place.

"Well," said Hieronymus d'Arcy, as he cast a cold, grey gaze across the distance between them. "This is a start, I suppose."

THE SOUND of Martin's tray hitting the ground seemed to spur everyone into action, but Laurence was still reeling, still trying to grasp how the duke had appeared here, where they were supposed to be safe. He stared numbly as Quen and Ru leapt to their feet; watched Angela withdraw a mirror from her purse, and Martin crouch down to retrieve the tray. Windsor launched himself into the air, screaming bloody murder as he gained altitude, and the dogs leapt to their feet to growl at the intruder.

Myriam let out a small sigh and remained seated.

Laurence met his mom's eyes, and all he saw there was sadness. While Quentin attempted to adopt some sort of defensive stance and Ru had already unleashed a spell under his breath, Myriam looked up at Laurence and swallowed tightly as her skin paled just a little.

Laurence wished he could ask what she knew, or even what she felt, but if he didn't do something right this moment there was going to be a war in his garden, and he wasn't convinced that anyone would get out of it in one piece.

The duke gave Quentin his word. It was his only hope, but he was willing to grab at it, and wring the life out of it if he had to.

"Stop!" Laurence yelled. He forced himself to let go of the chair he'd been trying to crush in his hands, and ran past Quen to put his body between the duke and the people in his life who were — pretty reasonably — about to try and kill him. "Wait!"

Standing with his back to the duke was the last place Laurence ever wanted to be, and sure as hell not to *defend* him. The man who had forced Freddy to put Laurence through hell, who had intended to kill Laurence with his bare hands, and who had raped his own son was *behind him*, and his skin itched so badly that it took all his willpower not to lower his hands and start scratching at his elbows.

Somehow, the scene in front of him was awful, too: Quen, unsteady on his feet but still with his left hand raised, palm toward his father; Angela, opening the compact mirror and facing it away from herself so that Laurence caught sight of his own reflection, with the duke looming at his back like an omen of death; Rufus, the most powerful witch on the West Coast, laden with turquoise spells which all waited patiently for the right trigger and could be unleashed with nothing more than a whispered word.

Laurence felt so exposed, but he knew he was right.

The duke wasn't about to attack them.

"Why are you here?" Quentin barked, glaring straight past Laurence's right ear. "What do you want?"

Rufus's cheeks tightened, and his fingers flexed. "This is your father," he breathed to Quentin as he seemed to connect a few dots.

The situation was stable — for now, at least. Nobody had fired off more magic, and there wasn't any blood, so Laurence took a breath and turned on the balls of his feet to come face to face with the single most evil piece of shit he'd met in his entire life.

The duke gazed impassively at him, not a speck of fear in his features or the way he held himself. The tendrils of void that seethed in his shadows were almost hypnotic.

"Why *are* you here?" Laurence raised his chin and forced his hands to hang loosely at his sides, to try and hide the terror he really wished he wasn't feeling.

"You have a problem," the duke replied, his deep voice carrying well despite him not raising it at all. "I have come to ascertain whether or not you also have the solution."

"And if we don't?" Laurence trapped the inside of his cheek between incisors and bit down just enough to keep his focus where it needed to be instead of running screaming into the sea.

The duke unleashed a frigid smile which featured far too many teeth for Laurence's liking.

"Then I will offer it to you," he said.

A trickle of sweat trailed down the small of Laurence's back at the malice in the duke's eyes, and he couldn't help but feel that whether they could beat Harrow or not, the last thing they should do was accept whatever fucking help the duke thought he could provide.

"Out of the goodness of your heart?" Laurence growled.

"Don't be ridiculous, child." The duke snorted. "There are things at stake here which are far more important than your injured pride."

Laurence's fingers curled until his hands were fists, and he already regretted stepping in to stop Ru unleashing hell. "Like what?"

The duke shrugged. "Your enemy targets mothers. Are you certain that you can protect yours?"

Laurence's flesh prickled, and every hair on his body stood up at once as the duke's words rang true. He saw with sickening clarity the look on the face of Vincent Harrow's possessed victim as she drove off a cliff and plummeted to her death in the rocky sea below, her own murdered child in the seat behind her. He saw the horror in Amy Jenkins' eyes when Harrow walked into her home and forced her to leave it with him. He saw the scream Paula Grant unleashed while Todd tried to avoid the car crash that would kill them both, and he saw the sadness in his own mom's eyes just two minutes ago.

The breath fled his lungs and left him lightheaded.

What Laurence *wanted* was irrelevant.

13

LAURENCE

"What do you know about any of this?" Rufus snarled. "*How* do you know about any of this?"

The duke ignored his question, though he did turn his callous stare on Ru, which lifted the oppressive weight of it from Laurence for a moment. "Rufus Grant," he stated. "Quite a stockpile you must have in that sanctum of yours, considering the time and resources Paula and Todd devoted to accumulating it."

Rufus looked like he'd been backhanded across the cheek, and he surged toward the duke, unleashing a word — except, whatever it was, he didn't get to finish it. The duke tossed Rufus over his shoulder and into the pool without lifting a finger, and there wasn't the slightest change in him that hinted he'd been about to do it. Laurence saw no shift in his breathing, his posture, the blood flow to his skin, or to the dilation of his pupils, and that meant the reaction had come to him so casually that it hadn't quickened his pulse, or even interrupted his train of thought.

Laurence let out a soft breath. This wasn't the man he'd watched Quen grind down into defeat. The duke was prepared, alert, and fully in control of the situation, which only reinforced Laurence's gut instinct that attacking him would be a super bad idea.

"I see that Mr. Grant is not blessed with maturity," the duke sighed, and turned his laser focus on Quentin instead. "What is your plan for resolving this problem?"

"Get out of our home," Quentin breathed. His voice shook, and he remained rooted to the spot.

Laurence sidestepped toward Quen, to offer moral support if nothing else. Quen was a grenade of rage, terror, pain, and meds right now, and if the duke wanted to yank out his pin, he could explode in all their faces.

"I am not *in* your home," the duke huffed. He gestured to the mansion without turning to look at it. "We are outside."

Outside.

Laurence took a second to be sure that Ru could get himself out of the pool without any difficulty — all those childhood swimming trophies in his bedroom had to be good for something, surely — and once he was satisfied to see Ru already springing out of the water he turned his attention on the house.

The building he could see above the hedge was threaded through with the green strands of his magic, protecting the mansion from esoteric entry. There were extra wards over the windows to stop anyone peeking in through them as a workaround. None of the people living here could be directly targeted so long as they wore the talismans Laurence made for them even if they weren't inside, but the house itself was an extra layer of defense. The only way the duke could possibly bypass any of that...

Quen's blood.

Laurence swallowed, and turned his head again, swiveling to watch Quen.

Quentin didn't have any of Laurence's magic on him at all. He'd been sitting outside, unprotected, this whole time, and Laurence had no idea where his talisman could be or why Quen wasn't carrying it. But the duke *did* have Quen's blood. Had he taken to spying on Quentin whenever he felt like it? Quen didn't have any perception magic; he was limited to his own innate senses, which had obviously worked well enough a moment ago when the duke had teleported in or projected himself or whatever the fuck he was doing right now, but what if scrying was too subtle to trip Quen's alarm bells?

"I said," Quentin hissed, his entire body stiff with rage, "get out!"

"Wait." Angela's voice was calm as ever. "I understand," she added with a nod in Quentin's direction. "He is here without invitation or permission. But he *is* here, and offering assistance. We should at least hear what he has to say."

Laurence saw the microscopic shifts in Quen's posture, the way the tips of his ears pinked along with his cheeks as his temper started to fray, and he felt the cold breeze that lifted the tips of Quen's hair and stirred Laurence's own curls.

That grenade pin was starting to wriggle loose, and if Laurence didn't do anything, this whole situation would go sideways really fast.

"I hate to say it, hon, but I think Angela's right." Laurence spoke softly, and stepped closer to Quen to get into his field of view, but he didn't reach out. Goddess only knew how Quen might react to being touched without warning while his dad was ten feet away from him. "Vincent's a warlock. If anyone can give us some insight into how that fucker's mind works, it's..." He waved a hand toward the duke, but didn't look away from Quentin. "It's this shithead. Why don't you take the girls inside, and I'll handle this?"

"I'm not leaving you with him." Quen didn't take his eyes off his father, but he at least unwound slightly at Laurence's words. "Pepper, Grace, go indoors."

Pepper whined, but she did as she was told, and Grace followed, her nose to Pepper's tail.

"I want to know what you know and how you know it," Quen continued. "Now."

Laurence glanced past the duke at Ru as the witch drew himself upright. Water cascaded off him and darkened the poolside. Laurence tried his best to make eye contact, to convince Ru to stay silent and still behind the duke so that they at least had a tactical advantage if they needed one.

Ru's lip curled, but he stayed where he was, moving only to

wipe the water from his eyes and push his curls back away from his forehead.

Okay. Laurence could shift his attention back to the duke at last. *So far so good. Everyone's still breathing.*

If he could keep it that way, he was willing to call it a success.

"If you really want to help us," Laurence murmured, doing his best to sound reasonable, "I think answering those questions is a good place to start."

Hieronymus grunted at him, but he reached out with one hand, and while everyone tensed up at the motion, all that happened was a manila folder appeared out of nothingness like he'd plucked it off a bookshelf. He flipped through it, idly skimming the contents until he picked out a single piece of paper and held it up, facing them.

Laurence made out the headline easily.

Mother and child die in tragic road accident.

"While you were enjoying your tour of American hospitals," the duke intoned, "this unfortunate young woman was murdered. The coroner has ruled it an accident, of course, and failed to notice that her son died several hours before she was killed." He returned the paper to his folder, and dug out another.

Neil & Amy Storm in helicopter crash.

"Getting named by the press was careless." Hieronymus clicked his tongue in disappointment. "It would be enough to advertise your absence even if your enemy was not already observing you and testing your capabilities. But allowing yourself to be injured so drastically, too?" He shook his head. "You are weak. Of course he has chosen to strike now. How do you intend to stop him in this state? You can barely stand, boy!"

"That's enough," Laurence said firmly. He closed the distance to Hieronymus, stopping barely inches away from him and blocking the line of sight between both d'Arcy's. There was sharing information, then there was straight up provocation, and the duke had quickly tipped over into the latter. It was like he couldn't help himself. "You're stalking us?"

"I'm not the only one."

"And now you've decided to get off your ass." Laurence licked his lips and jabbed at the duke's chest with his pointer finger, but had to tamp down his alarm when the tip of his finger disappeared into the illusion. He'd been so sure that the duke was physically here, that he'd teleported in, but now Laurence was this close he realized he couldn't smell him at all. "You're not gonna help out for free, right? You're bound to have a price. What is it you want from us? 'Cause I'm telling you right now Quen's not gonna learn magic, and he's not going home."

The duke's gaze was like a basilisk's, unblinking and unnerving, and Laurence hated everything about it, but he refused to back down.

"I want Vincent Harrow's sanctum, and everything in it," Hieronymus said.

"No," Rufus snapped, and jolted into action, stalking around the pool edge and toward the duke.

"It seems unwise," Angela agreed, more cautiously.

"Assess the future." The duke only looked at Laurence; he didn't spare even a flicker of his attention to anyone else. "Can you afford to reject my terms?"

Laurence ground his teeth. If the duke was right — if Myriam was in danger — did Laurence *want* to look?

I don't need to.

Goddess, he knew in his bones that he didn't need to. The way Mom had spoken to him on the phone this morning, the sadness in her posture right now, and the fact that she hadn't said a word since the duke popped into existence told him that she already knew.

Maybe they could beat Harrow without the duke's help, but not without losing Myriam, and there was no way Laurence was going to let that monster lay a finger on his mom.

"No," Laurence sighed. "I can't." He offered his hand before he remembered the duke wasn't really here. "Fine. You're on."

Hieronymus took the hand somehow, wisps of black coiling around his sleeve and along his fingers as he shook Laurence's hand firmly. His steel eyes were alight with triumph. "We have a deal?"

"Deal," Laurence agreed. The word tasted bitter on his tongue.

There was absolutely no way this wasn't going to bite him in the ass sooner or later, but as he withdrew his hand he had the sinking feeling that the fangs had already come and gone.

All he could do now was wait for the venom to take hold.

14

QUENTIN

Everything was wrong.

Everything was wrong and there was nothing he could do about it. Father was here, and that was wrong. Laurence shook Father's hand, and that was wrong. Myriam was in danger, and that was wrong. All of it was *wrong* and Quentin felt sick and the pain from his shoulder was thrumming and throbbing and his painkillers were wearing off and

people

kept

using

magic

and Quentin wanted to scream, but what was the use? He had spent thirteen years screaming and it hadn't changed a thing. He was supposed to be safe here but he wasn't. He carried a talisman and it didn't help, because Father was *here* and he refused to *leave*.

Rufus was angry about this, at least. Quentin hadn't expected such stalwart defiance from the witch, yet he seemed to be the only other person here truly incensed by Father's arrival. Even now he was attempting to throw himself bodily at Father, though he passed harmlessly through the illusion despite it having made physical contact with Laurence's hand only seconds ago.

Quentin could have told him that it would be fruitless. He had no idea how it worked, but he was already familiar with Father's capacity for transferring physicality from one location to another at will. Father had passed him the spellbook to help with locating the spell which trapped Lethe as if he had been in the same corridor, and yet he was not lit correctly for that to be true.

He was not lit correctly now, either. The San Diego morning sunlight was of a slightly cooler color temperature than that which illuminated Father, though thanks to the darkness of his suit and Quentin's familiarity with his father's features, the wrongness was only truly evident in the cast of his skin and reflections in his eyes.

Rufus nearly collided with Laurence. Laurence jolted back and *did* collide with Quentin.

The contact was only light. But it was at his right elbow, and the pain in his shoulder turned sharp. It made the sickness in his stomach churn that much more quickly, and when he flinched back the world began to slide away in all the wrong directions.

But then someone had him. Someone warm, and short, and surprisingly strong, who smelled of peat and flowers.

"I've got you," she whispered.

"Quen?" Laurence blurted. "Fuck! Baby! I'm so sorry! Are you okay?"

"Sit down," Myriam murmured gently. "Here. The chair is right behind you. I won't let you fall."

"No, I—" Quentin struggled to remember why he didn't want to sit, why he needed to fight her, but there was darkness at the corners of his vision, and all he could see was Laurence's worried face and it was too much.

"Sit," Myriam said. Her tone was still soft, but with that motherly undercurrent of firmness beneath it which brooked no argument. "I won't let you fall."

He couldn't resist her steerage for very long. He was far too unsteady on his feet, and not certain enough of which way was up. Ultimately he was forced to relent, and he allowed her to guide him down into the chair until his back nestled against it and he was able to breathe without wondering whether he was about to empty his stomach.

"Hon?" Laurence sounded worried. "Are you okay?"

"The acetaminophen," Myriam said. "It's in your room."

"I'll get it," Martin said.

Quentin did everything in his power to focus on Myriam's gaze. She had settled on another chair facing him, her back to everyone else. Her hands clasped around his and held on tightly. Her hazel eyes were warm and caring, her grip stalwart, so he allowed her to become the center of his world.

The blackness began to recede. The breeze faded away. But he still felt sick.

It would have to do.

"Thank you," he breathed.

Myriam nodded to him. "Take your time."

Father snorted in the distance. "Still overly dramatic, I see? Well, no matter. Where were we before we were so rudely interrupted?"

"Goddess—" Laurence snarled.

"Ah yes. An exchange of information." Father continued as though Laurence hadn't said a word. "Harrow has been 'stalking' you — as you so eloquently put it — since you sought out Mr. Grant as your tutor. I only truly began to pay attention to his activities after he used a Black Dog to take Quentin — presumably to Annwn?"

Laurence's breath hitched. "You're sure it was him? Like, you *know* that was him?"

"All evidence is circumstantial, but certainly points to him. I also don't doubt that he was instrumental in putting Mr. Delaney onto Quentin's scent. Likewise he patently orchestrated the encounter which led to Quentin's current physical condition. He has been testing you, Mr. Riley. He is working out the extent of your abilities and resources so that he may account for them in his plans."

"Testing... *me?*" Laurence's tone was incredulous. "Then why's he targeting Quen all the time?"

"You cannot be this naïve, boy," Father grumbled.

The sickness began to die down, although it did not diminish entirely. Quentin supposed that perhaps lemonade may not have been the best drink to fill up on. It was highly acidic, and he was generating quite enough bile on his own.

But it meant that he was at least able to think a little now.

"Because I am your weak spot," Quentin murmured. He didn't look away from Myriam. "Just as you are mine. You will push yourself to your very limits if it is my life in danger, just as I will for you. Harrow has forced you to show him your hand, little by little, so that you cannot surprise him."

"Therefore you require an ace," Father said. "And now you have it."

"You're not an ace," Rufus snarled. "You're a *warlock*."

"And we should consider fighting fire with fire," Angela replied.

"Yeah, well, you would say that. You were raised by one, just like he was."

Quentin had no doubt that Rufus' comment was aimed at him, but he wasn't interested in rising to the bait. Instead, he turned his attention to Martin as the butler returned with paracetamol and a fresh glass of water, and he murmured his thanks as he took both.

"Information!" Father was terse, evidently tired of the bickering. "It is your turn. What do you have?"

Instead, there was more bickering. Quentin focused on swallowing the pills and washing them down with as much of the water as he was able to drink, and then he gave the glass back to Martin.

"Enough!" Laurence yelled. "Ru! Do you want Amy back, or not?"

The crash of waves against the wall at the bottom of the garden was the only response Quentin heard.

"Great. Then can it. You don't get to bitch me out for 'wasting time' then piss and moan when we're actually trying to help you. Am I ecstatic about any of this? Of course I'm not! Do I wanna work with this shitstain? No fucking way! But am I gonna let what I want get in the way of saving people we care about? No, I'm not! Are *you*?"

Quentin let out a light breath. There was no way in hell he

would ever have used such language to refer to his father, and absolutely not with the man in earshot, but he certainly didn't object to Laurence doing so. He could even appreciate it — so much so that he managed to tear his gaze away from Myriam for a moment, just to look across at Laurence.

Laurence, who was radiant in the morning sun, his golden hair a halo, and his tanned skin so perfect. His back was to Quentin now, but even so he was breathtaking, and Quentin's body began to unwind a little further.

"This is on you," Rufus finally snarled. He pushed past Laurence in a manner which made Quentin want to toss him right back into the pool, and came over to sit back down next to Angela. He hunched over, and glared daggers at the duke.

"Information," Father prompted.

Laurence sighed and threw up his hands. "Harrow took Amy Jenkins. He's holding her hostage. He wants Ru to go to him."

Father's eyes narrowed. He turned his attention on Rufus for a short while. "Amy Jenkins the potter? Mr. Grant's surrogate mother?"

That didn't provoke a positive reaction from Rufus. If anything, the witch's attitude became frostier still, and Quentin felt a pang of sympathy for the young man.

"Yeah, well, it turns out she's his birth mom," Laurence said. "And Harrow's his dad. Warlocks, am I right? Just can't keep a hold of their kids."

"Made considerably harder if one gets shot of them the moment they're born," Father mused. "Was it to hide the boy, or to protect him?"

Laurence shrugged. "Harrow wanted Amy to get an abortion. She refused. That's all I know." He glanced over his shoulder to Rufus, then back to the duke. "He killed Ru's parents. If he wanted Ru back, why not take him then? Why wait until now?"

Father turned to face Quentin. "Well?"

Quentin sucked in air and straightened in his seat, then hated that he'd done either. Worse, he loathed that his brain was already turning the question over, examining it, probing it, attempting to extrapolate from what little data he had, and when the answer came to him, it seemed so clear that he sighed. "Because something has changed," he said. "Harrow's situation, or his needs, perhaps even his mindset. But there has been a change, and it has prompted him to reassess his relationship with Rufus."

"There *is* no relationship!" Rufus said through gritted teeth.

"But now he seeks one, although the nature of said relationship cannot be deduced from what we have thus far. I would suggest that his need is not urgent, if he has had this much time to poke and prod and test before making his move." Quentin pinched the bridge of his nose slowly, as though he could squeeze the rest of his thoughts free from their congestion. "If he only wanted Rufus, he would not have needed to test Laurence so thoroughly — or, in fact, at all. Therefore he anticipates that Laurence will also be in attendance, and either wants him there, or wishes to be able to neutralize him." He hesitated, then added, "It is possible that Laurence's appearance in Rufus' life may even be the change which prompted Harrow to take action, but I would not say that is anything more than a wild stab in the dark: we have no proof other than somewhat suspicious timing."

Father grunted. It *sounded* like approval, but Quentin wasn't sure he'd ever received approval from Father before, so he couldn't be absolutely certain.

"And you must be..." Father moved on to Angela now. "If you are his daughter, why did he keep you and not his son?"

"I am adopted," Angela intoned. "I do not know who my birth parents were."

"He was willing to raise *a* child. But not *his* child." Father mulled it over. "And he did not raise you as a warlock. You are older than Mr. Grant?"

Angela inclined her head slightly. "I am."

"Curious." Father nodded to himself, then walked past Laurence.

Towards Quentin.

Except he was not looking at Quentin. Instead, he offered his hand to Myriam, and even bowed his head a touch.

"If you would care to come with me, Mrs. Riley, I shall see to it that you are protected throughout this affair."

Myriam reached for Quentin's hand instead. She held it tightly, and he automatically closed his fingers around hers, returning her grip as best as he could. He liked absolutely nothing about this: not the closeness of his father, nor the fact that he appeared to be suggesting that he would take her somewhere else.

"Assuredly not—" Quentin began.

"Quentin," Myriam said. She spoke calmly, and offered him a small, apologetic smile. "I love Eric with all my heart, but I'm in no rush to be with him again so soon."

"Mom!" Laurence rushed over and hovered by her shoulder, looming over them both with a look of pure anguish on his face. He wrung his hands together. "You can't just go with him!"

"This is true," Father said. "You will need to remove your ward first."

Laurence shot him a look of pure malice, which Father ignored.

Myriam's fingers squeezed Quentin's softly, and he frowned at her in time to catch her as she made direct eye contact with him. Her lips were pressed together lightly, and her eyebrows were raised.

Was she asking him something?

Quentin blinked slowly as his fingers returned the squeeze. If she *was* asking what he thought she was, he despised it, but it *did* make sense.

He was of no use here. He could not use magic. Worse, he would become easily overwhelmed were he to be surrounded by it. He had already narrowly avoided one episode this morning, and he doubted there had been anywhere near as much of the stuff as there would be at Harrow's sanctum. And while he had absolutely no desire to leave Laurence's side, what else could he do? He could not fight, could not protect Laurence; in fact, he was an active hindrance to Laurence's next move. Harrow had shown repeatedly that he would toss Quentin into the pit to force Laurence's hand, and Quentin was in no fit state to prevent Harrow from using him that way yet again.

Myriam was right. Curse everything about this horrific situation, but she was right.

"Myriam is not going alone," Quentin finally said. He raised his chin and stared directly up at his father, daring him to disagree. "I'm coming with her."

Laurence yelled in protest, but Myriam gave Quentin the faintest of nods.

"Fine," Father said. "Obviously there's no need to dispose of *your* ward, since you aren't even bothering with it right now."

Quentin's pulse raced. Where was his talisman? Surely he hadn't left it indoors? It went with him everywhere, safely tucked into his—

His jaw clenched.

The talisman was in his wallet.

It didn't matter whether Father had his blood, because he'd idiotically left the house without his talisman, and that meant Harrow would be able to pick him off without even trying. It was in everyone's best interests for Quentin to take advantage of the magical protection on offer, and it would allow him to tackle multiple problems at once, so he rose to his feet with care.

He would go with Myriam.

He would find what remained of that bloody shirt, and incinerate it.

Then he would work out what exactly his father wanted from Harrow's sanctum, and make damned sure that Laurence destroyed it before the duke could get his hands on it.

"Obviously," was all he said.

15

LAURENCE

Laurence's skin felt like ice. He hadn't meant to bump into Quen, but everything had happened so fast, and like a butterfly flapping its wings in a forest five thousand miles away, somehow they'd gone from an accident to Quen agreeing to go home with his dad — the thing Laurence had literally told the duke less than ten minutes ago wasn't ever going to happen.

He was still grappling with the guilt of having hurt Quen, the fear of losing his mom, the terror of yelling at Rufus, and of shaking the duke's hand. Somehow now he needed to cope with the decision Quentin had made to be somewhere else while Laurence tried to hunt a warlock and rescue a hostage.

It's for the best. He can't be around all this magic. Look at what it's already doing to him. Never mind seeing a ghost, he looks like he is *the fucking ghost.*

It was true. Quen was deathly white, with pink splotches on his cheeks and knuckles, and a faint sheen across his face. Even his lips were pale, almost bloodless. Laurence was sure the only thing keeping Quen upright was Myriam.

"Quen," Laurence croaked. "You… You can't…"

He trailed off. What could he possibly say? *Don't go, your dad's evil?* They both knew it. What was the point in retreading familiar ground? *Mom will be fine without you?* The thought of his mom alone in that massive house with the duke made his flesh crawl. *I want you here, with me?*

Yeah, that was the sticking point. It wasn't that Laurence *needed* Quen here for this. It was selfishness. He *wanted* Quen by his side, even though it could do way more harm than good, and that wasn't right. It wasn't fair to Quentin. And in the end it would give Vincent all the ammunition in the world while offering Laurence none of the protection.

This really was for the best, 'cause if the duke could manifest himself in their back yard, there was nothing to stop Vincent from doing exactly the same. Only the house was safe from magic, but it couldn't keep a god out, or a psychopomp, or ghosts.

Hieronymus lived in a fortress. The only time Laurence had been there was before he'd learned the perception spells he used now, and he'd thought Castle Cavendish was under-defended. Now he wasn't so sure. Rufus' house was lit up like a Christmas tree, and Laurence could only imagine what defenses the duke's home might have lurking inside its walls.

Quentin raised his head and turned to face Laurence. Every inch of him radiated exhaustion and it wasn't even noon, yet he held himself with a level of dignity Laurence knew he wouldn't be able to muster if he was in Quen's position.

"It's all right," Quen said softly.

Laurence closed the distance between them and cupped Quen's cheeks in his hands. "We're going to fix this," he growled, gazing into those eerie, silver eyes.

Quentin tipped his head back faintly so that he could maintain eye contact. "You are," he agreed. "Call if you need me."

Laurence sighed faintly and dipped down to kiss him, then lingered against his lips even once the kiss was done, reluctant to break contact. "You too, baby."

"I shall." Quentin's lips brushed faintly across Laurence's. "Soraya has my wallet," he added.

If there was a train of thought that had led from one statement to the next, Laurence couldn't figure out what it might be, but he groaned anyway. "Shit. The kids. Where are they?"

"Shopping. I'll let them know they need to come home and

stay home until you are finished." Quentin closed his eyes for a little bit too long for it to be just a blink, even if it had started out as one.

"Forgive me for intruding, but... I can take care of that, if you wish?" Martin's voice came from beyond Quentin and Myriam.

Laurence nodded. "Yeah. Okay. We'll get everyone back here and inside. You just... look after yourself, okay?"

Quen opened his eyes, and he nodded faintly between Laurence's palms. "Of course, darling."

Laurence kissed him again, on the cheek this time, and pulled back so that Quentin could go do what they both knew he had to, and both undoubtedly hated.

"Bambi." Myriam moved in closer, and she pressed her talisman into Laurence's hand. The small brass pentacle was warm from her skin. "I'll be back for this, so don't lose it."

"You better be." His fingers closed around it, helped it keep that warmth for now, and he moved in to give her a one-armed hug. "I love you, Mom."

"I love you, Bambi," she whispered. "Be careful."

"You bet I will," he breathed.

She smiled a little as she stepped away, one hand still wrapped around Quentin's, and she turned to face the duke so that she could offer him the other. "We're ready," she said.

Hieronymus snorted. "Finally."

Without waiting around for any last words, he took Myriam's hand, then sliced his own through the air.

And, just like that, all three of them were gone.

"WHAT THE FUCK ARE YOU THINKING?" Rufus bellowed the moment the duke was gone. "Laurence! We all know what he did!"

"I don't," Angela intoned.

Laurence snapped a hand up to stop Ru before he could say another word. "Don't you fucking *dare*," he snarled. Ru might've accurately guessed what the duke had put Quen through, but he had no right to put it into words. "If Quen wants people to know, he'll tell them. We don't have time to argue; we have to work out what the fuck we're going to do about this!"

"Do about it?" Ru threw his hands up. "You said you wouldn't betray me, yet here we are!"

Angela let out a faintly irritated huff of air. "Calm down."

"Calm down," Ru echoed.

"Yeah." Laurence got in between them before they could start trying to kill each other. "Goddess, Ru, that asshole might be back any minute! We need to be on the same page before he gets here! We have *got* to trash Vincent's sanctum, right? I don't care what Quen's dad wants, we can't let him have it, surely?"

"You—" Ru cut himself off, then blinked at Laurence, and screwed his nose up. "Wait, what?"

"If you hadn't been so busy losing control of your emotional state, you would have seen clearly that Laurence was not betraying you," Angela stated. "He handled the situation well under the circumstances. We know nothing about that warlock's skill or readiness, and antagonizing him would have been foolish. We are already dealing with one problem; we do not require another."

Laurence ran fingers through his hair and tried not to pull on it too hard. He hadn't had a chance to talk to Quen about using the spell he'd found at Ru's to help him heal faster. The man he desperately wanted to kill with his bare hands had just taken his mom *and* his fiancée to England, using magic Ru didn't have access to, which meant Laurence couldn't chase after him. Ru could just about send something the size of Windsor, and even so the closest he'd get was Paris, because Ru's spell relied on an emotional connection to a place the caster had been before.

I go?

Win swooped down from the cloudless sky like a hawk hunting a mouse, his wings so dark and wide they seemed to blot out the sun.

I don't know. I don't think it's a good idea, Laurence thought back at his familiar. He raised an arm for Win to land on. *I don't want you falling into a warlock's hands.*

Warlock here, too, Win argued.

Yeah, but I want you to stay with the kids when they get back. I need to know they're safe.

Windsor chattered loudly and let loose a massive jet of droppings that narrowly missed Laurence's knee. "Fuck," he said out loud.

"Yeah." Laurence couldn't really disagree with that, but he still didn't appreciate it. "Look, we know Quen can kick his dad's ass if he has to. Let's just… focus on the problem at hand, okay?" He drew Win to his chest and petted the bird, mostly to soothe himself, as he looked between his two teachers. "I guess we start with everything you know about Vincent's sanctum," he said to Angela. "Address, layout, wards, defensive magics, the works."

"And his coven," Angela added.

It was Laurence's turn to witlessly repeat her own words back at her. "His coven?"

"Not that they possess free will," Angela replied. "He owns them all, to some degree. Only three retain any mild pretense at independent thought, but the remainder are still very capable witches capable of impeding or even halting most intruders."

Laurence exchanged a look with Ru, but Ru was finally quiet, like he'd had all the anger drained out of him. Now he just looked as confused as Laurence felt.

"How many in total are we looking at here?" Ru muttered.

"Thirteen, plus Vincent himself."

"Traditional." Ru's lips twisted in disgust. "How is he controlling them?"

"For most, they no longer possess a true sense of self." Angela gave a faint shudder, though she smoothed it away swiftly. "I do not know the technicalities of how this was achieved, but it is safe to assume that magic was involved."

Laurence nodded as he listened. "What you're saying, though, is that once this was done, it's remained in place. There's no active spell controlling them that we might break?"

"That is correct."

He clicked his tongue as he patted Windsor's head. "So we can't just destroy a sigil to get them off our backs."

"Which means we have to know who they are, and what they can do, too." Rufus sighed and finally sat at the table. He planted his elbows on it, and rested his face in his hands. "Fine." His voice was muffled by his own palms. "You were right. Rushing in might've gotten us killed."

It was as close to an apology as Rufus ever got, but Laurence was willing to take it.

"It's all good," he said, settling down in the chair next to Ru. He waited for Win to climb up to his shoulder before he gestured for Angela to join them. "When I watched Vincent take Amy, he had another woman with him. She did all the driving. She was white, and her hair was cut into a bob?" Laurence did his best to mime the severe haircut with both hands. "No tan, so she doesn't see the sun much. Wore a suit?"

"Marcella," Angela said while she lowered herself into a chair that faced them across the expanse of the tabletop. "One of the three who can still act reasonably independently. She is competent, but more suited to administration than magic. She is also reasonably strong for her size. She is much more likely to perform a physical attack than a magical one."

Laurence was about to ask her to go on, but then he figured if he was about to get twelve other names thrown at him, he'd better start taking notes, so he pulled out his phone. Once he'd jotted down what they had so far, he asked Angela to continue, and tried not to think about what could happen if they screwed this up.

16

MYRIAM

Maybe she hadn't really thought this magic would work, or at the very least it was probable that some small part of her might have believed that all Quentin's father really meant by his very British version of 'come with me if you want to live' was that he would guide her to a waiting limousine, because when the morning sunshine cut out and left her blinking Myriam momentarily wondered whether she'd had a bag put over her head.

There's been so much kidnapping lately that my imagination has run wild.

The duke released her hand. She clung to Quentin's, which was much cooler to the touch than his father's, and blinked a couple more times while she adjusted to the loss of sunlight.

Quentin made a choking sound, then breath exploded out of him in a single word.

"Really?"

Myriam began to see that they were in a large office, and though the enormously tall windows weren't covered, they looked out onto a dark world which was made even harder to see by their reflections in the glass, so she turned her attention to the room itself.

It belonged in another time. The décor was all beige and

brown: beige carpet; cream walls; wooden cabinets and shelves; plush leather chairs; an enormous wooden desk that took up almost a quarter of the remaining space. Every finial and every handle was brass, which meant that the brown was metallic here and there. Even the lamps were brass, with cream lampshades over their warm bulbs. The only doors were to Myriam's right, opposite the windows: a pair of them, paneled with wood, almost as tall as the room itself, and firmly closed.

"What did you expect, boy?" The duke circled them and strode to the doors.

Myriam felt the flinch in Quentin's hand when the duke pulled the doors open, but all he revealed was an octagonal library around the same size as the office. Still, she looked up to Quentin, and frowned softly. "Do you need a moment?"

Quentin stared out into the library while his father passed through it and tugged open the doors at the far side of it. "No," he breathed. "The sooner we're out of here, the better."

Myriam nodded and adjusted her hold so that she could take his arm rather than his hand. It would let her support his weight a bit better. "Then let's go," she said.

She waited for him to take the first step, though.

"GUEST APARTMENTS ARE in the east wing," the duke said as he stalked ahead of them along a long, wide corridor lined with statues, paintings, and furniture Myriam could only guess at the age of. "I'll have Thorne prepare the Emerald Bedchamber for you."

"Where is Higson?" Quentin frowned at the back of his father's head.

"He passed," the duke replied.

Quentin glanced down at Myriam. His frown darkened. "I'll take the Crimson Damask Bedchamber," he finally said.

"Your own is far more appropriate—"

"The Crimson Damask Bedchamber," Quentin repeated tersely.

The duke snorted. "Suit yourself, boy. Why not show Mrs. Riley around until your rooms are ready?" He stopped as the corridor opened up into an enormous hall, and turned to face them, one arm outstretched like he was welcoming them into the vast space beyond. "Do not leave the grounds. I cannot protect you beyond them," he added, making eye contact with Myriam.

He wasn't telling the whole truth, that was for sure, but his words didn't feel like more than a white lie either. Myriam suspected that what he really meant was that he didn't want the bother of trying to keep her safe if she went out into the world beyond these walls, which she supposed was fair considering that he didn't have to offer her any shelter whatsoever.

"Thank you," she said, and gave him her most practiced customer service smile. "I'm sure you have a lot to be getting on with, and it must be late. We won't keep you."

"You're too kind," he said, managing to almost sound like a decent human being for all of three seconds. "Good evening."

He set off again, breezing past them on the way they'd just come without another word, let alone sparing a look at his own son. Myriam turned slightly so she could watch him go, but she suspected he was going right back to his office, so she sighed and looked into the hall instead.

"Why the change of bedroom?" she murmured.

"My rooms are in the west wing," Quentin said just as quietly. "It would take far too long to reach you in an emergency."

It wasn't difficult to see that he was only telling a half-truth. Myriam wondered whether it was worth pressing for the other half, but he still looked white as a sheet, and she decided that it was not important.

"Then a tour sounds ideal." She smiled and drew him into the hall proper so that she could take it all in. "Tell me about this room?"

"The Great Hall?" Quentin moved alongside her, drifting like a lifesaver in a pool. "One of the oldest parts of the house. Standard reception hall, to be honest."

Myriam nodded along as he began to talk about the house's construction, the architect's original plans, and how many generations of his family it had taken to complete. Truthfully it was all going in one ear and out the other, because she was paying much more attention to the space around her than the lecture poor Quentin must've had drilled into him since birth.

The floor was covered in black and white tiles, laid out in a diamond pattern. Across the hall from the corridor they'd emerged from was another, an open stone archway leading to yet more art-lined walls. To her right, a pair of enormous black-painted doors, and on her left were two wide wooden staircases which curved around the outer edges of the hall and led up to a balcony level. She figured that was the way to go to reach Quentin's bedroom, or rooms, or apartment, or whatever it was. Most likely Freddy's, too, and that of their youngest brother, about whom Myriam knew surprisingly little now that she thought about it.

Above it all, a chandelier hung from the distant, ornately painted ceiling, with hundreds of crystal teardrops suspended like an extremely expensive sword of Damocles over the center of the hall.

What a cold place to raise a family. Myriam's gaze fell to a doorway between the staircases, which held a pair of cream doors. They were closed, and she wondered how easy it would be to get lost in a place like this, especially for a child.

Even at Samhain, when the veil between worlds was at its thinnest, this house felt like a spiritual void.

Why am I here?

She had followed her instincts, and they wanted her to come, but there was more to it than a nebulous threat to her life. Much more.

Was it to take Quentin away, to keep him safe?

No. That's not it.

She wasn't here to learn about the ins and outs of eighteenth century architectural choices, surely?

No, that wasn't it either.

Myriam smoothed a hand down over her dress while she mulled it over, then looked down at herself. "I'll need fresh clothes," she mused.

"I... Yes. Oh, I'm so sorry." Quentin winced. "I suppose we can't head out to buy any, either."

Myriam chuckled. She very much doubted that Quentin wanted to spend his time accompanying her while she tried to find underwear in a country she'd never even visited before. "We'll work it out. Is there somewhere we can sit?"

"The, um..." He began to wander towards the corridor across the hall from them. "Library?"

It was as though the stars had aligned inside Myriam's thoughts, and she beamed brightly up at him. "That sounds perfect, dear."

Whatever she'd come here for, if it wasn't in the library itself, it sure led on from there, so she walked with Quentin and gave the chandelier a wary eye as they passed underneath it.

The click-clack of her shoes on the tile floor echoed dully around them, and she idly wondered just how lonely the duke must be, living in this enormous house by himself.

The library was, of course, massive. Myriam shouldn't have been at all surprised by it, but she couldn't help herself. There were more books than anyone might read within their lifetime, stacked on shelves so high that there was an entire mezzanine floor overhead to reach them from. The room had armchairs and sofas dotted around it, as well as a couple of desks, and even a grand piano, all resting on vast red rugs that protected the wooden floor.

Quentin led the way to the nearest armchairs, and Myriam helped him sink into one.

"I suppose this library has a name?" She teased him gently while he got comfortable. "The Brown Library? The Ostentatious Library?"

Quentin let out a ghost of a chuckle. "No, it does not."

"Well, that won't do." Myriam stepped back and rested her hands on her hips as she turned slowly to take in more details.

"There's more than one library, for a start. How are you supposed to tell them apart?"

"Father's library is..." Quentin paused. "His personal collection."

"You mean it's where he keeps all the books on magic?"

"Just so."

Myriam began to stroll along the room, eyeing the shelves. Many of them were open, but several had decorative doors made from wrought iron, so that the books within could be seen but not reached. "And what about these ones?" She nodded to one of the doors. "Are they rare? Expensive? Or are the bars for show?"

"I don't really know." Quentin slumped a little in his chair and propped his elbow on the armrest. "Can't say I paid much attention in here, other than..." His gaze drifted past her, to the piano at the far end. "This was largely Freddy's domain," he concluded.

"I see. Where was yours, then?"

He raised his pointer finger off the arm of the chair to point vaguely in her direction. "The stables."

"Ah, of course." Myriam chuckled to herself and continued to peruse the shelves, drifting from one to the next as she listened to her instincts and allowed fortune to guide her.

She figured this was, in some way, kind of like a hunt. She'd never had the compulsion that Eric and Bambi shared — the unstoppable urge that had driven them both to addiction — but she sure could follow a trail of breadcrumbs without even noticing, and maybe it was time to seek out the path more deliberately. She was a Child of Herne and a Priestess of the Old Ways, bearing gifts and wisdom passed down through centuries from the Old World to the New, and now that her son was following his calling at last, there was no longer any danger that listening to her own could throw him from it.

Freddy's domain.

Myriam sucked her teeth at the thought. If anyone *had* read every book in here it would be Frederick, with his photographic memory and hunger for information, but what would she even ask for? Anything of use in rescuing Amy Jenkins would be in the duke's personal collection, wouldn't it? And Myriam couldn't use magic.

A look back at Quentin showed the poor young man had already dozed off in his chair, which wasn't wholly unexpected, but Myriam was wide awake and ready to delve her hands into earth that had long lain fallow. She drew her cellphone from her purse and gazed at the screen while she puzzled it over, but she slipped it away again. There really was no point bothering Freddy at this hour when she hadn't narrowed down what it was she was looking for, and until she did, he couldn't help her.

Instead she jolted back into motion, walking past shelves as she allowed her eyes to drift over spines without focus. If it was a book she required, it would leap out at her. All she needed to do was be patient.

But not for long.

A spine caught her eye. It was small and slim, cloth-bound, with no title or author that she could see. The book wasn't behind bars, imprisoned like so many others here, so she reached for it and traced her fingers down the spine. It was uneven, and had a smoothness that only came from age and handling.

Myriam took it down from the shelf and carried it to a desk, where she placed it on a blotter and turned on the desk's lamp, then sat. She took great care with the front cover as she gingerly opened the book. It was obviously old, and she didn't want to damage it.

When she exposed the title page to the light, she held her breath and took a moment to make sense of it. There was an ornate, woodcut header, below which read:

DAEMONO-
LOGIE, IN FORME
OF A DIALOGVE,
Diuided into three bookes.
VVritten by the high and mightie Prince, IAMES by
the grace of God King of England, Scotland,
France, and Ireland, Defender
of the faith. &c.

She let out the breath as dread replaced her curiosity, slowly creeping up from her gut as if she'd just swallowed something rotten. Myriam scanned the first couple of pages, but they only confirmed her worry.

While the English it written in was archaic, the preface wasted no time in making it clear that the book was intended as a manual for recognizing the many servants of the Devil, including witches and their familiars, as well as what kinds of magic the reader might reasonably expect to encounter while hunting them.

Myriam pressed her lips together. If this book was not in the duke's personal library, did that mean it was nonsense? Or simply that it contained nothing of magical value? And if her gifts had guided her to it, was it because it was relevant to Bambi's troubles, or was it important for some other reason entirely?

Either way, the upshot seemed to be the same: if she wanted to figure out what relevance the book had, she would have to read it.

She grimaced and did what she could to prepare herself for whatever horrors had been committed to print, then moved on to the first chapter, and after five minutes of squinting at what seemed to be a back and forth pontification between two fictional characters she gave up and reached for her phone again.

It was time to call on someone who had already done this part.

17

SORAYA

Soraya had appointed herself adult in charge of Quentin's wallet, but honestly she doubted any of them were going to go wild with his bank account. When you grew up poor, spending didn't come easy, and while there were plenty of jokes about all the things they could buy right now, it wasn't hard to see how everyone was holding back and staying on-mission. Even Alex, while they were new to the house, had that hesitancy about spending that suggested they hadn't had a whole lot of ready cash in their life.

Hell, Soraya hadn't even thought about where they were going to go buy clothes; she'd driven right out of La Jolla and gone to the nearest Walmart. It was practical, she reminded herself, and if there wasn't anything here, they weren't far from a Target.

"I don't know why these places have to have sections for men and women," Alex muttered. "I mean, I do, but it's frustrating." They pulled a coral hoodie off a rack and held it up against themself to peer down at it. "Don't you feel sorry for cis men?"

"Not usually," Soraya said. She looked at the hoodie and shook her head. "I don't think the color suits you."

"I do," Kim murmured. "Don't they get tired of only having boring clothes?"

"They could fight back any time they wanted," Alex said. They slipped the hoodie back onto the rack and drifted forward, hands idly touching and testing other hoodies and sweaters they passed. "But then they wouldn't conform, and a lack of conformity leads to a loss of privilege."

"I think Quentin looks good in boring clothes." Estelita grinned.

"He's British. They invented boring." Soraya smiled slightly, but teasing him was a lot less fun if he wasn't there, so she changed the subject. "Want to grab something to eat once we're done here?"

There was a chorus of uhhmms and ahhhs, so when Soraya's phone rang she was grateful for the escape. She answered it without checking the screen, and moved a few racks away so she could focus on the call. "Yeah?"

"Soraya. I'm so sorry to call while you're busy." Martin sounded like he was keeping his voice down, for some reason. "Would it take long for you to all come home, do you think?"

Oh yeah, the idiots had *definitely* gotten into trouble already, even though she'd only been gone for like three hours. "Sure. What's going on?"

"Quite a lot. It, um." Martin sounded shaky for a second. He stopped, and cleared his throat. "It seems there's a wizard of some kind who might be dangerous? I believe the specific word used was 'warlock?'"

Soraya grunted. She didn't really care about the different words Laurence used for other witches, but she did know he reserved that one for severely bad people, and since she'd only just come back from being murdered by a psycho neo-Nazi magic-user she was actually okay being asked to exercise caution for once. "A'ight. We're on our way. You gonna call everyone else, or do you want me to do it?"

"I'll take care of it," Martin said. "Please be careful?"

She blinked slowly at the worry in his voice, and was half-tempted to rib him for the un-butlery behavior, but if he was upset enough to lose his cool like this she could stand to take his warning more seriously herself, so she just nodded. "We will."

She ended the call and looked over to the others, with a cart that was only half full of clothes, and made an executive decision. If they abandoned the cart and went straight to the SUV they could be home in twenty minutes, but checking out would only add five minutes at most and it'd let Alex have some goddamn dignity, so Soraya snapped her fingers and beckoned them over.

"Okay, we gotta move," she said. "The dads have gone and started shit again, and it sounds like the shit might try and come for us, too. Time to buy this stuff and go home."

"Whaaaaat?" Estelita grabbed the cart and turned it toward the line of checkouts. "We've been gone like three hours at most! How do they even do it?"

"Beats me, but Martin sounded shook, so I figure it's bad." Soraya scanned the checkouts for the shortest line, then made a beeline for it, dragging the cart from the front while Estelita hung on to the back. "He's gonna round up everyone else, so it sounds like an all hands on deck kind of day."

Alex chased after them and tossed a multipack of underwear into the cart. "If it's urgent, have we got time to pay? Shouldn't we just leave?"

"I didn't come all this way for nothing, and I'm not going back empty-handed. Besides, Martin says it's a warlock, and we've all got our talismans on us, right?" She eyed them like it wasn't her who'd habitually left the house without magical protection for months on end, and very sensibly nobody called her on it; they all just nodded and patted pocket or neckline, depending on where they kept the stupid little brass pentacles that were probably about to save all their lives. "Great. Then let's pay up and get the hell outta here."

It wasn't until she opened Quentin's wallet that she found his talisman in the coin pocket, and she sighed deeply.

MARTIN MIGHT'VE SAID he'd do it, but Soraya called everyone she could on the way home anyway, just to double-check the message got out. By the time she pulled into the garage it was obvious that Laurence and Mia were home, but the rest were unknown and there was nothing she could do about it from inside the SUV, so she killed the engine and jumped out to go find Martin.

She didn't have to go far. He met her at the door into the house, looking like everything was perfectly fine: either he'd got the butler face back on, or it had all been fixed in the last twenty minutes.

"Where is everyone?" She dropped the keys into the bowl on the other side of the garage door on her way past him.

"Messrs. Navarra and Pierce were on the beach, and are currently scrubbing up," he replied, turning to take Alex's bags from them. "Misses Torres, Turner, and Anderson returned moments ago, and are in the kitchen. Mr. Riley and his colleagues are in the living room."

Soraya ground to a halt and turned to look at him over her shoulder. "And Quentin?"

Martin's skin paled faintly. "I *believe* he's in England, with Mrs. Riley, and his father…" He hesitated, then added, "I shall take these upstairs, and return in a moment to prepare lunch and refreshments."

"You…" She barely got the word out when she felt her blood pressure skyrocket. "He's supposed to be resting!"

"Events took a turn," Martin replied.

"What actually happened?"

He took a breath, then recounted a series of events which sounded maddeningly normal, even if they probably didn't seem that way to poor Martin. Myriam and Quentin sat out in the garden, resting, and then Angela turned up, and Laurence came home with Rufus a few minutes after. From there shit obviously got weird, what with Quentin's dad teleporting in, telling them all Myriam was in danger, then teleporting out again with Myriam and Quentin. Soraya had to fight to keep her mouth shut, because there was nothing Martin could've done differently, and the guy was holding it together surprisingly okay for someone who'd seen a magical disappearing duke.

"Then I contacted you," Martin said. "Mr. Riley and his colleagues came indoors to continue their conversation, everyone else returned home, and that is how the situation currently stands."

Soraya rocked her jaw, but she nodded to him in thanks. He might be new to all this weirdness, but his debrief had been efficient and calm, and she appreciated it. "Okay. I guess now we go figure out what shit they've got themselves into this time."

Martin only said, "Good luck," and then he disappeared off up the stairs, taking Alex's bags with him.

Soraya closed her eyes and searched for Quentin. She had no idea if she could see him so far away, but it turned out the answer was *yes* when she found him fast asleep in an armchair, surrounded by books, definitely still alive and not in any danger, so she opened her eyes again and gestured toward the kitchen. "Okay. You wanna get everyone, and I'll go kick Laurence's ass?"

"I think I'd like to see the ass-kicking," Alex replied.

"I'll go get the boys," Estelita said.

"Perfect." Soraya cracked her knuckles, then marched into the living room. She didn't knock.

BY THE TIME Soraya had a handle on the rest of what was going on that Martin either hadn't known or hadn't understood, everyone else had arrived in the living room, and it was cramped as hell.

"I cannot believe this," Mia said. "It doesn't matter who can and can't use magic, Laurence. You still need us. Three of you is not enough to face fourteen opponents, especially when they control the terrain."

"The odds are not in our favor," Angela agreed.

Laurence rolled his shoulders, but at least he kept his cool. "This guy is seriously bad news, Mia. I can't ask you to come with us. I need you to stay here and keep everyone safe."

"I don't mind staying safe," Clifton said.

"I'm okay with being *kept* safe," Lisa mumbled.

Soraya exchanged a look with Kim, but she didn't need to ask anything. The look in Kim's eyes was a mix of fear, concern, and determination; she was brave, and smart, and those were just two of the things Soraya loved about her. Kim held out her hand, and Soraya took it, then she looked to Mel, who just nodded like there was no question about it.

The boys weren't fighters. That was good. It meant they could stay home and hold down the fort: look after the dogs, Martin, Lisa, and each other. Soraya turned her attention to Alex, the untested quantity in the room, and noted that their shoulders were stooped and their frown uncertain.

Good. Alex could stay here too, then. They could use magic, so they added another level of defense to the house.

"Okay," she said, and stepped up to Laurence's side. "Here's what's gonna happen. You're gonna call everyone who works at the shop, and get them to come here."

Laurence blinked at her. "Wait, what?"

She waggled a finger at him. "Shop's closed, right? Myriam closed it. So they're available, and if this Vincent guy is going to target people you care about, your mom's staff are in his crosshairs. Plus if he really does hate moms, Maria and her kids are in danger, and they don't even know. Get everyone here."

Laurence sucked in air. "That means telling Maria—"

"Yeah? What's your point?" She glared up at him, and watched him wrestle with it until his shoulders slumped. "Great. Also get Sebastian and his family in here, just in case Vincent decides to go after his kids instead."

"Goddess…" Laurence grabbed his phone and started tapping out messages. "We can't protect everyone."

"We can do our best to protect the highest priority targets." Soraya gestured between the people in the room. "Me, Kim, Mia, and Mel are coming with you. Everyone else stays here and battens down the hatches once Ethan, Aiden, Rodger, Maria, and Sebastian arrive. Then we go up to LA and kick this guy's ass. The quicker and harder we hit him, the less time he has to react, and we can steamroll through there like a SWAT team." She turned her attention on Angela, and added, "Right?"

Angela paused, which suggested either diplomacy or refusal was inbound. Soraya stared at her, silently daring her to try either, but instead what Angela came out with was a third, other thing.

"What if we don't do any of this?" Angela raised her hands, and made a motion like she was sweeping their whole conversation aside. "We are making assumptions about what he wants, and we are half ready to give it to him. But what if, instead of going in, we bring him out?"

Soraya lifted an eyebrow, then she began to nod slowly. "And just *ask* him what his problem is," she said, "and what he wants." She looked up at Laurence. "Reduces the risk of losing Amy as collateral damage. Maybe we can play this right and get the odds moving more in our favor."

Laurence shifted his center of balance and paused all his texting. His lips pursed as his dark eyes flickered back and forth, but then he turned to face Rufus. "Well?"

Soraya turned, too. Rufus was the only person in this room she didn't trust, and letting this whole thing hinge on *his* thoughts was probably a really bad idea, but if this Amy Jenkins lady was his mom, Soraya supposed they could at least hear him out.

Rufus snorted, and gave Laurence the stink-eye, but he shrugged, too. "I guess," he muttered. Then he looked to Angela, and added, "Though I don't know why you didn't suggest this sooner."

Angela eyed him, but her tone was neutral when she said, "It would require that I relay a message to him."

Laurence let out a choked noise. "You mean, go in there? On your own?"

She inclined her head. "Yes."

Soraya didn't like it. It sounded like the direct opposite of a great idea. But before she could say so, Laurence said it instead.

"No. No way. What if he takes you hostage, too?"

The mood was turning sour, and rescuing it wasn't Soraya's specialty. If she started yelling, things would only get worse, but she couldn't figure out how to make things better.

"Have you been to Miss Jenkins' house?" Kim asked. She spoke quietly, but she was looking at Laurence like she'd had an idea.

"I looked back on it, saw Vincent take her," Laurence said.

"But did you go to the house?" Kim gnawed her lip lightly. "What if there's something there you missed? Something she left behind, or... or a scent, maybe? Something you can't see, but you can use?"

Laurence opened and shut his mouth again, before shoving his phone into the pocket of his pants. "It's... not the worst idea," he said slowly. "Right?" he asked Rufus and Angela.

They looked at him, then both shrugged.

"It is worth investigating," Angela concluded.

"Great. Everyone else stay here." Laurence picked his way through the crowded room to get to the door. "We'll go check it out. Soraya, make sure everyone gets here, and make sure they're comfortable and safe, okay?"

She watched him, and narrowed her eyes. "You better not be putting me on babysitter duty."

"Nuh-uh. Just want to make sure everyone coming in through the front door is who they say they are. After that, we can figure out our next move."

She nodded, but grabbed his arm before he was out of the room, and held up Quentin's wallet. "He's at his dad's without this," she said, lowering her voice and hoping only Laurence — and Estelita, sure — could hear her. "You know what he keeps in here."

At least, she sure *hoped* he knew.

Laurence frowned down at it, then he nodded faintly. "Thanks, Soraya. Hang onto it. He should be safe without it for now. You be careful, okay? Win, stay here, let me know if anyone needs me!"

She nodded and let him go as she stuffed the wallet back into her pants. Rufus and Angela got up and followed him out, and she looked around the room at everyone who was left.

She was on babysitter duty for sure, and there wasn't anything she could do about it other than be the best damn babysitter available right now.

But she was going to stay mad about it.

18

MYRIAM

THE REPLY SHE RECEIVED FROM FREDDY READ *I'LL BE WITH YOU momentarily*, so Myriam put her phone away and resisted the urge to ask how soon 'momentarily' might be. It was replaced with the urge to make a cup of tea, but where would she even begin? She hadn't seen anything remotely resembling a kitchen on her way through the parts of the house she'd seen so far, and Quentin needed his rest much more than he needed to take her to a kettle.

She huffed to herself and contemplated a solo exploration, but if Quentin woke and found her missing he might panic.

Her eyes fell on the book in front of her, and she came close to forcing herself to start reading again when she heard footsteps echo in the Great Hall. There was no decision to be made: she closed the book, tucked it into her purse, and made her way through library toward the corridor so that she could listen in — or, potentially, ask whoever it was where she might find the tea.

The sound out in the corridor changed in a way that made it softer, and at the same time there was a tinkle from what was most likely the chandelier. Myriam figured the front doors must have been opened, and her suspicion was proven correct as she stepped out into it and overheard a woman in the hall.

"Good evening, Master Brennan. Please, come in. You're alone?"

Myriam's eyebrows climbed. This was quite the coincidence. *Unless it isn't.*

"Yes. I'm afraid Frederick's working tonight. I'm just stopping by to pick up some of his things." Mikey's accent was so British that if Myriam hadn't met him before she wouldn't know he was American.

"Very good. Do you need rooms for the night?"

"Possibly. Better safe than sorry. Thank you."

The doors closed just as Myriam reached the hall, and put on the politest smile that she could muster. "Michael."

Mikey turned, and smiled at her like he was surprised to find her here, which she doubted. "Myriam! How are you?" He hurried across and offered his hand. "We should catch up."

She shook it, perfectly willing to go along with whatever this was so long as it was Freddy's promised 'momentarily.' "We should," she agreed.

The lady in the hall who had greeted Mikey turned to face Myriam and folded her gloved hands together behind her back. "Do excuse me, ma'am. I was on my way to inform you that your chambers are now prepared. Is there anything else I can do for you?"

Myriam looked at her and took in the neat lines of her black suit, and the way her brown hair was held firmly under control in a neat bun. She was around Myriam's age, with warm white skin and even warmer brown eyes. "You're Thorne?"

"At your service, ma'am," Thorne said.

Myriam smiled and nodded. "Then if it's not too much trouble, I'd love some tea and a bite to eat?"

"Of course. Would you like them in the library, or in your rooms?"

"Oh, the library would be perfect. Thank you." Myriam took Mikey's elbow, drew him down the corridor and into the library, then dispensed with her smile and lowered her voice. "How did you get here so fast? Were you lingering in the bushes?"

Mikey laughed a little and shook his head. "No. Freddy, uh…" His accent was slipping, but it didn't go all the way home. "You remember Hades?"

She searched his green eyes for his meaning as she led him over to the chairs by Quentin. "I do," she murmured.

"Not the kind of thing you forget, I guess." He sat down and eyed Quentin. "After we both left, Freddy told Laurence who and what Mnemosyne was. He told Laurence that if he drank more than we all needed to just to get home, it might make Laurence's oracular gifts stronger."

Myriam settled slowly and rested her purse in her lap while she added together Mikey's words with the context he was saying them in until it all aligned. "Freddy did it too, and now he can see things?"

"Hole in one," Mikey said. "He saw you'd be here tonight, so he sent me over. Gotta say it's a real fun time being in the house of the guy who beat me half to death last year—" He cut himself off as he stared into thin air with an aggrieved look, but he huffed and turned his attention back on Myriam. "Anyway, Freddy doesn't think I'll run into him tonight, so we better get to work. What's the problem?"

Myriam was very tempted to get straight to work, but details were tugging at her attention, and she decided to allow them to have it for now.

"If he knew this was coming, why isn't he here himself?"

"He is." Mikey tapped his temple with his pointer finger. "He's always anywhere I am."

"You know what I mean," Myriam said dryly. "Spit it out, either one of you."

Mikey glanced sideways for a second, then nodded. "Okay. He's keeping tabs on the Marlowes." He looked at Quentin for a second, likely to make sure he was still asleep, before he added, "Quentin might think they can be trusted, but Freddy doesn't. He's digging up everything he can about any disappearances or deaths that might be attributable to them, as well as tracking their movements so they don't just up and disappear like they usually do. It's taking up a lot of his bandwidth, and he didn't want Quentin to know about it."

Mikey's hint wasn't subtle, even though he stopped short of asking her to keep it a secret, but Myriam wasn't about to make any promises that she couldn't know whether she would keep. She simply nodded and took the book from her purse, and handed it to him. "What can you tell me about this?"

He opened it to the title page, then sat in what looked like deep thought for so long that Thorne had time to arrive, deposit tea and sandwiches, then withdraw again before Mikey spoke.

"It's a treatise written by King James VI of Scotland, also King James I of England, as a reaction to a supposed plot by witches to assassinate him." Now it wasn't only Mikey's accent that had changed, but also the pace and inflection of his speech.

Freddy was at the wheel.

"It's written in the form of a Socratic dialogue," Freddy continued, "because James thought it would be more entertaining, but the core of it is a conversation about why it's necessary to hunt and punish witches; descriptions of what witches, sorcerers, and necromancers can do; how they gain their powers from Satan; and a dose of why popes are bad thrown in for good measure. Most of his 'evidence' is either testimony from people who claimed to be witches, or passages from the Bible. It's all really quite horrible, before even contending with the Early Modern English it's written in." He raised Mikey's head to meet her eye. "Why do you ask?"

"Of all the books in this room, it's the one I picked up," Myriam said softly. She reached for the teapot and began to pour it into cups.

"Mmm. And you are attempting to divine the relevance of this text to the current situation?"

"That's right." She added milk for herself and Quentin, then passed the milk over to Freddy. "But Vincent Harrow isn't a witch hunter, he's a warlock."

"From the Old English, *wærloga*," Freddy drawled.

Myriam nodded. "Oath-breaker. Deceiver. Although later it was…" She tipped sugar into her tea and stirred it slowly as her instincts bit onto her words and held fast.

"Also used to mean 'in league with the Devil,'" Freddy said, finishing her thought for her so neatly that she had to remind herself she still wore the ward against telepathy.

"It can't be," she breathed. "There's no such..." But she stopped herself.

Herne existed.

All manner of gods had come and gone, and many were still around.

So who was she to say the Devil couldn't exist?

Freddy pursed Mikey's lips, then reached out to place a hand against Quentin's knee. "Wake up, Icky," he said gently. "I'm afraid you're needed."

"Freddy—" Myriam began, but it was too late.

Quentin stirred, and opened his eyes just in time to catch Mikey's hand pulling back from him, which led to him sitting up so fast that he winced.

"It's all right." Myriam leaned in to pick up the tea she'd prepared, and offered it to him. "I'm sorry. You weren't asleep for long. I thought it best to let you rest." She shot a look at Freddy. "But I think we're going to need your help now."

Mikey's whole posture had already shifted, shrinking back from Quentin, and he grabbed his own tea like it could protect him from an angry d'Arcy. "Freddy says Quentin can read EME easily, if you need more detail out of the book."

Quentin took the tea, his gaze flitting between Myriam and Mikey, but at least nothing flew across the room, and nobody got set on fire. "Book?"

Myriam sat once more. She nodded to the book Mikey still held, hoping no tea had gotten spilled on it, and explained briefly how she'd pulled it down from a shelf and then asked Freddy for assistance with the contents, but Quentin was far too bright, and also asked how Mikey happened to be here — with a great deal more distrust than Myriam had asked it. Once Mikey explained that half of the situation — and notably left out why Freddy couldn't be here in person — Quentin took the book, suspended it in midair, and began to flip through the pages while his hand was occupied with his teacup.

"I hope you aren't asking me to read the entire thing," he groused soon enough. "There's a lot of waffle. Is there something particular we're looking for?"

Myriam withheld the urge to smile with her fondness. Quentin was clearly tired, and didn't handle recovery well at the best of times, so she was not unsympathetic to his childishness. But he also likely wouldn't take well to her maternal feelings either, so she stuck to the facts.

"I think really we want anything about making pacts with the Devil," she said.

Quentin stared at her over the top of the book, and his incredulity was hardly subtle, but Myriam shrugged at him.

"Humor me," she said. "If you'd be so kind, dear."

She sipped her tea and feigned innocence at his continued stare, but in the end he capitulated, and turned his attention back to the book.

Now all Myriam had to do was wait to find out where her instincts had led them all.

19

LAURENCE

Laurence drove the truck to the 5 then joined it way more carelessly than he would on a day when he wasn't trying to face off against one warlock while another had his fiancée and his mom in a castle on the other side of the world.

Goddess, the duke better not be claiming to be able to protect them if he couldn't.

"Watch out!" Ru grabbed for the dashboard as a truck honked at them and sped past.

"There was plenty of room," Angela said dismissively. "He could have moved over sooner."

"Eh, technically I'm the one that should've…" Laurence shook his head. "Sorry. I just… It's okay. I'm focused. We're not gonna —argh!"

He *should* have expected the duke to appear in his rear-view without warning. It was the kind of shit the asshole did for fun, so Laurence figured he could've done less of the whole screaming like a child thing and more of the cool stoic stiff upper lip stuff Quen usually had a handle on, but damnit, this guy had been ready to murder him and now he was sitting in the back seat like that wasn't totally weird.

Laurence huffed and shook his head as he tried to put his

attention back where it needed to be: on the damn road. "How are you even doing that?" he muttered. "We're all warded."

"Do you forget that I have your spittle?" The duke sniffed, obviously still unimpressed with Laurence's magical skills.

Ru groaned. "Seriously?" He looked at Laurence, and Laurence practically felt the disapproval melting that side of his face off under the glare. "You gave your spit to a warlock?"

"Not my proudest moment, okay?" Laurence adjusted his grip on the wheel and waited for his heart to get down from the back of his throat. "You're one hundred percent sure you can keep Mom and Quen safe, right?"

The duke turned to gaze out of the window with the idle curiosity of a child watching an ant farm. "Correct. Where are you going?"

"Amy's house, where she got taken from. I'm hoping maybe we spot something in person that I might have missed..." Laurence paused, unsure whether the duke knew the full extent of his gifts. "From a distance," he finished.

"Logical." Hieronymus seemed to bore of the other traffic quickly enough, but that meant his cold stare was back on Laurence's reflection in the rearview. "What is your plan for a lack of further data?"

Laurence felt his cheeks grow hot from the subtle British insinuation that a failure to plan would lead to yet more disapproval.

Man, fuck this guy. I don't need him to like a damn thing about how I do shit.

He ground his teeth together a second, but went with the answer he really wanted to give, not the politically sensitive one. "I don't have one."

Hieronymus's silence was the kind that could send men screaming if they weren't already trapped in a car with him.

"It's aggravating," Rufus growled. "But it's how he works. He goes with his instincts, and it almost always pans out for him. If you want to be here and help out, you're just going to have to get used to it."

The duke gave a soft snort, but he stopped talking, which meant Laurence owed Ru his thanks, a favor, or maybe even both.

BY THE TIME Laurence killed the engine, Rufus was already out of the truck, and Laurence had to hurry to catch up with him. But all Ru was doing was standing ten feet away from the front door and staring up at the house in horror.

Laurence tried to see what Ru was looking at, but it was just Amy's house: no signs of forced entry, no blood seeping from the walls, no magic, nothing weird at all.

"What's wrong?" he murmured.

"No wards," Rufus whispered. "Her wards are gone."

Laurence heard another door shut, and Angela and the duke joined them moments after, but while Angela stopped by Laurence's side, the duke walked on in through the front door like he was a ghost. Except moments later, the front door opened for them, and the duke left it to move further into the house.

Laurence shook his head and glanced at Angela. "How is he doing that?"

"He is shifting his balance between two locations," she replied. "As easily as you might place your weight from one foot to the other. It is complex spatial magic, requiring an abundance of willpower and focus to decide from one second to the next where the majority of your physical existence is located. If he has chosen to specialize in the study of such magics it explains how he is able to transport two living people so readily, too."

Laurence flexed his jaw as he watched Rufus storm in through the open door, but he held still, tugging on the strand Angela had offered to him until it unraveled enough for him to see it. "Can that magic be worked on a smaller scale? To use his gifts somewhere he isn't?"

"I am not as conversant with the use of innate human gifts, but I do not see why not." She watched Laurence, a speculative cant to her head. "Why do you ask?"

"I think I just figured out how he killed Quen's mom," he growled.

It fit together so neatly. Laurence had watched the duchess drop like a stone, dead in seconds from a cardiac arrest, and even though the duke admitted to killing her, Laurence hadn't seen him anywhere near her when it happened.

But if he could be in one place, and use his telekinesis somewhere else, did that mean he'd used that combination to take hold of her heart inside her chest and just… stop it?

The thought was horrible, and disturbing, and he couldn't imagine how anyone could stand there and callously murder their own wife from both the inside *and* half a mile away just because she'd arranged to talk to a journalist. But Laurence knew he was right.

That was how the duke had done it, and it was a stark reminder that the guy leading Rufus through Amy Jenkins' house right now was a merciless bastard who wouldn't hesitate to kill them all to get what he wanted.

He glanced at Angela. Made eye contact with her. And he saw only the same, grim comprehension in her bright blue eyes.

They didn't need to say anything more. They had a viper on their team, and they both knew it.

Instead, Angela gestured to the open door, and said, "After you."

Laurence paused to take a deep breath and sift through whatever scents he could dig up, then stepped over the threshold.

THE SCENT TRAILS inside were far easier to pick out. Those outside were long gone, but the lack of fresh air moving through the interior had trapped what remained from the kidnapping and let it linger below the new traces of Rufus and, sporadically, the duke up ahead.

Laurence picked out Amy, which meant the other had to be Vincent — or, rather, the poor woman he'd been using like a suit before he discarded her. Neither scent was useful, so he hurried on through to the living room where Ru was scouring the bookshelves and Hieronymus seemed to find the kitchen far more interesting.

Steered mostly by a wish to stay the hell away from the duke, Laurence headed for Ru. "Hey," he breathed. "Find anything?"

"I can't say anything's missing," Rufus muttered.

"Hmm." Laurence glanced across the shelves too, in case anything snagged his attention.

There wasn't a whole lot of magic here. He found the little glass marble pendant on a gold necklace she'd once used to test whether or not he could perceive magic, and while it still glowed with that soft sunlight trapped within, he now saw the warm yellow threads of magic that held it in place, too. He moved on and found other items — mostly trinkets and a small handful of books — that also bore the gentle yellow weaves. There was no sign of any item or book which carried different threads, so Laurence figured it was pretty safe to assume that this was Amy's work and she didn't collect other people's stuff, unlike either Ru or the duke. That made sense, since she really didn't seem to care too much about magic, or even want to use it anymore.

Laurence stepped around Ru, over to where he'd seen Amy backed up against the bookshelves, and then he turned on the spot and searched the carpet. He'd watched Vincent take something out of Amy's pocket and throw it aside, and he found it again now, resting exactly where it had landed: a small silver charm, shaped like an old desk telephone.

He went over and crouched to pick it up. The small loop attached to the handset hung to one side, and it was exactly the right size to attach to a bracelet, but there was no sign of magic on it, so he swiveled on the balls of his feet and held it towards Rufus. "What's this?"

Rufus turned, looked down, and pressed his lips together so tightly that all color drained from them. "Our communications talisman," he said, and drew a matching charm from his pants pocket — except that his still retained tiny turquoise threads around it. "I tried to call her when she didn't show up, and she didn't answer."

Laurence chose not to ask why Ru hadn't bothered mentioning *that* before. Maybe Rufus didn't want anyone to know that he had a magical working phone inside his sanctum after all, or maybe he was just so self-involved that it hadn't occurred to him that telling Laurence about this might have been useful. Either way, there was no point complaining about it. Ru would just have an excuse, or shut him down.

Instead, he said, "So it should have a spell on it. Like yours."

Rufus returned the silver charm to his pocket. "And that spell is gone, but these aren't." He pointed to the trinkets on the shelves.

Laurence huffed. "Vincent said something when he reached the house, and he waved his hand at the door before he used another spell to unlock it. Was he destroying spells, maybe? Is that possible?"

"Child's play," Hieronymus drawled from the kitchen. "Was he reciting an incantation, or merely activating a trigger?"

It had been short. One word, maybe two, even though Laurence didn't know the language. "A trigger," he said.

"So we cannot discern the type of magic he used to destroy the wards, or this spell," Angela concluded.

"Yeah." Laurence figured the *how* was probably something bad anyway. "But it does look like it works on anything he touches once the trigger is activated."

His skin prickled, and the hairs on his forearm lifted swiftly just as the world around him felt sluggish and expectant. He sprang to his feet and turned, searching out the source of the magic, but nobody here seemed to be casting anything: there were no words, no hand motions, no activating any talismans that he could see.

But in the living room, by the windows, a flicker of light like a candle's flame hovered in mid-air, and then burned a hole in reality until the universe regained its breath and a woman Laurence didn't recognize stood there.

But when she smiled, it was that malicious, shit-eating grin he'd seen in his visions.

"Well," Vincent said as he looked out at them through a stranger's eyes. "This took you long enough."

20

LAURENCE

Vincent made a show of raising his host's wrist to look at her watch, and looked unimpressed. "Honestly, I thought you'd get here sooner."

Laurence would've spat out a sarcastic response if Rufus hadn't already started yelling. Instead he watched as Ru charged at Vincent like an arrow, and was startled when Ru collided with Vincent and tackled him to the carpet.

All Vincent did was laugh. "Amazing."

It all happened so fast, but even though Laurence's pulse was racing, his instincts didn't seem to think there was any immediate threat. That made a twisted kind of sense. Why would Vincent go to all this trouble to draw Ru out of hiding only to kill them all? He'd had plenty of opportunity to take Laurence out way sooner than this, and if drawing Rufus out of the house without then wanting something from him was on the cards he would've killed Amy instead of taken her hostage.

People only took hostages when they wanted to make an exchange.

Laurence took a second to check on everyone else. Angela was where she'd been seconds ago, immobile, and the only way he could tell she hadn't turned to stone was the extremely faint movement in her gut as she used her diaphragm to breathe. The duke, though, had disappeared completely — not even a wisp of his magic remained.

Smart, he thought. The duke wasn't a coward. Laurence figured he'd killed his own spell the moment he detected Vincent teleporting in to prevent Vincent finding out he was involved.

He's tucked the ace back up my sleeve.

Laurence turned his attention back to the bodies on the carpet and found Rufus looking about ready to try some more violence, so he darted in and put a hand on Ru's shoulder. "Hey. The host's innocent. You can't go whaling on her, dude!"

Vincent seemed totally at ease lying on the floor with his son pinning him down. He didn't try to break free or get more comfortable. There were threads of magic that wove in and out of his host's whole body, faint and flickering like dying candlelight, and Laurence wondered whether that meant the spell was already wearing off, or if this was what Vincent's magic looked like all the time.

"Ru," he said firmly, raising his voice a little to try and get through to him.

Rufus snarled, but at least he didn't make a move to strangle her, or punch her, or whatever the fuck else had been running through his mind. He didn't move, either. "Where is she?"

"She's safe." Vincent pursed the host's lips, then added, "Alive. Fine. She's okay. She's not dead yet. I'm sure she'll stay that way. Probably."

Goddess, is this how all warlocks treat their own children? Laurence had to tug on Ru's shoulder to remind him not to lose his shit. *What is wrong with these people?*

"What is it you want?" Laurence said, hoping he could steer this whole thing somewhere more productive before Rufus made the worst mistake of his life.

The host's mid-brown eyes turned on Laurence. "Paula and Todd spent most of their time together traveling the length and breadth of this continent. It's obvious they were looking for something. I don't think they ever found it, and I don't care. They *did* bring back something interesting, and buried it among all the trash they filled that house with. Like anything magical they got hold of, it went inside and never came out again. You fetch it and bring it to me, and you get Amy Jenkins in return. It's that simple." Vincent's malevolent grin was back in a flash. "Best if you do it before midnight."

Laurence didn't want to ask. He didn't need to ask. But he did it anyway, because Ru might not be paying enough attention. "Why before midnight?"

"Well, otherwise you'll be taking her dead body away with you, and most people don't enjoy sharing a car with a corpse." Somehow, his grin just got worse. "Most people."

Laurence's very clear memory of Amy's face when she'd seen the dead child she was trapped with flashed in front of his eyes, and he ground his teeth. Vincent wasn't making a joke; he had direct experience, and he was flaunting it in their faces.

Rufus only snorted. "Fine," he said. "Tell us what it is and we'll bring it, and then we'll fucking kill you while we're there."

"Sure. I bet you've got a plan and everything. Oh, but, Laurence doesn't make plans, does he?" Vincent chuckled. "He goes with his instincts, and it usually pans out for him?"

Laurence tried not to look as alarmed as he felt. There hadn't been any magic in the truck he didn't know about, right? Everyone had protective or perception spells on them, and while the duke had appeared out of nowhere, Laurence would've noticed Vincent spying on them while he was driving, wouldn't he?

Unless he isn't using magic to do it.

His blood ran cold.

Was his truck *bugged*? Was Mom's? How about the SUV? The house?

Just how much did Vincent know? How many of their private conversations had he listened to?

"It's not going to pan out for him this time," Vincent gazed up into Rufus' eyes. "He'll get her killed. So just do what I'm asking you to, don't get ideas, and everyone wins."

Rufus nodded. "Fine. Tell me what it is, and we'll bring it."

"The Book of Yew."

Laurence hadn't ever heard of it, but that wasn't a surprise;

most magical books weren't titled by their authors, so far as he'd seen, and just came to be referred to by some key defining feature. At least it wasn't called *The Nasty-ass Book of Murdering Everyone*.

"The Book of Me?" Ru pulled a face. "Haven't got it."

"Y-E-W," Vincent said with a sigh as he checked his host's watch again. "Clock's ticking, children. And your token adult, I suppose," he added, with a smirk past Laurence.

Laurence didn't turn. He knew Angela was there, and was grateful that she didn't grace Vincent's statement with a reply.

"Don't be late," Vincent added. "Anything could happen. Well, not strictly anything. Amy Jenkins will die is what will happen." He grinned at Ru. "Bon voyage."

The threads around him — around his host — snuffed out, and the change was immediate: she screamed and grabbed for Rufus' shirt, then broke down sobbing the second she had it in her hands.

Rufus stared at her like he had no idea what to do about this, and Laurence dropped to his haunches to touch her shoulder. "Hey," he breathed. "It's okay. He's gone."

"Is any of this real?" She gasped between sobs. "Did he even…" She didn't look like she could finish her question, but instead of trying, she shook her head.

"Get off her," Laurence hissed at Ru. "I know this must be so scary," he said to the woman, his voice gentle again. "But we're gonna get you somewhere safe, okay?"

"Nnngh!" Her head still shook, and her jaw clamped shut, but then she managed to gasp, "Coffee!"

Ru moved aside and stood. "Yeah I'm not sure coffee's going to solve our problems," he muttered.

"I don't think she *wants* coffee," Angela murmured.

Laurence stared at Vincent's host and took in everything he could: the rigidity in her jaw; the tremble of her head; the sensation of skin twitching under his fingertips; and the tightness in her facial features.

If he stopped looking at her as someone reacting to

possession, and instead like he was doing first aid, the klaxons all screamed one thing and one thing only.

Poison.

"Stay with her," he said as he shot to his feet and grabbed his cellphone. He hurried away, hoping to save the woman from having to hear this call, because if he was right, it was only going trigger even more anxiety.

"911," said the dispatcher the moment she answered.

"I've got a patient with muscle spasms and lockjaw," Laurence said as clearly as he could, trying not to rush it. "I think she's been poisoned."

If Vincent really wanted them to get this book to him before midnight, dumping a dying stranger in their arms was a weird way of making that happen, but it wasn't until Laurence stepped back into the living room that the horrible possibility occurred that this was a distraction, a way of making sure they didn't have enough time to come up with a plan or gather resources. Worse, if they waited around here until the ambulance arrived, they could get tied up with the cops taking statements and eating up their day.

As the potential outcomes of his phone call spun out in front of him and piled up on top of each other, it looked like he had two choices, and both were horrific. He could leave her here, with the door open, so the paramedics would find her while he ran off to get this book to Vincent before Amy died. Or he could stay here and leave Ru and Angela to go get the book while he got snarled up in red tape, police interviews, maybe even an arrest if they decided his story didn't hold water.

The wrong decision here could screw everything up and cost Amy her life, so he crossed to a chair and sat, and said, "Paramedics are on the way."

Then he closed his eyes, searched for the right future, and prayed that this trap hadn't already closed in around him.

21

MYRIAM

"Here we are," Quentin murmured after a few minutes of skim-reading. The pages stopped flipping themselves, and he put his teacup down. "The Devil's contract with Magicians. I presume that's what we're after?"

Myriam raised her chin. She was aware that this wasn't Quentin's preferred reading material, and that he was both in pain and exhausted, so the sooner she could get to the bottom of what it was the universe was attempting to show her the better it would be for them both. "Yes please, dear."

"Mmm." He didn't take the book into his hand now that it was available, and clearly had no desire to touch it at all, so Myriam was faced with the slightly odd sight of the book floating a foot away from his nose. "All right. Apparently once a magician enters into a contract with the Devil—" Quentin's nose crinkled in distaste "—this contract can bestow forms and effects, where forms is defined as the shape the Devil takes when he answers the magician's call, and where effects is defined as the way in which he binds himself to their service…" Quentin broke off. "This is nonsense. Magic isn't the Devil in a ring or tablet bound to do the magician's bidding."

Myriam nodded in agreement. Quentin was right, from what she understood of magic, but she couldn't even use it herself;

what little she knew was very dilute second-hand knowledge at best. And while Quentin could use it, he refused to, and did not actively participate in the study of it. Therefore neither of them could possibly know for sure how all magic worked for all people.

She took another sip of her cooling tea, then said, "But what if, for some magicians, that's exactly how it works? The power is not from the universe listening to them, but because they have hold of some artifact, item, or perhaps even contract with a third party that lets them..."

"Fake it?" Mikey offered.

Myriam nodded. "Or at the very least to use something they otherwise can't."

Quentin still looked like he wasn't convinced, and returned his attention to the little book. "Ah, I see he's using *Devils*, plural, as distinct from Lucifer. Presumably, then, one may summon any one of these Devils with which to enter into a contract, according to this highly fictitious diatribe—"

"Icky!" Freddy sighed.

The trouble was that he used Mikey's body to do it with.

Quentin stopped abruptly and turned a lethally sharp stare on Mikey, as though a bug had suddenly crawled out of the woodwork in front of him.

Mikey cleared his throat and shrank back into his chair. His skin whitened in a flash. "Uh, I mean, uh..."

This was no good, for so many reasons. Myriam didn't have the time to juggle two fractious brothers who were at each other's throats, especially not when one of them didn't even have the guts to be here in person. She also found Quentin's sudden capacity for such an intimidating glare to be deeply troubling, and wondered what he thought it would even achieve — though she was sure nothing good would come of letting him use it on Mikey this way, regardless of Myriam's own complex feelings about the young drug dealer.

Former drug dealer, she reminded herself.

She returned her cup to the saucer a bit too loudly, making it clink in a way she hoped might attract Quentin's attention, then grabbed her purse and stood up.

It didn't make Quentin back down, or even turn his death-ray stare down a notch.

"Mikey," Myriam said. "Could you do me a favor, dear? Please find out whether we can get a refill?" She gestured to the teapot and smiled at him.

"Gladly," he squeaked, and skittered out of the room as fast as his legs could take him.

Myriam watched him go, then moved across to the chair he'd just vacated and pulled it closer to Quentin before she sat in it. She cleared her throat until she had his attention, and was relieved when he dialed the rage down before he gave it to her.

"Frederick isn't here," she said calmly. "And terrifying the living daylights out of Mikey just because you can't reach your brother is not only unfair to Mikey, it's also needlessly cruel, don't you think?"

Small dots of pink touched Quentin's cheeks and the tips of his ears as he met her gaze. He didn't look away, and more of his anger seemed to bleed out of him, until he closed his eyes for a moment. "You are entirely correct," he breathed.

"I am," she agreed. "And I understand. You've been through hell this year, and now here you are." She gestured to the library around them, though she hoped he understood that really she meant the entire building. "The last place you ever wanted to be, and without warning. But Mikey doesn't want to be here either, and honestly nor do I. None of us are in any position to face a warlock, and as much as I don't want to admit it, we're in need of the protection that your father has given us." Myriam pressed her lips together, then reached out and placed a hand lightly on Quentin's knee. "I know I'm asking a lot, dear, but I think that you need to hear this: Do better."

He sucked in a deep breath, like he was about to argue with her.

"Do better," she repeated gently. "You *cannot* let your pain out for it to hurt others. It is not a tool to be used, or a whip to raise. It is an invitation for you to put out into the world more of what was put into you, and you *must* decline it."

The breath escaped him in a rush. The book tumbled to the

floor. Quentin's working shoulder slumped, and he stared down at her hand on his knee a while before he moved his own to rest over it.

"I'm so tired," he whispered, and there was the faintest sob in his words.

"I can't even begin to imagine how tired," Myriam murmured. She shuffled her chair forward until their knees touched and she could see the tears in his eyes. There was nothing else to say, so she leaned in and slid an arm around his uninjured side in a silent invitation. She might have only raised one child, but it took a heart of stone not to understand what this one needed the most.

He didn't resist for long. Quentin sagged into her hug, and his fragile frame trembled with crying that he almost managed to keep quiet.

Myriam cradled the man who would soon be her second son, and resolved to give the duke a piece of her mind the first chance she got.

When Quentin pulled back from her, he did it slowly, and used the back of his hand to brush lightly at his eyes. Myriam bent down to pick up the book to give him some personal space to compose himself in, and by the time she sat back up and nudged her chair away slightly, he held his head high despite the way his reddened eyes and mussed hair made him look an absolute wreck.

"I do apologize," he murmured.

"I'm not the one you owe it to," Myriam said with a sympathetic smile. She held up the book. "Do you think you can go on?"

He tilted his head slightly. "I will try. Thank you. For the... reminder."

"You aren't alone," Myriam said softly. "You have a new life, and a new family who all love you very much. You make my Bambi an incredibly happy man, and I can't wait to join your hands together before the people who care about you both. Now, for that to happen, we need to make sure Bambi kicks this warlock's ass, okay?"

Quentin blinked slowly at her, then the book rose from her hand and returned to its position in the air in front of him. "Agreed."

Myriam nodded and sat back in her chair, satisfied that she had defused the bomb and perhaps even prevented it from building a home inside Quentin's heart for the time being. She watched him skim through the pages, still unwilling to physically touch them, but he was more focused now and that could only be a good thing.

All she could do was wait, but Myriam was patient, and she'd had years of practice.

QUENTIN READ out the occasional sentence from the book, but none of it really grabbed Myriam, or struck her as the reason the book mattered. She started to doubt her instincts altogether, half worried that she was wasting all their time with a gut feeling that might just be shock from being transported to the other side of the world in the blink of an eye, but how could she have told Bambi his whole life to trust his intuition only to ignore her own?

No. The answer was in here. All they needed to do was find it.

Quentin frowned faintly, and read out, "'One word only I omitted: Concerning the form of making of this contract, which is either written with the Magician's own blood, or else being agreed upon (in terms his schoolmaster) touches him in some part, though peradventure no mark remain, as it doth with all witches.'" He gritted his teeth for a few seconds, then added bitterly, "Don't worry, I'm sure you can find it if you just keep pricking them for long enough."

Myriam squeezed his knee, and tried to pull him back from that particular ledge. "Peradventure?"

"Ah." He cleared his throat. "It's an archaic form of 'perhaps.' The author is claiming that the devil may touch a part of the magician's body, which may or may not show a visible mark after, but which must exist on all witches somewhere."

"To seal the deal," she mused.

Quentin only nodded.

Myriam considered the information she had at hand, then asked, "And the author considers Magicians and Witches to be different, yes? He's saying that all witches bear a mark, but a magician may have a mark — visible or otherwise — or may have instead a contract signed in their own blood?"

"That is the claim, yes," he replied.

She felt like the pieces were slowly forming a bigger picture, except that the new questions this picture raised were ones she was sure that Quentin didn't have the answers to. Worse, trying to enlist his help in finding them might do more harm than good; he was already fully at his limit and in dire need of more rest, and exposing him to the books in the duke's personal library would undoubtedly push him far beyond his mental capacity for the day.

But if it *was* possible for someone to enter into a contract with some kind of god, demon, devil, or other entity in exchange for magical power, was there a kill clause in the fine print, or were ancient non-human entities not very clued up on modern legal terms and conventions? If Vincent Harrow had made such a deal, and if Myriam could unearth the exact wording, could there be a way to nullify the contract and strip him of his power, or was she barking up the wrong tree?

All contracts can be breached, she reasoned. *Intentionally, accidentally, it doesn't matter. What counts is what comes next if it happens.*

"All right," Myriam said. She stood and brushed crinkles out of her dress, then tucked her purse under one arm, and offered her hand to Quentin. "Would you show me to these rooms of ours, please? I think I'd like to freshen up, and you could do with a good night's sleep."

The book floated to land lightly on the table between the empty teacups, and he took her hand, though didn't tug on it at all as he stood. "It's barely lunchtime," he protested.

"Back home," she agreed. "But here it's late, and even if it wasn't you still need sleep. Come on, dear, take me to my room, and don't argue about it." She said it with a smile, but also with enough authority that he couldn't possibly mistake her for anything but determined.

He eyed her, relented, and retained hold of her hand as he guided her toward the Great Hall then up the grand stairs within it, and Myriam gave him absolutely no hint at all that she wasn't going to stay put once he was in bed.

It was better if he had no clue what she meant to do next, or he would definitely try to stop her.

22

LAURENCE

Laurence sifted through futures which led to disaster. If he waited here for the paramedics, he'd definitely get caught up answering questions long enough for cops to arrive, and then they'd try to find out why he was here when the homeowner wasn't. If Ru stayed instead... Well, that wasn't even an option, since the moment Laurence proposed that idea to Rufus in the future, Ru would point out that if anyone tried to enter his home while he wasn't there, the house would do something awful to them, and he refused to specify what that would be. If they left Angela here for the cops to interview, she'd get just as caught up, even though she'd largely refuse to talk to them, but the cops would then latch on to the fact that the 911 call came from a man who wasn't here anymore.

He sighed, and changed tactics. If he stopped trying to look at futures which matched all the actions he could think of, maybe instead he could just look at the ones that would succeed?

"How long will this take?" Angela intoned.

Laurence held a hand up, but he couldn't answer her. Vincent would hear it. Shit, he couldn't even tell her he thought they were bugged, because it'd blow the fact that he'd figured it out right out of the water.

All he could do was try to finish what he'd started before it all became moot by the ambulance's arrival, so he dropped the hand to his lap and dove back in.

"This is cold, even by my standards," Angela said as the three of them sprinted to the truck.

"Yeah," Laurence said. He looked unhappy, features carved into a grimace. "I fucking hate it. But it's the only way we're going to make Vincent's deadline."

"She'll be fine," Ru said dismissively. "They can't be far now."

Laurence nodded. "A couple of blocks." He tapped his ear before he wrenched the truck's door open and leapt up into the driver's seat. "Let's go."

"Fuck," he spat as he pulled himself out of the vision. There wasn't any need to watch more of it. He'd already got his answer.

They had to leave this poor woman to wait for the ambulance on her own.

Laurence felt the grimace already forming on his face, but there was sickness in his gut to go with it. He sprang to his feet as fast as he could and tried to come up with the least horrifying statement possible.

Goddess, just when I really need Quen's way with words.

Well, Quen wasn't here, and of the three of them, Laurence was the best they had. He could lie with ease, convince people to buy flowers or plants they might have only half wanted when they walked into the store, so maybe he could just... convince a traumatized woman who'd been through Goddess knew what to wait for paramedics all on her own.

"Fuck," he said again. "Okay." He turned to the woman who was still in spasm on the floor, then hurried to her side and crouched next to her so she could see him. "Hey," he said. "Hey, it's going to be all right. We're going to wait outside for the paramedics to make sure they find the right house and come to you as fast as possible. I know this is scary, but I promise you, once you're feeling better, we'll talk about this, okay?" He shifted so he could pull his wallet out of his pocket, and tugged a crumpled business card out of it. "I'm gonna leave you my card.

Call me once you're in the hospital. I'll come see you and I'll answer any questions you've got, I swear." He ran his eyes over her, looking for an appropriate place to put the card, and managed to tuck it into the pocket of her pants. "You are going to be okay," he added.

He didn't know whether it was true. He hadn't looked that far ahead, and he didn't have time to.

Laurence rushed away from her and knew that the grimace was back on his face. He couldn't do anything to stop it. This was horrific. Leaving her was the absolute worst thing he could do, but if he didn't, they weren't going to get to Vincent in time to stop him from killing Amy, and the grotesque catch-22 Vincent had put them in by dumping a poisoned innocent in their laps was nothing more than a game to the warlock.

Laurence was going to kill him.

He beckoned to Ru and Angela on his way past, and grabbed a random book from Amy's shelves so he could put it in the jamb of the front door to stop it from closing and locking the paramedics out. Then he picked up the pace and sprinted to the truck.

"This is cold, even by my standards," Angela said.

"Yeah," Laurence agreed. "I fucking hate it. But it's the only way we're going to make Vincent's deadline." He could already hear the sirens in the distance, screaming through the neighborhood, and he grabbed his keys.

"She'll be fine," Ru said, with a tone that made it clear that he didn't give a shit. "They can't be far now."

Laurence nodded. "A couple of blocks." He tapped his ear to indicate how he knew this, then pulled the truck's door open and leapt inside. "Let's go."

He fired up the engine and hauled the truck onto the street seconds before the ambulance turned onto it. By the time it passed them, Laurence was doing his best to look casual until it was in his rearview.

Then he offered up a silent prayer for the health of Vincent's victim, and headed for the 5 as fast as he could go without getting caught speeding.

He made it to Rufus' house in what felt like record time, and nobody spoke for the entire drive, which Laurence figured might be some kind of miracle. Once they were inside the gates and out of the truck, Laurence hurried to the front porch, then took a deep breath.

"The truck's bugged, right?" he said to them both.

Rufus nodded. "Has to be," he grunted. "There was nothing magical in there other than the three of us."

"He does frequently engage the services of civilians for their technological aptitudes," Angela mused. "When might he have gained access to your vehicle?"

Laurence shook his head. "I dunno. Quen and I were only just away for a few days, but it's the store's truck, not mine. It could've been parked outside the store, outside a customer's property, outside Mom's house…" He sucked his lower lip as that thought led to others, and he winced. "And he's been on us for a year or more. Fuck. We've had all kinds of tradespeople in the house to renovate it, re-wire it, bring in new furniture… And literally anyone can walk into the store any time. It's a shop." He groaned at them. "And if the truck's bugged, he knows the duke's helping us, too. He just didn't say so."

So much for my ace.

"I have to go outside." Laurence pointed at the gate. "I need signal. You go in; I'll catch up."

Angela eyed him like she might say something, but instead she only nodded. Ru didn't even do that much, and pushed the front door open without hesitation.

Laurence pulled out his cellphone and ran for the gate to slip outside and get enough bars for what he had to do.

He pulled up Sebastian's number and texted him the second he could.

I think the house is bugged. Can you check it over? Maybe vehicles, too.

Laurence danced from one foot to the other while he waited for a reply, and had to fight the urge to go back inside without one.

I'll have to go get some equipment, Sebastian replied. *I'll report back.*

Thanks! Don't leave the house without a talisman. Martin has got Mom's. I'll text him and ask him to give it to you. The last thing he needed was Vincent overhearing such a simple request and working out that Sebastian was up to something.

Sebastian replied with a thumbs up emoji, and Laurence switched to his chat with Martin, which was usually about groceries.

I need you to give Mom's talisman to Sebastian and say absolutely nothing out loud about it, don't even say hello to him or acknowledge you're in the same room. Laurence hesitated, debating whether or not to tell Martin more, but Martin was extremely professional, so Laurence added, *I think the house is bugged. Sebastian is going to go out and get some gear for detecting listening devices. Keep a lid on this until Sebastian's fixed the problem.*

Martin's reply came back within seconds: *Understood.*

Laurence let out a soft breath, then decided to text his mom while he was out here.

Hey. We're okay. Let me know you're okay too? Quen's dad might be there with you, he can't come back to us while we're in Ru's house. He hoped, anyway. *I've got to go inside. Love you, Mom.*

He was just about to push the gate open when his phone pinged at him, so he quickly checked it.

We're safe, read the message from his mom. *I love you too, Bambi. I might have something useful for you soon. I'll let you know once I'm sure.*

Laurence bit his lip and wondered what it could be that his mom had found in the duke's home that could possibly help, but she obviously wasn't going to tell him more until she was ready to, and pushing would get him nowhere. Instead, he sent, *OK. Thanks!* and went back inside.

But the question still nagged at him.

HE RAN up the huge wooden staircase and in through the door to Ru's library, all the while trying to ignore the incredibly faint smell of his own vomit from earlier. They wouldn't need to be here long, and then it would be fresh air all over again.

Laurence skidded to a halt the moment he crossed the threshold.

The library had changed.

He'd spent the last year coming here, studying in this room, staring at the bookshelves and out the windows when he wasn't nose-deep in a book, and he felt like he knew every inch of it.

He absolutely didn't know that one of the stacks opened up into a whole other room.

Laurence stared at the opening. The bookshelf faced the window now, showing him a back of dark, heavy wood. It hung off a complicated-looking hinge mechanism of multiple curved metal struts that let the door swing out so it didn't crash into the shelves next to it. Strands of Ru's turquoise magic crisscrossed over the opening left behind, like a vault laser security system from a heist movie, and there was a glimpse of more shelves on the other side.

He stumbled toward the doorway, and saw more of the room.

It was nothing *but* shelves in there. No windows, no chairs, not even a rug on the floor. It was a walk-in closet, but for books, trinkets, and scrolls.

There wasn't a single item that didn't have its own glow.

Ru and Angela were already inside, so Laurence let out a low whistle and stepped through the security spell, hoping it wasn't about to dice him into tiny pieces. When he made it out the other side, all he could do was stare at the collection that he'd had no idea existed.

The shelves were stuffed, but tidy — probably organized by theme or objective, the way the main library was. And just like the main library, the magic in here was all different colors, though the threads mostly looked darker, or writhed in ways that made Laurence's skin itch, or straight up seemed to slice through reality itself.

His hair stood on end when he realized what he'd walked into. This wasn't a private collection. It wasn't even a vault.

It was a prison full of artifacts from countless warlocks.

"Oh shit," he breathed.

23

MYRIAM

It rapidly became clear why people in this house referred to a bedchamber as *rooms*, plural.

Quentin had shown Myriam to what was effectively a whole apartment, despite it being behind a single and somewhat unimpressive door on the mezzanine level which surrounded the Great Hall. It was named the Emerald Bedchamber because the walls were covered in a rich, gemstone-green silk, and all the soft furnishings in the room matched it flawlessly: bedsheets, curtains, drapes at the corners of the enormous mahogany four-poster bed, and even the upholstery on the chairs were the exact same color. Every piece of furniture was the same rich, dark mahogany as the bed, and all the metal in the room from door handles to light fittings was golden. Tall windows looked out over a landscape which contained no other buildings that Myriam could see, and the main source of light outside came from an ostentatious fountain below, where sculpted stone animals spewed water into a pool surrounded by a gravel square large enough to park twenty coaches.

It only reinforced her feeling that life here was incredibly lonely.

She had a private bathroom, although it was not green at all, apart from the enamel on the outside of the claw-footed bathtub. And there was also what Quentin informed her was a drawing room, which very much seemed to be a living room, with couches and table and a nice desk by the window so that fancy guests could gaze outside while they wondered what to put in their handwritten letters, she supposed. Finally, there was also a small dining room, with a large mahogany table in the center, and eight chairs around it.

Bambi's old apartment above the store would have fit inside this one five times over. It was ridiculous, though Myriam wasn't rude enough to say so out loud. Instead she had insisted on accompanying Quentin to the Crimson Damask bedchamber, which was unsurprisingly covered in crimson-colored damask over walls, sheets, and curtains, though it was about as close to Myriam's apartment as was physically possible.

"All right," she said, satisfied that she didn't need a tour of Quentin's other rooms. "I'll leave you to go to bed, and I'll ask Thorne to bring you some acetaminophen." She gestured to the door with a smile, and added, "Do you need anything else?"

She felt the vibration from her cellphone in her purse, but ignored it for now. If she reached for it, Quentin might decide it was more interesting than sleep, so she acted like nothing had happened and relied on his exhaustion to keep him from noticing it.

He had the look of a small child who had been caught with his hand in the cookie jar, all wide-eyed and petulant, but Myriam maintained her serene smile and eye contact until his lip jutted out.

"No. Thank you. You're quite right. It's probably best that I…" He struggled to contain a yawn, then hid it behind the back of his hand. "Yes, all right. But you will send for me if you need me, yes?"

"I promise," Myriam said, and she meant it.

But she would prefer not to need to.

She saw herself out, closed the door, and was forced to accept that she would have to visit her bathroom before she got back to work.

After which maybe she should cut back on all the tea.

ONCE MYRIAM HAD ANSWERED both Bambi's text and the call of nature, she made her way back down the stairs to find Mikey, who had made it easy for her by returning to the library now that Quentin wasn't in it anymore. Thankfully there was no more tea, which meant that either Mikey or Freddy had understood her words to be an escape route rather than a genuine request for a refill.

"Quentin is in bed," she said softly. "Or, at least, should be, but I think we all know how headstrong that boy can be when he wants."

Mikey's nose crinkled. "Yeah. Okay. Did you get anything else out of the book?"

Myriam nodded. "I suspect that Vincent's power comes from a deal he's made, but I don't know what with, when, or whether it's something breakable."

Mikey nodded slowly, but after a while, he narrowed his eyes at her. "But you've got an idea for how to find out," he said.

"I think if anyone knows how to get hold of power they shouldn't have, it's the duke." Myriam was aware that her full height wasn't imposing, but she raised herself to it anyway, and held her head high. "Plus I have some things I'd like to say to him."

Mikey's green eyes grew so wide that they seemed to take over half his face. "Are you out of your goddamned mind?"

Myriam snorted. "No, and I'm about to make that his problem. Now, you can either stay here, or come with me. Which does Freddy prefer?"

It was a low blow to point out that she knew Mikey was only here as Freddy's puppet, but Myriam had some hope that it might remind Mikey that he should have some say in the matter too, especially since he was even more terrified of the duke than he was of Quentin. If he wanted to put his foot down, this was his chance.

Instead, he glanced off to the side, then got to his feet with a sigh. "He can't keep an eye on things if I'm not with you," he muttered.

"And is that what matters the most?" she asked, much more kindly.

He gave her the side-eye and shoved his hands in his pockets, then huffed and pulled them out again, probably because of chiding inside his head that only he could hear. "What matters most is your safety," he grumbled. "I can't protect you. Freddy can't, either. But maybe if I'm with you, the duke might think twice about, you know, straight up killing you in front of a witness. He knows what Frederick can do; he'll know that even if he kills me too, there's still someone out there that can tell Laurence what happened to you faster than he can stop it. And whatever it is he wants from all this, he's not gonna get it if Laurence knows what happened. So, yeah, Frederick wants me to go with you, but I want to, too. You're a good person, Mrs. Riley. I always wanted a mom like you, and I was always jealous of Laurence, because he had you. I'm gonna do whatever I can to make sure he gets to keep you, even if all I am is a pair of eyes."

Myriam regarded the young man in front of her, with his bottle-green suit, and his neatly trimmed red curls, and wondered at how much he had changed from the teenager Bambi used to call a friend. He had gone to Hades — alone — to rescue Freddy, despite having no gifts or power of his own. He'd been the first to drink from Mnemosyne, just to be back to the real world in time to warn Quentin about Rufus' intention to kill Angela. And here he stood, willing to do his absolute best for Myriam, again without gifts or power of his own to call on if things went wrong.

She'd underestimated him. He wasn't a puppet, not at all. Instead, he had flourished into an incredibly courageous individual, and there was nothing left of the boy who had taken advantage of her son.

"Then I'd be honored to have you with me," she said.

But she drew the line at offering him her arm.

MYRIAM MARCHED across the Great Hall and down the corridor that led back to the duke's office. If he was in there, all well and good, but if he was not she supposed that she could rely on serendipity to lead her to useful books in his personal collection, and then put Freddy's linguistic skills to use. It was the best plan she could come up with on the spur of the moment, and her instincts agreed with her on it, so she had no cause to try for a better one.

She stopped at the doors which led to the octagonal library and looked up at Mikey. "Are you ready?"

He shrugged. It wasn't a careless gesture. The set of his jaw gave that away. "Never will be," he replied. "Let's do it."

Myriam gave him a smile that she hoped was at least slightly reassuring, then she pulled on the doors and stepped through them.

Mikey made a soft huff as he moved alongside her, and his posture shifted while he raised his head to look over the books they were surrounded by.

"Father's sanctum overlaps this space," Freddy said, sounding thoughtful. "It's only accessible from inside his office, through the use of an astrolabe in his desk." He indicated the office doors with Mikey's right hand. "When the path is open, it replaces these doors, and the outer doors to the corridor are sealed shut and cannot be used. Beyond that, I have little understanding of how it works, save to point out that the fact we were able to get this far suggests that Father is not presently in his sanctum."

Myriam tightened her hold on her purse and dipped her chin to acknowledge the information. "But you can't say where he is?"

Freddy shook Mikey's head. "No. Everyone in my family is immune to telepathy. I cannot sense them, let alone read them. Out of mind, out of sight," he added, sounding terse rather than flippant.

She pursed her lips, then turned to look at him directly. "I appreciate what you're doing," she said. "But you don't have to stay."

He gave her a sardonic smile. "Yes, I do. Michael wishes to be here, and so do I. But please, bear in mind that..." He took a deep breath. "Whatever power Icky holds, Father also wields, and he lacks Icky's restraint. If he wishes to harm us, there is absolutely nothing we can do to stop him."

"What you're telling me is that he's a bully." Myriam smiled sadly up at him, and reached out to squeeze his forearm. "I already know. And I'm not about to pretend that he doesn't scare me, but where will we get in life if we let our fears dictate our actions?"

Freddy clicked Mikey's tongue. "There you go again," he grumbled. "This wisdom of yours will get us all into trouble."

"Right this very second, I expect," she agreed. "Let's go."

She waited for him to nod before she pushed open the doors to the duke's office, and then she barged on in to find the most dangerous man in England sitting behind his desk eating a sandwich.

"Good," she said. "You're here. What do you know about making deals with demons to gain magical power?"

The duke blinked slowly as he continued to chew, and once he swallowed his mouthful he set the sandwich down on his plate, and reached for a cloth napkin with which to wipe his fingers.

Eventually, he spoke.

"You think Harrow has chosen this path," he concluded. An eyebrow lifted speculatively. "That's certainly one way to do things."

"Better than your way?" Mikey's voice trembled, even though he was probably trying to sound cocky.

The duke gave a languid tilt of his head, then rose slowly from behind his desk like a dark cloud cresting the horizon. "Our way creates no debt. The price is paid, and it is done."

"The price," Myriam echoed. All she could see in her mind's eye were the scars on poor Quentin's body as he lay bleeding out on the floor of her shop after Jack's attack.

The duke circled his desk and approached her, seeming to grow larger with each step he took. "Every warlock makes the same sacrifice."

Myriam felt small suddenly, like a fly snared in a spider's web. But she'd come here for knowledge, and she meant to get it, so she forced herself to stand tall again. She met his grey, dispassionate eyes. "And what sacrifice is that?"

His answer was spoken matter-of-factly, which only made it all the more horrific.

"Love, Mrs. Riley," he said. "We sacrifice our hearts."

24

LAURENCE

As much as Laurence wanted to ask what kind of books were so bad they needed to be locked up under so many layers of security, he figured now wasn't the time. Besides, he already had an idea of the shit warlocks thought was A-okay, so he was willing to cut Ru some slack for keeping it all hidden from him. Laurence *did* come into his life out of nowhere and demand to be taught magic; why should Ru mention this room at all, even after a year of being Laurence's mentor? Hell, if it wasn't for Vincent, Laurence might never have found out it existed, and maybe it was none of his business either, so long as Ru kept all this evil out of the hands of people who would use it without hesitation.

He puffed out his cheeks, then nodded at Ru and Angela. "What's the Book of Yew, and why would Vincent want it?"

Rufus stepped aside and pointed to a thick spine on a shelf he'd been standing in front of. "This is it," he said. "As for why?" He shrugged.

Laurence was about to push for more detail than a shrug, but Angela spoke up quickly.

"To save him from having to repeat himself: Rufus has not read any of the materials in this room," she explained. "He sensibly does not expose himself to them, nor has he added to the collection since the loss of his parents."

Laurence nodded at her, grateful for the answer, and returned his attention to the book.

The spine was around twelve inches tall, and four inches thick. It was dark, uneven, and it took Laurence a second to work out that it wasn't what he'd usually think of as the spine of a book; instead it looked like the folded edges of the sheets of paper that made up the pages, bound to thick wooden-looking covers by several cracked leather bands. The threads of magic woven through the bindings were a deep, glistening red that made the spine look as if it might be bleeding, even though there wasn't any evidence of blood on the shelf.

He gritted his teeth and reached for it, but hesitated with his hand still several inches away, and licked his lips. "Wait. Is it the Book of Yew because it's bound in yew wood?"

"That is precisely what we were discussing before you arrived," Angela said. "And I am not certain that it would fit into my purse."

Her quip had to be tongue in cheek, because this book was at least twice as big as the purse she had with her today, but it sounded deceptively like she'd really considered whether she could cram it in there to avoid touching it.

Laurence rocked his jaw and stared at the wood. All he could see was the edges, far too dark to make out color or texture. Either they'd accumulated a whole lot of grime before Paula and Todd got their hands on the book, or someone had stained or painted it for cosmetic reasons. Either way, it meant he couldn't tell what the wood was just by looking at it.

"You see the problem," Angela said.

He nodded. "Yeah. There's not a single part of any species of yew tree that isn't poisonous. I mean, other than the meat of the berries, but that's obviously not relevant here."

"So we don't eat it," Rufus said with a roll of his eyes. "I wasn't planning to, anyway."

Laurence snorted softly, but Ru did have a point. Laurence wracked his brains trying to remember whether the toxins in yew wood could be absorbed through skin, but he came up empty, so he finished the motion he'd paused, and tugged the book off the shelf.

The damned thing weighed a ton. He whipped up his other hand to catch it before it could fall to the floor, and he stared down at the cover. It was a sheet of wood, close to ten inches wide, with ornate metal fittings on the corners which were just as grimy as the rest of it. There were a pair of locks on the right-hand side, and as Laurence tilted the book, he saw thick struts of brassy metal cross the edge and meet with hinges attached to the back cover.

He turned away from the shelves, but didn't move further than that when he saw the spell across the doorway. "Is that thing going to try to kill me if I walk out of here with this?"

"No," Rufus said. "It won't *try*. It will succeed. Your wards are not capable of preventing it." He reached for the book, empty hands outstretched. "Only I can remove anything from this room. You will have to leave first."

"Goddess, Ru! What if I hadn't asked, huh?" Laurence handed the book to him with a heated glare. He figured it'd wash off Rufus like rain off a tent, but he could at least try to make his teacher understand what might have happened.

Ru tucked the book under his arm and raised his eyebrows at Laurence like he didn't see a problem. "Your instincts saved you."

Laurence opened his mouth, but all he had was frustration, so he threw his hands up in the air to accompany the strangled noise he made. "Fine. But we're also gonna have to have a talk about how my only wards are the ones *you* taught me, except it turns out they can't protect me from lethal death trap magic, and I find this out hours before I'm about to walk into a warlock's sanctum."

Rufus didn't say anything at first, but Laurence didn't stop glaring at him.

"That's a valid complaint," Ru mumbled. "Though I could not have foreseen this situation."

"Yeah, and I can't spend my whole life watching every single possible future, or I'll never get to live any of them." Laurence sighed and gestured for Angela to go first. "Fine. We'll go wait by the truck so we don't hear your super secret password that lets you leave Evil Book Jail with one of the prisoners."

Angela smirked faintly as she passed him on her way out the door, her back to Ru so that only Laurence could see the expression, and he knew damn well that was intentional; whether a show of solidarity, or approval of Laurence's words, though, he couldn't be sure of. He moved to follow her, and as his gaze traveled across the shelves that had been behind him all this time, something caught his eye. It was a book, unsurprisingly, but the magic woven through it was a subtle olive-beige, and the glow it produced was soft.

That book did not belong in this room. Laurence knew it like he knew water was wet. It didn't radiate dread, it wasn't watching him, and it didn't leak blood. It was just a normal, small grimoire, tucked away in the shadow of books that *did* give off all the wrong vibes.

Something made him carry on like he hadn't seen it. He didn't say a damn word, didn't hesitate or make a sound. In fact, he almost went the other way, into full stealth mode, and had to stop himself in case it worked. Nothing would freak Rufus out more than Laurence vanishing in his vault of evil shit, and it might only take a word to turn the death trap ward up to eleven, so he stepped through it and breezed past Angela, then said lightly, "Actually, you go ahead. I'm gonna use the bathroom before we leave."

"The *downstairs* bathroom," Ru called after him.

Laurence waved a hand over his shoulder without looking back. "Of course. I'm not an idiot."

He could feel Ru's stare drilling into the back of his head, but fuck it. There was a truth demanding to be uncovered, and Laurence wouldn't make it wait.

Angela followed him down the stairs, but if she had questions, she didn't ask them. All she did was hold out a hand outside the bathroom and say, "Keys."

Laurence passed them to her. "I won't be long." He thought a second, and added, "I don't suppose you know how to find bugs?"

"It is not a spell that I have ever had cause to memorize," she mused. "But I can destroy electrical signals nearby without knowing where they are."

"Is that going to kill the truck, too?" He frowned at the thought of what could happen if Ru came downstairs and found the truck wouldn't start.

"Probably." Angela let out a little sigh of annoyance. "We'll have to drive in silence, then, which will tell him that we know he's listening."

"Yeah, but he basically told us that he was. He knows we know. Why else would he try to provoke Ru with something Ru said in the car just before we got to Amy's place?" He shook his head. It was something they could figure out later, because surely it wouldn't take Ru much longer to leave the vault, swing the door shut, and do whatever he had to do to lock it. "Anyway, I really gotta go before I burst."

She stared at him like she knew damn well he was lying. Hell, she probably did. But he didn't have time to care. He hurried into the bathroom, locked the door, and closed the toilet lid to sit on it. Then he took a breath and closed his eyes as he tried to bait time.

He visualized the book, and its soft, almost comforting glow. How long had it been there? Who put it there? Did Paula and Todd store it, or had Rufus?

Rufus was searching his library. He looked fidgety, on edge, like something was eating him from the inside, and his motions were abrupt when he pulled what seemed to Laurence like totally random books from the shelves to pile up on the table.

Ru didn't look a day younger than he did today, so this couldn't have been too long ago. Laurence watched him while he gathered up books, skimmed through them, and scowled as he went back to his search. In the end he stopped flicking through a book that was the same size as the one that didn't belong in the vault, and he ran his fingers down a page as he read it.

Laurence hurried closer to peek over his shoulder, and barely caught what was written at the top of the page before Rufus flipped to the next one.

On the Matter of Protection from Movement of the Potent

Laurence had no idea what language it was in, and that was the best translation the spell resident in his cellphone gave him before Ru turned the page, but Ru kept on reading and so did Laurence.

It is of no surprise to me that the Potent bear a variety of unnatural skills, but the most disturbing of all to a Practitioner must be that of Movement, for with this skill a Potent is able to render a Practitioner virtually powerless.
I find it imperative therefore to devise protection against these beings, since they pose effortlessly as men, and pass unnoticed to even our most clever observations. Such creatures would be able to overpower us before we are able to act, and while they are few and far between, it is not a risk I dare countenance.
The spell, therefore, is the best that I can make it, yet still it requires those components which are common to most such endeavors, most notably the blood of the Potent. I can find no way around this need, which suggests that there already exists somewhere another spell which performs the same function, yet I cannot uncover it.
This will have to suffice, and I pray that I never need it, for I cannot conceive of how to take blood from these creatures without their awareness, and by then it will surely be too late.

Rufus snapped the book shut as his eyes blazed with triumph, and he crossed to the bookshelves to open the door to the vault.

Laurence gasped as he surfaced from the vision, and he leapt to his feet to flush the toilet and wash his hands in the sink in case anyone was listening at the door, but the vision replayed itself inside his head like a klaxon, leaving him with the sickening feeling that Rufus had deliberately set out to arm himself against Quentin for some reason. And, yeah, Ru didn't like Quen — was jealous of him, even — but did he really feel like Quen was a serious threat to him? That Quen would seriously try to hurt him?

You came back from Hades, and Quen was holding Rufus so tight that Ru couldn't use magic, he reminded himself. *Shit, he could barely even breathe, and he was furious.*

Sure, Quen had blacked out almost immediately, but Ru had tried to use magic to kill Angela, and Quen stopped him with nothing more than a thought. So maybe Rufus had a right to be scared, angry, or a mix of both.

Laurence ran his hands over his face and checked himself in the mirror. He forced his features to relax before he left the bathroom, but he couldn't shake off the discomfort at knowing Ru had gone to the trouble to dig up a spell to target Quen with, and Laurence especially loathed that it made him grateful that Quen was in England right now.

25

MYRIAM

"And was it worth it?" Myriam tried her very best not to sound judgmental or angry, but it wasn't for the duke's sake.

It was for her own.

It wouldn't serve her well to let him get under her skin, or to lose her temper over events she could never change. She didn't wish to be sidetracked from her investigation, or earn the enmity of a warlock who had only offered to protect her until Bambi took care of the situation back home, so she held her nerve.

The duke took a while to answer, though he didn't break eye contact at all. "I can't say," he finally admitted in a surprisingly soft tone. "I was raised to believe that the answer must be 'yes,' but now I have failed, and it was all for nothing." He took a deep breath and exhaled slowly through his nose. "Because of the twins."

Mikey's posture shifted as Freddy took over. "Because of your greed," he said bluntly. "Our ancestors were satisfied with preserving the gifts we already had, but that wasn't enough for you. You had to reach for more, didn't you?"

"I must say I'm impressed that your plaything is still alive," the duke murmured, though this time his voice bore a hint of a threat, matched by a sharp glint in his eyes. "And you've sent him right back to me, too. Either you failed to learn from his last hospitalization, or you don't care for him as much as he believes."

"That's enough." Myriam took Mikey's hand, and hoped it would keep Freddy from snapping at the bait. "You might have given up your ability to love your children, but that doesn't mean cruelty is the only language you have left."

The duke turned the full coldness of his stare onto her, and Myriam wasn't sure whether he was attempting to frighten her, or simply saw no further need for his mask of humanity. If he thought this was a battle of wills, though, he was mistaken: Myriam wasn't here to prove she had cojones, whatever metric he might measure them by.

She was here to help her son, and no petty tyrant could frighten her off.

"You are correct, of course," he finally said, as though her being right about something was irrelevant. Still, he brushed past her and made his way out to the library to peruse the shelves, which Myriam was ready to take as a sign that he wasn't about to kill them all and was still invested in helping them, for whatever reason.

She gave Mikey's hand a soft squeeze before she let it go, and looked up at him. "Will you be all right?" she whispered.

He grimaced, but jerked his head up in a nod. "Yeah. We're okay. Thanks."

"You're doing well," she said. "Both of you. Remember, the people who have hurt us always want us to be who we are inside *their* heads. But we aren't, and we don't have to let them pound us into the shapes that suit them best."

Mikey scrunched his nose up, then gave her a small, crooked grin. "Freddy says you should bill him for the therapy."

Myriam huffed in amusement and patted his arm. "Not every kindness must be purchased, dear. People can take care of each other for free."

At that, Mikey looked extremely skeptical, but at least he didn't argue, so Myriam returned her attention to the duke and found him already heading back to his desk with a couple of books in his hands.

He sat, placed the books down, and returned to eating his sandwich as the books began to flip through pages of their own accord, exactly as Quentin had made the little book on demonology do in the library earlier this evening.

It was not a reminder of their similarities which Myriam appreciated. Not so soon after Freddy's warning. She pushed it to the back of her mind, took a seat in front of the desk, and settled her hands over the purse in her lap while she waited, since he gave off the air of a man who would speak when he was good and ready.

Eventually, Mikey came to stand by her shoulder, and the only sounds in the room were of breathing, pages turning, and the relentless destruction of a sandwich.

EVENTUALLY, the duke finished eating and pushed the plate to one side. Skim-reading the books didn't take him much longer, and he gave a small nod of satisfaction before he moved them aside too.

"Allow me to lay out a little context," he began as he sat back in his enormous leather seat. "It will save time in the long run, but forgive me if I retread ground you are already familiar with. The universe is an ebb and flow between order and chaos. Many believe that it is a balance, but balance itself is actually a manifestation of order, so if the universe were truly in balance, order would have already won out." He paused and eyed Myriam, perhaps to see whether she would question him or otherwise interrupt.

She did neither, and instead nodded for him to proceed.

"If order wins, we all lose. Everything becomes uniform. Static. Unmoving and undying, but also not alive. In physics terms that would be the heat-death of the universe: when thermodynamic equilibrium is achieved, all energy is bound up, and entropy cannot increase. An eternal state of nothingness, with all energy spread out equally across the entirety of space. But without *some* order — such as energy forming into matter, and matter taking on repeatable and predictable properties — life cannot exist."

Myriam nodded to show that she was listening. This was, so far, rudimentary high school science. While she hadn't been a high schooler for many years, nothing he had said so far was new to her.

"Humanity is a microscopic facet of this far larger ebb and flow, but we do like to think of ourselves as the center of it all. Regardless, this ebb and flow plays out in and around us, in nature and in our actions, both as individuals and as societies. Humanity's specific manifestation is, as Frederick has already pointed out, one of greed." The duke made a sour face as he laced his fingers together in his lap. "Many of us want more than we need, and some of us act on those wants."

"To the detriment of ourselves, and others," Myriam said, as diplomatically as she could.

"Precisely." He idly cracked a couple of knuckles. "One of the larger scale ways in which this has shaped our world through the centuries is the imposition of one set of cultural values and norms onto others, whether through warfare, colonization, faith, or propaganda. The most effective impositions use all four tools, and ultimately the result is that — over time — some humans have stripped others of their identities, their power, and their existence. In the context of access to gifts and magic, the imposed order saw those things as a threat, and so set out to exterminate them."

"You're talking about the Crusades," Myriam murmured.

The duke shrugged his broad shoulders. "The Crusades came a thousand years after the Roman conquest of Britain, which itself was an attempt to homogenize the world in Rome's image, two hundred years after China's first unification, another thousand years after the formation of the Median empire. What's relevant here is much more recent: monotheism can become inflexible, with the existence of things beyond the scope of what is ordained to be 'good' or 'normal' often taken as a threat to faith, society, and control. And when your religion states that anything 'miraculous' is wholly the purview of your god, a human being who is able to call on powers that not everyone has access to is deemed to be 'bad,' and must either be exiled or destroyed."

"And so, over the centuries, we were all largely purged," Freddy concluded. "To the extent where, no matter how much power one of us might hold individually, we remain very much in a minority, and are capable of being overwhelmed by sheer weight of numbers."

"One cannot also overstate that, once done with purging internally, we turned our gaze outwards, because other cultures we encountered had not done away with their mystics, wise women, or shamans. Those cultures still integrated the gifted and the magicians, and so we had to invent ways to paint them as inferior, just as the Romans had done to us." The duke rose from his chair and wandered around his desk to go stand by the windows, where he clasped his hands together behind his back and gazed out into the night. "This homogenization attacked by codifying people into right and wrong, obfuscating its intentions under multiple layers of prudishness, acceptability, and rationale. It whittled humanity down based on sex, sexuality, color, behavior, fashion, wealth, and other metrics, all to impose order and destroy any danger to that order."

Myriam swiveled her seat to watch him, but she didn't follow. "And so, with your context laid out," she said, "what is it you're about to say?"

If he was bothered by her gentle reminder to get back on track, he didn't show it in any way. "What I am saying is that there is nothing more antithetical to the facility for supernatural talent in the human species than the enforcement of heteronormativity, which is why it is so deeply entrenched in most systems of control." He twisted so that he could glance at her over his shoulder. "Those outside the system embody chaos."

"You're suggesting that only people outside of heteronormativity possess the use of gifts, or of magic?" Myriam frowned softly at him, still unsure of where he was going with this.

"Yes. There are, of course, those who would never admit it of themselves. Every regime attracts quislings. But centuries of pogroms and selective breeding have left humanity where it stands now, whereby the universe only bestows such power on those who do not fit in." He gestured around his office, palm upwards, and added, "Many of us found ways to survive, of course, either within the system or beyond it. But my match with Margaret was not borne of greed." His gaze shifted to Mikey. "It was one of desperation. Privilege is no longer enough to protect us, because collaborators always end up with their backs to the wall, even if it took three hundred years for us to get there. We are outnumbered by an order of magnitude which is utterly unprecedented. We *will* become extinct."

Myriam sighed. "You thought that you could combine the power from two families, and put off your extinction for a few more generations?"

"It was a losing battle right from the start," the duke grumbled. "The first duke of Oxford set out to exterminate the plague of Witchfinders who were slaughtering us all, but then the damn fool married a Hopkins, and every single one of his children was born without magic." His lip curled. "We're fortunate that his hubris didn't snuff out our psychokinesis, too, but it was drastically weakened. It took generations of careful matches to bring us back to the strength we have today, but our capacity for magic never returned."

Mikey took a sharp breath. "You're saying your whole line has been warlocks ever since then?"

"I am the thirteenth duke," Hieronymus said. "It has been this way since the second. We always test our firstborn sons, but none of them are capable, so we must bestow it upon them because the ritual itself requires magic." He turned more fully to face them, and added, "But if one does not have magic to begin with, it can be bargained for, instead."

Myriam rose slowly to her feet as the duke's history lessons lined up into a single, clear train of thought. "Sometimes we want things we don't have, even though the culture we grew up in says those things are bad," she said slowly. "So when you're the kind of person who will do what it takes to get what you want, you'll follow the path your culture laid out for you." Her eyes fell to the little book from the main library. "You'll make a deal with a devil, and exchange your soul for power." She looked to the duke, and found him frowning at her. "But," she added carefully, "you said that he has yet to pay his price. He has the magic, but still possesses his soul, too?"

"It's invariably the case that the soul passes to the entity after the death of the supplicant," the duke agreed. "Therefore, while Harrow remains alive, he has his soul, but he also holds magical power. I'm afraid that there is no contract to break which would strip it from him."

A sinking feeling permeated Myriam's core, as the truth the duke spoke weighed heavily on her hope of another way, slowly smothering it.

He hadn't been giving her context. Not really.

He'd been preparing her for the worst, and doing everything that he could to let her down gently.

"There's no way to cut Vincent off from his power," she said, with more peace than she felt in her heart.

"None but the usual way," the duke agreed.

Myriam opened her purse and retrieved her cellphone, unlocked it, and called her son, all while she tried to work out how to tell him that the only way to stop Vincent was to kill him.

Although she suspected that was already his plan.

LAURENCE

HE MADE IT OUT THE FRONT DOOR AND FOUND ANGELA AND RU hadn't gotten as far as the truck. Instead, they were sitting on the doorstep, with the Book of Yew on Rufus' lap, and Angela shoulder to shoulder with him as she ran a hand over the locks.

"Uh," Laurence said.

"Here's how it went," Ru said without looking up. "We figured if Harrow wants this so bad, we should open it up and find out what's in it."

"And we can't do that inside the truck because it's bugged," Angela added.

"Right," Laurence said slowly. "Except we're in a pocket realm, so the bugs can't transmit. Or, at least, he can't receive, right? They're not magic or we would've seen them."

"That's what I said." Ru nodded. "But miss fancy pants here said some techno nonsense which amounted to 'yes, but.'"

"I said that it's possible they might store information internally until they're able to transmit," Angela said dryly. "Either we spend our time tearing the truck apart trying to find them, or we just sit here while we try to crack open these locks. Except, of course, they're password-protected."

"You mean there's a spell on them that requires a verbal trigger," Laurence translated. He closed the door as he stepped around them, then held a hand out for his keys. Angela tossed them to him. "And we've no way of knowing what the right word or phrase is."

"If we had time, we could probably pick it apart," Rufus said as he traced around one of the locks with a fingertip. "But whoever cast these was smart. Everything's interwoven. If we destroy the lock spell, we kick off a bunch of others that'll try to kill us *and* destroy the book at the same time. If we tackle any of the booby-traps, the locks go into meltdown *and* the whole thing still tries to kill us and destroy the book. They didn't want anyone getting in here without a warrant." He lifted the book up so he could squint at the edges, and added, "Judging by the thickness of the paper, there's at least five hundred pages in here. Maybe it's a warlock's book of shadows?"

Laurence bit the inside of his cheek to help him focus as all the possibilities presented themselves. Did he want to know what was in the book, or would he prefer to get the listening devices out of his truck? And how much could he afford to worry about Ru's anti-Quen spell if Quen wasn't even around right now?

"Okay," he began, "Vincent basically told us he's listening in on us, which means he can't be upset about it if we do something about it. Keep trying with the book, see if you can figure something out. I'll go look for the bugs."

Ru grunted at him and lowered the book to his lap.

Laurence crunched his way across the gravel and unlocked the truck, then hopped inside and rested his hands on the steering wheel. He closed his eyes, and hoped that having a physical connection to the truck was enough to overcome trying to see events which took place on a different plane of existence from the one he was in right now.

This truck. Unattended. Then someone does something to it they shouldn't, and we didn't notice. He was struggling to figure out how exactly to bait the hook, but he stuck with it. *They get inside, and hide devices...*

A vision bobbed close enough to touch, so Laurence immersed himself without hesitation.

The truck's hood was open, and a service tech in dark blue coveralls was leaning over the engine.

Laurence took a look around, but this was obviously an auto shop, and he spied Ethan in the waiting room with his nose glued to his cellphone. Laurence kept on searching for some clue about when this had happened until he found an oil-smeared calendar nailed to a wall, and he took a sharp breath.

It was almost a year ago, back while Laurence was in London, or Manchester, or wherever the fuck it was Freddy had taken him.

He scowled and turned back to the truck just as the tech finished topping up the oil and dropped the hood, and couldn't shake how gross it felt to watch this happen while knowing what he was going through halfway around the world at this moment in time: tortured because of one warlock, with the next one lining up like Laurence was some kind of prize to fight over.

The tech went to go get his clipboard, then looked like he'd just remembered something, and grabbed a paper bag from the desk instead. It was plain, rolled over like it might have his lunch inside, except he took it over to the truck and climbed into the passenger seat.

Laurence leaned in through the window and watched the guy take a tiny black plastic device out of the bag.

The tech peeled off a tab to reveal a sticky surface, then reached down and tucked the bug underneath the glovebox, as far back as he could get it. Another went under the driver's seat, then the mechanic moved into the back seat and stuck a couple more in places they wouldn't be accidentally discovered: the back of a headrest, and tucked under the drinks holder in the central console. Once he was done with the cab, he walked calmly to the back of the truck and climbed in to plant four more, easily hidden underneath shelves, presumably just in case Laurence ever had an important conversation while on deliveries.

Laurence backed out of the vision and snarled. It was safe to assume Vincent had gotten to the other vehicles in much the same way, and there had been so many builders coming and going at the mansion that it might prove easier to ask when *hadn't* Vincent had the opportunity. The shop could get bugged by anyone walking in off the street, though the back room would be harder, and Laurence felt sick at the idea that someone might've got into the farmhouse while Mom was at work.

Right now, it didn't matter. He was right about being bugged, so he searched the truck everywhere he'd seen the devices get stuck, and picked them off their hiding spots one by one until he was in the back with all eight in his palm, and used a pair of pliers to crush each and every one of them until all he had left was a mass of cracked plastic and broken circuitry which he swept into an empty plant pot.

It didn't change the past, but at least they could talk on the move again without Vincent listening in on them, and that was the best he could do for now.

THEY GOT on the road again and drove north. Laurence's stomach growled and burbled as Ru and Angela sat together in the back and debated how to find out what was in the book without wrecking it and dooming Amy.

The route only made him think of Disneyland, and all the fun they'd had before shit went sideways in the desert, so he was grateful when the GPS took him off the 5 to avoid LA traffic and head northeast instead. He was even more grateful when he saw a drive-thru without much of a queue.

"What are we doing?" Rufus asked sharply as the truck pulled off the freeway. He leaned forward to peer at the GPS, and added, "This isn't the turn."

Laurence pointed to the Baker's drive-thru the other side of a gas station. "I gotta eat, man. You should, too."

"I wasn't sick," Ru huffed.

"We should also get water," Angela said.

Ru made an angry, wordless noise, but Laurence ignored it and pulled up to order some tacos, sodas, and bottled water.

By the time he got them, his cellphone started to ring, and he hurriedly distributed drinks and food into the back before he thumbed the button on the steering wheel to answer. "Hey?"

"Bambi," Mom greeted warmly from the truck's speakers. "How are you?"

He exhaled with relief that it wasn't anyone he wanted to punch, and balanced his bag of tacos in his lap while he made his way back to the freeway. "Yeah, we're okay. You're on speaker. I've got Ru and Angela with me. How're things with you?"

"Quentin's asleep, so Freddy, Mikey, the duke, and I have all done a little digging."

Laurence's mouth opened. He had questions, but his mom didn't give him time to blurt any of them out.

"I had hoped that with the resources at the duke's disposal we might find a way to cut Vincent off from the source of his magical power, but I'm afraid there isn't one."

He shut his mouth. Now he had even *more* questions, but at least this time there was a pause, so he leapt at it.

"What made you think of that, Mom?" The bag in his lap was making his thighs too hot, so he shifted it, then dug out a taco and crammed it into his mouth.

"Well, to cut a long story short, we believe that Vincent was born without magic, and that he traded his soul for it," Myriam said. "I hoped this meant that there were terms and conditions he might be nudged into breaking, which would then nullify the contract, but I'm afraid it doesn't work like that." She sighed a little, and added, "The only way to take away his power is… well, the duke calls it 'the usual way.'"

Laurence swallowed the taco. "Kill him?"

"Yes," she said simply.

"Gonna do our best." He sighed as he dug out the other taco, and squished the soft shell a bit harder than he'd meant to. "Mom, there's a good chance the farm is bugged. And the store, and the mansion, and your truck. Vincent's been on me for over a year. I've got Sebastian looking into the house and the SUV and stuff, but it's probably best not to call them until he's dealt with all of that shit."

"Motherfucker," he heard Mikey say in the background.

"I see," Myriam replied, far more levelly. "Well, I'm sorry I didn't have better news for you, dear. It's quite late here, but I'm sure one of us will be awake to answer if you need anything. Be careful, won't you?"

"I will. I promise." Laurence paused, then added, "Tell Quen I love him."

"Of course," she promised. "I must go. The duke will be with you in a moment."

"Thanks for the warning," Laurence grumbled. "Love you, Mom."

"I love you, Bambi. Blessed be."

She ended the call before he could say anything else, so he shoved the taco into his face just as the duke reappeared, in his passenger seat this time.

Laurence's lip curled. He screwed up the empty bag and stuffed it into a cup holder, then washed his taco down with a gulp of soda. It wasn't like Mom to hang up so abruptly, but he didn't have time to dwell on it either.

"What did Harrow have to say for himself?" The duke eyed the empty bag with a disdainful crinkle of his nose.

"A bunch of shit that led to us figuring out he'd bugged the truck, so we had to root all that crap out and destroy it. Smart move to vanish when he was busy arriving, but it turns out it was a waste of time: he knows you're involved." Laurence checked on Ru and Angela in the rearview, but they were studiously ignoring the duke and poring over the book again.

"Disgusting," the duke growled. "Do you know how long he has been eavesdropping on you in this manner for?"

"Yeah. It's been at least a year." Laurence put the soda down before he added, "This truck got done when it was in for maintenance while I was a guest of your shitty hospitality." He shot the duke a sideways glare. "I figure he got our home during renovations, probably hit up our other vehicles during maintenance, too. I can't check right now. I figure it's safe to assume he's listened in on just about every damned conversation I've had at home or at work since then, though. Hope he enjoys hearing me and Quen fucking."

The duke snorted. "I doubt it." He didn't elaborate. Instead he routed the conversation back to where it had begun. "He did not go to the effort of speaking with you only to tell you that he's been spying on you, and he would have known that you were already on your way to visit him, which means he contacted you because he wants something. What is it?"

Laurence bared his teeth. Quen and Freddy sure both got their brains from someone, and it was a real shame it was their dad. "The Book of Yew," he muttered.

Hieronymus' eyebrow lifted faintly. "You have it?"

"You know what it is?" Laurence countered.

The duke shrugged, and finally turned in his seat to regard the witch and the sorcerer in the back. "Locked," he concluded. "Resoundingly."

"Very funny," Rufus grunted.

Laurence eyed the GPS as it flashed at him to take the next off-ramp, but they still had maybe thirty minutes to go to the address Angela had provided. He flicked the turn signal and checked his mirrors. "I'll try again. What the fuck is the Book of Yew?"

The duke took his eyes off it and faced forward, and his expression was every bit as neutral as Angela's usually was. "Not a tome I have personal experience with," he said. "But I think we can hazard a guess. You're a witch, Mr. Riley, you tell me: what does the yew tree symbolize?"

Laurence adjusted his grip on the wheel while he grappled with the question. He'd looked at it from a botanist's perspective, worried about the toxicity of the wood and whether they were in any danger if they touched it. But this was magic they were dealing with, and he hadn't even thought to engage his faith.

"Death. The Crone aspect of the Goddess. Access to Annwn. The power to reach our ancestors. And..." He groaned weakly. "Rebirth. Regeneration. Immortality."

A chill ran through him.

It all made sense. If Vincent owed his soul to a demon, and that demon wouldn't get paid until Vincent died, all Vincent had to do was stay alive. He got to keep his soul *and* his magic.

"Goddess," he breathed. "He wants immortality, and we're taking it right to him!"

27

LAURENCE

"That's it." Angela spoke quietly as the truck stopped, and she pointed at a house across the street.

Laurence didn't kill the engine just yet. He followed the line of her finger to an ordinary-looking two-story home and didn't see a single thread of magic anywhere.

"Huh," he breathed.

The house was all browns and greens, nestled behind a front yard overflowing with trees and succulents all neatly planted in beds raised up on sandy brick walls. The spaces between plants were artfully arranged with boulders and rocks on ornamental bark mulch, and a clean white stone path led through them to the steps up to the front door. Off to the right-hand side was a wider white stone driveway, which ended at a garage. Morning glory climbed up and trailed along the porch, casting it into shade and protecting it from the harsh desert sun. The cursory nod to Halloween decor was a single plastic pumpkin in among the rock garden, though Laurence figured it could've been blown there from a neighboring yard.

Whatever Laurence might have expected, it wasn't this. He didn't feel comfortable about pulling up into the driveway, so he finally cut the engine and took a deep breath. "Any last things we should know?"

"The entire building is a facade," Angela said. "If you enter, you will cross the threshold into a sanctum, and if you attempt any offensive magic, it will kill you without hesitation."

Laurence's mouth dried up. "Is it gonna decide the book is offensive magic?"

"It shouldn't," she mused.

"Promising," the duke grumbled. "Very well. I cannot go with you. Message your mother to let us know when you have returned."

"Wha—" Laurence whipped his head around, but the duke had already vanished, and he growled. "Damn it!"

He hated this. Rufus had stressed time and again that a witch could kill anyone in their sanctum with complete impunity and hardly any effort, and now Laurence had to go inside a warlock's personal murder realm without using magic to do anything but defend himself — and without the help of the other warlock who had invited himself along for the ride.

He released his seatbelt and jumped out of the truck, waited for Ru and Angela to join him, then rocked his jaw and crossed the street.

The sooner they got this over with, the quicker they got Amy back. He could figure out how to kill Vincent another day if he had to.

HE HEADED up the path and approached the stone steps up to the porch with mounting caution. There was something eerie about this quiet suburban street with the cancer hidden at its heart, and Laurence felt the hairs raise on his arms and the back of his neck as he slowly mounted the steps.

Even though he couldn't see any magic, the place definitely felt off now he was on the porch. He eyed an old brass doorbell set into the doorframe, but he didn't press it.

This street wasn't where his vision of Marcella and Amy had cut out, and that made him even more uncomfortable. He'd figured Marcella drove into a sanctum area like Rufus', but if they'd crossed that space themselves already, nobody had felt it, and it hadn't cut the duke's projection off.

Did Vincent have access to some kind of apotropaic magic, like the Marlowes? Was that why there weren't any wards at Amy's house by the time Laurence and Ru had got there? Had Marcella taken a route that drove over apotropaic marks like the one that had stopped Quen using his telekinesis to protect his bodyguard?

Laurence ground his teeth. He had no idea, and it just emphasized how outmatched he was, so he stepped to one side and waited for Ru and Angela to join him.

Rufus held the book to his chest, both arms coiled around it, and Angela clasped her purse in one hand as she raised the other to the doorbell.

She paused, her finger on it. "Ready?"

"Let's get this over with," Ru grunted.

"I guess," Laurence agreed.

He wasn't ready at all, but Angela pushed the button, and their time was up.

THE DOOR swung inwards and revealed several things at once: the threads of dying candlelight across the open doorway; Marcella, folding her hands neatly together as she looked them over; a hallway which was far too tall and wide to fit inside this house; and a musty odor which made the place smell like a disused abattoir.

Marcella's eyes fell to the book in Rufus' arms, then she stepped aside and gestured to the hallway beyond her. "Come in."

Rufus didn't move. "Give us Amy," he countered.

"The wording of your deal was specific," Marcella said, sounding for all the world like she'd expected this. "You bring the book to him, and *then* you get Jenkins."

"Fine." Ru held out the book, almost touching the threads at the threshold, but not quite. "Here."

"You bring the book *to* him," she repeated.

Laurence fidgeted on the spot and closed his eyes to try and see whether crossing the threshold would kill them, but — as he'd anticipated — he couldn't make out any future inside that house whatsoever, so he opened them again and relied on his gut instead.

"He wants us," he whispered to Ru. "He hasn't been fucking with us all this time just to murder us in his hallway."

And you're his son, he thought, but he didn't want to add it out loud in case it pushed Rufus into doing something reckless. *He wants more than just the book, and until we find out what, we're just fumbling in the dark here.*

Angela shrugged and stepped inside. She breezed past Marcella like the woman didn't even exist, and only stopped once she was in the center of the hallway, surrounded by dark wooden paneling. She turned to face them, waiting, with her emotionless wall in full effect.

She isn't going to betray us, Laurence reminded himself. *We know she isn't.*

"Let's get this over with," he said, and followed her inside.

It felt like stepping into any other sanctum, with that brief disruption to equilibrium that he was now used to enough to handle without losing his balance. The flickering threads caressed his wards, curving around them, but once his foot landed on the carpet inside it was still attached to the rest of his body, and he hadn't been burned to a crisp.

He let out a breath and took another, but the odor was worse inside, and he immediately regretted letting it into his lungs. His skin started to crawl, too, as he made out more of the candlelight magic all around himself, woven through walls and across doorways like it was part of the fabric of reality itself. And, in here, maybe it was.

Rufus seemed to be weighing up his options, but then he held the book against his chest again and stepped inside, shuddering like someone had walked over his grave. "Urgh," he muttered. "Gross."

Marcella closed the door, then breezed around them, and said, "This way."

Laurence glanced between Ru and Angela, but they were looking at him now, so he made an executive decision and followed Marcella through another doorway and into an even darker room where her heels clicked on hardwood floor, and the only light came from clusters of candles spread around the vast, horrifying space.

There was so much to take in. Sigils and circles were carved into the wooden floor, all filled in with dark, crusted matter that stank of dried blood. Amy Jenkins was slumped against one wall, her wrists locked into rusting manacles that were fixed to a metal loop in the floor through an extremely short chain. There were other women, too, vapid-eyed and naked, all kneeling in supplication around the outer ring of the circles in the center of the room. And at that center, a huge, wooden, throne-like chair with a small table either side of it, and a tall, wide man in his forties looking way too comfortable on it, with countless threads of magic converging on him like he sat in the heart of his web.

"Your guests, Master," Marcella announced, bowing deeply.

"So I see," said Vincent Harrow. His voice was gravelly, and sonorous, like he had all the time in the world.

And if he gets this book, he might, Laurence reminded himself.

Harrow rose from his seat and took a step forwards. Some of the threads came with him, some stayed with the throne, and a few stretched out between him and it as he moved. He was clothed, wearing a rumpled shirt and dark pants, both of which were stained with old blood he obviously never bothered washing out. "You have time to spare," he mused. "Plenty of margin for error. Wise." He snapped fingers at Marcella, then pointed at Amy. "Release her."

It wasn't until Harrow took another step that enough light brushed his features for Laurence to see his face, and his pulse quickened.

He *knew* this face. He'd seen it before, years ago, when he'd been dying of a heroin overdose.

Somehow, at some point, Laurence would hunt this man down through a forest, with a raven overhead to guide him, and Harrow would reek of fear.

Laurence straightened up as the familiar thrill ran through his veins, and he couldn't stop himself from unleashing a wolfish grin.

Vincent Harrow was his prey now, and once Laurence began a hunt, he would not stop until it was done.

28

QUENTIN

He stirred, aware of the dull throb in his shoulder before anything else pierced his consciousness. The temptation to try and ignore it was strong, but the longer he lay in place, the more other sensations seeped in: the heavy duvet over him, weighing him down; a mattress firmer than that which he usually slept on; utter silence all around.

Quentin forced his eyes to open, at least, so that he could assess his situation, but the dark expanse of canopy over his head was all it took to remind him of where he was.

And why.

He turned his head until he could make out the faint outline of his phone on the bedside table, and he summoned it to his left hand and checked the time, but it had either already somehow switched itself to Greenwich Mean Time, or he'd been out like a light for ten hours. At least in the light from the screen he could also see a fresh glass of water and a pack of paracetamol, so he sat up with care, fumbled with the box until he could take a couple of pills, then he threw the duvet off and slid his silk-clad legs out of bed.

He had to use telekinesis to help himself get out of bed, and once he was up, he was in no state to try to get dressed. Instead, he threw a robe over his right shoulder, threaded his left arm through the sleeve, and telekinetically fastened the belt for decency's sake. That was as much as he was willing to manage, and once he had slippers on, he used the bathroom, then made his way out of his bedchamber on a mission.

THE WINDOWS which weren't curtained showed darkness outside, which meant that he hadn't slept until midnight San Diego time, thank goodness. He picked his way downstairs with care and poked his nose into the library, but nobody was there. That was to be expected, he supposed, since it was quite late, and he allowed his gaze to linger on the piano at the far end of the room. He could readily recall the names of several works commissioned by and composed for Wittgenstein — a concert pianist who had lost his right arm in the First World War — but was not familiar enough with them to attempt to play without the sheet music in front of him.

Now is not the time, he reminded himself, and tried at least not to feel too frustrated that his mind was wandering. *You're in a lot of pain. Give the paracetamol time to work.*

Quentin sighed and backed out again, then padded his way through the back door and into the servants' corridor to find the kitchens. While he wasn't hungry, he really shouldn't be taking too many painkillers on an empty stomach, so if he could scrounge up a sandwich he would at least have practiced some of that self-care Violeta kept talking about.

It was quite a hike, and by the time he made it, he was slightly more alert. He dug into cupboards and refrigerators and unearthed both bread and fruit, so in the end he toasted a couple of slices of bread and made a banana sandwich out of it all, then stood and ate it like a raccoon who had gotten into the bins.

By the time he made it back upstairs — not that physical stairs were involved — he was much improved, and finally realized that if he wished to find Myriam, he could simply text her to ask where she was, but her reply was extremely unfavorable.

The duke's office, she said.

He dropped his phone into the pocket of his robe and made his way there at once, before he could change his mind.

Quentin barged through the outer library and through to the office with barely a glance at the books he passed by. Once inside, he shut the doors at his back, and took stock of the situation.

Myriam, Michael, and Father were all in here, all sitting around Father's desk with tension in their bodies and strain on their faces. Myriam set her handbag down on the floor and stood to come towards Quentin and offer him a hug, and he slipped his arm around her to squeeze gently.

"What's happening?" he murmured.

"Bambi has arrived at Vincent's sanctum," Myriam said softly. "We're waiting for him to contact us."

Quentin nodded a little and moved with her as she returned to her chair, but there were no others, so he perched on the edge of Father's desk instead. Father huffed at him, but Quentin ignored the complaint. "All right," he said. "Fill me in."

It was Myriam who did so, gently and efficiently, without any interruption. When she was done, she turned to Father, and added, "Surely you have some way of helping Quentin's shoulder?"

Quentin scoffed faintly. "If he had, I'm sure my childhood would have been far more tolerable." He didn't bother looking towards his father. He was quite capable of heaping scorn in that direction without turning to face it, too. "Do you really think there's a spell for immortality in this book Harrow has demanded?"

"All things are possible," Father rumbled thoughtfully. "Though I cannot imagine what that might look like, or how one is meant to endure eternal life."

Quentin decided not to think about that too hard. Instead, he retrieved his phone and typed out a message to Sebastian to check on his progress in removing bugs from the house, and murmured, "We must find a way to level the playing field, or even to tip the scales in Laurence's favor. Any warlock worth their salt will be protected from magical and physical attacks. What other options do we have?" He finally glanced to his father, and raised his chin. "You sent Black Annis to do your dirty work. Are there any such entities we could work with on this matter? Preferably ones less inclined to eat children?"

"I might have an option," Michael said, though clearly with Freddy's intonation. "But it's an incredible risk."

Quentin looked to the redhead and found him leaning forward with his elbows on the arms of the chair, hands clasped together and propping up his chin. His brows were drawn together in doubt, or worry.

"Really," Quentin said levelly. "And what might that be?"

Michael's expression soured even further. "Katharine Marlowe."

Quentin's pulse quickened at the thought of letting that woman anywhere near Laurence. His lips parted, and he was ready to object, but he couldn't deny the brilliance of the idea.

Harrow's magic was the problem.

Marlowe would literally shut it down just by standing in the same room.

"Who, or what, is Katharine Marlowe?" Father asked.

"She's a Witchfinder," Freddy drawled as he leaned back in the chair and crossed Michael's legs. He gazed up at Father. "She attempted to kill Icky."

"She's still alive?" Father didn't seem too impressed.

"She is," Freddy said smoothly. "I have been keeping tabs on her whereabouts to ensure that she has indeed changed her ways. So far, so good, but it's only been a few months." He paused, then added, "She's a direct descendant of whichever Hopkins managed to escape to the Americas before they could be finished off completely. Which, it transpires, makes her a distant relative to us. Fancy that."

Quentin blinked sluggishly at Freddy. "I'm sorry, *what?*"

Freddy waved a hand at Father. "It transpires that Nicolas

d'Arcy, first Duke of Oxford, fell for one of the Hopkins women and married her, and that's why none of us since him have been born with the ability to use magic. Kept that one quiet, didn't you, Father?"

The duke snorted at him. "Hardly. It's all right there in the family archives."

Quentin stared at Father in growing horror. All these centuries of hurt and hatred, and they were *family*?

You're acting as though we haven't already been inflicting hurt and hatred on ourselves all those years. We're willing to do it to direct family, why wouldn't we do it to distant relatives too?

He eased carefully to his feet and adjusted the robe to ensure that none of it had wriggled loose with the motion, and he nodded to Freddy. "Very well. Do you have a means of contacting her that won't cause friction?"

"That would be a significant part of the risk I mentioned," Freddy sighed. "If any of us contact her, she will know that I have her under observation, and it could cause her to go to ground. If I lose track of her, it might be some time before I find her again, if I'm even so fortunate as to do so, and who knows what damage she could cause in the interim."

Quentin's heart sank when he realized what that meant. Freddy could call her, or email, or reach out some other way, but Marlowe had made it abundantly clear that she knew how to disappear into desert, or forest, or any other enormous and uninhabited area in the United States, and all a message did was give her plenty of time to do so.

The only way to circumvent that was to go there in person, unannounced, and hope that she could be reasoned with.

Quentin tried to assess his options. He was at a significant physical disadvantage against the Marlowes already, before throwing a broken shoulder into the mix, but Freddy wasn't here, and Father wouldn't go. It couldn't be Myriam, or she would no longer be protected by the castle, and Quentin would never even consider asking such a thing of her in the first place.

No. It had to be him.

"All right," he said softly. "I'd best get dressed, then you can give me the address, and Father can set me down as close to it as possible."

He made his way to the door, and hoped that he wasn't about to throw his life away for nothing.

29

LAURENCE

"I've been watching you," Vincent drawled as he stopped a couple of feet away, still well within his circles and sigils. "Tell me: how *did* you retrieve your lover from Annwn?"

Laurence shrugged, and did nothing to hide his grin. "Maybe you weren't watching closely enough."

Vincent eyed him, but didn't respond to the provocation. Instead, he turned his attention to Rufus, and reached out his hands for the book. "I'll take that now."

Ru clung to it and stayed still. He didn't even acknowledge Vincent. He was busy watching Marcella unlock Amy's manacles.

Laurence glanced over, too, just in time to see Amy jerk awake at the touch on her arms.

"No," Amy moaned when her gaze settled on Rufus. Her eyes grew wide, and she snatched her hands back from the manacles as she tried to take in the situation around her.

"It's okay," Laurence said to her. "We're taking you home."

"You are," Vincent purred, "if you give me the book."

It seemed like the absolute worst kind of standoff: the sort that would go around in circles until someone lost their shit and started a fight. Laurence had been in enough bars and clubs late at night to know how this would play out without taking a peek at the future, and since he wasn't convinced Ru would be the one to win if this all went sideways, his only option was to break the standoff before everyone became entrenched.

Laurence put himself between them, turned his back on Vincent, and met Rufus' eyes. "You don't have to give it to him," he murmured. "You can let me do it."

Ru's lip curled, and his hold on the book remained tight.

"It's what we came here to do," Laurence added softly. "The time to change your mind was on the drive up here, and you didn't. Amy's our priority. Let's focus on her for now." He beckoned with his fingers, just slightly, and dipped his head in a faint nod. "It's going to be okay."

He prayed silently for Vincent to keep his mouth shut, and either the gods were listening, or Vincent wasn't a total fucking idiot. Either way, Laurence was able to remain focused on Rufus without Vincent throwing a spanner in the works, and after a few more seconds he saw the slow unwinding of Ru's shoulders, and the stiffness in his lip melt away.

Ru held the book out, and Laurence took it from him with another nod, and a gleam in his eye he hoped conveyed what he couldn't say out loud.

This isn't over.

Whether Ru got the message, though, Laurence couldn't tell.

Laurence turned back to Vincent and offered him the book, arms outstretched. "Here," he said simply. "This is the deal we made. The Book of Yew, for Amy Jenkins, within your deadline. You take it, we take her, and our business is concluded."

Vincent moved to the very edge of all his circles and reached out with both hands. Either those sigils etched into the floor were protective, or he wanted Laurence to believe some implied weakness without them, but right now it didn't matter. Laurence stepped closer so that Vincent didn't have to make any unpredictable moves, and as he leaned in to place the book in Vincent's hands, he parted his lips and inhaled deeply.

The mixture of scents was horrific, and he gagged on it. There was rotten flesh and old semen, sickness and death. He struggled not to retch as the weight was lifted from his hands, but it was all he could do to stagger back from Vincent without choking. By the time he felt the hands on his elbows that held him upright, and managed to blink tears out of his eyes enough to focus again, Vincent had retreated to his throne with the book in hand, and settled into it like a guy who'd roofied Laurence's drink and was waiting for it to kick in.

Laurence swayed on his feet while Angela held onto him, the world swayed around him. "We don't have the password," he croaked. "We can't help you open it."

Vincent shrugged. "If I needed that, it would have been part of the arrangement, wouldn't it?" He rested the book in his lap and laid one hand on the front cover, then used the other to gesture graciously to Amy. "You may go."

Laurence glanced that way in time to see Ru help Amy to her feet, and for her to cling to him in a desperate hug, but his attention went back to Vincent, because Vincent was the main source of danger.

"Разрушать," Vincent said.

Every single spell woven around the book died at once. The threads cut out of existence like they'd never even been, and when he murmured, "Открыть," the locks popped open without hesitation.

"Now, if you don't mind, I have some reading to do." Vincent met Laurence's eye and gave him the exact same grin Laurence had flashed at him only a minute ago, like hunter and prey had just switched places. "You don't want to outstay your welcome."

Laurence had to agree. He drew his elbow away from Angela's hand so he could take hers instead.

"Let's get the fuck out of here," he muttered.

Nobody objected, and Laurence somehow herded them out of the hell house and back to the truck without argument, which had to be a miracle.

He was going to need more of those.

THE DRIVE south was terse for well over an hour. If anyone attempted to strike up a conversation, someone else made a sound that cut them off.

It was like nobody wanted to say anything within fifty miles of Vincent Harrow, even though there was no way he could be listening in on them now, but once they passed San Clemente Laurence cleared his throat to give them all some warning that he meant to break the embargo, then he glanced to Amy and Ru in his rearview. "Are you okay?"

He knew it was a provocative question, but it was the best way to get people talking, even if it meant frayed tempers.

"How can she be?" Rufus spat. "We all saw what it was like in there!"

"Ru," Amy breathed.

"It was a stupid question," Ru growled.

Angela took a breath, but Laurence cast her a glance, and a faint shake of his head, so she let it out with a confused frown.

"I'm okay," Amy said quietly. "He didn't…" She paused and shook her head, letting her curls fall forward to hide her face. "I'm okay."

"I saw… a lot," Laurence told her, as kindly as he could. He returned his attention to the road ahead, though the 5 southbound was pretty quiet this time of night. "I saw him take you," he added, leaving the rest unspoken, because there wasn't any gentle way to say *I saw the dead baby he made you ride with*.

He heard Amy's quiet sob, and a glance confirmed that Rufus had had the decency to put his arms around her, so Laurence fell quiet again and gave her space to grieve.

It would probably be a mistake to take Amy and Ru to La Jolla right now. Amy was fragile, Ru was volatile, and immersing them in the chaos of the mansion might overwhelm them. Laurence didn't want to go anywhere near Amy's house, either; it could still be crawling with cops, and might remind Amy too much of the horror she'd been put through since Vincent walked through her front door.

That left Myriam's farm, or Ru's sanctum, and Ru's sanctum

was way better protected, so Laurence pulled off at Carlsbad and took them straight to it. Angela got out to open the gate, and once Laurence was safely parked outside the front door he killed the engine and gestured to the house.

"Why don't you go get comfortable?" he said as he turned to face Amy. "Whatever it takes. Bath, shower, change of clothes, a bite to eat, anything you need. After that, we can work out what our next move is gonna be. Does that sound okay?"

She hesitated, and looked at Ru like she was waiting for him to chime in.

"I don't have any food," Ru muttered.

"It's fine," Laurence said smoothly. "You both go inside, and me and Angela will go hit up whatever we can find that's open this time of night. We'll get groceries, clothes, whatever you need, okay?"

He didn't want to leave them alone, mostly because he doubted Ru would be all too sensitive about Amy's needs, but he also knew Amy needed a break, and there was no way Ru would willingly leave anyone alone in his sanctum without being there himself. This was the best way to give Amy her space, so he'd have to deal with it.

"Fine," Ru grunted. "Whatever."

Laurence waited until they were out of the truck, then he pointed Angela at the gates again, and waved her to follow him as he drove through them.

He absolutely wasn't going to leave Angela with Ru, either, because he didn't trust that Ru wouldn't blame her for everything that had happened and try to kill her.

Again.

THEY FOUND a 24-hour grocery store easily enough, but it didn't seem to sell so much as a t-shirt. It *was* overflowing with Día de los Muertos decorations, candles, and gifts, but Laurence figured some sugar skulls and an ofrenda tablecloth weren't ideal replacements. No matter how much he dinked around on his phone while Angela pushed the cart along the aisles, he struggled to find anywhere in Carlsbad that sold clothes this late at night.

This wasn't how he preferred to spend Samhain.

He sighed and hoped Amy could wait until Target opened in the morning, because driving further afield seemed like a waste of everyone's time.

"Are you ready to talk," Angela said as she tossed a bag of instant coffee into the cart, "or do you want to wait some more?"

Laurence snorted and shoved his phone into his pants pocket. "About what?"

"About why you went and took a deep whiff of Vincent Harrow's rancid stench right when it was about as bad as it could possibly get." She threw in a couple of varieties of tea bags after the coffee, without seeming to bother checking what they were.

"Toothpaste," Laurence muttered as it popped into his head. "Toothbrushes, too. Probably toilet paper. Ru hasn't done any grocery shopping this week; we don't wanna get caught short."

"Noted," she intoned. She didn't change the subject, but the way she held her head high as she pushed the cart to the end of the aisle made it clear she still expected an answer, just like she did whenever she was teaching him magic.

Laurence debated her question as he strode alongside her. His gut — and what little common sense he actually possessed — told him Ru still wasn't in a place where thinking straight was on the cards, and none of them had taken a break all day either. Laurence was tired, and he doubted that would change any time soon, so he rocked his jaw and looked Angela in the eye.

"Back when my power to see the future kicked in, I was dying of an overdose, and I saw a whole bunch of things all at once. I saw my dad's death, which didn't happen until a year later. I saw Quen, and I didn't meet him until three years after the overdose. And I saw Vincent Harrow, except I only met him tonight, so I had no idea who he was."

Angela tilted her head to indicate that he should continue.

"I was hunting him, and he was *terrified*." Laurence kept a lid on the thrill that tried to stir in him. Now wasn't the time. "We were on foot, naked, running through a dark forest, and he didn't

— doesn't — see me until it's too late. I had his scent, and that's how I tracked him down." He scratched at the stubble along his jaw as they turned up the next aisle.

"And to ensure that future, you first need to *obtain* his scent," Angela mused. "Did you succeed?"

He nodded slowly. "I think so. I didn't have a lot of time to pick through it all but I'm pretty sure I'll be able to find it again when I need to." He ran the tip of his tongue along his lower lip, then trapped it between his teeth. "There's something else."

She tossed toiletries into the cart as they moved. "What?"

Laurence pinched the inside of his cheek with his canines as he wrestled with the sense memory, but the more he honed in on it, the more certain he became.

"I think he's sick," he breathed.

Angela eyed him. "I think we all know that," she deadpanned.

"Ha ha," he said flatly. "No, I mean physically." He gestured like he could put his thoughts into words by dragging them out of his brain with his bare hands, grasping at the empty air and wishing he'd swallowed even half the number of dictionaries Quen had. "There were a bunch of scents that were external, like all the blood and, uh, whatever the fuck else was rotting away in dark corners in there," Laurence muttered, lowering his voice even though there wasn't anyone else nearby to hear him. "But there was something else I couldn't put a finger on. Something wrong with the way *he* smelled." He took a breath. "When we're sick, it can disrupt our hormones, change what chemicals are in our breath, sweat, or waste, and all those things smell different. Not to humans, of course, but..." He trailed off for a second. "I'm not trained, and I don't go around hospitals sniffing the patients, but I know there's something wrong with him, and I think that's why he's doing all this."

She slowed to a halt, and turned to face him fully. "He's dying," she mused.

Laurence straightened up and raised his chin. "Yeah," he agreed. "I think he's sick, and whatever he's got is killing him."

"And we've handed him the key to immortality," Angela breathed.

"Uh-huh." Laurence crinkled his nose and set off again. "He made sure we had no choice. But now we do. He's all out of leverage."

"And we'll soon be out of time." Her eyes narrowed.

"Looks like it's all going to come down to how fast he can read, and how deep into it he has to get to find his immortality spell, huh?"

They exchanged a loaded look, then hurried to finish the shopping in grim silence.

This was going to be an all-nighter, and that meant no rest after all.

30

MYRIAM

Myriam was torn between the wish to chase after Quentin to try to talk sense into him, and the urge to slap Freddy in the face for suggesting such a dangerous idea. The main thing that prevented her from doing the latter was that it wasn't at all fair to Mikey.

She watched Quentin leave, then rounded on the men in the room with her hands clenched into fists, which was preferable to letting them loose on anyone's cheekbones — even in a family overburdened with them.

"What are you thinking?" she demanded of Freddy. "He's in no fit state to face any of the Marlowes, or to think clearly about ridiculous suggestions that could get him killed. You're usually so full of plans. Tell me that you have one now!"

Mikey's mouth opened and shut, and his cheeks blazed pink.

"That isn't a plan," Myriam huffed. She tried to relax her fingers, but it seemed as though they weren't ready to give up their anger yet.

"It's an *idea*," Mikey mumbled, shuffling defensively.

"Not the best he's ever had," Hieronymus drawled. "There are far superior alternatives."

Myriam felt like telling him exactly what she thought of his *superior* approaches to life, but like most expressions of anger, it would help no one. She took a breath and focused on loosening her hands on the exhale, then flexed her fingers as she asked, "Such as?"

The duke shrugged idly. "I'm sure that between the four of you you can work something out. Pool your resources. They are not as limited as you are telling yourselves."

She pressed her lips together as she eyed him, but he clearly had no intention of helping them solve this problem, not even to save his son's life.

And why would he? As far as he's concerned, he's already destroyed the family's legacy. His world has ended, and all he has left is personal power.

Myriam picked up her purse and tucked it under her arm. It gave her an excuse to break eye contact, to focus on something other than the face of a man who didn't care whether or not his children died.

"All right," she said as she beckoned Mikey to follow her. "Let's be out of the duke's hair. I'm sure he has more important matters to attend to."

She turned on her heel and followed in Quentin's footsteps, while taking the opportunity to breathe out more of her frustrations and clear her thoughts.

If they had the means to solve this problem, then solve it they must.

She closed the door behind Mikey once he'd followed her into the duke's personal library, but grabbed his elbow before he could continue out into the corridor.

He blinked at her and his red eyebrows launched themselves towards the ceiling.

"There must be something in here that we can use," Myriam whispered. She pointed to the nearest shelves. "Find it."

Mikey's head tilted. "Unless you have a very specific secret that you have yet to share, none of us are able to use what is in here," Freddy murmured.

"Your father knows something that we don't, and most of what he knows is in these books. Find it. If it turns out it's magic…" Myriam puffed out her cheeks and shook her head. "We'll cross that bridge when we come to it. Go digging; I'll talk Quentin out of throwing his life away." She scowled at him, and added, "What were you *thinking*, Freddy?"

"I was thinking that Katharine Marlowe could kill Vincent Harrow without so much as batting an eyelid," Freddy drawled. "It seems an obvious solution to a thorny problem."

"Except that you don't *want* her to go back to killing, and that's why you're monitoring her, isn't that right?"

Freddy's gaze wavered, then he sighed and turned his back on her. Mikey's hands drifted across the spines of books, then plucked one from its shelf and flicked through it at speed. "You have a point," he finally said. "This would be quicker with two pairs of hands, if you care to remove your talisman?"

"Or just come here in person, and use your own hands, for once," Myriam huffed.

His only response was to flick through the next book just as quickly, so she left him to it, and hurried out into the corridor in the hope that she could track Quentin down in a house the size of a small village.

HE HAD SAID that he was going to get dressed, so Myriam made her way up the stairs and to his apartment, where she knocked politely on the door. She gave it fifteen seconds before upgrading to banging on it, but there was still no response, so she turned the handle and stepped inside.

The crimson felt oppressive, surrounding her on all sides like a bloodbath, and Myriam shuddered at the unpleasant mental image. While Quentin wasn't here, his robe and slippers were, so he had to be in one of the other rooms.

Myriam stepped further away from the door before she called out, "Quentin?"

No answer.

Myriam set her purse down on a chair and tipped her head until she heard the faintest of splashes from the bathroom, and she groaned to herself. Quentin *wasn't* thinking straight, and getting dressed meant that he had to bathe first, because goddess forbid anyone see him in anything less than an absolutely pristine state.

She crossed to the bathroom door and rapped on it with her knuckles, then cracked it open a few inches so that he would be able to hear her without her seeing him. "Quentin," she called out. "Do you need any help?"

"What? No!" His voice rang out in alarm. "Absolutely not!"

Myriam held the door steady and wondered how best to proceed without invading his privacy or upsetting him further.

He is about to become my son-in-law, she reminded herself. She was every bit as responsible for him as she was for Bambi, and she would hardly let Bambi struggle alone in the bathroom with a broken shoulder.

"All right," she said levelly. "Did your doctors say that you were allowed to bathe unattended just yet?"

His silence spoke volumes.

"Are you even supposed to let water anywhere near those sutures?" she pressed on.

"Myriam," Quentin said, though there was a whine in his tone.

"Well, you're in there now," Myriam sighed. "And your assistance options are limited. Would you like me to go get Thorne to help you?"

"No!"

"Then it will have to be me. May I come in?"

"Myriam!" The whine was much stronger now.

"I have seen it all before, dear. I need you to put aside your pride and accept help, because I don't want to be the one to tell Bambi that I let you slip and crack your head open. Do you wish to put me in that position?"

He was quiet a while, until he let out a sullen, "No."

"All right. I won't look anywhere that I don't need to, dear, I promise. I'm coming in."

She gave him a few more seconds before she slipped into the

bathroom, and she closed the door so that nobody else could peek in on him. From the corner of her eye she could see that Quentin sat in the bath with very little water, but she walked briskly to the tub and perched on the edge with her back to him so that he could adjust to her presence in his own time.

"I don't doubt that you can manage," she said softly, after a drawn-out silence. "You are telekinetic, after all. But you are also injured and recovering from surgery and anesthetic, and aren't allowing yourself the time or rest that your body needs. Have they given you iron supplements for blood loss?"

Quentin sighed faintly. "Yes."

"Anesthetic, painkillers, iron supplements... You must be producing the most horrendous stools," she said gently, hoping to ease his discomfort with a light joke. But she didn't give him the opportunity to butt in, and pressed on. "Your digestion is sluggish, your body isn't able to move oxygen or nutrients around as quickly, you have a cocktail of medications lingering in your system, and all your energy is being spent on repairing your wounds. You are not thinking clearly, and can be forgiven for getting it into your head that traipsing off to find the woman who tried to kill you is an excellent idea, but I am here to tell you that it is not, and that you aren't going to do it."

Myriam could almost feel the glare that burrowed its way between her shoulder blades. Quentin didn't take kindly to being told what to do at the best of times, and this was certainly not one of those.

"Here's what we'll do," she continued. "We'll get you cleaned up and presentable. I'm sure it will help you feel much more comfortable, which will let you concentrate on the real problems. Freddy is busy searching for anything in your father's library which we might be able to use to our advantage, and once you are dressed, you and I will help him."

Quentin hissed. "I won't use magic."

"Not even to save Bambi's life?" Myriam folded her hands together on her knee while she waited for his response.

"Potentially," he eventually mumbled.

"You're a good man, Quentin. But you're not firing on all

cylinders, and you are not alone. That must be extremely hard for you to accept after having spent so long without..." She took a deep breath as her heart ached at the thought of him traveling the world with nothing more than clothes and his piano for so many years, and it was not difficult to see how he had turned to alcohol. "Without support," she said, unable to keep the slight crack from her voice. "But you have it now, and we won't let you fall. Do you understand?"

He was quiet for over a minute, but Myriam didn't push, or fidget, or even turn to face him. She simply waited, and used the time to process her feelings, to let them run their course, so that she would be better able to work once he was ready for her to.

"I understand," he eventually replied, in little more than a light whisper.

"Good, because your father believes that there are ways to make this omelet without breaking the eggs we don't want to lose." She finally began to turn, twisting on the edge of the tub until she could look into his eyes.

He met her gaze, though he'd taken great care to cover his crotch with his left arm, which left him with no way of hiding anything else. The poor boy looked exhausted, desperate, and far too fragile to be unattended in a bathtub. The irony that such a startlingly powerful psychic was in this extraordinarily vulnerable state was not lost on her, and Myriam made a mental note to have another talk with Freddy at some point about saying ridiculous things to his overconfident brother while Quentin was in no position to differentiate good ideas from bad ones.

It was clear that Myriam would have to take over the decision-making for the time being, and that meant corralling a fractious pair of twins who were barely on speaking terms, while their abusive father refused to offer much in the way of assistance at all.

"That would be you," she clarified, and reached out to run fingers through his thick, heavy hair and push it back from his forehead. "We're not going to lose you, Quentin. Now, why don't you wash what you can, then I'll help with your hair, and we can talk through what we know about Vincent to see whether we've missed anything obvious, all right?"

Quentin nodded faintly. "All right."

She let him get on with it while she searched the bathroom for the tools she'd need to clean his hair in a bathtub, and by the time he was finished, she was at his side with a towel so that he could protect his modesty.

"Now," she said, once he'd pulled the plug and arranged the towel in a way that satisfied him. "If you would like to call on other people for help, why don't we start with those who have helped you before, instead of the ones who've tried to murder you?" Myriam filled a porcelain bowl with warm water, then used a cup to scoop it over his hair, and guided the water with her hand to keep it out of his eyes. "What about young Basil, from New York? He might be able to help you. He uses magic, doesn't he?"

Quentin tipped his head back with his eyes closed, and frowned softly. "He does," he said slowly.

"Tell me more," Myriam said.

Quentin began to ramble about Basil, and Jon, and Annwn, and Myriam couldn't help but wonder whether a necromancer might be exactly what they needed.

31

FREDERICK

Aggravatingly, as was her habit, Myriam was entirely correct. The more brains Frederick could apply to the task — preferably in their own bodies so that they came with hands and eyes attached — the faster he could catalog Father's entire library. But he was an hour and a half from Castle Cavendish, and unwilling to leave Delaney unattended. Furthermore, it was damn near sunrise outside; they'd been up all night, and Frederick had spent the entire time stretched between three bodies.

Sooner or later, he would need to take a break.

He pushed himself to his feet and padded quietly through the house, making his way downstairs to the kitchen on the ground floor. This was a problem which required tea, and Frederick had no staff at this particular abode to make it for him.

This home was for privacy, not creature comforts.

Michael dutifully flicked through book after book, and Frederick's brain filed away everything that it saw, but it would take time to process, to inventory, and he didn't want to cock it up the way he'd done with his bloody idiotic idea that Icky go talk to the Marlowes.

What *had* he been thinking?

Myriam was quite right to chew him out for it, as she tended to be whenever she gave him a piece of her mind, and he sighed as he filled the kettle.

What is it? Michael asked, nothing more than a thought from forty miles away.

I made a mistake, Frederick admitted. He sat the kettle down on its base and switched it on, then set about preparing cups. Delaney wouldn't drink tea, but Frederick had instant coffee on hand to cater to the American's underdeveloped palate. *The pieces fit together too neatly, but I forgot to factor in that those pieces were violent psychopaths.*

It's late. Hell, it's already morning again, Michael replied. *Myriam's had eight hours more sleep than we have. We'd already had a full day before they got here.*

"Mmm," Frederick agreed out loud. The water began to boil, and he watched the turbulence of it in the clear level indicator up the side of the chrome kettle. It was hypnotic, and the spell didn't break until the kettle switched itself off with a loud click, which spurred him back into action. He poured the coffee first so that the water had cooled enough for his tea by the time he moved on to it. *You're right,* he thought to Michael as he stirred both drinks. *We have to maximize our capacity before we lose it altogether.*

Uhhh... What're you thinking? Michael paused in flipping through books as concern took over.

You need more hands, Frederick answered. *I'm going to get them for you.*

Michael's mind swirled with worry, but he got back to work, and Frederick carried the cups upstairs.

FREDERICK USED his elbow to push open the door to Delaney's bedroom, then gave the side of his bed a hefty kick. "Rise and shine," he barked as he moved on and set the coffee down on his bedside table. "How can you possibly need ten hours' sleep a night? You're not even twenty, for crying out loud."

Delaney was a scruffy little oik. Frederick had cleaned him up as much as possible, of course — got a stylist to take away his ridiculous mullet, and curate a far better wardrobe — but the boy was breathtakingly idle about his personal grooming in ways Frederick had thus far failed to comprehend, and he was equally difficult to rouse in the mornings.

How am I still here? Every day I open my eyes and it still isn't a fucking dream. Delaney's waking jumble of thoughts was as banal as ever. *Is that coffee?*

"Yes," Frederick said. He backed away to a chair and sat, then crossed his legs and blew on the surface of his tea to cool it. "We have a problem."

Delaney groaned and pulled the duvet up over his head. "My only problem is you," he spat, though his voice was muffled by the bedding.

"Hardly. Your main problem is that you are an odious little creature whose sense of entitlement far outstrips his willingness to work for it."

Delaney snorted. "Says you, who gets it all handed over on a silver platter. This is illegal. It's kidnapping. Imprisonment. Coercion. Slavery."

Frederick sipped his tea. "You're welcome to prove it in court, but I'm afraid I cannot represent you. It would be a conflict of interest. Besides, I have a proposal for you."

The caution and curiosity that warred within Delaney's puerile thought processes all but filled the room, so Frederick turned his attention back to Michael's page-flipping until the duvet eventually moved aside, and the crumpled thing that was Cameron Delaney finally emerged from his cocoon.

Alas, he had not become a beautiful butterfly overnight.

"What?" Delaney grunted. He grabbed the coffee and downed half of it, then had the temerity to be surprised that it was hot. "Ow!"

"I want you to think about what it is that you want for your life," Frederick drawled. "Is it fame? Money? Power? Or do you crave something deeper? Friendship. Love. Connection. People who listen to what you have to say, and respect your opinions. You spent so much of your life attempting to punish others for being more interesting than you, Cameron. Would you like to be interesting?"

There was about to be a whole stream of effluent out of the boy's mouth, so Frederick put a stop to it at once.

"Here's what I can offer," he continued smoothly. "An education. Connections. Wealth. Therapy. I can put you in touch with whoever you need to speak to. I can open doors that would never unlock for you otherwise. You can *choose* all of this, Mr. Delaney."

The boy's analytical brain grabbed hold of Frederick's words and began to churn them over, and swept his rage aside in the process. He really was excellent at collecting and sifting through data, and his thoughts were alight with what could be possible if he really had everything Frederick suggested.

"I want to go home," Cameron said, though the tremble in his voice would've made it clear how uncertain he was about that even if Frederick wasn't reading his mind.

"You know you cannot," Frederick replied, not unkindly. "How will your family react to your return? You were instrumental in the kidnap and torture of a foreign national, and while you have been released from custody, they won't ever treat you the same way again. They won't trust you."

"You can *make* them trust me."

Everyone seemed to think telepathy was a magical panacea for all their woes, and Frederick sighed faintly. "Until you break their trust again. But…" He leaned forward slowly, and wrapped both hands around his cup as he gazed into Delaney's eyes. "If you return home once you have grown, gained your fortune, or your fame, or whatever it is you truly want, you won't be the same person, and they will welcome you with open arms."

You're so full of shit, Michael chuckled fondly.

Indubitably, Frederick replied, but he kept the smile from his face.

Delaney fidgeted in his uncertainty, but thoughts of walking in on his parents with a variety of ostentatious displays of wealth dripping from him so that they would smother him with the praise he'd never received as a child were all-consuming, and he shrugged. "I'm not having sex with you."

Frederick rolled his eyes and stood. "Of course not. But you *are* going to stop fighting me, and you will do as I say without requiring that I be inside your head all day, every day." He took a sip of tea, then added, "You have a great deal of promise, Mr. Delaney. Allow me to nurture it, and the rewards will last a lifetime."

There was something distinctly American in the way that Delaney's thoughts turned to private jets, piles of gold, and incredibly gaudy cars, but in the end he drained the rest of his coffee and slammed the cup down on the table.

"Fine," he said. "What do you want in return?"

Frederick shrugged. "Exactly what you are already giving me, but with far less arguing about it all day, every day."

I don't know why you haven't just given him a whole new personality, Michael grumbled. *It's not like the one he's already got is great.*

The one he's already got is intrinsically woven around his detective skills, Frederick reminded him. *If I tabula rasa him, we might lose the very skills we need him for.*

Is tabula rasa a verb?

Frederick sent him the telepathic equivalent of a withering stare.

"Okay." Delaney snorted at him. "Sure. Why not? I'm already buried in student debt and trapped in a foreign country. Might as well try and make the best of it, right?"

Frederick eyed him, then tapped the side of his own nose before pointing at the boy with the same finger. "There you are," he rumbled. "That wasn't so difficult, was it?"

Still, he checked that all the controls he'd buried deep in Delaney's brain hadn't shaken themselves loose in any way so that the boy wouldn't think to run or get messages out to anyone who might be inclined to try to help him, and then he pulled his own wallet out and tossed it to the boy.

"Get dressed, then go shopping. Buy yourself whatever you'd like. Be back by five o'clock."

Cameron almost fumbled the catch, and only recovered it by clutching the wallet to his chest. He stared down at it as though Frederick had opened a door to Narnia. "No limits?" he squeaked.

"No limits," Frederick assured him, while also embedding some reasonable limits deep into Delaney's consciousness. "Go wild. Consider it a promise of what the future could hold if you're able to behave yourself."

What're you doing? Michael asked.

Frederick turned his back on Delaney and left the room. He closed the door far more gently than he had opened it, and retreated to his own bedroom, whereupon he locked the door and hauled a chair in front of it to provide an additional barrier to entry.

I need him gone for the day, Frederick told Michael. *I cannot focus if I must control him too. I'm too tired, and cannot risk another mistake.*

He finished his tea and left the cup on an occasional table by the door, then settled down in the center of his bed and closed his eyes.

Can I help?

You're already helping, Frederick assured him. *Carry on. You'll have company soon enough.*

Michael was quizzical, but he continued his task without further questions, and Frederick used him as a starting point.

From there, he sought out Thorne, who was the nearest member of Father's staff, and swept into her mind without her even noticing.

Once he had her, he was able to use her to seek out the next nearest staff, and the rest fell one by one. Every single mind he took over expanded his reach exponentially until he had maids, kitchen staff, groundskeepers, and stablehands under his control. It was far too many people to fit in Father's personal library, of course, so they formed a human chain and emptied the whole thing out into the main library, where they could spread out and skim thirty books at once.

If Michael had anything to say about it, he was sensible

enough not to, and Frederick lost himself completely in the task of committing tens of thousands of pages to memory.

A subtle ache blossomed into existence at the back of his eyeballs, and he did everything in his power to ignore it for now.

32

QUENTIN

Quentin couldn't decide whether he was deeply humiliated at having Myriam wash his hair while he sat naked in a wet bathtub, or oddly comforted by the presence of a mother who — while not his own — clearly cared for him in a way he hadn't experienced in years.

Or, in fact, at all, he thought, somewhat bitterly. *Mama was hardly the angel I once believed her to be.*

What a state he was in. If he wasn't hallucinating his own father, he was reliving the moment he'd killed Nathan Anderson, as though if he simply picked at that wound enough it would unravel him entirely and he could stop fixating on it at last.

Was that what you wanted to do? Throw yourself on the mercy of Katharine's judgement as punishment for your crime? She already considers you guilty. There would be no trial.

Scorpions sting. It's in their nature. That was what she said.

Were you trying *to get yourself killed?*

He groaned as Myriam rinsed the conditioner from his hair. The water was warm, and her fingers strong, and as the stream ran down his spine he drew a thin trickle of heat from it to try and make up for his utter lack of strength.

When did you last eat?

Quentin had some vague memory of a banana sandwich, but

that was all. He certainly couldn't take Myriam's warmth; despite her gifts, he didn't think she was as overflowing with life as her son, and Quentin wasn't willing to find out.

The towel around his waist soaked up a great deal of the water that sloshed past his hips on the way out of the bath, and grew heavy on his skin. Warmth, soothing touch, grounding weight... he almost dozed off again.

"There," Myriam said. "That will do for now. Wait there."

He stirred slowly and cracked an eye open in time to see her return with more towels, her gaze politely fixed on the ceiling overhead while she held them out to him.

So much for not allowing her to see me in an inappropriate situation prior to officiating at my wedding, he thought.

Quentin kept his eyes down as he took the smallest towel and wrapped it around his head. He took the sodden one from around his waist and pushed it toward his feet so that he could quickly replace it with the fresh one Myriam held.

Once he was done, she offered her hands.

"Move carefully, dear," she advised him, still looking up. "Lean on me if you need to. Once you're safely out of this tub I will leave you to it and wait outside, all right?"

He struggled to figure out the logistics, and cursed softly under his breath. Getting *into* the bath with one working arm had been simple. Leaving it again now that everything was wet was next to impossible, even with a helping hand.

He was forced to use his gifts.

How ridiculous.

Be quiet.

Quentin pulled himself upright and rested his hand on Myriam's shoulder for stability so that he could step out of the bath without beaning himself. When both feet landed on the soft, dry mat, he released her, and moved his hand to hold the towel around his waist so that he could stop using his telekinesis for such a silly task.

She met his eyes and inclined her head to him. "I'll be outside," she repeated.

"Thank you," he rasped.

Then he was alone, and hollow, and tired of being quite so feeble.

He heard a phone ring.

Quentin had managed to brush his teeth, to dry himself and moisturize, even to shave and apply deodorant. His next task was to leave the bathroom and make it to some clothing, but Myriam's voice spoke softly after the ringing sound went away, and he was sure he heard her say *Bambi*.

Clothes forgotten, he pushed his way out to the bedchamber and rushed to Myriam's side. "Laurence?" he asked of her.

Myriam smiled dryly. "He's here," she said into the phone. "I'll put you on speaker, dear." She lowered the device and tapped it. "There we go."

"Quen?" Laurence's voice was so small, coming from the speaker, but he sounded excited, not upset. "Hey! How are you?"

"Quite alright," Quentin said. It wasn't even a complete lie. Laurence's voice had lifted his spirits enough that he was able to fool himself into believing that he hadn't been about to do the stupidest thing ever conceived of. "What's happening?"

"We saw Harrow. Gave him the book, got Amy. Then I took Ru and Amy back to Ru's place. Now Angela and I are just getting groceries, then we'll head back to Ru's and probably stay awake all night trying to come up with a plan to go kill Vincent before he manages to make himself immortal."

Quentin scrunched up his nose while he fought to grasp what Laurence had just said.

"Would you like me to tell the duke that you're available again?" Myriam asked.

Laurence sighed. "Maybe not the worst idea," he grumbled, "though the drive back is only gonna give us about ten, fifteen minutes tops, if he wants any kind of conversation. Once I get to Ru's, he can't come in with me. I don't suppose he's had any ideas and passed them on to you so I don't have to look at his smug fucking face, right?"

"Of course not," Myriam sighed. "He wouldn't dream of missing out on telling you how brilliant he is himself."

"Urgh." Laurence sounded like his huff had turned into a yawn, and there was a pause before he continued. "Okay. Quen, get some rest. I love you, hon."

"I love you too, darling. Be careful."

"Always am. Love you, Mom. Bright blessings."

"And you, Bambi. Blessed be."

The phone went dark in her hand, and Quentin gazed at it until she put it into her purse, as if it still somehow bore some afterimage of Laurence so long as it remained within his line of sight and — once it was gone — the connection to his fiancé had finally cut out.

"I had best pass on that message," Myriam said. "Will you come downstairs once you're dressed?"

He nodded sluggishly and watched her leave, then turned away to find out exactly how much of his long-abandoned wardrobe Thorne had relocated into these chambers while she'd had the chance.

Everything felt so disconnected, so dreamlike, that he wasn't wholly certain he was awake at all.

His clothes here were so outdated. How could they not be? It was everything that he left behind when he fled, the items that eighteen-year-old Quentin had not prioritized. And, of course, every shirt or sweater had long sleeves. The only items without were thermal undershirts, so he maneuvered his way into one of those, then pulled a sweater on over his sling and allowed the unused sleeve to dangle like a scarf.

By the time he was fully dressed, his hair had almost dried, and he was willing to call it a day. He felt slightly refreshed, which would have to do, so he left his chambers and made his way to the stairs.

The Great Hall was flooded with cold morning sunlight and the peculiar sound of flapping, or scraping; something familiar and yet confusingly different at the same time. It was only once he followed the noise all the way to the library that he was able to identify it.

The room was jam-packed with what had to be every member of household staff, all of whom were methodically flipping through pages of softly glowing books.

Nobody uttered a word.

Quentin entered the library and assessed the situation a little more closely. There was some order to it: the majority of staff stood by one flat surface or another with books piled nearby, and skimmed through one at a time; two groundskeepers darted back and forth, taking away used books, or delivering them to another table; Michael and Thorne were at that final table, seeking out pages in books which had already been skimmed then using their phones to photograph them.

The whole thing was eerie and mechanical in a way that only had one cause he could conceive of.

"Freddy?"

"He's busy," Michael said, sounding distracted himself. "This is everything from your father's personal library. It would take way too long to catalog alone, so Frederick recruited extra help. We're collating any and every spell he thinks might be useful."

Quentin crinkled his nose in distaste, but he'd already been quite clear about his unwillingness to use magic, and he wasn't going to rehash it. It was safer to presume that this information would be passed on to Basil, regardless of Freddy's intent.

"We've found the one the duke uses to be wherever he wants," Mikey continued without looking up from his work. "He doesn't think it's hard to cast, but it's extremely difficult to use effectively. Needs a whole lot of concentration, which he doesn't think you've got right now." He put one book down and reached for another. "He says you should go outside and pick up some energy or whatever it is you need, 'cause all the kitchen staff are here. Nobody's making breakfast, sorry."

"And Myriam?" Quentin couldn't see her here at all.

"Came by a few minutes ago, didn't stay. I figure she's gone to the duke's office."

"Thank you." Quentin inclined his head softly, though Michael wasn't looking, and he turned to leave the library as quickly as he could.

Freddy's suggestion, while annoying, wasn't the worst, and so Quentin popped out into the courtyard to steal some ambient warmth from the air, the ground, and the ornate water fountain in the center of it all. It didn't take long to freeze the fountain and fill the air with tiny flurries of snow, and by the time he was back inside and marching toward his father's office he was considerably more on the ball — or, at least, far less convinced that he might still be dreaming.

He pushed open the outer office doors and strode into the almost-barren library. Stripped of all its books, only trinkets and talismans remained, scattered across otherwise-empty shelves.

Quentin's step faltered slightly at the utterly alien sight, but he pushed on through to the second set of doors, and entered the office without knocking first.

Myriam sat in front of Father's desk, and Father was behind it. It might have seemed quite mundane if not for the faint prickle of magic which made the hair on the back of Quentin's neck stand on end, and he ground to a halt, still several feet away.

"I wouldn't recommend it as a course of action," Father said, though he didn't seem to be addressing either Myriam or Quentin. "Even if you were able to identify the correct demon and speak with it, it cannot take action beyond the bounds of its contract. It can't preemptively terminate Harrow just to ensure it receives the soul it was promised." He spread his hands slightly. "All you do is expose yourselves to it, and it will attempt to rope *you* into a contract instead. These things aren't worth it."

Myriam turned and gave Quentin a warm, welcoming smile. "Quentin," she said quietly. "Do you feel any better?"

Quentin nodded. "Yes, somewhat. Thank you." He glanced to Father, then added, "Laurence?"

"And Angela," she confirmed. "They're on their way to Rufus' house."

Quentin bobbed his head again. He understood what that meant: that soon they would lose contact once more, hidden behind the wards of Rufus' sanctum, and cut off from the world so that not even a text message could get through.

Father grunted with a shrug, and dropped his hands into his lap. "Dismantling one spell is simple, especially if it is anchored by sigils. But once you are in another's sanctum you are very rarely faced with a single spell, and it is not uncommon to interleave several so that they function as back-ups, booby traps, or alarms. It would take skill which — between the four of you — you *may* possess, but I very much doubt that Harrow will allow you all to enter his sanctum and tamper with it at your leisure. Witchfinders would be a viable solution, but—"

The duke looked mildly annoyed as he cut off his sentence halfway through, and his gaze briefly flit across to Quentin before it returned to the thin air he'd been addressing before.

"Yes," he said. "I agree. Exposing *yourselves* to something which would neutralize you too *is* an extremely bad idea."

Quentin huffed and shoved his hand into his pocket.

"Hmm. If he is able to negate spells completely, you are best off not to rely on any at all." Father sighed. "Very well. Let us know once you are reachable once more." He listened a moment, then raised a hand and drew it through the air in front of himself, and the hair-raising sensation died away.

Negate spells completely echoed in Quentin's ears.

"Harrow knows how to... what, exactly?" He blinked slowly and regarded his father. "Destroy magic?"

"So far as Mr. Riley can tell," Father agreed. "It may be best for your lover to lean into his gifts, instead."

His gifts.

Quentin blinked again as puzzle pieces softly shifted themselves around in his brain, and while he wasn't sure he grasped what the larger picture was just yet, it felt as though he'd managed to glimpse a corner.

"I see," he mused. "Then, as there's little I can do from here, I must ask that you relocate me to somewhere far more useful."

Myriam stood quickly and frowned at him. "No," she stated, her head held high. "You are *not* going to find Katharine Marlowe, Quentin."

"I am not," Quentin agreed. He knew only one person whose gifts could negate anything they touched, and he certainly wasn't a Marlowe.

Father rose far more slowly, hands on his desk until he reached his full height, and he turned the full force of his glare onto Quentin. "Then where?"

Quentin didn't shrink away. He didn't even flinch. He looked Father straight in the eye, and answered the question.

"New York."

It was time to pay Jon Dwyer a visit.

33

LAURENCE

Laurence parked the truck and waited for Angela to return from closing the gate, then he grabbed the grocery bags and joined her out on the driveway.

"Do you think his suggestion is sound?" Angela asked as she led the way to Rufus' front door.

Laurence shook his head and followed her. "Go in without using magic, against a whole coven under Harrow's control, and in a sanctum absolutely dripping with spells? I'm the only one of us here who has gifts to fall back on, and I can't protect the rest of you. They're not those kinds of gifts."

Angela knocked on the front door, even though they both knew there was very little need: Rufus' wards and alarms would've already told him they'd opened and shut the gate, and arrived inside his sanctum. "Perhaps if we could obtain a rocket launcher," she mused, though it was impossible to tell whether or not she was joking.

The door opened, and Rufus stepped aside to let them both in. He even reached out to take some of the bags from Laurence and lighten the load.

Laurence used his foot to nudge the door shut behind himself, and he followed Ru and Angela through to the kitchen. He hefted his bags up onto a countertop, then started helping Ru to put groceries away. "I think whatever we do, we can't be as coordinated as an entire team under one man's control, and they outnumber us three to one. Maybe a rocket launcher isn't the worst idea."

Rufus glanced between them as he stocked the fridge. "Amy said a couple of things I found concerning," he grumbled.

That didn't surprise Laurence all that much. The poor woman had been Vincent's prisoner for a couple of days, and Laurence suspected he'd only scraped the surface of the horrors she might have seen since she was taken from her home. But any information at all could be critical, so he raised his chin and looked Ru's way. "Oh? What'd she say?"

"And where is she?" Angela took a seat at the nearby dinner table and rested her hands together on it.

"Spare bedroom, asleep," Ru said. He frowned to himself. "She doesn't think this is the end of it."

"Well, no. We're going back and we're going to kill Vincent." Laurence stuffed cereal boxes into a cupboard.

"From Vincent's end," Ru explained. "He told her he'd been waiting for me. Waiting for a long time. Like he couldn't reach me here, and I was never away from home long enough — or with too many wards — for him to get to me." He took a deep, shaking breath, and rested his hands on the countertop. "He *wants* me, Laurence. I don't know why, but it sounds like it goes beyond wanting a book I had. It sounds like…" His fingers curled faintly until his nails pressed against the counter. "I don't know. It sounds like I'm the goal, and the book's just a distraction, maybe."

Laurence felt like there was something missing, something Ru wasn't being totally honest about, but had to admit that this lined up with what Vincent had said to Amy when he'd kidnapped her, so he nodded in agreement. "And what was the other thing?"

Ru rocked his jaw, and got back to filling the fridge. "He wants you, too. Apparently he's been waiting for you to be 'ready,' though he didn't say what for."

Laurence grunted at that. Vincent hadn't spent all these months testing the boundaries of Laurence's resourcefulness for nothing, after all. "Well, I've got something, too. He smells sick. I mean that he smells like he's dying, not that..." He flattened out empty bags and then left them on the counter, unsure where Ru might want to put them. "I think that's why he wanted the book, because if he dies, the demon he made a deal with for his magic gets his soul. But it makes sense that he's not going to just sit around doing nothing after that, right? He's still got stuff he wants to do with his immortality. He must have." He turned his attention to Angela. "What *does* he do when he's not fighting to stay alive?"

"I try not to wonder," she replied flatly. "He spends the majority of his time inside his sanctum, and when he does leave it, it is never in his own body."

Rufus snorted. "Possession is disgusting, dark magic."

Laurence patted his curls down absently. "He's a disgusting, dark magic kinda guy," he reminded Rufus. "But there must've been a time when he went outside. How else could he have met Amy in the first place?" He hesitated, then frowned at Ru, as he was sharply reminded that Rufus had only just found out who his birth parents were, after having spent ten years desperate to avenge the deaths of parents it turned out had adopted him. "How're you holding up?"

Ru finished putting away the last of the groceries, then he collected all the empty bags together and tossed them into a drawer. He busied himself with filling the coffee machine's water tank for so long that Laurence wondered whether he'd ever get an answer, but once Ru changed the filter and switched the machine on, he sighed and crossed his arms as he leaned his ass against the counter and gazed sullenly at the floor. "Not great," he admitted.

Laurence lifted an eyebrow. This had to be the first time he'd ever heard Ru claim to be anything other than totally fine. "I'm sorry, man," he murmured. "This has to be so hard. I can't even imagine what you're going through."

"Everything in my life is a lie." Ru didn't look up, and he didn't raise his voice. He sounded more resigned than angry. "All of it. And it all goes back to him. He fathered me, then never wanted me, except he wants me now. Amy had to give me away, and let me think she was taking care of me after Mom and Dad..." He paused, frowning, like he was considering whether to call them something else, but in the end he carried on without doing it. "Because she was their friend, not because she was the woman who gave birth to me. She never told me, never even hinted. But then, here I am thinking I've always been alone, except it turned out I had this amazing friend when I was younger, and she made me forget her." He still didn't move, didn't so much as look Angela's way. "And, again, it's because of him." He unfurled his arms and pushed fingers into his rust-colored curls. "Why did he kill them? Why go to the trouble of keeping me alive? He can't have known back then that he'd need me in the future, surely?"

Ru's voice raised sharply, and he cut himself off, turning back to the coffee machine to ready some mugs and watch coffee drip slowly through the filter into the jug.

"I don't know," Laurence murmured after a few moments passed by. "I don't have any of the answers. But maybe I can look back and try to find out?" He bit the tip of his tongue lightly. "I might not see much if he's spent all that time in his sanctum, but..." He gave a small shrug. Sometimes, if he had the person or object he wanted to look back on nearby, he was able to see things that had taken place on other planes, but that didn't mean he was eager to go searching through time to watch yet another warlock getting up to evil shit.

Ru grunted and kept watching the coffee.

Laurence waited a while, but all Ru did was pour the coffee once it was ready, so he made his way to the table and sat next to Angela while he tried to figure out how they could possibly take down Vincent when they were outnumbered and outmatched. He raised his chin in silent thanks as Ru brought the mugs over, and turned his attention to the nearest window. It was too dark outside to see the faint, brassy color the edges of the sanctum tainted the sky with, but he knew it was out there, and he frowned slowly.

"Paula was a great planar engineer," he murmured as his thoughts began to align themselves in a new direction. "She probably had books on it."

"Several," Ru muttered.

Laurence wrapped his hands around his mug and drew it closer. "Do you know what happens if you break the link between a sanctum and the mortal world?" He tore his gaze off the window and switched to looking between Ru and Angela. "Would it be jettisoned from reality, like a lifeboat? Or does it reappear wherever it was cut out from?" He sucked in a breath as he remembered something both Ru and the duke had told him. "Can we seal them up in there and wait for all the air to run out?"

"Depends on what it's made of." Ru propped one elbow on the table. "This sanctum would reappear. It was carved out wholesale and an illusion left in its place. The real world basically has a crater where this house sat. But for sanctums that are created instead of transposed…" He raised his hands to try and illustrate his point. "All sanctums are closed systems when the path between them and their anchor point is not in use. They are a whole plane of existence, on a very small scale. A universe all to themselves. They aren't really lifeboats, because there is no sea beyond them. There's *nothing* beyond them. A *created* sanctum has no limits on size or scope. It doesn't have to match the real space it overlays, because the only connection is the doorway, and that only exists while the door is open."

It was Laurence's turn to groan, and he resisted the urge to try and drink his coffee, because it was far too hot right now. Metaphysics was hardly his favorite subject, even less so when it got downright weird, and *every sanctum is a closed universe* was definitely weird. "Does that help us?"

"Rufus is saying that Vincent's sanctum is created, not transposed," Angela said.

Laurence narrowed his eyes, but the answer came to him a second later. "Because it's way bigger on the inside," he realized.

She nodded. "Correct."

"So if we break the link, he's trapped in his own rotten universe?" He didn't dare get his hopes up yet. "He can't just build a new door from the inside, right? Otherwise people would have one door for everywhere they ever wanted to go."

Angela gazed at him, her expression neutral.

Laurence's shoulders sank. "Marcella drove Amy up into the mountains before they disappeared. There's definitely another door."

"And if we close the one we know of, it's us who lose track of him, not the other way around," Ru sighed.

"Okay, well," Laurence began slowly, "if we're outnumbered and outgunned, the only thing I can think of is to increase our numbers and get bigger guns." He finally gulped down some coffee. "I know a guy. We should go talk to him."

Rufus sat back in his chair and looked distinctly unhappy. "Quentin's no good for this. There's too much magic. He won't be able to keep his shit together."

"Quen's in England," Laurence reminded Ru, and chose not to touch the rest of what Ru had said. "And Sebastian is way more willing to put a bullet in someone if he has to." He downed the rest of his coffee in a hurry, and hoped it had enough caffeine in it to keep him going for a few more hours. "I think we've got to stop trying to fight magic with magic."

"You think we should fight it with bullets, instead?" Angela arched an eyebrow.

"Maybe." Laurence pushed his chair away from the table and stood up. "Who's with me?"

Rufus pulled a face like he'd accidentally touched poop. "Amy's asleep; I better stay here."

Angela got up, though, and reached for her purse. "Sure, why not?"

Laurence tried not to feel underwhelmed at her lack of enthusiasm. He just grabbed his keys and made for the door. "Sit tight," he said to Ru. "We'll be back as quick as we can."

The whole idea was well outside his comfort zone, but if all it took to stop Vincent was a pyrokinetic with a gun, Laurence wasn't going to complain.

34

QUENTIN

"All right," Quentin barked as he strode into the library and made a beeline for Michael. "What do you have for me?"

Michael used his phone to gesture to the growing stack of books at the end of his table. "These are ready to go back where they came from."

"Other than a request for logistical assistance." Quentin cast his eye across the pile, but any glows were diminished by the cold light of day, so the books seemed almost mundane.

"I'll collate everything and send it to you." Michael snapped another photo. "So far we've got that co-location spell, some personal protective wards, a couple of perception spells, one that lets you temporarily fake a sympathetic connection, one for *spotting* sympathetic connections, uh…" He closed the book he'd been working on and added it to the pile. "Freddy's skipping over any spell that replicates your existing gifts. Turns out there are a *lot* of spells for moving stuff, making fire, flying, that kind of thing." As he flipped through the next book and snapped another picture, he added, "Plenty for summoning or interacting with gods, daemons, psychopomps, or ghosts, too."

Quentin suspected none of that was remotely useful, but he could at least offer it all to Basil for the necromancer to pick and choose from. Perhaps it would do as an olive branch for waking him and Jon in the middle of the night. "Thank you," he said. And, as he'd effectively been asked to do so, he gathered up all the books that Michael was finished with and used his gifts to carry them out of the room and across the Great Hall.

He encountered Myriam as he continued on into the west corridor, and nodded to her as she turned on her heel to accompany him.

"Is this wise?" Her voice was gentle. "New York, I mean."

"Jon is able to negate energy with a touch," Quentin murmured to her. "If it transpires that he can do it to magic, too..."

Myriam nodded thoughtfully. "All the benefits of a Marlowe, with none of the drawbacks," she finished. "But what if he can't do it, and you're stranded in New York?"

"Freddy has identified the spell Father uses to appear and disappear at will. I will share it with Basil." Quentin paused to open the doors to Father's library, then he shoved the books into arbitrary piles on the nearest available shelf space, sorting them together by size to fit as many on as he could. He had no intention of even trying to restore whatever order Father had imposed upon them. His task, as he saw it, was merely to save staff from having to run up and down both corridors all over again, especially since he doubted Freddy would allow the poor sods to remember having done so.

He grimaced a little and turned to face Myriam. "Will you be all right here?"

"Of course, dear." She reached for his available hand and gripped it tight. Her skin felt hot to the touch, though it was more likely that it was he who was cold. "You should eat," she added, which only meant that she'd felt it, too.

"The kitchen staff are busy," Quentin sighed.

"Whatever will we do with you?" Myriam gave him a dry smile and used her hold on him to drag him back out into the corridor. "Come along. Show me where this kitchen is, and we'll see what we can pull together. For everyone, not just you," she clarified, as though she'd foreseen his coming complaint and knew exactly how to fend it off.

He rocked his jaw, but she had a point: according to Michael, there had been no breakfast made this morning.

"This way," he said.

MYRIAM MANAGED to make food preparation for thirty-odd people look easy. All she had done was evaluate the contents of cupboards and refrigerators, and then she had him slicing and buttering stacks of bread, which she filled and turned into sandwiches. They were not, perhaps, everyone's idea of an ideal breakfast, but they were food, and Quentin had little interest in eating at the best of times. A sandwich would at least give him some extra energy, then he could abstract more out of the air until he was ready to leave.

She made him carry plates the same way that he had moved books, and he stood by while she told Freddy to feed the people he was using. Eventually, he allowed her to sit him down in a chair and put one of the last two plates in his hand, and she ordered him to eat.

She was right to do so. He knew it. But, god, how he did not want to force his way through a whole sandwich right now.

One look at the patient expectation in her eye convinced him that he should do his best.

"Once you're in New York," Myriam eventually said, halfway through her own breakfast, "I won't be there to stop you rushing off to do something ridiculous."

Quentin impelled himself to chew his way through the sandwich, which bore the favorable side-effect of rendering him incapable of answering her until he was done. It saved him from embarrassing himself with well-meaning nonsense about how he would never do such a thing.

Your shoulder is held together by pieces of metal, you are barely functional even with painkillers, and you wish to go to New York — alone — in the hope of recruiting a necromancer and a child of Arawn into a battle with a murderous warlock. That is, surely, the epitome of ridiculous.

He made it to the end of the sandwich without even registering what had been in it, set the plate aside on a scrap of spare table space, then turned to face Myriam and reached for her hand. Once she took it, he met her eye, and murmured, "I owe you a great deal. You have done so much for me, of which talking sense into me is merely the tip of the iceberg. All I can do now is promise you that Basil and Jon are extremely competent, and that I will listen to their judgement as keenly as I would yours."

She searched his gaze as she squeezed his hand, then her head bobbed faintly. "I suppose that's as much as I can ask for, isn't it?"

"No." Quentin blinked owlishly at her. "You can always *ask* for anything. Whether or not I can promise it, though, is another matter entirely."

Myriam laughed a little. "Then I *ask* that you do everything you can to stay alive, Quentin. Bambi needs you. Don't leave him."

His lips parted slowly.

He *had* almost left Laurence. On multiple occasions. Myriam's request was a fair one, with a great deal of precedent, whether she knew all of it or not. But was her question innocent, or did she mean to ask him to kill if that was what it took to survive?

You are experiencing what we call a moral injury.

The image of Nathan Anderson's frozen, ruptured skin was there, waiting for him the moment he blinked, and Quentin withdrew his hand.

"I'll do everything I can," he breathed.

But he didn't know where the line was anymore.

He carried most of the rest of the books back to his father's personal library and stacked them wherever he could, then barged on into the office without knocking. It was rude, and he meant for it to be.

The desk was largely covered in accounting ledgers, and Father was in the midst of poring over them, pen in hand.

Had he really decided to use this lull in his time to get on with some bookkeeping?

Quentin halted in the middle of the room. He had no concept of what he'd expected to find Father doing in here, but for some reason, finances wasn't remotely near what he might have imagined.

"That's it, then?" The duke snorted. "You expect me to drop everything just to take you on a day trip?"

Quentin refused to be baited. He was too tired of the belittling and sniping, and the sooner he could get away from it, the better. "Yes. You aren't helping Laurence out of the goodness of your heart. You want something. And if you wish to obtain it you'll do whatever is necessary. Take care of Myriam, and don't harm Michael." Then he did something he never could have imagined of himself: he offered his left hand toward his father, palm up, with the full understanding that he was asking his abuser to use magic in his presence. "Let's go."

Father eyed him with the sort of disappointment which had been present throughout Quentin's entire childhood, but he emerged from behind the desk, and approached until he was within spitting distance. He loomed as though he was attempting to convey the full force of his irritation, and he grabbed Quentin's hand in a crushing grip, but Quentin refused to so much as flinch.

He couldn't. He was too busy focusing all his will on preparing himself for what would come next.

"Non est ad astra mollis e terris via," Father said.

And then they were both somewhere else entirely.

Quentin reeled as a tsunami of sensation threatened to drown him. Magic had flared to life and taken hold of him, the air around him shed several degrees of warmth, he heard remote sirens and closer cars, and the sunlight was wiped out in an instant, replaced with night sky and distant skyscrapers.

Father released his hand and stepped away. "Will this do," he said, his tone scathing, "or did you have a better spot in mind?"

Quentin recoiled and backed into a tree, which jammed a sharp reminder through his shoulder that he couldn't fumble around without looking where he was going. He leaned against it until the world stopped trying to make him throw up and, in the meantime, squinted as he took in his surroundings. This place was so familiar to him that it didn't take long at all to recognize it.

He was in Central Park.

"This will do," he said, and hated how weak it sounded. Then he supposed it wouldn't do any harm, so he added, "Thank you."

Father sniffed at him, then sliced a hand through the air, and both he and his magic vanished.

That was it, then. Quentin was utterly alone. He had no wallet, no passport, and no idea of where Jon and Basil actually lived, so he pulled out his phone and waited for it to stop bombarding him with messages about roaming charges, data limitations, and clock changes, so that he could dredge up Basil's number and call it at four o'clock in the morning.

He had no doubt that he was about to become incredibly unpopular.

35

LAURENCE

"Where are we going?" Angela asked once she was back in the truck's cab and pulling her seatbelt across her chest.

"Eh, just around the block," Laurence admitted. "I don't see the point of driving all the way to La Jolla, but I don't know this area well enough to say whether it's safe to stand out on the street at one o'clock in the morning, and I figure you don't want to be alone with Ru in there." He pulled away from the curb and thumbed the phone button on the steering wheel. "Call Martin Flynn," he said, once the truck beeped at him.

"Your butler is a trained assassin?" Angela rested her purse in her lap, then her hands on her purse.

Laurence chuckled at her and shook his head. "No, but if I call Sebastian I might wake up his whole family. Hey, Martin," he added when the call connected. "Sorry to wake you. I really need to talk to Sebastian. Is there any way you can get him on the line without, uh…"

He trailed off and realized that Martin walking into wherever Sebastian was sleeping would be just as disruptive as ringing Sebastian's cell, and groaned to himself.

"Of course," Martin said smoothly. "Please give me a moment, and I'll return your call once I have him?"

"Sure. Yeah. Totally. Thanks, man." Laurence hung up and

studiously avoided looking across at Angela while he felt his cheeks burning.

Thankfully, she didn't say a word.

MARTIN CALLED BACK in only five minutes, and when Laurence picked up, it was Sebastian on the line.

"Hey," Sebastian grunted. "What's the latest?"

Laurence nearly went straight for answering the question, but managed to stop himself at the last second, and instead he asked, "How'd the bug hunt go?"

"Great," Sebastian said. "Got everything, without a doubt. It's all commercially available gear, nothing off-market or in need of a permit, so tracking it all down was relatively easy once we got the right equipment in. Took half the day, but it's done now. We haven't done your mom's store or farm, though."

"That's fine," Laurence said. "I want you all inside those wards until this is over."

"And how close are we to it being over?"

Laurence puffed out his cheeks, then gave Sebastian a rundown of everything he'd gone through so far, until he finished with, "I figured maybe if we're gonna lose at a magic fight, why not change the game completely?"

"You want to Indiana Jones it," Sebastian mused. "Not the worst idea."

"I, uh..." Laurence tilted his head faintly, but it was his turn not to get a reference. "What?"

"You want to take a gun to a sword fight," Sebastian explained. "Kids. What movies are you even watching these days? Don't answer that. Okay, from what I understand, magic takes a little time to get warmed up, is that right?"

"Usually," Laurence agreed. "But a lot of people can have spells stored up and ready to unleash with a movement or a phrase, or have them already active or imbued into talismans..."

"So we can't count on a speed advantage, is what you're saying," Sebastian mused. "But if they've got magic that protects them from gifts, or bullets, or getting punched in the face, what then?"

Laurence huffed in irritation and his fingers tightened on the wheel. "I don't know, man. I only started to learn magic last year, and this guy's got like twenty years on both my teachers. His whole sanctum is a web of wards and defenses, I don't think he goes outside unless he absolutely has to, and even then he possesses some innocent victim to do it with so that his body stays safe."

Sebastian grunted at that. "Have you considered playing dirty?"

"I mean, I figure dirty's all we've got left," Laurence reasoned. "What're you thinking?"

"We could SWAT him."

Laurence wanted to come up with a response to that, but he had nothing, and he almost ran a red light trying to figure out how he even felt about the suggestion.

"That *is* dirty," Angela said, sounding like she was considering it.

"But..." Laurence struggled to put his nebulous doubts into some kind of order. "If cops can't hurt him, but they go in there and see everything I saw, it'll end with the cops getting killed instead, surely?" He shot a quizzical look to Angela. "He's not going to let them leave if they've seen all of that?"

Angela pursed her lips and furrowed her brows in thought. "If he can make them think they didn't find anything, they might leave again and assume they were responding to a prank call."

"Can he do that?" Sebastian asked.

"I... don't know," she said. "He tends to kill anyone that isn't useful to him anymore. I've never seen him alter memories. I don't doubt he could bind Lethe the way that I did, but she can only erase; she can't create new memories."

Laurence heard the faint huff Sebastian made as the air from it hit the microphone of his cell, and he briefly bit the tip of his tongue. It was as frustrated as he'd ever heard Sebastian, and he felt the same way.

"I gotta say, I think if we try to SWAT him it'll blow up in our faces somehow," Laurence groused. "Either the doorway we know ends up crawling with cops so we lose him, or he uses them against us somehow, or he murders them all..."

"We're at a significant tactical disadvantage," Sebastian stated. "Our primary tools in such a situation are attrition and exhaustion, though it sounds like he's winning the exhaustion battle. Have you had any sleep?"

"No, but I've had a *lot* of coffee."

"Not the same thing, but I'll allow it. The problem as I see it is twofold. First, a web of unknown spells, and second, an entire coven of unknown spellcasters. My suggestion would be to catch them off guard, overwhelm their senses, and take out as many as you can as fast as you can. That means going in hot — with superior numbers if possible, preferably a few stun grenades to get the party started — and tasking some of your team with destroying any and all sigils they find, while the remainder takes out any spellcaster they encounter. The faster the sweep, the more resources you rob him of, and the more off-balance he will be. Then when both teams converge on him, the numbers balance will be in your favor, and you can get the job done."

Laurence nodded slowly as he listened. Everything Sebastian said was the opposite of how Laurence would normally act, but there was no way he'd be able to sneak in alone and slip a knife between Vincent's ribs. It wasn't going to happen, and holding out hope for familiar tactics wouldn't help him at all. "Okay," he breathed. "You want in?"

"Obviously," Sebastian said, without a second's hesitation. "Mia will, too. Soraya, possibly?"

Laurence winced. Soraya had been killed only a few days ago, and he was uncomfortable at the idea of it happening again. "I don't know…"

"I'll ask her. It should be her choice. I'll ask this Alex kid, too; they could be useful, but they seem pretty skittish, too. And you know I hate to say it, but you'd stand a much greater chance of success if we had Quentin with us."

"There's too much magic," Laurence breathed. "It'll set him off. It's not worth the risk."

"I am inclined to agree," Angela said.

"Fine. I'll see who else volunteers, and we'll come to you. Where are you?"

"Ru's sanctum. Mia knows where it—" Laurence cut himself off the second that red and blue lights flashed in his rearview mirror, and he checked it to see what it was. He was hoping for an ambulance, on its way somewhere else, passing him in the night.

What he saw was a police cruiser.

"Laurence?"

"You've got to be fucking kidding me," Laurence spat. "I'm getting pulled over by cops."

"Okay. Take it easy. Maybe your taillights are out. I'll stay on the line."

Laurence checked the rearview again, but the cruiser was absolutely tailing him, so he sighed and slowed down to search for somewhere safe to pull over. The closest opportunity he had was a church up ahead, so he hit his turn signal to show he was going for it, and turned in to the parking lot once he got there. He parked the truck in the center of an empty row, switched on the interior light, opened his window halfway, then killed the engine and put his hands on the top of the steering wheel.

The cruiser pulled up behind him, and Laurence regretted having the coffee as his heart picked up the pace.

Don't panic. It's just a bored cop wasting time.

A cop got out of the cruiser and made his way toward them. Laurence watched his approach in his wing mirror until he was by Laurence's shoulder.

"License, please."

Laurence moved one hand slowly to the pocket of his pants and wriggled his wallet out, then he brought it up to the wheel and dug into it for his license. He passed it out through the gap in the window, all without saying a damn thing.

The cop took the license, eyed it, then looked at Laurence. "Bambi Riley?"

"Yes," Laurence said.

"Were you in Encinitas at all yesterday?"

Laurence's heart skipped a beat. Had someone seen him leave Amy's house? "Am I being detained?"

"Yes, sir. Please step out of the vehicle."

He opened his mouth to protest, then remembered everything he'd ever learned about interacting with cops, and shut it again. He had to stay calm, because yelling that he had a warlock to stop wasn't going to help any, and might just get him shot instead. He unfastened his seatbelt and eased slowly out of the car.

The cop handed him his license back and waited for Laurence to put his wallet away. "Mr. Riley, you're under arrest for the rape and murder of Diane Lloyd. Turn and face your vehicle, please, and put your hands against it."

Laurence stared at him in growing horror. "*What?*" he blurted.

"Turn around, Mr. Riley," the cop said again, except now his hand moved to rest casually over his holster.

Laurence turned slowly and put his hands up against the side of his truck, and his thoughts descended into chaos while the cop patted him down then handcuffed him.

Was Diane Lloyd the woman Vincent had poisoned and then dumped on them all at Amy's house? If so, what the hell made the cops think Laurence might have assaulted her?

"I want to remain silent," he stated, the well-rehearsed words coming out of him almost by themselves. "And I want to speak to a lawyer."

But all he could think of was the fact that he'd told Lloyd she'd be okay, left her alone and afraid, and now she was dead.

36

QUENTIN

"I am so sorry for disturbing you at this hour," Quentin blurted the moment Basil answered the phone. "I have rather an urgent matter, and need to speak with you both. Would you be so kind as to text me your address?"

"Uhhh," Basil said, then yawned loudly. "Quentin? What time is it?"

"A little past four o'clock," Quentin murmured apologetically. "I must press you for that address, if you don't mind?"

He heard a cat chirp in the background, and Basil mumbled something to it, then said, "Are you here? Uh, in New York, I mean?"

"I am, yes." Quentin did his level best not to sound terse, and he stepped away from the tree at last to search for the nearest lit pathway through the park. He was, by his estimation, somewhere in the Ramble, reasonably close to the Lake, which meant Father had effectively set him down in a maze. If Quentin headed downhill, though, he should find the water's edge, then he could follow it to a path out of the park.

"Okay, but, uh..." Basil sucked in a breath. "My place isn't super fancy or anything. If you want to meet somewhere else..."

"It's a sensitive matter," Quentin said. "I'm sorry. I wouldn't ask unless it was important."

"Yeah. Yeah, okay. I'm in East Harlem. 125th Street is the nearest subway station. I'll send you the address. How long do you think you'll be?"

Quentin squinted while he tried to figure out if he'd ever been that far north, then plucked a number out of his arse. "Half an hour, perhaps? At the most?"

"No problem. We'll throw some clothes on. See you soon."

Basil hung up, and then Quentin's phone started to bombard him with even more notifications. At first he thought Basil might have accidentally sent his address twenty times, until he realized that it was Michael instead, forwarding all the spells Freddy had deemed worthwhile. Quentin grimaced and dismissed each one with his thumb until the address arrived, and then he tapped on it to open a map and work out the quickest way for him to get there.

Only once he looked up again did he notice that reading the screen had wrecked what little night vision he'd begun to develop, so he sighed and turned on the phone's torch to light his way, then carefully picked his way through the trees in search of a way out.

Quentin made it onto one of the narrow, winding paths through the Ramble, and continued weaving his way down the hill. There was the occasional streetlamp, but never anywhere terribly useful, and too few and far between in the woods for him to put his phone away. He was half convinced now and then that he was being watched, but he didn't care, and the sooner he got out of here the better.

So when he turned a bend and walked into the path of a young Black man approaching from the opposite direction, he almost leapt out of his skin.

"Damn, bro!" The stranger whipped his hands up to shield his eyes. "The hell you playing at? Put that away!"

Quentin thumbed the torch off and slid the phone into his

pocket. "I am so sorry. Do excuse me, I didn't mean to cause alarm."

Now, without the torch, the stranger was little more than a dark blot on a dark path surrounded by dark trees, and Quentin flexed his jaw as he resigned himself to waiting for his eyesight to adjust after all.

"British, huh? You lookin' for something in particular?"

"Just a way out," Quentin murmured.

The stranger's laugh was warm and gentle. "Yeah, you an' me both. Maybe we can help each other out?"

"That's most kind of you." Quentin blinked a few times as the afterimage of the torch started to recede. "Am I headed in the wrong direction?"

"Are you..." The stranger hesitated, then cleared his throat. "Hold up, are we on the same page here?"

"I need to get to East Harlem," Quentin explained.

The man laughed again. "Oh. *Oh.* Okay, well, uh..." He cleared his throat. "Man, you are *lost*. Don't you know it's against the law to be in this park before 6AM?"

Quentin quirked an eyebrow. "You appear to be here too," he murmured.

"Yeah, well, don't ask me nothing, and I won't ask you nothing. Deal?"

"That seems very fair." Quentin smiled faintly and offered his hand. "Deal."

After an awkward dance before the stranger managed to hold out the correct hand, Quentin found that the man's hand was warm around his own, and the handshake lasted all of a second before the touch was gone again. "A'ight, let's get you outta here without either of us catching a ticket."

Then, oddly, he turned to head the same direction Quentin was facing, which suggested that Quentin hadn't been heading the wrong way at all.

True to his word, the stranger didn't ask a single question, and once he'd led Quentin to Fifth Avenue, all he did was offer Quentin his phone number for "the next time you're in town and lookin' for a way out," so Quentin politely added it to his phone's notes in case it would be rude not to, and they parted ways.

His phone said that it was over three miles to Basil's address. Ordinarily he would hail a taxi, but there were none to be found which weren't already occupied, and he didn't know whether he could use his phone to pay for them either, so he decided to do it on foot. He memorized the majority of the route to set off at a jog, but it jolted his shoulder too much and made him feel sick. In the end he confronted his reticence about using the subway and made his way east instead.

He was almost at the entrance to the 77th Street station when his phone rang. He reached for it, preparing himself to apologize to Basil for the delay, only for the screen to announce that the call was from Sebastian Wagner.

Quentin frowned as he answered the call. "Sebastian?"

"Yep. I know you're in the UK right now, but I thought you'd want to know: Laurence just got arrested."

Quentin stopped immediately and took a sharp breath. His tiredness and pain seemed as though they'd been switched off in an instant. "What? When?"

"Barely five minutes ago. I was on a call with him when it happened."

Quentin felt utterly blindsided. If he'd been there, with Laurence, he could have...

What? What could you have done?

His jaw worked uselessly for a moment, then he shook his head and blinked. "Why?"

"I'm looking into it, but it sounds like there was an alert out for his license plate after a 911 call yesterday. He's going to need a lawyer, fast. Have you got one on retainer?"

"No, I..." Quentin sucked in air. "Have Martin contact Freddy. This is absurd! Is it Harrow's work, do you suppose?"

"Don't doubt it," Sebastian grunted. "Look, even if we find a lawyer who's awake this time of night, there isn't going to be an arraignment until morning, assuming there's a judge available to hear it. But it sounded like Laurence is in a time crunch for taking down Harrow, and eight hours in jail is going to eat it up. We were hashing out an idea when the cops caught up to him, so I've got to ask: if we can pull together the numbers to rush Harrow's sanctum, do you want in?"

Everything swam. His shoulder throbbed, and his gut lurched as the world turned circles around his head. Quentin took a few steps so that he could put his back to a wall for stability. "I'm doing what I can to try and find additional help," he breathed. "I'll know more in a short while." It didn't quite answer Sebastian's question, and Quentin wasn't convinced that he could do so right now anyway, so he added, "Is he all right? Laurence? Does Soraya see him?"

"I haven't woken her yet, and I won't until it's absolutely necessary. Call me when you've got this help you're going for."

"I shall. Thank you."

Quentin numbly ended the call, and was sorely tempted to ring Laurence, but he supposed that the police would have taken his phone away if they'd arrested him. Instead he fired off a text to Freddy, and called Myriam.

She answered quickly. "Quentin? Blessed be, dear! That was quick!"

"Laurence has been arrested," he blurted. "Sebastian is looking into the details, but I thought you'd want to know as soon as possible."

There was silence on the end of the line for a moment, before he heard Myriam take a deep breath. "On what charges?"

"I don't know." Quentin did his best not to chide himself for not even thinking to ask. "I've asked Freddy to help, and Martin will be calling him shortly, but…" He floundered for words and screwed his eyes shut. "If Harrow's behind it, that means he wants Laurence out of his way for a while, which suggests we have little time to waste."

"Go," Myriam said, her voice firm. "I'll speak to Freddy. Bright blessings, Quentin."

"Thank you." He dithered for an awkward moment over how

to respond to her blessings, then ended the call and put that worry aside for later.

All he could do now was head down into the subway, hope it was easy to work out which train he needed, and that he could pay with his phone.

LAURENCE

Laurence squirmed in the back of the cruiser, trying to get comfortable on the hard, molded plastic seat, but those things weren't designed for comfort: they were made to stop people hiding evidence down the back of a cushion.

He gritted his teeth and watched the officer go back to the Jack in the Green truck to speak to Angela, holding out hope that she had some way of fixing all this and making it go away, but a couple of minutes later the cop left her alone and strolled back to the cruiser, then got behind the wheel and looked over his shoulder to Laurence.

"You wanna tell me who your lady friend is?"

Laurence wanted to tell him to get fucked, but he'd already exercised his right to remain silent, and he wasn't going to revoke it before the cop had even read him his rights. That was dumbass behavior, and Laurence had spent too many years doing drugs to fall for basic tricks like that one.

The officer eventually shrugged, cited Miranda at him in a bored tone, then pulled the cruiser out of the parking lot. Laurence twisted to check on Angela as best as he could, and was relieved at least to see that she'd moved to be behind the wheel of the truck and turned off the interior light. With any luck she'd head straight to Ru and together they could figure something out.

Or he'll take the opportunity to kill her.

Laurence clenched his jaw and closed his eyes so he could focus on reaching out to Windsor. *Hey, Win. I'm in trouble. Are you awake?*

It was a couple of seconds before Windsor responded, and the sleepiness in him was so obvious that it would've been adorable if Laurence wasn't in so much shit. *Awake now. Trouble?*

Yeah. I got arrested by a cop, I'm being taken... uh... probably to a police station, I guess. He huffed. *Tell Sebastian I'm OK. Tell him they arrested me for murder.* Laurence clenched his jaw, unsure whether Windsor would be able to convey all this information, then his eyes snapped open, and he added, *Use Clifton and Lisa if he doesn't understand you, okay?*

Okay! What is arrested?

It means I've been taken by a cop and can't leave. Laurence trapped his lower lip between his teeth. Windsor had seen cops before and knew Laurence was cautious about them, but explaining everything he knew about the legal system to a bird he wasn't in the same room with seemed like it'd just lead to more frustration, so he didn't try to. *Sebastian can tell you more about what it means and how it works. But first tell him what I was arrested for. Tell him I need a lawyer. And...* He sighed to himself. *Tell him if we don't stop Vincent fast, Vincent's going to become immortal, and then we're all fucked.*

That was way too much for his familiar to be able to say to anyone who couldn't understand him. Windsor's mimicry was good, but he was still young, and he'd only mastered saying a few dozen words out loud, half of which were swears. The raven would have to rely on Clifton, and maybe Lisa too, and all Laurence could do was leave it to them to work together.

I will, Windsor declared, full of confidence.

Thanks, Win. Love you.

Love, Windsor agreed.

Laurence drew back into himself and opened his eyes, but the only thing left for him to do was watch the streets go by.

THE CARLSBAD POLICE DEPARTMENT had a pretty sizable building, with a sandy stone front, and tidy lawns. Laurence didn't get to stare at it from the outside for too long, though. Once the cruiser passed through gates and into a far less public-facing yard he was faced with the suddenly more real fact that he'd been arrested for murder and was about to spend the rest of his night in a cell.

And, depending on how busy a night this place was having, he might not be alone.

He swallowed tightly and struggled to think of a way out of this, but his door got opened, and he was helped out of the back into cool, fresh air before he'd moved on from the stupid fantasy of summoning his knife and stabbing his way to freedom.

He was led inside, processed at a desk, and patted down again, except this time they took everything away except his clothes. His wallet, his cellphone, every talisman in his pocket, every thong around his neck or wrists, it all got removed piece by piece and laid out into a tray until they were far enough away from him that he couldn't even see the individual threads of his magic around them anymore. Every item was noted down and added to a clear plastic bag, and by the time Laurence was being electronically fingerprinted, his stuff was way out of his range.

Eventually, they took his clothes, too, though they gave him the privacy of a small room so he could get changed into drab grey replacements. But in the end it all led to a small cell through a heavy security door, and Laurence was left in it like he'd been put into storage.

At least he wasn't sharing it, though. That was a relief. There were other cells, and he could hear breathing and snoring from some of them, but his was blessedly free from other detainees.

He had a bed that looked like it'd be hard. The mattress was thin and wipe-clean, and there was a single pillow at one end. Three of his walls were concrete; the fourth was bars, with a sliding door he'd entered through. The wall facing the bars had a metal toilet and a small sink, right next to the edge of the bed.

Nice.

It wasn't the worst, he supposed. If he wasn't screwed for time he'd probably put his head down and get a few hours' sleep until lawyers and courtrooms woke up and the procedure for getting him the fuck out of here could swing into action, but instead all he did was pace in the tiny floorspace not taken up by bed or toilet, and run his hands through his hair while he tried to work out what the hell he could do about any of this. So when he felt the universe begin to hold its breath, he had a second's confusion before he realized he wasn't the one doing it.

Without his talismans, he couldn't see much more than a dull, brief, ruddy flicker of magic that was gone as soon as it had arrived, and as a cellphone fell onto the mattress with a dull *pat*, time jerked back into motion like nothing had happened.

Laurence tilted his head and approached the phone cautiously. He didn't doubt that if he got caught with it in here he'd be totally fucked, but what could he do other than grab it before it made any noise?

Ru hadn't sent it. What little Laurence saw of the magic sure hadn't been turquoise. Angela, then? Her magic was red.

Laurence eyed the phone, and squinted when the screen lit up. It wasn't anything fancy or expensive, and he had to fumble with it a bit to figure out how to turn the brightness way down and the volume off before he could even try to use it. It seemed brand new out of the box: no customization, nothing in the contacts list, no files on it. He was about to try and call the first number he knew off the top of his head — his mom's — when it lit up again with an incoming call.

He squeezed himself as far back in his cell as he could, thumbed the button to answer the call, and hissed into the phone, "Who is this?"

"I heard you were arrested," Vincent purred. "And — this is the interesting part — you actually allowed it to happen. I *must* hear your rationale."

Laurence's scalp prickled, and a shiver ran through his chest. He sat on the edge of the bed slowly and fought to keep his voice low. "You got the book. What more do you want?"

"A witch of your resourcefulness, and you're in a jail cell?" Vincent sounded amused. "Very disappointing."

"Did you frame me for murder?" Laurence ground his teeth. "Why?"

"You framed yourself, I think. Using your own cell to call 911. Driving your mother's truck everywhere you go. Leaving your business card in the victim's pocket. What did you think would happen?" Vincent chuckled. "I find myself fascinated by the way that you behave, the actions you choose to take. It's all rather irrational."

"Yeah, well, there's also some evidence I *didn't* leave," Laurence growled. His grip on the phone grew tight. "What did you do to her, Vincent? Did you fucking rape her?"

He could hear the shrug in Vincent's voice, like Laurence's anger was irrelevant. "Insemination is a necessary component of the possession ritual."

Laurence stared at the far wall in horror, and found himself at a total loss for words.

"Regardless, I put a lot of time and effort into accelerating your magical education, and it's time to recoup that investment. You're going to extricate yourself from this nuisance situation and go back to Grant's sanctum, where you will dismantle each and every one of the wards that defend it."

Still reeling from the knowledge of what Vincent must have done to every single one of the women he'd possessed and then murdered, Laurence almost missed the enormity of what the warlock had ordered him to do. When his brain caught up, he sucked in air and came close to unleashing a stream of vitriol every bit as scathing as Vincent deserved, and the only thing that stopped him was the sound of a grunt from another cell.

"That's not gonna fucking happen," he snarled, barely above a whisper.

"It is. You aren't the only person out in the world without wards right now."

Laurence curled his lip. Was Vincent threatening to start murdering random strangers until he got what he wanted?

"Seems like your lover has also decided to spend the night unprotected," Vincent said. "Time for a new deal. You dismantle

Grant's wards within the next two hours, and I'll spare your lover's life."

Heat tore through Laurence's chest and into his gut, where it churned and boiled like it would utterly consume him. He had no idea where Quen was right now, why he wasn't warded, or whether Vincent was lying about it altogether. The threat was enough to stoke his rage, and he leapt to his feet. "Don't touch him!"

"Two hours," Vincent repeated, "or you'll be the one who never touches him again."

"I'll kill you!" Laurence screamed into the phone, like he could rip Vincent's insides out with the power of his voice alone. "If you lay a finger on him, I'll fucking kill you!"

Vincent laughed. "That seems unlikely. I *do* have the Book of Yew."

"Vincent—" Laurence roared, but the phone beeped in his ear to tell him that the call had ended, and he almost threw it at the wall as the rage threatened to consume him.

Keep it, some tiny part of himself managed to whisper. *Use it.*

His thoughts were getting drowned out by the yelling of other prisoners, angry at getting woken up in the night, and seconds later the security door that led out here buzzed and clicked. A cop would come in and check on what was causing the ruckus, and Laurence had a split second to figure out what to do about it.

He stuffed the cellphone under his pillow, sat his ass down, and struggled to rein in his fury before the cops could decide he was a problem.

38

QUENTIN

Thankfully the station he had entered showed clear signage to inform passengers of which platform was for the northbound trains, so all Quentin had to do was make his way down to it and wait for the next train, though it took so long to turn up that he'd almost circled back to the idea of walking all the way to Basil's home.

He managed to talk himself out of it moments before a rush of air emerged from the tunnel, and once the train arrived he found himself a seat which gave off all the appropriate signals to indicate that it was clean. There were very few other people on board, and it only took around ten minutes to reach 125th street. From there, it was a ten minute walk at a brisk pace to reach his destination.

That was about as near to half an hour as he could get it, and while he felt horrible about his lateness, all he could do about it was apologize on arrival. He hurried along relatively deserted streets with slightly uneven paving and lined with brick buildings until he found the one he was looking for.

All in all, the area felt distinctly unlike any part of New York he had ever been to, but he had no time to explore it. He hurried up the steps to a door, found the correct intercom button, and pressed it.

It buzzed within seconds, and he blurted out, "I am so sorry I'm late!"

"Hey, it's okay. Top floor," Basil said.

The door gave off an angry buzzing noise, and Quentin heaved on it until it let him through, then took the staircase two steps at a time, as though racing through this final leg of his journey would make up for the time spent waiting for a train.

When he reached the top floor, though, Basil was already waiting at an open door, with a grey tabby cat in his arms. He blinked at Quentin, looked him up and down, and said, "Holy shit, what happened to you?"

"It's a very long story?" Quentin offered.

"You better come in." Basil stepped back and used a foot to keep his front door propped open, then he closed it the moment Quentin was through. "Take a seat. If you can find one. Then you can fill us in."

Quentin was not ungrateful, but he desperately hoped he didn't have to recount a year's worth of events just to get to the point.

Basil's apartment was smaller even than the one Laurence used to live in above Myriam's shop, though it was possible it only seemed that way due to the library's-worth of books stuffed into it. At some point Basil had given up on using the shelves which lined the living area because they were out of space, and so books were piled onto most other surfaces, too: the coffee table; side tables; windowsills; the floor.

Quentin found an available spot on the couch and sank slowly into it, and within moments Jon had pressed a hot mug of tea into his hand, which Quentin sipped from gratefully. It was dreadful tea, the sort that tasted like it was made from the tea dust swept up off the factory floor at the end of the day, but it was wet, and he didn't wish to be rude.

"Your energy is off," Jon stated, without any kind of greeting or other preamble. "Are you injured?" His near-black eyes flicked meaningfully to the empty sleeve of Quentin's sweater as he asked it.

"My shoulder was broken. It's been put back together with surgery, but that was earlier in the week, and I'm..." Quentin drew a deep breath to try and clear away the brain fog. "I may heal swiftly, but not *that* swiftly," he concluded. "But that's not why I'm here."

Basil set his cat down gently on the floor, where she darted off to play with another. "Okay," he said slowly. "That begs the obvious question." He picked up a chair from the kitchen table and brought it over so that he could sit on it and face Quentin.

Jon sat by Quentin's side on the couch, though — thankfully — he left a good amount of distance between them. "Why *are* you here?"

Quentin shifted slightly in his seat so that he could better see them both, though he crossed his legs as he moved, as if he could add just an extra couple of centimeters of space between him and Jon by doing so. "There is a warlock whose sanctum is incredibly well-protected," he began. "I wondered whether your power to negate some forms of energy made it at all possible for you to destroy wards, too." He looked at Jon. "And," he added, "if that doesn't work, I wondered whether you might be able to do it with magic, instead." He turned his gaze on Basil. "Though I think the idea is to rely on magic as little as possible."

Basil nodded slowly. "And this warlock is in New York? Why didn't you tell us you were in town?"

"Ah, no. He's in, uh..." Quentin hesitated. "California, I think? I'm not certain, truth be told. I would ask Laurence, but he's been arrested..."

"What?" Basil leapt to his feet so quickly he almost kicked his own chair over, but thankfully a stack of books caught it in time. He flapped his hands through the air so fast that it turned his pink nail polish into a bright blur. "That's... Nope. From the top. Tell us everything!"

Quentin sighed, and forced down more of the tea to fortify himself.

Then he did what he could to get through the salient points as efficiently as possible.

Ultimately, he ended up recounting almost a year's worth of events.

By the time Quentin was done, he had long finished his tea, and begun to feel the pain and exhaustion creep up on him once more.

"Therefore," he managed to murmur, "if you are able to assist I would be most grateful, but I understand if you cannot." He fumbled for his phone. "I can forward these spells to you, if you wish?"

"Can't hurt to take a look," Basil said with a shrug. "Doesn't sound like many of them are in my wheelhouse, though."

Quentin frowned as he focused on sending them to the right number, one by one, and only once he had finished that task did he notice that Jon had leaned in to scrutinize him.

"Take the sweater off," Jon said.

"I, um... I... I'm hardly decent under it," Quentin stammered. The thought of undressing to nothing but a thermal undershirt was enough to make him far more alert.

Jon blinked every bit as languidly as a sloth. "That does not matter."

"I think it matters to Quentin, hon," Basil said. He cast a small smile to Quentin, then turned back to Jon. "Why do you want the sweater gone?"

"Arawn stipulated that healing falls under his dominion." Jon pointed to Quentin's shoulder with one bony finger. "Before we encountered him, I had already used my own life energy to restore yours," he said to Basil. "Now that he has significantly improved my gifts, it is worth evaluating whether or not I too am able to repair a living body, but I would prefer to be able to see what I am doing."

"Oh!" Basil gasped, and covered his mouth with one hand as his hazel eyes grew wide, then both hands flapped again, and he smiled so brightly at Quentin that it was almost contagious. "That's got to be worth a try, don't you think? I can leave the room? Give you some privacy? I mean, only if you're willing for Jon to go ahead, obviously!"

It was difficult to really piece together all the separate components of this idea and what it would entail. Some of his scars would be readily visible below the sleeves of the undershirt, but Quentin was largely at peace with them these days, so he supposed that it was his tiredness which made him worry. There was the effort involved in removing his sweater, but he was psychokinetic; it really was no hardship. Perhaps what he fretted about was the indecency of allowing himself to be seen in a state of partial undress, but these were friends, and they were trying to help.

He took a breath, and as he exhaled, he eased the sweater off before his brain could throw up more pointless objections to the idea. The garment slid off the arm he raised overhead, and he settled the arm down into his lap while the sweater seemed to fold itself in mid-air then land neatly on top of a stack of books.

"There," he murmured, though he was not able to meet anyone's gaze. "We won't ever find out if we don't try it."

"That is correct," Jon agreed. "Are you ready for me to proceed?"

Quentin considered saying no and writing this whole experiment off as ridiculous, but Laurence was in jail, and Sebastian seemed intent on attacking Harrow no matter how poor his odds. Myriam would not be safe until Harrow was dealt with, and it very much sounded like a house of cards which Quentin could not stabilize in his present state.

He raised his chin and forced himself to face Jon.

"I'm ready," he said.

39

LAURENCE

"Knock knock," Freddy said.

Laurence jerked upright and looked toward the door of his cell in the low light, but there was nobody there.

"I realize the irony that I must already be inside your mind to be able to ask permission to enter," Freddy continued, "but needs must. May I?"

Uh. Yeah? Sure. Laurence's thoughts were a mess, but he was able to at least answer Freddy's question while he was playing catch-up with hearing voices.

Freddy manifested inside the cell, standing with his back to the bars, and he nodded faintly. "We're inside your mind," he said. "You can speak; it won't wake anyone."

Laurence shuddered. Having Freddy do this to him was high on his list of least favorite things, but at least the telepath had thought to ask permission for once. Maybe he was improving.

Freddy snorted, though it only seemed half-hearted. "All right," he murmured. "What a pickle. If I can get in, Harrow can too. And already has." He strode to the bed and sat by Laurence's side. "Priority must be to return your talismans, then," he concluded.

"And get me the fuck out of here," Laurence breathed, not entirely comfortable with raising his voice, even though it should be safe. "You're all caught up, you know Vincent gave me two hours or he's going to kill Quen—"

Freddy dipped his head faintly. "You're right. I apologize, I have a migraine brewing. This is a stretch. Once I'm done here I doubt I will be of much use for a few hours." He grimaced slightly. "Priority is to return your talismans *and* get one to Icky."

"The kids have got his. Quen gave them his wallet so they could go shopping, and that's where he keeps it." Laurence sighed and scratched at his stubble. "Ru has a spell that could send it to him, but Quen would have to be somewhere Ru has an emotional connection to, and the nearest to Quen he can get is Paris."

"Perhaps not," Freddy said. "Icky is now in New York."

Laurence blinked at him, then joined the dots himself. That was why Quen wasn't warded: he wasn't at the castle anymore. And if he'd gone to New York, it had to be because he thought either Basil or Jon might be able to help somehow, though why he couldn't just call them from the UK, Laurence couldn't figure out.

"I suspect because he wishes for Basil to use a spell to transfer all three of them onward to San Diego," Freddy mused, "after which they will all be within the wards of your house. Knowing Icky, he isn't taking well to sitting around waiting for everyone else to fix the problem, particularly with you at risk."

"Basil's a necromancer. Does he want to cut through Annwn or something?" Laurence narrowed his eyes. "Your dad's teleportation spell," he concluded.

"Correct. I located that spell, among others, and passed it on to Icky." Freddy waved a hand. "This is all largely irrelevant to the present problem, however." He stood and idly paced back towards the bars to scrutinize them. "If I make the desk sergeant release you, questions will be raised. If I give you Father's co-location spell, different questions will be raised." He squinted past the bars and added, "Though the security camera only covers the corridor outside the cells, to afford detainees the privacy to use the bathroom. If you take yourself off and then return before the shift change you might get away with it."

"And if I don't make it back, that's going to cause bigger problems once they put a warrant out for my arrest and start grilling me about my escapology." Laurence grimaced. "Getting the sergeant to let me out is safer."

"For you," Freddy agreed. "How you then get away from here is another problem." He sucked his teeth, then turned his back on the bars and stuffed hands into the pockets of his cream-colored pants. "All right. I have an idea. Play possum, will you?"

Laurence raised his eyebrows. "Like, on the floor?"

"Mm. Best if you can fall over dead with an arm through the bars, too. That will help immensely. Oh, and tuck that phone somewhere the sun doesn't shine. I'm sure those buns of yours can grip it well enough." He flashed a smile, though it wasn't half as sharp as usual, and disappeared.

Laurence grunted. He was *not* going to shove a cellphone between his ass cheeks.

He took it out from under the pillow, stuffed it down his pants instead, then arranged himself on the floor like a corpse and let his forearm fall out between cell bars.

Man, you better know what you're doing.

THERE WAS a flurry of activity around him. First a cop came in to feel for a pulse, then he entered the cell and checked Laurence over. After that, paramedics came instead, and hauled him onto a stretcher. He kept his eyes closed while they wheeled him out of the station; only the changes in airflow, temperature, and sounds told him where he was.

Then doors slammed shut, and the ambulance he was in started to move.

Smart, he thought. *But what about once I get to the hospital?*

"You're going to have a miraculous recovery while waiting for triage," Freddy murmured, "and you're going to slip out while nobody's looking. Everything they confiscated from you is in a locker at the back of the ambulance. Once you are at the hospital they'll move the bag with you, and it might end up close enough to start working, so we shall have to assume this will be the last time I can speak to you. It may well be anyway; I'm not sure how much longer I can do this, and I'll have to move several pieces once you arrive to ensure they leave you alone long enough for you to sneak off. I can't buy you more than a few minutes, alas."

They'll still put out a warrant once they realize I've escaped.

"Correct, but it doesn't come with a side-order of video evidence to show that anything untoward was involved, and by the time they find you again we'll have a local lawyer lined up for you. It's only five miles to the nearest emergency room, so this shouldn't take long. I'll have to hop to your EMT so as not to lose you."

Thanks. What then?

"I will arrange something. Also, if I may be so bold…"

You usually are, Laurence thought dryly.

"Ha. If Harrow wants Mr. Grant's wards destroyed, I'd put money on it being so that he can go there, or at the very least send one of his flunkies. It may present you with an opportunity."

I'd say you read my mind, but that's a given.

"Very true. All right, hang tight."

Laurence figured that hanging tight was the same as continuing to play dead, so he stuck with it.

IT ALL WENT ACCORDING to Freddy's plan, which didn't surprise Laurence at all. He was taken into what sounded like a busy ER, transferred to a bed, then left to wait for a doctor, and the second he heard the clatter of curtain rings he snuck an eye open to check that nobody could see him.

He was alone.

Laurence sat up and saw the bag at the end of his bed, nestled safely between his feet, so he reached for it and dug out all his talismans first. Once they were on, he hopped out of bed, shucked the jail clothes, and shimmied into his own. Then, for good measure, he tossed the bland grey shirt and pants into the trash, but he rolled up the bag and crammed it into a pocket of his pants. He couldn't see any magic on the cellphone Vincent had sent him, and he debated tossing that, too, but decided to keep it, in case he had to call Vincent at some point.

Satisfied that he'd done everything possible as fast as he could, he eased aside the edge of the curtain just enough to peek outside.

It *was* busy out there. Clinicians, patients, friends or family of patients, all clogging up the route between Laurence and the exit. But he'd arrived in a prison uniform and he'd be leaving in casual civilian clothing: that should be plenty enough cover for his stealth gift to work with.

He slipped out past the curtain, made sure it was neatly closed in his wake, then drifted casually down the white corridor like he was leaving. Despite the yammering of his pulse, nobody seemed to hear it, and nobody paid any attention to him.

A minute later and he was out in the fresh air just in time to see a grey cab pull up into the patient drop-off bay. While he was still wondering whether this was Freddy's doing or completely unrelated, the cab driver waved to him, so Laurence hurried on over and slunk into the back of the cab.

The driver didn't even ask where to. Of course he didn't. He pulled out of the drop-off bay and continued on past the parking lot to the exit, so Laurence hunkered down and checked his own cellphone over, then began firing off text messages.

He was so close to his own freedom that he could taste it, but he wasn't out of the woods yet. He'd have to stay out of sight, convince Rufus to take down his wards, and hope it really would be enough to lure Vincent out of his own sanctum at last.

Then, finally, they'd have him, and all this would be over.

40

LAURENCE

The cabbie dropped him one block over from Rufus' place, and drove off without asking for a dime, so Laurence sprinted through an eerie neighborhood that was mostly plastic skeletons and carved pumpkins looming in the darkness.

He paused at Ru's gate to check his phone, but there weren't any new messages. Sebastian was already on his way, Mom had confirmed that she was still safe at the castle while Quen had gone to New York, Mikey told him Freddy was out of juice and resting, and according to the clock he still had an hour of his deadline left before Vincent would try to kill Quentin.

Laurence tapped out a new text, this time for Quen.

Hey baby. Vincent's spotted you in NY without any wards. If Basil has any, put them up ASAP. If not, I'm going to send you a couple of spells for him to use. I'll be unavailable after I send them. Please stay safe!

He scrolled through his photos, all the way back to the last year, when he'd snapped shots of the spells Rufus showed him so that he could ward the mansion, and he forwarded them to Quentin.

There wasn't any immediate reply. Laurence tapped the edge of his phone against his chin and debated whether to just call, but every moment he spent standing out on the street not only wasted time he'd need for yelling at Rufus, it also increased the risk someone would call the cops on him for loitering outside an empty lot.

He sighed, then sent an extra *I love you* to Quen before he nudged the gate and slipped through the opening the second it was wide enough for him.

The only relief he felt as he shouldered the gate closed was that his truck was in front of him in the middle of Ru's driveway, which meant that Angela had come here.

With any luck, she was still alive.

Rufus hauled the front door open while Laurence's hand was still an inch away from it, and he stared like he was meeting a ghost. "So many questions," he muttered.

Laurence gestured past Ru with his eyebrows raised, and once Ru stepped aside for him, he hurried inside. "Looks like the woman Vincent poisoned and threw at us at Amy's house didn't make it," he explained. "Cops put out an alert for my license plate, we got unlucky. I was arrested, processed, then Freddy busted me out in a way that doesn't leave any evidence of magic or gifts or a paper trail, but it does mean they'll probably issue a warrant for my arrest once they realize they've lost me, and that means we can't use the truck to go places, either. But Sebastian is coming, so we'll at least have the SUV. Quentin's in New York, so I'm hoping we'll have Basil, too. And I figure where Basil goes, Jon goes. So..." He sucked in a deep breath, then tried to sound nonchalant. "How's your night going?"

Rufus closed the door while he stared at Laurence. "Unbelievable," he muttered. "Angela came, said you'd gotten arrested, we had something to eat then hit the library. We both figured if we carried on with the plan you'd get out of jail sooner or later, though we didn't figure it'd be *this* fast."

"Great." Laurence made his way to the stairs. "Vincent's threatened to kill Quen an hour from now, but I've sent Quen the ward spells so Basil can use them to protect his apartment. I figure that means we've got an hour before Vincent finds out his threat has been nullified and loses his shit about it."

He heard Rufus follow him up the stairs, his footsteps light despite his mood. "What does he want?"

Laurence chewed lightly on his lip and didn't look back at Ru. The other witch was way too smart. Of *course* Vincent wanted something; otherwise he'd just kill Quen outright if that was his idea of fun. The moment a threat came with a countdown, it meant there was a deal on the table, and Rufus had spotted it immediately.

"You're gonna need to sit down and promise not to kill me," Laurence finally answered as he strode into the library. When he caught sight of Angela at the table, he added, "Hey!"

"Impressive," she said with a dry smile.

"Not my doing, otherwise I'd absolutely take credit." Laurence rested his hands on the back of a chair, then decided he might look less confrontational if he sat down, so he pulled the chair out and settled into it.

"Spit it out." Rufus didn't sit, and Laurence hadn't really expected him to. He loomed a couple of feet away and crossed his arms, probably to try and look scarier.

He didn't need to try. Laurence was all too aware that Rufus could kill him before he made it out of his chair.

"Vincent wants me to destroy all the wards in your sanctum," he said levelly, leaning back in his seat so that he could raise his chin and meet Ru's stare.

Rufus stared at him like a cat that had just seen a bird. "And how does he expect you to do that?"

Laurence shrugged with care, and didn't break eye contact. "I don't think he cares how, he just wants it done. But, listen: if he wants your wards out of the way, that means he wants to either come here himself, or send some of his coven in. And *that* gives us an opportunity."

"An opportunity," Rufus echoed, with the kind of calm that probably meant he was way beyond angry and well into murderous.

"If his forces are split, we're not outnumbered," Laurence said.

"Suppose we do take down the wards. Lure him in, take him out, restore the wards, go over to his place, mop up the rest of them." He spread his hands slowly, careful not to give the impression that he was casting a spell. "I can check the future, see how that might play out, and we can take it from there?"

"Or we can just not do it," Ru said. "He threatened Quentin; you made sure he can't act on that threat. Where does he go from there?" He uncrossed his arms, and his shoulders slowly unwound. "Can't carry out his threat, can't come here either, can't get Myriam, can't target your home. He's got no power over us. Giving you so much time was a mistake. He already..." He trailed off with a pensive expression, then finally made his way to the table and sat cautiously. "He's made it clear that he knows the best way to give out a deadline is to have already kidnapped the person whose life he's threatening. You're sure he hasn't taken Quentin?"

Laurence took a sharp breath. "I mean, he *hadn't*, but... that doesn't mean he *hasn't*... Okay. You're right. I'll check that first."

Rufus nodded. "Otherwise it's just a distraction to throw us off what we *should* be doing, which is stopping him before he becomes immortal."

"He has a point," Angela agreed. "It's possible this threat on Quentin's life isn't even sincere."

Except he didn't answer my messages.

Laurence held a hand up briefly and closed his eyes to concentrate.

Quentin. New York. Visiting Basil. Right now...

A moment or two passed by as he searched for a vision, and then he found what he was looking for, and dove into it.

"Perhaps it is not possible," Quentin murmured sympathetically. He was on a couch, wearing only a thin white undershirt, and surrounded by so many books that it looked like someone had stolen an entire bookstore and tried to cram it into a single apartment.

Jon sat next to him on the same couch. His pale fingers were spread across Quentin's shoulder and upper arm, touching shirt, skin, and sling, and his gaunt features were etched into a frown. "Perhaps," he intoned. "Remain still," he added when Quentin tried to wriggle.

"My phone—"

"—Can wait." Jon's dark eyes narrowed, which was about as annoyed as Laurence had ever seen him.

"I can check it, if you want?" Basil came closer and indicated Quentin's pocket. "In case it's important?"

"Please," Quentin murmured.

Basil leaned in and used pointer and middle fingers to tug Quen's cell from his pocket, then he held it in front of Quentin's face to unlock it. "Oh, hey, it's Laurence!"

Quen's features lit up, and his fatigue seemed to melt away for a moment. "How?"

"No idea..." Basil's smile faded. "Oh. Um, okay, oh my god, no, he's fine," he added when Quentin tried to stand up. "He says this Vincent guy knows you're here. You're not warded? And he's... Oh, he's sent some spells for you to give me so I can ward the apartment, okay! Let me just..." He ran fingers over the phone, flicking through images. "Okay, well, it's all Latin, so that should be easy. I just need to do windows and doors and..." His gaze darted around the apartment quickly, then he nodded to himself. "Kiss my security deposit goodbye, I guess. You two stay there, keep going, I'll start on this." He bounced away with Quen's phone in hand, then searched the pockets of coats that hung by the front door until he found a Sharpie.

Quentin watched Basil with some caution, but he settled back down on the couch. "At least send Laurence a message to acknowledge his, or he'll be worried."

"Oh, yeah." Basil laughed easily. "That'd be a good idea, huh?" He ran thumbs over the screen. "Done."

Quentin nodded gratefully, then turned his attention back to Jon. And as Basil began to cast the first spell, Quentin screwed his eyes shut and resorted to taking slow, deep breaths.

Laurence couldn't do anything to help him get through this, and it hurt his heart to watch Quen do his best to endure the nearby spellcasting, so — albeit reluctantly — he withdrew from the vision.

"He's still there," he said as he opened his eyes. "Basil's just starting to put the wards up now. It looks like a pretty small apartment; it shouldn't take him long."

"Great. Then Vincent's got nothing, and we've got everything he wants." Ru leaned back smugly in his chair. "What's he going to do about it?"

"Become immortal?" Angela lifted an eyebrow slightly.

"I bet he'll be willing to step outside his sanctum once he is," Laurence agreed. "Then I guess it doesn't matter how many of your wards try to kill him when he walks in through the gate; they're not gonna work."

Ru's expression soured again, and he grunted. "Stalemate," he realized.

Laurence's mouth felt dry all of a sudden as he too saw the nature of the trap they were all in.

Both sides were stuck inside their own fortresses until the moment Vincent got his immortality, and once he did, it was game over.

41

QUENTIN

THE SITUATION WAS SWIFTLY BECOMING UNTENABLE. THE WORLD was crowding in, threatening to overwhelm him, but if Quentin lost control in Basil's apartment, he could damage or destroy a whole library, harm people and cats alike, and ruin whatever wards Basil had established.

But he shared a seat with someone who was in physical contact with him, and that someone was not Laurence. He heard Basil reciting the same spell over and over, in Latin, and felt each and every hair on his body lift each time the ward was cast. He heard distant car horns or sirens along with the closer whistling of wind over the face of the apartment block. It was all so much.

Too much.

He did his level best to meditate his way through it. It seemed to help, or perhaps he was deluding himself. All he could think of was how desperately he wished he had some of those noise-cancelling earbuds Mel had talked about. Then, perhaps, he could listen to music and it might distract him. Here and now, however, he had no such help.

He inhaled sharply as the urge to berate himself for not being prepared reared its ugly head and nudged him further toward the ledge, but something else happened instead.

The pain in his shoulder melted away.

Quentin hadn't truly appreciated exactly how much it had been wearing him down. More than the obvious pain, there were lesser aches which had spread out from it, muscle tension and fatigue in equal measure, and the constant drain on his consciousness it all created. When it all disappeared, he was left with the stark appreciation of how much it had taken from him, and how foolish he had been to think he could do anything other than rest.

He let out a soft gasp as Jon's touch withdrew, and his eyes slowly fluttered open of their own accord. He found them focusing on his shoulder, though of course it was impossible to see anything beneath all the straps and dressings.

"Is that it, do you think?" Quentin asked softly, unwilling to try and move until he had the answer. After all, if what Jon had achieved was advanced pain management, it would be a spectacular error to make any assumptions.

"Yes," Jon said, though he sounded slightly mystified. "I cannot confirm success without an X-ray or CT scan, which I am unavailable to provide, but to the best of my knowledge your life energy is flowing correctly now, albeit below capacity. I can replenish that, if you wish? It will prevent you from taking what you need from those around you."

Quentin blinked slowly, and while his response was interrupted by the hair-raising sense of Basil casting another ward, it was much less overpowering this time. "You can do that?"

"Readily," Jon agreed. "Though I do not carry anywhere near as much of it within me as Laurence does."

"And recouping your expenditure?" Quentin frowned faintly.

"I must take it directly from another living source," Jon said. "I do not convert other forms of energy as you do, and cannot pull it out of the air."

"Ah." Quentin looked down at himself again, then reached for the nearest Velcro fastening and tugged on it with care. "Then I shall decline your offer, thank you. I can get what I need from your radiators."

"So long as you do not get it from Charon or Hades," Jon said.

It sounded like perhaps he meant it as a warning, but it was not a harsh one.

Quentin thought for a moment, then realized what Jon meant. "The cats?"

"Correct."

"I will not, I promise you." He tugged the first strap free, then set to work on the next, until finally he had released them all and was able to ease the sling off of his arm.

He moved carefully, testing the weight of his arm each step of the way, but his shoulder felt absolutely fine. He flexed his fingers, slowly bent his arm, then raised it over his head, and it did as he asked without a single complaint.

"Well," he said with a soft smile. "It seems as though you were thoroughly successful. Thank you, Jon. This is truly astonishing."

"It is," Jon agreed.

Quentin chuckled faintly and lowered his arm, then set to work on removing the dressings.

Now if only Basil could hurry up and finish the wards, Quentin would be well and truly comfortable at last.

QUENTIN MOVED across to rest his backside against a radiator once Basil had finished warding everything near it, and he set about gently leeching warmth from it without freezing either the metal or the room. The cats had emerged from their hiding spot and finally chosen to investigate him, too, which left him wondering whether they had somehow determined that he may have posed some sort of risk to them until now, but he appreciated the distraction from Basil's ongoing work — though, thankfully, Basil had moved on to the bedroom, which made it far easier for Quentin to allow himself to become occupied with petting cats.

"I do not think it plausible that I might be able to destroy magic," Jon mused. He'd gone from the couch to the kitchenette, and was refilling the kettle at the sink. "I cannot even perceive it."

Quentin clicked his tongue thoughtfully. "I hadn't considered that," he admitted. "However, with your newfound talent, I wouldn't wish to expose you on a front line anyway."

Jon put the kettle on, and turned back to the sink to rinse out the used mugs. "You consider me more valuable as a medic."

As with many of Jon's statements, it wasn't inflected as one usually might a question, but Quentin took it as one all the same.

"Yes." He nodded faintly. "All I can do is convert one form of energy into another and pass it around, but you can wield your life force like a scalpel and direct it to heal specific injuries. That's far more useful. And, should the situation warrant it, I'm capable of keeping you topped up, as it were."

Jon used a dishcloth to wipe the mugs dry. He seemed to be thinking, so Quentin stayed quiet, and remained focused on replenishing himself from the radiator beneath him.

"Do you always think tactically, or is it situational?" Jon mused.

"Ah." Quentin pressed his lips together briefly. "Almost always, I'm afraid. My therapist suggests that it's a... ah..." He turned his attention to the nearest window and looked outside, but there was now a faint blue glow across the glass, and he flinched at the sight. "Sodding hell," he gasped.

"What?" Jon sounded almost curious. "Oh. You are able to perceive magic." After a beat, he added, "Then why not apply additional manpower and assist with the wards?"

"Because I don't," Quentin muttered. He turned away from the window and frowned at Jon, but now he had two questions to choose between, and while the one he'd attempted to slink out of felt rather personal to be sharing with people he didn't know all that well, the second was absolutely a subject he wasn't willing to touch, so he returned to the first. After all, he couldn't always leave it down to the other party to perform the heavy lifting when it came to making friends, could he? That's how it had gone for the majority of his life, and the only good friends he'd obtained from it were Neil and Ames.

Maybe, for once, Quentin could put the effort in himself.

"My therapist says that hypervigilance is a symptom of complex post-traumatic stress disorder," he murmured with a soft sigh. "I am, as a consequence, almost constantly aware of the potential for danger in most situations, although it also comes with a tendency to work through possible solutions automatically. It's a defense mechanism, I'm told. So... Yes. I do almost always think tactically. I apologize."

"No apology is necessary." Jon poured water into mugs, and didn't seem at all bothered by Quentin's admission of illness. "I assess the world through an engineering lens. It is not very useful, but it is how my mind operates." He stirred tea and removed teabags. "Are you a successful tactician?"

Quentin grimaced at the question, and moved away from the radiator so that he could fetch his mug of tea and save Jon having to carry it to him. His last bout of tactical genius had cost him his shoulder, and Soraya her life.

"For the most part," he answered. "But not always."

"Good." Jon picked up the two remaining mugs and turned to face the bedroom, in time for Basil to emerge from it.

Basil almost skipped across the small space into Jon's arms, and took the tea with a broad grin. "Thanks! It's serious in here! What's going on?"

"We are discussing the strengths and weaknesses we bring to the table so that Quentin can work out how to defeat a warlock," Jon said, wrapping a gangly arm around Basil's shoulders.

"Well, there's always necromancy!" Basil grinned, and his nose scrunched up into a wrinkly button. He held his mug by the handle and almost drank from it, then pulled back at the last second. "I mean... There *is* always necromancy," he added, as though an idea had suddenly come to him. His eyes were growing wide, and he waved his free hand to fan himself. "Oh, wow. So, like, this Vincent Harrow is, like, super bad, right?"

Quentin eyed Basil in an attempt to discern any hint of sarcasm, but the necromancer seemed utterly sincere. "Yes."

"Killed people?"

Quentin thought he might have some idea of where this was headed, and he frowned thoughtfully. "Yes," he agreed.

"You know if those deaths were violent or horrific, odds are they left ghosts behind, right?"

Quentin raised his head and regarded Basil. "Are you suggesting that we gather them together and use them against Harrow?"

"You got it!" Basil snapped his fingers, then took a victory gulp of his tea, and whimpered at it. "Ahhh, hot! But yeah, if we know who he's killed, and where they died, we can go get them, and sic 'em on him. Don't worry," he added quickly as Quentin's eyebrows furrowed, "ghosts aren't people. Not really. They're just afterimages, like when you've stared at a bright light too long then look away. The light — the person — has already gone. All you've got is the impression they left behind. They're not good at understanding much, but they are often *super* into revenge, if their killer is still alive."

Quentin was far too aware of what a ghost's anger could feel like, and he hadn't even been the one who had killed whomever it was Derek Brooks had unleashed on him. The sensation of it seeping into his very bones, filled with nothing but malice, had been skin-crawlingly horrific, and while that ghost was old, perhaps a handful of much younger ghosts working in concert could have a similar effect.

Whatever the ghosts were able to do, it might knock Harrow off-balance enough for Laurence to do what undoubtedly needed to be done.

"All right," Quentin said. He withdrew his phone and suspended his mug in the air so that he could fire off messages with both thumbs. "Then our first task is to identify as many of his victims as we can."

It was a gruesome task which he was wholly willing to palm off onto someone else if at all possible, so he fell silent and concentrated on attempting to do just that.

42

LAURENCE

Here!

Windsor's cry was triumphant, and so unexpected that Laurence banged his knee on the table.

"Ow! Fuck!" He clutched his kneecap and sucked air through his teeth, and it was pure luck that he saw Rufus bounce to his feet at the same time, his face pinched in surprise.

It didn't take long to piece two and two together. Laurence prayed that he'd gotten four.

"Wait," he croaked. "It's Windsor."

Rufus turned his head toward the wall, and Laurence could see the tendrils of shimmering turquoise in the air that had manifested to connect Rufus to the house.

Someone must've opened the gate.

"It's Windsor," Laurence repeated, more firmly now the initial shock of the pain had died down. He wriggled his chair back from under the desk until he could stand up, then made his way to the door. "Sebastian and Mia, right?"

Rufus huffed. "Yes. And..." He frowned as he hurried across the room and beat Laurence to the exit. "Half a dozen children," he groused.

"I'm not sure they really count as *children*," Angela said as she followed them both. "Neither legally nor emotionally."

"Yeah, well, just don't slice and dice them before they even get out of the SUV, okay?" Laurence hurried downstairs after Rufus. "They're here to help."

"They're *in* my *sanctum*," Rufus growled. He strode across the hallway like a small tornado, but a fist banged against the front door before he could get to it, and all he could do was fling the door open in anger and point his finger directly up into Mia's face so close he almost shoved it up her nose. "You don't just—"

"You've got three seconds to take that away that before I break it," Mia cut in levelly, looking him in the eye the way she did most any time she was forced to be the only adult in the room.

"Ru—" Laurence was about to try and calm Rufus down, except a bolt of black zipped straight past Mia's ear and barreled right into Laurence's chest so fast that it almost knocked him off balance. He caught it, though, on pure instinct, and it cawed at him so loudly it made his ears ring. "Win! Win, calm down. Goddess, I'm right here!"

Chaos poured in through the front door like a tidal wave, sweeping up Rufus and Mia and depositing them further inside the hallway, now several feet apart from one another and with a horde of teens between them.

"I can't believe you're up to your neck in it. Who would've thought?" Soraya said to Laurence, sarcasm dripping from every word.

"And you didn't call us sooner?" Mel agreed. She placed her fists on her hips and stood by Soraya like they were the world's angriest cheerleaders. "Knowing you *needed* us?"

"All right, that's enough," Sebastian bellowed, cutting through all the noise. Either he knew exactly how to use the acoustics of a space he'd only just entered, or he was naturally loud when he wanted to be. "No time to waste. Sorry it took so long to get here, had to stop off for supplies."

Things that make noise! Windsor chattered in excitement.

Laurence hugged Windsor to his chest and quickly checked who Sebastian had brought along. Mia, Soraya, and Mel, of course, but Kim, Estelita, Alex, and Rodger were in the mix, too.

He blinked. He hadn't expected Alex, and he *definitely* hadn't expected Rodger, who was busy gawping at the hallway like he'd just discovered Narnia.

"I could've killed you all," Rufus complained. He slammed the front door shut. "Do you have any idea how dangerous it is to walk into a sanctum without—"

"Told Laurence we were coming," Sebastian said, firmly cutting Rufus off before the tantrum could fully manifest itself. "Brought Windsor so he'd know it was us. Now, we want to get moving." He jerked his thumb to the door behind him. "Where are we moving *to?*"

"Southern edge of the Angeles National Forest," Laurence told him.

"Two hours. Maybe less, if we don't care about a ticket." Sebastian gave a curt nod. "All right. Soraya, you drive."

"Yes!" She fist-pumped the air.

"I need to brief the wizards on how to use grenades," he continued with only the smallest smirk at Soraya's enthusiasm.

"Not a wizard," Angela said, with a dry tone that sounded to Laurence's ears like she was amused, at least.

"Grenades?" Rufus rounded on Sebastian. "In a moving vehicle? Whose side are you on?"

"Boom!" Windsor wriggled out of Laurence's arms and climbed up to his shoulder.

Laurence took a deep breath. All the noise was building to a crescendo, vibrating discordantly along the spaces between his tiredness and the coffee, reverberating around the hallway, ricocheting off its hard floors like it was coming back for round two, until he was forced to clap his hands over his ears to take the edge off.

He blinked, and Alex was in front of him. He knew it was Alex, even though Alex looked different in so many ways now: shorter, with softer features, and shorter hair.

They gazed into his eyes and placed a hand on Laurence's unencumbered shoulder, then just... breathed.

Laurence latched onto the lifeline Alex was throwing him, and let his breathing fall into synch with theirs until his head thrummed way less, and he was mostly on top of the caffeine jitters.

"Better?" Alex mouthed, lifting their eyebrows to make it a question.

Laurence nodded to them. "Thanks," he mouthed back. He risked taking his hands from his ears, and was relieved that the noise had died down to a lone argument now.

"I thought you were all about the vengeance," Sebastian said. At least he wasn't raising his voice anymore, though. "Well, now's the time. Everyone's here to help you get it, and it might kill some of us. Maybe even all of us. But we're here, and we don't have time for this, so tell me what the problem is, and I'll fix it."

Alex stepped aside and turned to stand by Laurence's side to reveal that just about everyone else had also moved away from the center of the hallway. Only Sebastian and Ru remained there, obstinate as each other.

Sebastian had a point, though: Rufus was so dedicated to getting revenge on Vincent for the death of his parents that the promise of getting it was the only reason he'd agreed to teach Laurence magic, and he'd done that last summer, not once letting Laurence forget that there was a bargain behind his tuition.

But all he'd wanted to do since they'd got Amy back was put the brakes on: sit in the library, read books, come up with one reason after the next as to why they couldn't go on over and kick Vincent's ass. *He's too powerful, he's in his sanctum, he knows too much, we don't know the extent of his defenses, I haven't got any food...*

Laurence's eyes grew wide.

Had Rufus been delaying them? Deliberately holding them back from getting this over and done with? And, if so, why? *Why did the witch who craved Harrow's death more than anything suddenly have no interest in causing it?*

Rufus's gaze wavered faintly. All eyes in the room were on him, and Laurence couldn't imagine the isolation he had to be feeling right now, but he also wasn't about to relieve him of it.

The truth was so close he could taste it. All he had to do was wait.

Rufus' shoulders lowered a fraction of an inch. His center of balance shifted with the motion, and he came off the balls of his feet to plant himself in a slightly more relaxed position.

There it is. Laurence pressed his lips together and prayed for the teens to stay silent.

"I lied to Angela," Rufus said with a growl. "Because if I lied to Laurence he might have noticed it. So I let her do it for me, because she didn't know it was a lie."

Laurence licked his lips as he took a cautious step forward. The last thing he wanted to do was spook Rufus, but he was drawn closer, and it felt like the jaws of fate were closing in around him. "About what?" he whispered.

"The Book of Yew," Ru muttered.

Laurence tried to figure out what there was to lie about, but the second he did, he swallowed tightly. "You've read it," he said.

"Of course I have." Rufus crossed his arms slowly and refused to make eye contact. "I've been in here ten years. You think I haven't looked?"

"You knew the password?" Laurence took another step, but didn't go any further. "But you didn't give it to him. You wanted to delay him?"

"Obviously."

"Then you know whether there *is* an immortality spell in there." Laurence's skin prickled slowly, and he added, "And you know what he needs to cast it. That's why you're trying to delay us, isn't it?"

A muscle in Rufus' jaw began to twitch as the tension crept back into his body. "I'm trying to find a solution," he snapped.

"Yeah, that's about as much of this shit as I'm willing to take." Soraya stepped forward with her hands raised, looking like an irate referee at a boxing match that had gone on too long. "Get to the point."

Rufus scowled at her, but he'd already admitted to his lie. How much more could there be for him to hold out on?

"It has three essential ingredients, beyond the caster himself," Rufus said. "First, it has to happen during Samhain."

Soraya sniffed. "Okay, so we're good for a year, right? It's technically November now, by like two whole hours."

Laurence shook his head. "Samhain starts on October 31st," he explained, "but it lasts through November 1st."

She groaned and dropped her hands. "Okay, then what else does he need?"

"Second ingredient is the sacrifice of a blood relation," Rufus muttered. He crossed his arms.

The world leapt into sharp focus as Laurence's heart began to race. "And the third?"

Rufus finally raised his head, and looked directly into Laurence's eyes.

"A suitable new body," he said thickly.

He wants me. He wants you, too.

Laurence felt sick to his stomach. He knew what Vincent did to his hosts.

Vincent needed Laurence's body — today — and once he had it, Laurence would be trapped in there with him forever.

43

QUENTIN

Your enemy targets mothers.

That was what Father had said to Laurence. It was the reason Myriam was in Castle Cavendish right now, protected by its wards. And it meant that Father had knowledge of at least some of Harrow's past victims. Whether or not anyone Quentin had messaged was able to convince Father to share what he knew, however, remained to be seen.

Quentin waited impatiently for any kind of response to his barrage of text messages, since Father himself did not possess a mobile phone, and it was Myriam who finally came back to him with information she had obtained from the duke. Quentin liked to think that she had chewed Father's ear off as part of her interrogation technique, but truth be told it was far more likely that all she'd had to do was ask — and withstand Father's disappointment that it had taken his heir so long to come up with the right question.

I've hardly been in tip-top shape, he reminded himself, before he could get wrapped up in self-recriminations over something which did not deserve them.

In the interim, he'd kept Sebastian updated with Basil's progress on the wards, and Sebastian had in turn advised Quentin that he, Mia, and some of the teens were en route to an address in

Carlsbad to liaise with Laurence. Quentin presumed it was Rufus' sanctum, as he knew of no other reason to go to Carlsbad.

Everything seemed under control once more, and with Basil busy at his laptop researching the list of names Myriam had furnished them with, Quentin was content to return to idly leeching heat from the radiator. He had already achieved a very comfortable level where he was certain that he was no longer drawing energy from the air around himself — not even slightly — but if they were off to scoop up some ghosts, there was little harm in taking extra.

Basil's pen rasped over the notepad next to his laptop with an air of finality, then he set it down. "There we go. That's everything."

Quentin's eyebrows lifted. "That seemed... quick?"

"All that is required is the ghost's name and location," Jon said flatly. "I am able to summon them once we have the correct name and are in the right place."

"And once Jon reels them in, I can grab 'em," Basil finished. He closed his laptop with a grin. "I've never been to LA before. You?"

Jon shook his head. "No."

"Yes," Quentin murmured with a slight tilt of his head. "Terrible air, horrendous traffic, beautiful beaches." He crinkled his nose as memories of his very short time spent trying to live in the city came to him. "Very confusing," he concluded.

"I hear it's more like twenty cities in a trench coat." Basil hopped to his feet and flipped back and forth through pages of his notebook, then closed it and crossed the room to a coat rack near the front door. "We've got some non-LA destinations, too, but plenty are in Los Angeles County."

Quentin eased away from the radiator with all the grace he could muster, considering that he knew what must come next: Basil and Jon would have to leave him alone here, stranded, while they gathered as many ghosts as they were able to. He watched as Basil dithered over what coat or jacket to wear, nodded approvingly when the lightest was selected, and stood by while Basil shrugged it on. Finally, the necromancer shouldered his courier bag and slid his notebook into it.

Jon seemed content not to bother with a coat at all.

"All right," Quentin murmured. "You're certain that you have everything you need?"

"Sure thing! And we'll be right back once we're done. Take care of my babies, and don't go outside." Basil grinned at him before whipping out his phone and unlocking it. "Okie-dokie then. How does this work…"

"I'll be… out of your hair…" Quentin stepped away, but rapidly had to face the fact that Basil's apartment was extremely tiny. If he wished to hide himself away while Basil set about his attempt at Father's co-location spell, Quentin would be forced to either invade the sanctity of the bedroom, or tuck himself into a closet. He couldn't even find a loo to hide in, which suggested that the bathroom was through the bedroom. Ultimately it left him standing in the kitchenette, feeling at a loose end.

"Okay," Basil said, though whether he was answering Quentin or talking to himself wasn't clear. "Oh, huh. Mmhmm. Okay." His finger swiped the phone's screen back and forth.

"What?" Jon sounded disinterested.

"The spell doesn't do the thing," Basil explained to him, rocking on his toes slowly while he gestured with one hand. "The spell makes a talisman; the talisman is then activated at will by whatever phrase or action you assign during the casting, and you turn it off again using a different phrase or action."

Quentin pursed his lips in concern. "Do you require an item suitable for the magic?"

Basil shook his head. "No, it's not an imbued spell, it's anchored with sigils, so it can be cast on anything and not wear off. It's fine. No need to go shopping."

Quentin did his best to hide his disappointment before remembering that if there were shopping to be done, he wasn't allowed out to do it regardless.

"The real problem," Basil continued, with a grimace at his phone, "is the level of concentration needed to use the talisman with any degree of success."

Jon crossed to Basil's side and loomed over him. "How so?"

"It'll be fine!" Basil laughed, and leaned up to kiss Jon's cheek quickly. "I just have to somehow pay attention to two totally different places, and how much exactly of my entire existence is real in each one, fine-tuning it second by second. *Then* I've got to add onto that *your* body, and make sure I don't scatter our internal organs all over the place." He let out a laugh that was only slightly frantic. "Talisman comes first," he added, seemingly to himself. "Worry about the rest later."

Jon remained impassive as Basil pulled away from him and started to search through drawers, and Quentin settled down at the kitchen table to occupy as little space as he was able to.

All he needed to do was stay well out of the way, and everything would be fine.

Basil had unearthed a plastic ruler and apparently decided that this would be the perfect item to create a talisman out of. It seemed ridiculous to Quentin, but then he wasn't the one who would be using it, and he supposed that it was not for him to pass comment on, so he didn't.

"Okay." Basil fiddled with his phone before he put the ruler down on a tall pile of books, and he had his ubiquitous Sharpie ready in no time. "This won't take long, but don't interrupt, okay? Otherwise I gotta find something else to use, and start over."

"All right," Jon said.

"Understood," Quentin murmured. He turned to face the fridge, and considered stuffing his fingers in his ears before he realized that he could doubtless go one better than that.

If he could draw sound waves towards himself, perhaps he might also be able to push them away?

He closed his eyes and honed in on the noises around him, from the winds outside to the persistent hum from devices in the kitchenette, then he wrapped them around himself as he might with warmth in winter.

If Basil had begun to recite the spell, Quentin could not hear it, but it wasn't until he felt the hairs on his arms begin to lift that he realized that his attempt was working: he had successfully blotted out all other sound.

Well, this would have been handy if I could have figured it out a little sooner.

Still, not to worry. He'd worked it out now, and that was what mattered. And as he felt magic fire off nearby over and over again, he simply clenched his jaw and gripped his thighs as he waited.

He could get through this.

He *would* get through this.

So fixated was he on this mantra that when a cold hand landed on his shoulder, he almost jumped out of his skin.

QUENTIN GASPED AT THE TOUCH, and his eyes snapped open. He looked up to find Jon leaning over him, lips moving, dark brows drawn.

There was no sensation of magic anymore. So why was Jon still here?

Quentin looked past him, to where Basil had been, but the necromancer hadn't gone anywhere either, and his freckled features were contorted in frustration. The ruler was clenched in his right hand, and the poor boy looked on the verge of tears.

Jon lightly shook Quentin's shoulder, and Quentin remembered why everything was so quiet.

"—me?" Jon said, the moment Quentin cancelled out his little bubble of peace. "Or anything else?"

Quentin blinked up at him, and gave him a faint shake of his head. "I am so sorry," he murmured. "Miles away. Are you both off now?"

"That's what I've been trying to tell you," Basil wailed. His cheeks were flushed so pink that they almost matched his nails. "I can't do it!"

Quentin tipped his head aside slowly. "I don't understand. The spell has worked, has it not?" It must have, otherwise how had he felt so much magic?

"Yeah. Yeah, that part's easy! But I can't—" Basil shook the ruler in frustration. "Maybe if I had time to practice, or... Or if I had a little more sleep, or... It's..." He sucked in air as tears crept in at the corners of his eyes. "This is ridiculous. I can put my head down and write five articles a day if I have to. I've got focus, I can concentrate. But this is... It's impossible! How am I supposed to be in two places at once, and pay attention to everything in both of them, *and* move from one to the other, *and* take anyone else with me? I can't do it!" He finally slumped into a chair and broke down sobbing, wiping at his eyes with his empty hand.

Jon rushed to Basil's side and crouched down to hug him. He said nothing, but Basil leaned into him anyway, and sniffled on his shoulder.

Quentin's heart went out to them both. He understood the pain of failure all too well, and had nothing but sympathy for Basil, but as the enormity of the source of Basil's upset truly began to sink in, it brought with it a chill that began to slowly squeeze Quentin's gut until it was truly oppressive.

If Basil was unable to control the magic, he and Jon could not set off on their task; the assistance Sebastian had hoped for would not come.

And that left Laurence without an ace up his sleeve after all.

44

LAURENCE

"That's fucked up." Soraya's words barged bluntly through Laurence's spiraling horror. "Let's go throw grenades at this motherfucker."

Laurence's breath hitched and he turned his head enough to face her. She was looking at him with a sympathetic crease to her eyes, and her fists were firmly planted on her hips. She was waiting for an answer, so he tried to formulate one.

"If you knew all this," he began, piecing the facts together as he went, "why didn't you tell us?" Laurence turned to look to Rufus again, and by the time his head got there, he had the answer. "Because saving Amy was your priority. That's why, even while we were in his sanctum, you had trouble handing the book to him, isn't it? Because you knew what was in it."

Rufus somehow managed to look increasingly irate, but at least he didn't say anything.

"But if Vincent's been watching us both, waiting for whatever he thinks 'ready' looks like, that means he knew what the spell needed way before he had the book." Laurence approached Rufus cautiously. "So why did he let us go? Why not use Amy, get us and the book, then hang on to everything he needs?" His skin itched as he remembered how Vincent had looked at him once he had the Book of Yew in his hands — like Laurence was the prey now

— and he took a deep breath. "Oh, Goddess. I've been looking at it all wrong, trying to see the logic in it. But that's only half of why he does anything, isn't it?"

Angela hummed faintly before she spoke. "Correct," she finally agreed, sounding resigned.

"So what's the other half?" Mel prodded.

"Entertainment," Laurence said quietly. "He enjoys what he does. He's amused by torturing and killing, treating people like toys." He pointed down at the floor. "This is a fucking game to him; he's been jerking us around for *fun*."

There was a moment's silence, broken by a grunt from Sebastian. "This is definitely a conversation we could be having while Soraya is driving. Come on. We need to move." He started back across the hallway.

Laurence set off after him.

"No!" Rufus yelled.

Laurence stopped in his tracks. He was about to round on Ru, to give him hell for trying to keep them stuck here for even longer, but his words died in his throat the second he saw the sheer panic on Ru's face.

Ru wasn't looking at anyone in the room; he was staring towards the wall by the front door.

"It's—"

Rufus didn't need to finish whatever he was about to say, because the world did it for him. There was an awful fluctuation in the very structure of reality, and the whole house creaked as a *crack* reverberated through it. Laurence heard items throughout the house fall from shelves or smack into each other in cupboards, little clacks and tinkles and shattering sounds that all took place at once as the floor under his feet was suddenly at a minutely different angle.

He, Rufus, and Angela were as steady on their feet as might be expected under the circumstances, but everyone else was far less stable, either stumbling forward or lunging to grab hold of a wall or doorway.

It was over in a second, but Laurence knew exactly what had happened. He'd passed too many sanctum thresholds not to.

Rufus' mansion wasn't in its own realm anymore.

They were in the real world.

"He— he's killing them," Rufus stammered, shaking his head numbly. "The wards, the defenses, he's..." His hands darted through the air, yanking on threads of turquoise magic that were breaking apart between his fingers. "This can't be—" He broke off, then croaked, "I've lost them!"

Sebastian's hand rested on the door handle, but he hesitated a second, then turned the bolt to lock it instead. "We're toast if we go out there one by one. Best thing we can do is hole up somewhere defensible and pick them off instead. Where's best?"

"The library," Angela said.

Laurence shook his head. "No. It's got huge windows," he added at her creased brows. "But what if we go out into the yard? Gives us room to move, there's a lot of overgrowth out there, we —" He paused as his cellphone began to ping and vibrate with all the notifications he'd missed while he was holed up in a sanctum. He was about to reach for it, and had to force himself not to, because this was *not* the time to catch up on his messages.

"We need to control their approach, funnel them down," Sebastian said, speaking with urgency. "Think, Laurence!"

"The library," Angela insisted. "This way." She turned on her heel and marched up the stairs without checking whether she was being followed, and Rufus chased after her like he was more worried she might steal a book than he was about Harrow destroying his sanctum.

Laurence winced as a car alarm sounded off outside. He was so used to the peculiar silence of this house that it threw him for a loop until he remembered it wasn't safe here any longer, and he jerked into action. "Upstairs," he ordered, waving his arms at the teens and willing them to move. "Go, follow Angela!"

Windsor launched from his shoulder and cawed raucously to help Laurence herd everyone up the stairs, and as Laurence and Sebastian brought up the rear, Sebastian drew a pistol.

"We're screwed," Sebastian breathed softly near Laurence's ear.

Laurence looked to him in alarm. "What? Why?"

Sebastian spared him a glance. "That alarm you hear is our SUV," was all he said.

Laurence stared at him so hard he almost missed a stair, said, "Fuck," then pulled out his cell and fumbled with it to try and call Quen as the front door unlocked itself and flew open. He heard some rattling, rolling noises like a bunch of heavy marbles had gotten dropped, and while his cell was still ringing in his hand and Sebastian pushed him up the last of the stairs and Windsor dove in through the library's open doors, his whole world turned into such an excruciating barrage of light and sound that he was half convinced he was still in the desert, being bombarded by Nate Anderson's lightning bolts.

He screamed.

He stumbled.

He fell.

And the world kept exploding.

Smoke.

Screaming.
Gunshots.
Sobbing.
Footsteps.
Silence.

LAURENCE DRIFTED toward consciousness on a wave of nausea. He drew in air tainted with smoke and blood and rotten meat. His whole body trembled at the lingering sense-memory of percussive sound and punishing light, and though he tried to roll onto his side, to curl up into a ball, he couldn't move. Worse, he had the horrendous feeling that something fundamental had been torn away, and he couldn't work out what it was.

"Riley wakes, Master." A woman's voice, distorted by the ringing in his ears.

"So I see," Vincent purred. "Keep working."

"Yes, Master."

Laurence didn't know whether he really wanted to open his eyes, but desperation forced his hand, and he opened his eyes into a tight squint to protect himself against more light. Thankfully there wasn't so much of it now.

He made out shadows that flickered back and forth across the edges of his field of vision. It took a while to work out that he was staring at a ceiling, so he tried to turn his head, and that worked.

Library, he realized. *This is Ru's library.*

Except there weren't nearly so many books left on the shelves.

Laurence's ear pressed against the cool, glossy, hard surface under him. He was on the desk, flat on his back. He couldn't see any magic anywhere: either Vincent had finally killed all the wards, he'd taken all Laurence's talismans away again, or both. The shadows were cast by an entire group of dirt-smeared women wearing the barest excuses for clothing — little more than an assortment of baggy nightshirts and dresses — who were plucking books from the shelves and carrying as many as they could out of the room. He strained to hear their footsteps descend the staircase, and picked out more breathing from places he couldn't see.

"I hardly expected you to go down so readily," Vincent said. His body came closer and blotted out Laurence's view. He leaned in to grip Laurence's jaw and force eye contact, and his stench washed over Laurence and made him heave. Vincent watched him buck and writhe on the table like he was pulling the wings off a butterfly. "Still, the less damage done to my new residence, the better. For entirely personal reasons," he added with a slow, malicious smirk that released the odor of sickness from somewhere deep inside.

"Residence," Laurence wheezed, echoing the weird word

choice. If Vincent was taking over Ru's home, why did he need to remove all the books?

He doesn't mean the house.

He means my body.

Laurence's eyes widened in terror. He wrenched against whatever was holding him down, but it was tight around his wrists, his waist, his legs, and all he did was wriggle a couple of inches on the slippery table.

"Careful." Vincent's smirk grew into a grin. "You and I are about to share eternity together, Mr. Riley. Let's not start off with any injuries. Marcella!"

"Yes, Master." Marcella appeared at his side.

Vincent gestured to Laurence and stepped away from the table. "Take it, before it has any ideas."

"Yes, Master." She came closer and — in an alarmingly easy motion — slid Laurence off the table, then threw him over her shoulder in a fireman's carry.

Laurence groaned and tried his damndest not to puke. He thought he saw bodies on the floor, strewn across the library like discarded trash, but before he could figure out who was down and who might still be standing, another waft of rot assaulted his senses, and his stomach gave up everything he'd put in it recently.

Marcella didn't react at all, and she carried him downstairs without another word.

Win? Laurence struggled to reach his familiar, to find out where he was and what had happened, but there was no answer. Worse, Laurence couldn't even feel him. He'd lost all sense of the bird. Not like Windsor was asleep, or even how it had felt when Win had left for Otherworld to try and get help from Herne.

Now there was nothing, like Windsor didn't even exist anymore, and as Laurence finally understood what had been ripped away from him, he knew in his heart what in meant.

Windsor was dead.

45

QUENTIN

Quentin rose from his chair and approached Basil slowly. The poor boy seemed to be falling to pieces, sobbing into Jon's shoulder as though the world were ending, and while this situation was not optimal, Quentin knew better than to say so out loud.

Instead, he perched on the arm of the couch, the other side of Basil, and rested a hand lightly against his back. "It's all right," he said softly.

"It's not!" Basil wailed.

"Basil," Quentin said. He spoke firmly, without raising his voice. "It is *all right*. Good heavens, I've woken you in the middle of the night, handed you a spell you've never seen before, and given you no warning or time to prepare. You're tired. I'm quite sure that under different circumstances you would have no difficulty with this whatsoever."

Basil sniffled into Jon's shirt, and mumbled, "You don't have to coddle me."

Quentin scoffed at him. "I'm not. It is quite acceptable not to master something new on your first try after only half a night's sleep." He rubbed Basil's back slightly, then withdrew his hand. "Have a break, then you can try again."

Basil seemed to inflate like a pufferfish as he sprang to his feet to round on Quentin, pointing at him with the yellow plastic ruler. His hazel eyes were reddened, cheeks damp from his tears, and he looked about ready to start screaming. "It won't work! I can't do it!"

"You *can* do it," Quentin replied calmly.

"What makes you so sure?"

"Because I know that you can." Quentin folded his hands together on his thigh as he met Basil's angry glare. "And because we have no other option," he admitted.

Jon made a faintly derisive noise. "Not strictly true."

Quentin turned slightly so that he could face Jon. "Within a reasonable timeframe," he clarified. "It's a six-hour flight, not including travel to and from airports."

Jon's stare was impassive and unblinking. "You can use magic," he stated.

"I'm afraid I cannot." Quentin shook his head faintly, but Jon was still staring at him.

"Ohhh," Basil breathed slowly. "You *can*! And you're intense! And you were still capable of drawing Gwyn ap Nudd's corruption out of all those souls in Annwn despite having it in yourself *and* being outnumbered." He waggled the ruler far less aggressively. "You should try!"

"I *can't*," Quentin said, a little more tersely than he would have liked to, but his phone rang before he could apologize for snapping.

"Saved by the bell," Jon groused.

Quentin stood, so that he could get the phone out of his pocket more easily, and the screen read *Laurence*, so he answered with a smile. "Darling!"

The sound that came out of his phone wiped the smile off his face immediately. It began with as loud a noise as he'd ever heard the device make, followed immediately by screams, a clattering sound, and what he was absolutely certain were gunshots.

What he did not hear was Laurence.

His heart pounded, and he tightened his hold on the phone as he struggled to figure out what he was listening to. There was muffled yelling, as though from several feet away and through a closed door, and it *sounded* like Soraya, but he couldn't be certain. He heard footsteps, unhurried, grow louder. Then there was a low, agonized groan, and Quentin knew without a shadow of a doubt who had made it.

"Laurence! Can you hear me? What's happening?"

He heard a scraping sound, then the call ended.

Quentin stared at his phone as if he could simply will it into giving him the answers, and when he attempted to return Laurence's call, it went unanswered.

He isn't going to answer. That sounded like a bloody war zone.

He gritted his teeth and raised his head to find Basil and Jon both staring at him, but there was no knowing what they had overheard, and even if Basil somehow managed to make his spell work on the next try, it was already too late. If they all rushed in like the Charge of the Light Brigade, it would end just as poorly, that much was obvious. Laurence was down, Soraya was off-balance, and their opponents were in no hurry. The *only* way to handle this was to persist with the original plan, because Basil and Jon were not suited to open warfare, and Quentin would crumble in the presence of offensive magic.

And if Laurence is dead?

Then he is in Annwn, and I will either avenge him, or join him.

Quentin forced his fingers to lessen their grip on his phone, then he took a shaky breath as he began a litany of steps in his mind.

Stay calm.
Go to Los Angeles.
Collect ghosts.
Drop them on Harrow.
Separate him from his team.
Unleash hell.

That seemed like a solid plan, so he got to work on the first step right away, and counted down from ten.

"He's doing that thing again," Basil stage-whispered so loudly that it barely counted as a whisper at all.

"Indeed," Jon said.

"Do you think this is where he, like, flips out and kills us?"

"I cannot say."

Quentin opened his eyes and blinked quickly. Neither Basil nor Jon had moved, though Basil now looked at him as though Quentin had just choked him again, and Quentin couldn't blame him in the slightest.

"We have to go," he said thickly. "They are under attack."

Basil's head bobbed, and he held out the ruler, offering it to Quentin. "I can't do it," he squeaked.

Quentin forced himself to look at it. It seemed innocuous enough at present, with black marks scrawled along its length, but he knew that it had a spell stuck to it, and he knew where that spell had come from.

"Time would appear to be of the essence," Jon stated, his tone flat.

All Quentin could think of was Myriam's soft, gentle question: *not even to save Bambi's life?*

Potentially.

There was nothing *but* potential now. If Laurence was still alive, this would be what it would take to save him, and that was that.

Quentin jolted into action. He reached for the ruler, and took it carefully. "Very well," he murmured. "How is it activated?"

Basil chewed his lip, and mumbled, "The trigger is, um." He eyed the ruler, then took a few steps back. "Get in, loser, we're going shopping."

Quentin frowned faintly at him. "We are?"

"It is a quote," Jon stated. "From a movie."

"Oh." Quentin nodded to himself. "And to end the spell?"

"Stop trying to make fetch happen," Basil said.

Quentin eyed him, but there was little point asking for an explanation, and even less time in which to do so, so he took a deep breath, screwed his eyes shut, and said as quickly as he could, "Get in, loser, we're going shopping."

Despite all his preparation, nothing happened.

QUENTIN CRACKED an eye open to confirm that he hadn't somehow triggered any magic. He was still resolutely in Basil's apartment, as were Basil and Jon. He saw no evidence of any other location, and sensed no magic in his presence.

He would have liked to feel relieved, but the truth was that he did not, because if he could not get to Laurence, he would not be able to help him.

"What went wrong?" He opened his other eye and frowned at Basil.

Basil chewed on a fingernail, then snapped his fingers and pulled the notebook out of his bag. He hurried forward and held it out to Quentin. "I forgot! You need to have a destination in mind! I'm sorry, that was on me."

Quentin transferred his phone to the hand which held the ruler so that he could take the notepad, and he used his gifts to open it and flip through the pages of names and addresses and was relieved that he recognized at least half of the locations on the list, so he selected one in San Diego, then tried again.

Still, nothing happened.

"Oh, this is ridiculous," he huffed, and thumbed at his phone to bring the spell up. If he could identify what Basil had done wrong, they could get on with the actual work, so he skim-read it and thumbed through the pages. There was a lot of guff about philosophy threaded through and around the instructions of the spell, but a line caught his eye, and he read it out loud. "'Hoc opus mentem valentissimam postulat…' Oh."

Basil nodded nervously. "Right. This work demands a very strong mind."

Quentin eyed him. "Which you interpreted as focused?"

Again, Basil's head bobbed in a quick nod.

Quentin clicked his tongue faintly. "No. A better translation would be, ah… Strong of will."

Jon gave him a glare which felt mildly more sarcastic than his more usual, deadpan glare.

"So, like... Stubborn," Basil mused.

"Persistent," Jon offered.

"Intense," Basil agreed.

They were both staring at him now.

Quentin huffed at them and continued to skim the document, then he groaned. "'Contra aliis amuletis quis simpliciter scientiam vegetationis poscunt opus tuum non alii nisi tibi est.'"

Basil opened his mouth and raised his hands as though he were certain he had a point to make, but then he seemed to deflate, and let out a faint whine. "Oh."

Jon blinked slowly. "What is the problem?"

"Unlike other amulets which simply require knowledge of enlivening, this work you made is no-one but yours." Quentin crinkled his nose and handed the ruler to Basil. "Only Basil can activate this talisman," he explained, for Jon's benefit.

Jon frowned at Basil. "An oversight?"

Basil waved his hands, then took the ruler, and waved them some more. "Vegetationis," he huffed. "I read it as vegetation and figured, well, I'm not doing anything with plants, so it's not relevant here."

"But vegetation is a later meaning," Quentin murmured. "Regardless, the result is that we are back to square one."

Jon turned that relentless stare on him, and one eyebrow raised faintly. "It means that you must create the talisman," he countered.

"No. Absolutely not—"

"We will skip the bit where you insist that you cannot, and move directly on to the part where you do it anyway," Jon stated, "because otherwise this will not be done, and we cannot help Laurence without it."

Quentin wanted to argue, to object to being bossed around, but Jon was right, and Quentin had to operate under the assumption that every second mattered until proven otherwise.

"Very well," he said with a sigh. "I will require an item to anchor the spell to, and a pen with which to inscribe it."

And once he had those, he would need the fortitude to not black out and destroy Basil's apartment.

He doubted Basil had *that* in a drawer, though.

BASIL HAD DREDGED up a folding compact mirror made of glossy black plastic, and Quentin had no real inclination to care whether or not it was a suitable object; it was large enough for all the required sigils, as well as portable, so it would have to do.

The difficulty was, now that he had something to cast the spell on to, he had to actually do so.

Stay calm.

Go to Los Angeles.

God, he was still only on step one of his plan, and now he had to insert *Use magic* as a new step two.

Laurence needs you. You can do this. You must *do this.*

Quentin huffed at himself. He had grown reasonably accustomed to sex. He had challenged himself, done what he needed to, and now he was able to communicate his needs and his boundaries. He had not gone about it the best way, perhaps, but he was capable of enjoying himself without destroying the bedroom, and he was improving all the time.

Magic was always going to be next. Neil had already ribbed him about it, and he did not have the luxury of putting it off any longer. This was not a theoretical scenario. All he needed to do was switch his brain off and follow instructions, and hopefully once he regained a modicum of awareness the task would be complete. It was a trick which had worked several times while he was still becoming accustomed to intimacy, and he could use it now.

Laurence had sounded as though he were in pain. Perhaps he was already...

He ground his teeth and focused on the pen in his hand. If he was too late, he still had to do this so that Vincent Harrow could be made to pay for his actions.

But if he was *not* too late, he had to stop farting around, lest it *become* too late. He could not mess it up, either, or they would have to find yet another item Basil could live without, and Quentin didn't want to resort to saucepans or dinner plates.

The best, most logical course of action was to get it right the first time.

"Very well," Quentin sighed. "Some quiet, please."

Basil mimed zipping his mouth shut. Jon remained absolutely still.

Quentin placed the mirror on the kitchen table, his phone beside it, and uncapped the Sharpie.

Then he tuned out, and got to work.

46

LAURENCE

Laurence was only dimly aware of the world around him. He was consumed with rage, with grief, and still shaken from the stun grenades, the stench of Vincent, and throwing up all over Marcella's ass; paying attention to where he was going was way down his list of capabilities.

He got jolted and bounced, then there was fresh air, gravel crunching, footsteps. It was dark, with the occasional sound of distant traffic or a dog barking. Then, without warning, a sanctum threshold was crossed, which set his head spinning all over again.

Now the distant sounds were gone, and the smell was back. Laurence groaned and tried to look around, but tears blurred his eyesight and the stink of his own vomit on Marcella's clothes only made it worse.

"You're fine," she said. "Nobody's going to hurt you."

"That's a lie," he hissed through gritted teeth.

Marcella shrugged, and walked for so long that Laurence wondered whether he'd slipped into a nightmare. Eventually, she deposited him onto a filthy wooden floor, and while Laurence twisted and turned to sit upright, she closed metal cuffs around his wrists and stepped back.

Laurence snarled. He blinked the tears away as fast as he could and pulled on the cuffs, but he heard the clink of chain, and bumped something soft.

"Will you stop it," Rufus growled. "This is bad enough without you making it worse."

Marcella turned her back on them and walked away, but another of Vincent's coven came in and set a stack of books on the floor amidst the rest of Ru's plundered library.

"Goddess," Laurence breathed as he stared at the books. "He's taking all of it! Ru…" He twisted to seek out Rufus, and found him with his back to Laurence, his arms similarly wrenched behind his back, barely an inch away. "Ru, what the fuck happened? Where…" His throat closed in. "Where's Windsor?"

"He's going to kill us, and you're worried about your familiar?" Rufus didn't sound like he had the heart to be angry.

Instead, he just sounded beaten.

Laurence gritted his teeth and faced forward. This was Vincent's sanctum all right. The enormous throne at the center of the room was maybe thirty feet away at most: Laurence and Rufus were being held in the same spot Amy had been when they'd come to rescue her. Ru faced the wall, which Laurence suspected was a deliberate choice.

"I don't understand," Laurence whispered. "How the fuck did we get here?"

"He's attached one of his doors to the house across the street," Rufus muttered. "All they have to do is cross the road. I've got no idea how long it's been there. He could've been watching my gate with his own two eyes for years, for all I know." He sighed, then added, "I don't know, and I'm not sure it matters anymore."

Laurence searched the rest of the room as best as he could, peering into the murk, trying to make out anything that might help them. "Maybe not," he agreed. "What happened?"

Ru was quiet for so long that three more piles of books were dropped off before he said a word. "I figure they used the stun grenades from the SUV," he finally muttered. "You went down so fast I didn't even notice. Sebastian hauled you into the library and shut the doors. Angela wanted us to break a window and go out that way, but she'd been relying on your gifts to get us there, and with out for the count all we could do was try and defend ourselves when they reached us." Rufus hesitated. "We failed."

Laurence shook his head slowly and let it hang forward. "That's on me," he whispered. "I'm sorry."

"How do you figure?"

"I hung back." Laurence was just about able to raise his knees, though he couldn't make out what the hell was binding his legs together. He rested his forehead against them and let his eyes close. "Goddess, I figured you and Angela were way more experienced than me, knew so much more magic than me, so I... I didn't want to get in your way, didn't want to ruin whatever plan you both came up with. I was so sure that I was in over my head, that Vincent had so many years of magic and practice and knowledge that I lacked, that there was barely anything I could do to help other than be there and do whatever you told me to. But you..." He wetted his lips with the tip of his tongue. "You've never fought anything before, and sure as hell not for your life. You've spent over a decade in hiding, reading books. You've never even gone grocery shopping on your own, and I should've stepped up. I should've recognized that it wasn't me out of my depth; it was you who was out of yours. I'm so sorry."

He heard Rufus inhale sharply, and wondered whether Ru was about to try and argue with him, but instead Ru just let the air out in a slow, deep sigh.

"You were always going to favor any plan that involved hiding in your sanctum," Laurence murmured, "because that's how you live your life. Especially if you thought you could wait for Samhain to pass: that would've given us a whole year to figure this shit out. And Angela? Man, she's so smart, but she spends her whole life chasing these vast, cosmic truths, some higher plane of existence she'd rather be on because this one's too horrible for her. She's had to fight for her freedom every single day, but she's lived with the monster so long she's never been able to face it, let alone defeat it. The best she ever managed was to not become one of his mindless coven groupies." He slowly raised his head to bump it against his knees a couple of times. "She's never used magic in combat, and neither have you. Nor have I, but if I'd seen that's where our weakness was, I could've…"

"Yeah, well. Soon I'll be dead, and you'll wish you were. At least the bird got off lightly."

Laurence bucked against the cuffs and twisted to glare at Rufus. "Lightly? *Lightly?* He's *dead*, Ru! What happened?"

Rufus still wouldn't face him. "Angela shot him," he muttered. "Once Sebastian fell, she took his gun, and shot Windsor."

Laurence stared in sheer, dumbfounded confusion. He'd assumed Vincent had murdered Win, or maybe one of his coven, but *Angela?*

"What the fuck," he gasped. "Why would she…"

He trailed off.

If Windsor had been shot, if he'd been killed with something as mundane as a bullet, that meant he'd been dispersed to Otherworld. Laurence didn't know how long it took for a familiar to reintegrate themselves once that happened, but it *would* happen, and Angela knew it. Hell, she'd been the one to explain it to Laurence, back when they were rescuing Quen from the Marlowes.

If Angela had shot Windsor, either she'd had an idea, or she was performing a mercy, but Laurence was done waiting around for his teachers to save the day. If he could only find a scrap of living plant matter in all this decay it would be something he could use, so he turned his back on Rufus and went back to desperately searching every nook and cranny he could see from his position on the floor.

"Where *is* Angela?" he asked as another pile of books got dropped off.

"I don't know," Ru replied. "They hit us with another couple of grenades, and snatched me before I could tell which way was up."

Ru obviously didn't know anything more about whether anyone else had survived the assault on his sanctum, and Laurence figured Ru was probably in shock about his fortress of solitude getting wrecked so fast, so he decided to change the subject.

"Okay. Okay... He's got us. Is there anything else he needs, or is he good to go?"

"That's it." Rufus's words were quiet. "We're already dead."

Laurence snorted at him. "You might be. But he's going to possess me, isn't he? And I'm going to be trapped in here with him, forever, while he uses my body to rape and murder and..." He shuddered violently enough that he almost fell over. "Fuck. Come on, man, we've got to be able to figure this out. How much time have we got?"

"Until he comes back? You're the Oracle, you tell me."

"No, asshole, how long does this spell take? It's got to be a ritual of some kind, right? It's not gonna be *hocus pocus switchus corpus* or he would've done it by now." Laurence spat some of the remaining taste of vomit out of his mouth and onto the grime-encrusted floor. "You know, the possession spell he's already been using was bad enough. He had to rape his victims to take them over." He bit the inside of his cheek and debated whether he really wanted the answer to his next question, but he had to know, so he asked it. "Does the permanent version need that, too?"

Rufus' silence was answer enough, and Laurence snarled.

The book piles continued to grow, but the books being placed on them now were the nasty kind, the ones Rufus kept locked up in his not-at-all-impenetrable vault, and among them he made out a slender tome that was out of place; one with the faintest of soft, olive-beige glows.

"Great," he muttered.

Vincent had taken everything worth having out of Rufus' sanctum, and if he hadn't been unstoppable enough already, he would be doubly so once he was in Laurence's body and started reading everything he'd stolen. Worse, now that the raid was done, there was no reason for Vincent not to come home soon, and once he was here he probably wasn't going to hang around on the whole body-snatching ritual.

Laurence returned his attention to searching for anything he could use to his advantage. Rufus might have given up, but there was no way Laurence was going to. He'd resist until it was too late, and then he'd spend eternity screaming in Vincent's head if he had to, but until then the only certainty he had was that Angela had saved Windsor the only way she could, so he clung to it and prayed that some of the others had found an escape route, too.

But the way that bodies had been strewn across the floor of Ru's library didn't fill him with hope.

47

SORAYA

ANGELA'S PLAN SUCKED.

Soraya assumed she had one, anyway, but the only part of it she'd heard was, "Stay down, don't move until they're all gone," and since Soraya was already on the floor by then it seemed like a much better idea than trying to get up.

It had to have been the grenades. The first couple had been loud, but outside the library, so everyone but Estelita seemed okay. The real problem came once Sebastian staggered in and fell over, and while almost everyone rushed over to find out whether he was okay, Angela had taken his gun and shot Windsor out of the air.

That sure got Soraya's attention, but before she could punch Angela's head off about it, the next grenades went off *inside* the library, and Soraya had gone down.

She didn't know how long she'd been flopping around like a landed fish. Her ears were ringing nonstop, and her eyes wouldn't stop running. It felt like she'd been this way for days, and whenever she tried to push away from the ground, her limbs turned to liquid and down became up. Once in a while she thought she saw figures stepping over her, but she couldn't focus on them, and had no idea whether they were real.

Had Angela even said that? Or did Soraya dream it up?

"Master, there is a problem downstairs."

Soraya didn't know who that was. It sounded like a woman, and it was the first voice she'd been able to hear past all the whistling in her ears, so she tried to listen in.

"What kind of a problem?" A man, a deep voice, in no hurry and without a care in the world.

"Water is overflowing from the basement."

"It's fine. We're about done here anyway. Take care of the trash, will you?"

"Of course, Master."

"No." This voice was raspy, another woman, but Soraya was sure she was Angela. "They are no danger. Leave them."

Soraya groaned faintly. She had no doubt that she was the trash in question. Maybe the others, too, if any of them were still alive.

"I raised you," the man said, half drowned out by the ringing noise. "But I do not follow your orders, Angela."

"But I could follow yours," she replied levelly.

Either there was silence, or Soraya couldn't hear what was said for some time. She clenched her jaw like she could will the tinnitus away, but it refused to go.

"That's your offer?" he asked.

"Yes. If you allow them to live, you will have my bond."

"Fine. Leave the trash, Marcella. Let's go."

Then there was nothing but the noise in Soraya's head, and she passed out.

SHE CAME TO WITH A START, and to the discovery that the noise had finally gone away. When she tried to move, her limbs seemed to work, so she pushed herself up onto her knees, then grabbed a chair. She'd meant to use it to help her stand, but the thick wood splintered in her hands.

"Ah, shit," she muttered, and tried again with a different part of the chair and a lot more concentration.

This time, Soraya made it up without causing any property

damage, and she took a shaky breath while she tried to assess the room. Half the windows were broken, glass almost totally missing. The shelves were bare, including in a small closet behind a secret door that was hanging open. And almost all the bodies were at the back of the room, furthest away from the door.

She jerked towards them, one hand on the edge of the enormous desk that ran down the center of the library to help her keep her balance, but she could see before she even got within touching range that everyone was breathing.

Well, everyone present.

She scowled and crouched by Kim first, and touched her shoulder as lightly as she could. "Kim," she whispered.

What the hell am I whispering for?

"Kim!" She raised her voice, and nudged Kim's shoulder gently. "Hey. You better not be dead!"

Kim groaned. "Feels like I am," she mumbled into the floor.

"Can we move yet?" Mel asked.

"Try and stop me." Soraya helped Kim to her feet, then wrapped arms around her and held on for dear life, using the warm body against hers to reassure herself that Kim was okay, that she was still alive.

You know this has to be how she felt in the desert, she realized.

"Worth it," Kim said, this time mumbling into Soraya's chest.

Soraya snorted at her, but didn't argue. She knew Kim had to be well aware it was the pain and fear that made her crack a joke at a time like this, so what would be the point of getting in the way of her letting off steam? Instead, she looked around again to work out who they still had, and who was gone.

Mia, Rodger, Alex, and Mel were slowly getting to their feet. Sebastian and Estelita stayed down.

Laurence, Rufus, and Angela were gone.

Soraya came to a decision quickly, and peeled herself off Kim. "Rodger, Mia, check on Sebastian. Kim, disappear and make sure the assholes are gone."

People began to move, with Mia the first to reach Sebastian, and Soraya crossed to Estelita and crouched by her side.

"Hey," she said gently. "Estelita?"

There wasn't any response, and for a horrible second Soraya thought she might've been mistaken about seeing Estelita breathe, but thankfully once she nudged Estelita's shoulder, Estelita opened her eyes and gasped.

"Oh, damn, girl," Soraya huffed. "Don't do that to me! You okay?"

Estelita grabbed her forearm and sat up sharply. Her face contorted in alarm, and she said, "What?" Then she paused, and added, more loudly, "What? Oh, god!"

"Okay, wait, stop." Soraya took hold of Estelita's shoulders and frowned at her. "Look at me."

"What?" Estelita grabbed Soraya's shoulders in return. "I can't hear you!" Then she cleared her throat, and added, "I can't hear me! Can you hear me? Oh my god this is so weird!"

Her volume was all over the place, like someone singing along to a song only they could hear through their noise-cancelling headphones, and Soraya shook her incredibly gently to try and get her attention.

Estelita stared at her.

It had to be her senses, Soraya figured. If her own ears had been ringing for ages after the stun grenades went off, Estelita must have endured ten times the damage, and now she was totally deaf. Whether it would last, Soraya had no way to know, but for now her hearing had been knocked out, and for someone with her senses it might be terrifying to hear nothing at all for what could be the first time in her life.

"You are okay," Soraya mouthed. She exaggerated the movement of her lips, hoping that Estelita caught on. "Just…" She didn't know how well *grenade* would come across, so instead she shrugged and tapped her own ear with a forefinger, then pointed to Estelita.

Estelita stared at her, then looked around the room. She sniffed the air, and raised fingers to her mouth to lick one. Then she nodded to Soraya, and pointed upwards.

Soraya gave her a nod in return, stood up, and helped her to her feet.

"They're gone." Kim reappeared in the doorway, her hands

balled into fists at her sides, and eyes hard with determination. "There's water everywhere downstairs."

Soraya nodded, then turned her attention to Sebastian, who was still out for the count. "How's he holding up?"

"Breathing in and out," Mia said. "Potentially concussed, though. Consciousness level is too low. He needs a hospital."

"A'ight. Call an ambulance. Can I move him?"

Mia shrugged. "The house is flooding. Better to get him outside than put EMTs at risk. Moving him is the lesser of two evils."

"Got it." Soraya steered Estelita across the room, then put her hand in Kim's, and pointed to the two of them. "She can't hear shit," she explained to Kim. "Hang onto her in case her balance is fucked, too, and get her downstairs, okay?"

Kim nodded quickly and offered Estelita a small smile, and Soraya moved to Sebastian so she could scoop the big guy up into her arms.

From there, it was pretty easy to urge everyone out of the room and down the stairs, and Mia and Mel worked together to help Rodger and Alex get out in one piece, but once they were most of the way down they all stopped on the stairs.

The lobby had turned into a fucking lake.

The woman had said something about this, hadn't she? Soraya wracked her brains as the half-heard conversation drifted into her thoughts, and she grimaced. "It's coming up from the basement," she said.

"And what if it's in contact with a power outlet somewhere?" Alex said.

"Mia? Mel?" Soraya looked at them both. "Is it?"

"Yes," they both said, without hesitation, then exchanged a glance with each other.

"But we might be able to do something about it?" Mia said.

"Yeah, I think so," Mel agreed.

"Get on it," Soraya said.

She watched them both crouch on the lowest available step and stick their hands in the water, and immediately heard popping, fizzing sounds from the walls. Something distant cracked, and all the electrical noises ended abruptly.

"Done," Mia and Mel both said at once. Then Mel offered Mia a high five, and Mia stared at her like she thought Mel had lost her mind.

"Oh, man," Mel whined. "Left hanging!"

"Let's go," Mia barked. She took the last couple of steps down to the floor, and began to stride through the water with a grimace on her face as it sloshed over the top of her boots. "Gross," she muttered.

Rodger stuffed his phone away and hurried down the last few steps to catch up with them. "Ambulance is on the way," he announced.

"Great. Thanks," she added to him. "Everyone outside, now."

She was the last to go, making sure nobody got left behind, and then she set off after them, wading through the icy cold water and grimacing as it saturated her socks and squished around her toes.

"Gross," she agreed to herself.

OUTSIDE WAS DRY, at least, but not how Soraya had left it. The SUV's doors were open, though the alarm had long since stopped going off. The enormous mansion didn't sit totally right, like it had suffered an inch or two of subsidence in the space of a second, and some of the windows had cracked under the strain. Others, downstairs, had blown out completely, which Soraya figured was down to the grenades.

She walked around the SUV so she could put Sebastian down much closer to the gate and save the ambulance crew having to go far to get to him, then she carefully put him in the recovery position, and tried not to let any gravel get into his mouth. Once she was up again, she checked her phone, and grimaced at it.

They'd arrived here barely thirty minutes ago. It might have *felt* like she'd been knocked out for hours, but it couldn't have been more than fifteen minutes.

Did that mean there was still time to get after this warlock guy, or was he long gone already?

"Okay," she announced to the rest of the crew. "Rodger, I want you to stay here with Sebastian and wait for the ambulance. Everyone else, we've got to find Laurence."

"And get Angela for what she did to Windsor," Mel added, as sparks flew around her fists.

There was a chorus of agreement, but Soraya held a hand over her head.

"Hold up," she said, raising her voice to get them to shut up and listen. "I don't know if any of you heard what happened in there, but Angela gave herself up to keep us alive. They were gonna kill us all while we were defenseless, and Angela made a deal to stop them. So let's just, uh, figure she did some kind of magic bullet shit to get Windsor out first. I mean, there was no body, was there? He just fucking evaporated!"

"He's a familiar," Alex said, features creasing thoughtfully. "What if they don't *leave* a body when they die?"

"You can use magic," Mel said to them. "You tell us."

"The closest thing in Norse mythology is a fylgja," Alex explained apologetically. "And very few people can see those, so we're already well outside anything I know."

Soraya grunted, then took to her phone again, and tapped away in her notes app so that she could show it to Estelita. *Do you want to go to the hospital with Sebastian and get your hearing checked?*

Estelita read it, then shook her head firmly, and wrapped her arm around Kim's.

Okay. Let me know if you need anything. She showed it to Estelita.

Estelita held out her hand, and took the phone when Soraya handed it over, then she typed away and handed it back.

I can smell them. They stink like rotten meat. We can track them.

Soraya read the note, and couldn't help but break out into a slow grin. "Okay, we've got a plan. Estelita says she can track the assholes who took Laurence, so we're gonna do that. Stay in touch," she said to Rodger, then she beckoned to the rest of them and hauled the gate open. "Everyone else, let's go."

Maybe this was a lousy idea, but it was better than standing around doing nothing, and Soraya hadn't gotten out of bed in the middle of the night to *not* kick a bad guy's ass, so she let Estelita take the lead, and fell in beside her.

She just wished she knew if the bad guy was out of grenades already.

48

QUENTIN

Everything was fine.

Quentin sat back, watching the world through a body's eyes, aware of the raised hairs on its forearms and the back of its neck as little more than a curiosity. It was speaking, reading from a phone, saying the words slowly and clearly, then it would pause here and there to write something on a small mirror, inscribing letters which were designed to be carved into stone or etched in clay, and so bore sharp angles and straight lines.

Quentin didn't even have to be here—

Yes, you do.

—because none of it involved him in the—

Yes, it does!

—slightest. And even if it did—

It does!

—it was best if it did not, otherwise things might go terribly wrong.

There. That seemed to have silenced the nagging voice which had been attempting to intrude into his safe, calm cocoon.

The body completed its task. The skin tingled, and then the hairs settled down, and everything was over.

Quentin considered leaving it behind. It made sense. There

was no knowing when the body might start doing... *that* again, and it was best to not be here if it did.

"Did it work?" The voice was distant, and sounded bored.

"I think so!" That voice was different, more excited. "Quentin?"

Quentin absolutely did not wish to respond to anyone speaking his name under such circumstances, and leaned more resolutely into the thought of walking away.

"Hey... Quentin?" A young man's face swam into the body's peripheral vision, then a hand waved in front of its eyes. "You're not gonna go postal on us, are you? Are you okay?"

"I believe that he is in a dissociative state," the other voice droned. "I do not know how to correct it."

The young man frowned, and a hand came to rest lightly against Quentin's forearm.

It's never the forearms. Never! Father knew that he couldn't risk the exposure. Summer uniform included shirtsleeves. You're safe. You're safe, don't leave!

Laurence needs you!

Quentin took a sharp breath, and the breath was in *his* lungs. This was *his* body, and Basil was touching *his* arm. He blinked rapidly as the world rushed in around him, and he managed to tear his gaze off the mirror to face Basil instead.

"I..." He blinked again. "I'm so sorry, I..."

Basil smiled tightly up at him and squeezed his arm gently. "You okay, buddy?"

Quentin inclined his head. "I shall have to be, shan't I?"

"Yeah." Basil winced and stood up, letting go of Quentin's arm in the process. "I'm sorry. I didn't get what you meant when you said you couldn't..." He broke off and flapped his hands dismissively. "Doesn't matter. You did it!" His eyes lit up with a smile. "You *did* it. Can you do the next part?"

Quentin hovered a hand above the compact mirror and gritted his teeth.

You can do this, and you will do this, and you cannot disappear from it this time. This requires control, and you have practiced control your entire life.

"I have no choice," he said simply.
You have no choice, he agreed.

QUENTIN STOOD, the compact in one hand. He had closed it, but the inscription remained on the glass, and he knew enough about magic to understand that he didn't need to see it to make it work. It simply needed to be within range of his aura, so he slipped the compact into the pocket of his trousers and double-checked the address he had chosen before he passed the notebook back to Basil.

It was now or never.

Alas, in lieu of any conscious decision-making during casting, the body had chosen to weave Basil's trigger phrases into the spell's casting. They were better than emulating his father in any way, and Quentin hadn't been present enough to choose something else. On the bright side, they were phrases he would never utter otherwise, so he stood no chance of unintentionally triggering the spell.

But it did mean that he had to talk complete nonsense.

Quentin straightened up, raised his head high, and said with all the dignity he could muster, "Get in, loser, we're going shopping."

Magic coiled around him in an instant, and the prickle returned to his skin.

HE WAS in two places at once. One was an apartment, cramped and over-filled with books, lit by a single bulb, with two men staring at him. The other was a razor-thin cliff edge overlooking an ocean, with salt air carried on a chill breeze, and a bright moon in a clear sky overhead.

Unlike when he observed his body from a distance, where he was aware of two spaces at once, both of these locations were real.

The cliff edge began to fade. His mind had been drifting, and he already started to lose track of where he was, but when he turned his attention to the cliff, it was Basil's apartment which slowly faded away, and he gritted his teeth as he attempted to concentrate on both, somehow.

The magic depends on will, he reminded himself. *If it were simply a matter of focus, Basil would have had no difficulty whatsoever.*

He raised his chin again, and put his foot down.

This *would* work. The magic *would* obey his command, because failure was not acceptable.

Both realities regained cohesion, and he released his breath slowly.

Headlights sped towards him, and he raised a hand to protect his eyes. The car horn blared out, but the car stuck with the bend in the road, and avoided Quentin by several feet.

"All right," he said carefully. "I think I have... the basics, at the very least. Would you hand me something you do not mind losing?"

"Uh," Basil said, and walked past the edge of the cliff into the kitchen.

Quentin's gut lurched, and he was about to reach out with his gifts to save Basil from the fall when he realized which of the two locations Basil was in.

Basil seemed quite unaware that he was hovering in a kitchen over crashing waves. He picked a knife out of a drawer, then brought it back and offered it to Quentin. "Will this do?"

"Let's see." Quentin took it from him, and it felt solid enough in his hand, so he turned with care and extended his arm over the cliff edge. He had to shift the core of his existence, and it felt oddly as if he were stepping onto an escalator, yet he hadn't moved his foot. Instead it was an internal sense, like balance or temperature; he simply *knew* that his physical form had swapped the majority of its existence to the place he willed it to be.

"Holy shit," Basil whispered.

Quentin released the knife, and it plummeted to the waters several meters below.

"That's as thorough a test as I am able to perform, I think,"

Quentin said. He felt a little dizzy, and the apartment began to fade. He had to exert his will once more, to reassert both locations, before he could turn back to Basil. "Pay close attention," he advised the necromancer. "This location is extremely narrow, sandwiched between a cliff edge and a road, and it is night-time." Then he brought his body back to New York and offered Basil his hand. "Are you ready?"

Basil let out a nervous laugh, but he took Quentin's hand tightly. "Sure, I think. What's the worst that could happen?"

"You could become disoriented, and fall to your death," Jon stated.

"I won't let that happen," Quentin assured them. "But for now I would prefer to only try this with one person at a time, if you don't mind?"

Basil nodded quickly, and his grip grew even tighter. "Let's do it."

Quentin inclined his head and shifted his balance without relinquishing either his determination or his grip on Basil.

Basil squealed immediately, but he also remained stock still as the tips of his hair fluttered in the wind. He swiveled his eyes so that he could look down, and only then did he wriggle his feet back from the cliff edge with slow care until the backs of his legs bumped against a poorly-constructed wooden fence which someone had tied a bouquet to. "Oh my god, this is, like…" He stared up at Quentin, his eyes wide. "Okay, okay," he said, seemingly to himself. "This is fine. Everything is fine."

Quentin couldn't help but smile softly. It was somewhat reassuring to know that he wasn't the only one who told such lies to himself.

"Are you ready for me to let go?"

Basil's throat bobbed. "Yeah. We got this. Let's do it!"

They both released their hold on one-another slowly, and then withdrew their hands with just as much care. Basil grabbed hold of the fence and nodded to himself.

"I assume that this has worked," Jon said.

"So far, so good," Quentin said. He gestured to a spot that would be safe to bring Jon to, and said, "Here, please."

Jon did as he was asked, took Quentin's hand without a word, and once he too was standing by the edge of a road on the west coast, he let go again as if completely untroubled by the experience. "Remarkable," he said, sounding as though it were anything but.

"Mmm," Quentin murmured. "Stop trying to make fetch happen."

The apartment was gone just as swiftly as the cliff had appeared, and the constant prickle of magic went with it.

"Uh, is that wise?" Basil blinked at him. "Shouldn't you stay in the apartment with the wards?"

"Very probably," Quentin agreed. "But I am willing to gamble on that being a misdirection intended to keep me out of the fight. Best if we hurry and don't linger long enough to find out whether I am wrong."

Neither of them argued. Instead, Jon assessed his surroundings, then closed his eyes and spread his arms wide. He seemed quite calm, and after a few seconds, he spoke in a low, even voice.

"Hilary Patton. I know you. Come here, now."

The wind seemed to pick up a little, though Quentin suspected he was simply imagining it. He saw or felt no other hint of spectral presence, but Basil smiled nonetheless and pulled a small, plastic trinket box out of his bag.

"You can't sit with us," Basil said as he opened the box. The prickle of magic came, and died down when the box was closed again, then Basil smiled up at Quentin and added, "Got it. Next stop?"

Quentin felt a glimmer of hope, and he clung to it as he readied himself to do this over and over again, as quickly as they all could manage it. The faster this step of the plan was complete, the more rapidly they could move on to the next one, and the sooner he would find his way to Laurence.

"Next stop," he agreed.

49

LAURENCE

Laurence heard footsteps, and this time there were definitely shoes included. He raised his head abruptly and tipped one ear towards them, where he'd already figured the door had to be, and in among the slaps of bare feet on floorboards from several people at once, he also picked out harder pats and clicks.

He closed his eyes to listen, to try and work out how many people were there.

One pair of shoes made dull clicks. They had to be flats, probably Vincent's.

At least two other pairs tapped more sharply, with duller echoes that snapped into place almost imperceptibly soon after the tap. Those were definitely heels, which were probably Marcella and one or more other women. Angela had said that Vincent had a couple of servants with more mobility than the majority, so Laurence supposed the shoes were theirs.

"They're back," he whispered to Rufus.

Rufus snorted. "Well, I'd say it was nice knowing you, but…"

Laurence opened his eyes and twisted around to peer at Ru, but Rufus kept his back turned. "Rude," Laurence chided him.

"Fine. It was okay knowing you. Would've been nicer if you weren't a package deal with Quentin."

Laurence stared at the back of his head and debated letting it slide, but if Ru was about to get slaughtered, and Laurence was next in line to lose all free will, he might as well go out with some grace. "Maybe," he said, trying to sound sympathetic. "Ru... I know I'm basically the first person you've gotten to know in ten years. If you want a relationship with anyone, crushing hard and saying nothing about it while being hostile to their partner isn't the best way to do it, but if we survive this I'm totally willing to help you get out more."

"I'm not going to make it out alive." Rufus hung his head with a sigh. "He has to use my blood to write the sigils on both of you and imbue himself with the spell, then he... I..." He cleared his throat. "I have to die at the same moment that he climaxes."

Laurence bared his teeth. "So, what, someone else has to kill you while he's..." He choked off the words and shook his head, then turned back toward the door.

The footsteps were coming closer.

But so was something else.

Laurence's breath hitched as he searched for it, for the tiny glimmer of hope he hadn't found anywhere in here yet.

There.

Someone had brought a piece of plant life in with them.

He had no idea what it was, or how useful it might be, but they were carrying it towards him and he dared to dream that it could help him get out of this shit.

Women flowed into the room. Each stopped just inside the doorway to shed what little evidence of clothing they'd been wearing. They dropped their garments into a growing pile before moving around the stacks of stolen books. They walked with blank faces, not even looking towards Laurence or Rufus, and knelt down along the outer circle around the throne, several feet apart.

Vincent was next. He kept his clothes on, and directly approached his prisoners with satisfaction radiating from his whole body.

Laurence clenched his jaw and watched the warlock come closer, but Vincent didn't have the plant. It was still outside.

"Sorry to have kept you waiting," Vincent said. "We're ready now." He circled past Laurence, and stopped by Ru, his back to the wall.

"I will prepare the space, Master," Marcella said as she entered. She, too, retained her clothes, which were far more passable than the dirty nightshirts most of Vincent's slaves had shucked.

"Not *totally* ready then," Laurence muttered.

Vincent scoffed. "I was always so irritated that Amy hadn't gotten the abortion. Who knew it would work out to my advantage?"

"Fuck you," Rufus spat.

"Unfortunately it's him I have to fuck," Vincent countered. "But needs must."

The last set of footsteps arrived, accompanied by the clip of heels and the glimmer of plant life.

Angela.

Her features were every bit as expressionless as those of the women surrounding the throne. She didn't meet Laurence's gaze, but she did approach him, her eyes fixed on Vincent. When she stopped, it was inches from Laurence's legs.

"Do you require assistance?" she asked him.

"You're forgetting something," Vincent said.

Angela blinked slowly. "Do you require assistance, Master?"

Laurence's heart sank. How long had she been calling Vincent that? Was he even really her adoptive father, or had that been a lie to cover up the true nature of their relationship?

Had she killed Windsor on his orders, not to protect him like Laurence had thought?

She'll betray us, you know.

She won't.

Laurence flexed his fingers behind his back and lowered his eyes to the ground at Angela's feet. His gift had been clear: Angela wouldn't betray them. And she *was* carrying something he could use.

This had to be a ruse on her part. He wasn't willing to believe otherwise.

"No," Vincent said. "Marcella knows what she's doing. Your job is to stay out of the way until this is done."

"Of course, Master," Angela said.

"Подчиняться." Vincent spoke the word behind Laurence, and Laurence felt time stretch and snap in a heartbeat as a spell was triggered. He heard movement, saw the warlock come to stand in front of him, and just as Laurence glared up at him, Vincent said it again.

The spell coiled around Laurence. It slid itchy tendrils in through his ears that felt like they were burrowing into his brain, and he gasped at the grotesque sensation.

"Don't make a sound," Vincent ordered. "You'll do what I say, when I say it. Now, sit still and wait for Marcella to remove your restraints, then follow her instructions." He released a toothy grin and a cheerful wave, then turned his back on them both and stalked away to the piles of books.

The writhing in his brain took over, and Laurence wanted to scream.

But he couldn't.

Angela watched Vincent walk away, then she stepped in closer, so lightly that her shoe barely made a sound. She crouched in front of Laurence, raised a hand to cradle his jaw, and gazed intently into his eyes.

Laurence stared helplessly up at her. If she was trying to communicate with him, she was doing a lousy job.

Wait...

She had something in her palm. It was soft against his skin, slightly cool to the touch, and the source of the fragment of plant life he could sense.

He blinked, and she lifted one eyebrow slightly, then used her thumb to part his lips and open his jaw half an inch. In a series of small, smooth motions, she eased the plant matter to his mouth and stuffed it past his teeth with her thumb as she leaned in closer with her head tilting aside. For a moment, Laurence thought she might kiss him.

She pushed his jaw closed and caged the tiny leaf — it sure felt like a leaf — on his tongue, then stood up, turning her back on him as she went.

"What was that?" Vincent asked.

Laurence couldn't see him. Angela was in the way. Which, he hoped, she'd meant to do.

Vincent had only ordered him to sit still. He hadn't said Laurence couldn't use his gifts, so Laurence gently coaxed a tiny fragment of his energy into the leaf to keep it alive.

"Something I have wanted to do for a while," Angela said flatly, "and will have no desire to do once his body is yours, Master."

Vincent laughed. "Well, well. Aren't you full of surprises today? Wait here, I'll be back."

"Yes, Master."

Laurence swiveled his eyes in the direction of approaching heels. Marcella had returned, key in hand, which meant he and Ru were out of time. If he tried anything right this second it wouldn't go his way: he was vastly outnumbered, *and* Vincent was in the room. Wherever Marcella was about to take them, Laurence hoped he'd be alone with her, if only for a few seconds.

That would be his final opportunity. If he could use the leaf and take her out, he stood a chance of laying some kind of trap for Vincent that the warlock couldn't get out of by destroying magic: Laurence wouldn't use any.

He prayed that the leaf in his mouth was from something tough, or else he'd be fucked.

Literally.

50

QUENTIN

THEY HAD FALLEN INTO A SMOOTH, EFFICIENT RHYTHM. QUENTIN would transfer them to the next location on Basil's list, Jon would attempt to summon the deceased, and then — if he was successful — Basil trapped the ghost. It was repetitive enough that they were through the entire list within minutes, and Quentin had allowed himself to tune out the response to every single time magic lifted the hairs from his skin. That or it happened every few seconds and he had simply become too overwhelmed by it to pay it any further mind. What mattered was that he *was* succeeding at this, so it was best not to think about it too hard.

The next destination had to be Rufus' sanctum, and Quentin wasn't sure whether the spell would take him there or to a nearby road — assuming it worked at all. He consulted his phone to glean the address from Sebastian's message, then glanced to Basil and Jon.

"I'll go first," he advised them. "If this location is indeed a sanctum, I don't know whether it will allow us to enter, and if there are defenses in place I would rather you not be hurt."

"I don't want you getting hurt either, though," Basil said with a petulant scowl.

"Time is of the essence," Jon reminded them.

Basil huffed, but he crossed his arms and dipped his chin.

"Get in, loser, we're going shopping," Quentin murmured.

The spell flared to life around him, and he immediately straddled two places at once: Griffith Park, with the twinkling lights of skyscrapers in the distance, and the subtle scent of oak and dust; and a gravel driveway with a large, colonial house looming over him, and both a black SUV and a Jack in the Green truck parked nearby.

There were no signs of a fight, and he heard nothing other than distant sirens, so he reached for Jon and Basil, then shifted them to the new location.

"Stop trying to make fetch happen," he said.

The spell was over, and he centered himself with a deep breath of the cool night air.

Jon raised his head, then moved abruptly. The gravel crunched as he walked around both vehicles, and Basil sprinted after him a second later.

Had Jon detected a ghost? Or spotted some sign of a fight, perhaps? Quentin frowned, and followed, only to notice soon enough what Jon had already detected.

Sebastian lay on the gravel, already in the recovery position. Rodger was staggering to his feet next to him, eyes wide with shock as he stared at Jon.

"Rodger?" Quentin hurried past Jon to try and mitigate some of the alarm the poor boy seemed to be feeling. "What happened? Where's Laurence?" He dropped to a crouch by Sebastian to feel for a pulse, and was relieved to find warm skin to go along with the heartbeat.

"It's all fucked," Rodger blurted, with an edge of panic in his voice. "We drove here because Laurence was going to raid some warlock's sanctum. Sebastian stopped off at a friend's to grab a box of stun grenades, then we got here and went in to hash out the plan, but the warlock arrived and broke into the SUV and used the grenades on us. It was like shooting fish in a barrel." He gestured wildly at the house. "We ran upstairs. Laurence and Sebastian hung back back to protect us, but that means they got hit first. Laurence went down, and Sebastian had to drag him into the library with the rest of us. Then it was grenades in our faces too, and—" Rodger blinked, then shook his head and waved a hand. "No, first the whole house shook, and they said the wards were getting killed. Anyway, basically once we got hit with our own stun grenades, we were done. When I came round, all the books were gone, Estelita had gone deaf, they'd taken Laurence and Rufus and Angela, and Sebastian wouldn't wake up. I called 911; an ambulance is coming. Everyone else went out." He pointed to a gate in the ten-foot-high wooden fence that hid the rest of the street from view.

It was a lot to take in, and Quentin was impressed by the clarity with which Rodger conveyed the information. It seemed at odds with his layabout demeanor whenever he was at work, so Quentin made note of the discrepancy to question at a later time, and stripped the data down to the bare essentials: Laurence had been taken, alive or dead; and if he wanted to find out more, whoever had those answers was on foot.

"All right," he said to Rodger. "Thank you. How long ago did they leave?"

Rodger shook his head. "Only, like, a minute or two, tops."

The siren drew nearer, but Quentin didn't wish to wait for it. One of his best tactical assets was out for the count, and he had the means to remedy this, so he turned to Jon and indicated Sebastian with an upturned palm. "Are you able to heal him?"

Rodger recoiled as Jon came closer, and fell onto his backside so hard that he winced. "Ow, fuck."

Jon, to his credit — or, perhaps, merely his familiarity with this kind of reaction to his presence — ignored Rodger entirely. He crouched by Sebastian and placed a hand on his neck, then another in his hair, and he remained there, holding still.

Quentin wanted nothing less than to wait here in the hope that Sebastian could be revived, but he had managed patience thus far; he could rein in his urge to rush in for just a little longer.

Sebastian groaned and began to stir, so Jon withdrew, and took several steps back until he was by Basil's side.

"Excellent. Thank you." Quentin extended a hand to Sebastian, and waited for the older man to regain consciousness enough to take it. "Concussion?"

"Repaired," Jon said. "There was also a proliferation of minor tears throughout upper body tissue, indicative of injuries caused by the blast force of a shock wave. Also repaired. Minimal expenditure required."

Sebastian finally came to and took Quentin's hand, but mostly heaved himself to his feet despite Quentin's assistance. He dusted himself down and plucked gravel off his cheek while he assessed his surroundings, then he looked Quentin in the eye. "Give it to me," he grunted.

Quentin gestured to Jon and Basil. "Sebastian, Jon, Basil. Protect them both to the best of your ability, please?"

"You got it." Sebastian patted himself down, then hurried across to the SUV and searched the back of it until he found himself a gun.

Rodger clambered up off the ground, and watched Sebastian arm himself. "Urgh," he said. "I better wait for the ambulance anyway, I guess."

Whether it was a request to not be taken into combat, or something less quantifiable, Quentin would respect his wishes. He inclined his head to Rodger. "Thank you," he murmured.

"Good luck," Rodger replied.

Quentin used his gifts to raise the latch and haul the gate open, then he stepped over the metal line embedded into the ground beneath the gate, and out onto the pavement.

QUENTIN HAD BEEN CONCERNED that he would have to part ways with his companions to search for whomever had left Rodger and Sebastian behind.

He needn't have.

The road beyond the fence was a residential street, not terribly wide by Californian standards, and on the far side of it he could see a cluster of teens — and Mia, thank goodness — gathered on the porch of a house which was just as large as the one Rodger waited outside of. Everything about the situation looked sinister, from the shadowy skulls and tombstones in the house's front garden, to the way that flickering orange lights made the dark shapes of the teens judder and slither in the darkness.

"Are they the good guys, or the bad guys?" Basil whispered.

"Ours," Quentin whispered back, unwilling to be drawn into a philosophical discussion at the present moment. He quickly checked for traffic, then strode across the street and hopped up onto the other pavement.

"Is jaywalking legal in California?" Basil huffed as he chased along at Quentin's side.

"Debatable," Sebastian grunted.

Quentin frowned faintly as he made his way up the path toward the teens, since none of them seemed to have noticed him, and he cleared his throat.

Kim and Mel were closest to him. They turned sharply, then squealed and threw themselves at him. It was enough to alert Alex, who at least only blinked in surprise instead of attempting to launch into a hug. Then Soraya and Mia turned, which prompted Estelita to do the same, and within moments Quentin was being squeezed tightly from all directions while Mia and Alex stood back.

"Shh." Quentin attempted to return hugs to anyone within reach, but he looked to Mia. "What are you doing?" He kept his voice down, lest they wake whoever was in the house.

Mia raised her chin to Sebastian. "Hey." Then she jerked her thumb at the house to answer Quentin. "Estelita followed the smell here. Of that Harrow guy," she clarified. "Apparently it's a distinctive smell. We were about to kick in the door and go rescue Laurence. You want in?"

Quentin frowned and tilted his head aside. "This seems... close, does it not?" He glanced back across the street, where ambulance lights were beginning to reflect off of windows ahead of the vehicle's arrival.

Did he really have the time to question how Harrow had set himself up directly opposite the home of a powerful witch? Would Rufus not have spotted this somehow? And if not Rufus,

Laurence, surely? If Harrow's scent was so distinctive, would Laurence not have detected it sooner?

"It does," Mia agreed, "but Estelita's one hundred percent on it." She cast her gaze across Basil, then Jon, and seemed to bristle. "Who's this?"

"Forgive me. Basil, Jon, Mia. Alex, Soraya, Estelita, Kim, Mel," he added, nodding to each teen in turn while also attempting to extricate himself from them.

The girls rearranged themselves in a flash, with Soraya and Mel putting themselves between Jon and the rest, staring up at him like they wouldn't hesitate to electrocute him whilst also knocking his head off.

"No," Sebastian said. "They're here to help. Healed me up on the spot."

Soraya sniffed, but she lowered her hands, then dug something out of her pocket and threw it to Quentin. "You went to England without this, dumbass," she grumbled.

Quentin caught it automatically before he recognized it as his wallet. He eased it into his pocket alongside the compact, momentarily baffled as to why Soraya insisted on returning it to him right this very moment, then groaned faintly to himself. Of course she thought he was an idiot; it had his protective talisman in it, and leaving hers behind had recently gotten her killed.

"Thank you," he murmured to her.

She turned and pointed at the door. "Let's go kick evil ass."

"That does sound like an excellent plan," Quentin agreed. "Jon, Basil, at the back. Sebastian, Mia, Alex, protect them. Soraya, Mel, with me. Kim, with Estelita in the middle, please."

The group parted for him as he made his way to the front door, and rearranged themselves to his order, with Kim taking Estelita's elbow. As the ambulance arrived, Quentin reached for the door of the house and shattered it into a thousand shards of wood, which he carried with him as he stepped over the threshold.

It was time for the *unleash hell* part of his plan.

51

LAURENCE

Marcella led Laurence and Rufus out through the hallway and upstairs, and while fighting her orders wasn't part of Laurence's plan, he tried anyway.

Unsurprisingly, It didn't work.

She steered them along a corridor and into a large room that could have made a decent bedroom if it wasn't bare of anything other than the sigils in the center of the floor. There weren't a whole lot of them, and they weren't contained within a circle, but Laurence smelled the lingering chemical odor of fresh marker pen: this had to be the 'preparation' Marcella had done.

Laurence focused on the leaf on his tongue instead, gently feeding his life into it and coaxing it to grow. He'd produced a slender stem, but all it did was sprout more leaves that were as tiny as the first, so he still had no idea what it could be. A fern, maybe? Did Angela think he could use a fern to escape somehow?

"Take your clothes off," Marcella said. "Leave them on the floor."

Laurence caught a look of raw fury on Rufus' face as they both began to strip, but Laurence was grateful for the range of motion the command afforded him. He pulled his t-shirt over his head, then spat the leaves into his palm while the shirt hung between his head and arms like a makeshift privacy screen.

He wracked his brains to try and identify the cutting. It didn't *look* like a fern, so he pushed even more of his life into the stem in the hope that it would take the shape of a much more useful clue, and it grew until it was several inches long. More stems sprouted, with yet more leaves, until by the time he had teased the t-shirt off his head completely, the garment was full of leaves, and he knew exactly what it was Angela had given him.

It was a Jacaranda.

Laurence dropped the shirt and moved his hand to his pants. He didn't have any choice about that. His body was doing what Marcella had ordered it to, and he shimmied his pants down to his ankles, then bent double again to unlace his sneakers so he could step out of the pants.

As he stood up again, he opened the floodgates, and shoved as much of his life as he could spare into the Jacaranda tree.

It tore its way out of his abandoned shirt, and he directed branches at Marcella with all his might while he pulled one of his socks off.

She yelped in alarm and grabbed the first branches to reach her. She twisted and snapped them, but Laurence kept on pushing, and the moment she opened her mouth again, he managed to cram a branch into it before she could trigger any spells or make him stop what he was doing.

He debated what to do now that he had her at least partially subdued. He still couldn't run out of here, and as he pulled his boxers down and stepped out of them, he realized he was all out of clothes to take off, which meant he was back to standing still and awaiting orders.

There was no way he could take the risk that she might force him to stop what he was doing, or kill the Jacaranda. That was the truth that helped him make his mind up.

Laurence commanded the tree branches to coil around her body, then wrenched it in opposing directions.

The sounds that came from her neck were like the pops and cracks of the driest firewood.

Her body went limp.

Laurence made the tree drop her and brought branches over

to himself. If he couldn't will his body into action, he would have make the tree carry it instead, like some bizarre organic exoskeleton. It encased him in branches and leaves, lifted him a few inches off the ground, and turned him so that he could see Rufus.

Ru was butt-naked, too. He eyed Marcella's body, then looked up at Laurence before he swiveled his gaze towards the door.

It could only be one person, and Laurence made the Jacaranda twist so that he could see what Ru saw.

Vincent had arrived, and he looked pissed.

Laurence flung branches at the warlock as fast as he could, pushing every last shred of energy he had into the attack. Vincent was alone, all Laurence had to do was—

"Stop!"

And, just like that, Laurence stopped. He wanted to snarl, to spit at Vincent, to tear him apart, but Vincent had got a single word out, and it was over.

No, it isn't.

Listen.

He heard faraway sounds, distorted by distance and reverberation. Snapping. Tearing. Crunching. It sounded like a small army on the march, destroying everything in its path.

"Get down on the floor," Vincent said.

Laurence stared as he worked his way free of the Jacaranda so that he could do what he'd been ordered to. By the time he got there, Rufus was already sitting, so Laurence sat by his side.

"Lie down."

Laurence lost sight of Vincent as his body laid back against the cold floor. He felt Rufus' shoulder touch his, but all he could see was dark ceiling overhead, and the Jacaranda at the edges of his vision. He heard Vincent move across the floor, then the rustle of clothes, and he wondered whether Vincent was undressing.

When Vincent came close enough to be seen, Laurence didn't have to wonder anymore, and he really wished he could look away.

Vincent was as naked as they were, with a large Bowie knife in his hand. He stepped over Laurence and straddled Ru, then sank down.

The distant chaos grew louder. Laurence was sure he heard Sebastian yell Quentin's name. Then — much closer — he heard the wet sound that only a knife slicing through living flesh could make.

"We'll have to be quick," Vincent said. "I'm sure we'd all like it better that way anyway."

The wet noise gave way to new, equally horrible wet noises. Vincent began to recite a spell, and as the universe began to hold its breath, Laurence's pulse raced.

Is Quen really here? He desperately struggled to make even the slightest sound, to scream for help and lead Quen to him, but he was as silent as Ru. Tears formed, blurring his view of the ceiling, and they tickled as they ran down his face into his ears. *Please. Please be Quen. Please be here. Goddess, please, show him where I am.*

I help?

Windsor's voice was so distant, and so weak. He seemed confused, even while he was offering aid.

Win? Goddess, Win! Are you okay?

Laurence heard gunshots and shouting, but there was nothing he could do about that, so he clung to Windsor's words with all the desperation of a man staring down the barrel of eternity as a prisoner in his own body.

Dead? Windsor's confusion rumbled across the thin, reedy connection. *Otherworld?*

Yeah. I'm so sorry, Win. I think Angela tried to protect you.

I come? Windsor was deeply unsure of this suggestion.

No. You gotta stay there, you have to heal.

You come?

No, I... Laurence hesitated. *I'm stuck,* he explained. *Bad man. He's going to possess me. I can't move, can't get away.*

You come!

The wet sounds from Ru stopped. Vincent made his way over to Laurence instead, and his chest was smeared with sigils in glistening, fresh blood.

Laurence felt sick. What if Windsor's suggestion was a good

one? Suppose it meant that Laurence wouldn't have to live the rest of eternity trapped in this body while Vincent used it to commit atrocities for the rest of time? The sound of a fight was raging downstairs, but what if it didn't end soon enough, or if Quen lost, or couldn't get to Laurence in time?

Is Samhain, Windsor added.

Vincent rested the blood-covered knife on Laurence's chest so that he could lean over and begin using Ru's blood to draw on Laurence's skin. It was warm, and the stink of it mingled with Vincent's rotten stench to drive Laurence half out of his mind.

Samhain, Laurence agreed.

The veil was at its weakest. Maybe it was weak enough for Laurence to go to his familiar in Otherworld. But Laurence was in a sanctum. Did the veil even matter here?

He stared at Vincent and unleashed the worst curse he could think of, even though it only existed in his thoughts.

May the Goddess turn her back on you. May the sickness within you devour you whole. May all your dreams come to nothing. May your past actions receive the payback they are due. So mote it be.

Then he reached for Windsor, and let his familiar drag him the rest of the way.

52

QUENTIN

The house seemed relatively unthreatening inside. The destroyed door led to a wide hallway in a Spanish colonial style, with arched doorways and a tiled floor. Much of it was smothered with fake spiderwebs, skeletal hands protruding from the walls, and plastic pumpkins which lined the edges of the floor, but Quentin found them far less unsettling than the front lawn had been.

He paused in the center of the hall and listened for anything which might tell him where to go from here, but the house was quiet, so he glanced back to Estelita.

She sniffed, then covered her mouth with her hand, and pointed to one of the arched doorways.

Quentin turned toward it and placed one hand against the door, ready to destroy it just as he'd ruined the last one, but the hairs along his forearm lifted, and he paused.

Magic.

His immediate thought was to destroy it, but if this was the entrance to a sanctum which was held in place with sigils, he might ruin his only point of ingress. He quashed the urge and pushed with his hand instead.

The door swung inwards, and he was rewarded by an outpouring of vile, musty air that reeked of decay.

"Kim, stay here with Estelita," he croaked.

"But—" Kim began.

"It will overpower her," Quentin stated. "She is safer out here."

Kim muttered something inaudible which Quentin took as assent.

He stepped through the doorway.

The planar shift was palpable. It rippled through him as he stepped from one world into another, and he had no doubt that it would leave everyone behind him a little more disoriented than it did him, so as much as he disliked doing so, he paused once he had progressed far enough to give those behind him space in which to follow.

Meanwhile, he assessed the sanctum he had entered. It seemed to be little more than a reception room of sorts, albeit with little capacity for welcoming visitors. The four walls were covered in dark, wood panels, and the floor was laminate. There were no windows, nor furniture. The only other feature was a door at the far end, facing the one he had entered through, and it was closed.

Quentin frowned slightly. This felt far too much like a killing zone, and he eyed the ceiling for murder holes or other signs that they might soon be on the receiving end of boiling oil, a hail of arrows, or magic which would wipe them out before they left this room.

He saw none, but then he hardly had Laurence's perception spells to hand.

The door closed at his back, and he checked to see who had followed.

Everyone but Kim and Estelita. Good.

Quentin looked to Alex. "Are you able to perceive magic?"

"Oh," Alex said, and blinked in surprise. "That might be a good idea." They closed their eyes and touched fingers to their own forehead, then murmured a few words before opening them again. "What do we have here..."

Quentin waited while Alex approached the door ahead, and he watched as they assessed it.

"It's everywhere," Alex said at last. They turned to look at Quentin, and their features eased into a worried frown. "This room doesn't have a lot, but the door?" They huffed. "It's like one of those movie vaults with laser beams everywhere. They've got to be alarms, if not traps."

"Are they anchored?" Quentin asked.

"If they are, it's not on this side."

"Very well. Thank you." Quentin indicated for Alex to re-take their position, and then stepped in to destroy this door, too. He shattered it completely, tore the frame out of the walls, ruined that too, and then tossed the fragments into the swarm of splinters he had accumulated thus far. "How about now?"

"Well, that did it," Alex gasped. "But there's more on the other side."

Quentin nodded, and moved through the ruined doorway into the corridor beyond, where he set about systematically destroying all the wood paneling, flooring, and decor which could feasibly hide a sigil as he proceeded.

Those ruins, though, he left in piles on the floor.

THE STENCH WORSENED the further down the corridor they went. It was so thick in the air that Quentin could almost taste it.

Perhaps if there were windows in this place, some of it could bloody well escape.

He doubted Harrow wished for anything to escape this place.

Soraya touched his arm, and he glanced to her. "Laurence," she explained. "That way." She pointed forward and up, toward the ceiling ahead of them. "He's in trouble."

"Shortcut?" he asked.

"If we're in a sanctum, the only routes that exist are the ones built into the sanctum," Basil piped up from the back. "There's literally nothing beyond these walls. Not even, like, outer space."

That sounded very much as though attempting to tear his way through the ceiling and up through the floorboards of whatever was above them was beyond Quentin's capabilities, so he ditched that idea as quickly as it had come to him.

"Forward, then," he murmured, and picked up the pace.

THEY REACHED ANOTHER DOOR, but this one opened out into a hallway, where there was more of the dark wood paneling, but also more doorways, a staircase, and flickering candle lights, so it at least seemed they had gotten somewhere at last.

If Laurence was indeed above them, the stairs were the only way up that Quentin could see, so he made a beeline for them. He did what he could to disregard the dubious stains on the floor, as well as the rancid stench which emanated from another doorway.

He was barely a handful of steps into the hall when something invisible coiled around him and held him fast, and for one absurd moment he thought he might be doing this to himself; that his telekinesis had misfired. A second later, as his skin prickled and tensed at the contact, he realized instead that this was magic, and he gasped at the hot, writhing touch against his skin.

"Ah, fuck," Soraya grunted. "What the shit?"

"Tactical error," Sebastian called out. "Wreck it, Quentin!"

Quentin gritted his teeth. In his haste to reach Laurence, he had neglected to tear the hallway apart first, and with magic feeling its way over his scars and touching his *everything* it became increasingly difficult to concentrate.

He lost hold of his swarm of splinters, and they rained down onto the floor. Wood hit wood, and it sounded like hailstones.

You aren't about to allow this second-rate warlock to beat you, surely?

Quentin had no answer to that. He had been through — and even used — an awful lot of magic in the last half hour. It was far beyond any previous limit he had been able to surpass, but now the magic was *touching him* and he couldn't process it.

There is a simple way to stop it, the voice reasoned.

Quentin knew what that was, so he rocked his jaw and asserted his will.

Wall panels cracked, shattered, then caught fire as a gust of wind blew them into the room the stench came from. Floorboards splintered and tore themselves asunder. Sconces fell from the walls, then twisted and glowed as they followed the rest of the burning detritus until there was nothing left in the hallway but the bare bones of a ruined floor, with smoke and sawdust in the air.

The magic which had trapped him was gone.

Quentin heaved for breath as his skin continued to twitch and spasm after the magic's touch, then coughed at the dust he inhaled. By the time he wiped tears from his eyes, there was a horde of naked women rushing towards him.

So he was less alarmed than he might otherwise have been when Sebastian began to shoot them.

53

LAURENCE

Most things vanished: the stench, the sounds of fighting, the anticipation of a universe that waited for magic to be cast. All were replaced in a heartbeat by the cool, soft grass under Laurence's back, the distant chatter of ravens, and leaves rustling in a faint breeze.

What didn't disappear was the weight across his hips.

Laurence blinked swiftly and stared up at Vincent, who had stopped chanting, and sat with his lips parted in shock.

Laurence gritted his teeth. It was a movement he hadn't managed to make a moment ago, so he tested his freedom with a slow flex of his fingers.

It worked.

He grinned slowly. He knew this forest — knew it as intimately as he did his own bed — and he belonged here.

"Run," he whispered to Vincent.

Vincent grabbed at Laurence's chest, then staggered back as his shock twisted into alarm. "The knife," he breathed as he shook his head. "Where is…"

"You don't have one." Laurence sat up slowly and glanced down at himself, but there was no blood on him here. He had no idea how the hell Vincent had come along with him, but he didn't care.

He deserved a hunt, and he was going to get one.

"Run," he spat more forcefully as he twisted onto all fours. He dug the balls of his feet into the welcoming earth.

Vincent stumbled to his feet. "Stop!" His voice shook, and he tried again. "Stop!"

Laurence didn't stop, and he laughed with glee as he rose from the ground far more slowly than Vincent had. "What's the matter? Spell stuck to my body? But my body isn't here, asshole, and neither is yours. *Run!*"

Vincent's lips drew into a snarl, and for a split second, Laurence thought the warlock might charge him.

He didn't.

Laurence sniffed the air and picked out the thin thread of fear Vincent shed like sweat, and he felt alive.

Eager.

Ready.

Vincent turned tail and sprinted into the darkness of the forest.

Laurence watched him leave. His heart sang with the hunt, but he held out an arm and waited for Windsor to land on it.

His familiar fell out of the sky like a brick. His claws dug in as he grabbed Laurence's forearm, and wrapped his wings around it for good measure. "Fuck!" he croaked.

Laurence blinked, derailed from his need to hunt, if only for now. He drew Windsor to his chest and ran a hand down his back, only to find that the bird was missing patches of feathers. Other areas were covered in the pins he'd first sprouted as a baby. He gazed down at the sorry state of his bird, and hugged him tenderly.

"I'm so sorry," he whispered. "Goddess, Win, I'm sorry."

"For what?"

The deep voice was unmistakable. Laurence whirled on the balls of his feet to face Herne as the god emerged from the trees.

Herne smiled warmly at him. "Did *you* hurt him?"

Laurence shook his head vehemently. "No! Never. It was someone else. I'm hoping she did it to keep him out of the warlock's hands."

Herne frowned. "He can come here whenever he has a message for me."

"Yeah. I don't think she knows that." Laurence swallowed tightly. "Can you help him get better?"

"I am no healer," Herne rumbled apologetically. "But I will care for him while you are gone." He reached for Windsor with his enormous hands.

Laurence leaned down to kiss the top of Win's head, and then he handed his familiar to Herne. "I'm sorry. I better go get that fucking warlock. I don't even know how he's here."

Herne cradled Windsor carefully, and Win cooed to himself as he settled into Herne's palms. "You are bonded together," Herne mused. "Where one goes, the other must follow."

Laurence flexed his jaw. "The ritual," he muttered. "I have to stop him before he finds a way back to finish the job." He lifted a hand to Herne's arm and squeezed it a moment, then turned to leave.

"May your hunt be fruitful," Herne said. "So mote it be."

Laurence cast a glance back to the god, thanked him with a nod, then gave himself over to the hunt.

THE TRAIL WAS STARK: a thread of sickness and of terror that wove through the forest so brightly that Laurence could almost see it.

He chased after it, sprinting around trees and leaping over fallen branches with all the ease afforded to him by keen agility and even keener senses.

To begin with, a handful of ravens joined in, chattering and cawing with excitement, but soon most of them had left him, either to stay behind or to race ahead. One remained, and settled in to match his pace as it flew overhead. He heard them all as they chattered back and forth like they were relaying messages along a chain.

They probably were.

Laurence flowed through the forest like he'd become one with it. He didn't need the raven to guide him; Vincent's stink was close now. Soon Laurence would be on him, and he would kill without mercy.

That was the hunter's way. Laurence took no pleasure in the killing; only satisfaction. But the hunt itself? It was *life*. It pounded through his veins. His heart thrummed to it. His senses were so finely honed that nothing could escape him, not unless it left one world behind and went to another, where Laurence couldn't follow.

A shape crashed its way through the forest up ahead, pink and naked and vulnerable.

The trail led straight to it.

Laurence laid eyes on his prey. It couldn't see him yet, and Laurence pushed himself to his limits to catch up. There was a time for stealth, for patience and silence.

This was not it.

Vincent stumbled as he ran. He cast a look of panic back over his shoulder, his eyes wide as they searched for his pursuer, and the stink of fear sharpened.

Laurence howled with joy as he launched out from the shadows. He threw himself at Vincent with all his might, and coiled arms around the broader man's waist, then kicked a knee out from under him and used his weight to drag them both to the forest floor.

Out of nowhere, a chill seeped into his bones. It felt eager and excited, like it wanted to help him kill Vincent. Maybe it was some fragment of a wild hunt. Laurence didn't know, but it was as thrilled as he was, so he welcomed it.

Branches overhead shuddered as ravens landed in them. Their raucous cawing sounded like they approved of the battle below.

Vincent writhed in Laurence's hold. He grabbed blindly at the ground around himself until he found a tree branch, but when he picked it up, his whole body jerked.

The branch fell to the forest floor.

Laurence had no such problem. The chill inside his bones took control of his arm, and his fingers closed around a branch he hadn't even noticed. It was crooked and covered in lichen, almost a foot long, but the edge was jagged and that was all he needed.

Vincent tried again. He picked up his branch, but this time his arm jerked through the air and made a sickening *crack* before the branch he threw away hit a tree trunk.

The ravens screeched loudly like they greatly enjoyed this turn of events.

"What the fuck," Vincent howled. "What are you *doing*?"

"Revenge," whispered a woman's voice.

"Revenge," agreed another.

"Revenge," a third chimed in.

There wasn't anyone else here. Laurence saw nobody, smelled nobody, but now the word *Revenge* grew louder. More voices joined in, overlapping and chanting and demanding and sobbing, and the chill in his bones pulsed through his body in time with their mantra.

It wasn't in his soul, he realized; this body he had here in Otherworld, with the branch in one hand, and Vincent under him.

The chill was in his physical body; the one still in Vincent's sanctum.

It was weird. Just like when Mikey had injected him with heroin to pull him out of Avalon, Laurence felt it, but he saw nothing, and as the chill intensified, the voices — the *women* — grew louder.

Revenge.

Laurence bared his teeth, and together with the voices, he drove the jagged branch into Vincent's gut, then twisted it up through his diaphragm and jabbed for the heart — or for whatever swiveled lump of meat the warlock had in its place.

Vincent gurgled at him, and grabbed at him with fingers curled like claws, nothing but terror in his eyes.

A second later, and the forest was gone. The sweet, clean air was gone. The branch in Laurence's hand was gone.

Instead, what he held was the hilt of the Bowie knife, and he was up to his wrist in Vincent's gut.

Laurence yowled in triumph as he shoved the warlock off himself, and kicked against the floor to roll onto him so that he could continue to ravage Vincent's insides and carve up his organs.

Revenge, crowed the voices in his head.

"Revenge," he agreed as the body around his hand went slack.

Vincent's corpse gazed sightlessly at the ceiling, and his blood stopped oozing out around Laurence's fist.

The chill abandoned Laurence's bones. It dissipated into the air like it was free at last, and the voices went with it.

Laurence shuddered with relief.

It was over.

54

LAURENCE

"Now," Quentin said.

Footsteps flooded into the room.

Laurence rasped for air. He wanted to take his hand out of Vincent's body, he really did, but he also didn't, like if he broke the connection, Vincent might spring back to life. So all he did was stare at the body and wait for it to do something.

Warm skin touched his own. It spread across his back and draped around his shoulders, and as Laurence looked at it he saw the scars that ran all the way to the thin arm's elbow, and the smattering of dark hairs along the forearm to the wrist.

He blinked.

"Quen," he croaked.

"I'm here," Quentin whispered.

Laurence tore his attention away from the bare arm. He turned in Quen's hold until he could see into those pale, ethereal eyes, and he searched them, though he couldn't figure out what for.

Quentin's brows tugged together. He cupped Laurence's cheek with his other hand, and leaned in until his forehead rested against Laurence's. "You're safe," he said quietly.

Laurence closed his eyes. He let himself unwind into Quentin's arms, to bask in his warmth, and his fingers slowly loosened around the hilt of the knife until his hand slid free and landed against the floor.

The enormity of what he was safe *from* hit him. His muscles began to shiver, to tremble, as the fight bled out of him, and he let Quentin bear his weight as he took deep breaths and did his damndest not to cry.

"Rufus," he groaned.

"Jon's taking care of him," Quentin murmured. "He'll make it. Are *you* all right?"

"No." Laurence let his eyes drift closed for a moment. "Let's get the fuck out of here."

"Of course, darling." Quentin pressed lips lightly to the top of Laurence's head, then he pulled back enough to sift through the pile of clothing he pulled across the room and into his lap. He picked out Laurence's items and handed them to him before turning slightly and passing the rest to Rufus.

"As cavalry go," Ru said quietly, "you aren't the worst."

"You are most welcome," Quentin replied, just as quietly, though he turned back to Laurence the moment he did so.

"Your house is flooded," Soraya added. "Basement and first floor, anyway. Nothing we could do about it."

Laurence pulled what remained of his t-shirt on quickly, and used the scraps of cotton to try and rub off some of the blood on his chest while he was at it, then he wriggled into his boxers. The rest he could pull on with slightly more care once his privates were definitely private again.

Quentin helped him to his feet, and Laurence wrapped arms around him for a tight hug before it even registered that Quen was wearing a thin tank top and missing his sling.

"Wait..." Laurence pulled back and looked him over at last. "You... What?" He rested his hands on Quen's waist and gazed at his shoulder, where there were definitely some new scars, but they were fully healed, without any bruises or swelling to show how recent they were.

"Jon is a child of Arawn," Quentin said simply.

Laurence ran his eyes down Quen's chest to assess him for any evidence of injury, then hissed through his teeth when he realized how much of Vincent's blood he'd smeared all over Quen's clothes. "Right, right," he mumbled. He remembered Arawn healing his broken wrist and the wound in his side from Gwyn ap Nudd stabbing him pretty much the same way he'd stabbed Vincent, and he gasped. "Oh, shit! He fixed your shoulder? And…" He twisted to search for Ru, who was barely three feet away: pulling his pants up, instead of bleeding from whatever wounds Vincent had inflicted on him.

Only then did he see how many other people were crowded in here, too, squeezed into what space was left after the Jacaranda tree's branches had swallowed half the room. He turned slowly and took in Sebastian and Mia, Jon and Basil, Soraya, Mel, and Alex, and tried not to think too hard about how many of them might have seen his junk.

"Angela? Kim?" Laurence asked. "Estelita? Rodger?"

"Downstairs, outside, outside, and dealing with the ambulance he called for Sebastian," Basil chirped. "Hey, Laurence! You wanna get the fuck outta here?"

"You bet your ass I do, but first we've got to go get Ru's library back." Laurence cast a final look at Vincent's body, but it had already turned grey, which was more than enough proof of death so far as Laurence was concerned.

Still, he flipped a bloodied middle finger at it, then stalked past it and made his way out the door.

THE PLACE WAS A MESS. Every piece of wall panel, every shred of flooring, every hint of furniture, doorway, or baseboard had been torn to pieces, burned, or disintegrated. Laurence picked his way along the corridor back the way he'd come, and once he reached the top of the stairs he looked over the ruined remains of the handrail to the hallway below.

That was even worse.

Angela stood by a ruined wall with her back to it, using her phone to light the space around herself.

The rest of the hallway was covered in wood shards and dead bodies.

"Goddess," Laurence breathed. "This is..."

Angela raised her head to look up at him, but thankfully had the presence of mind to keep her phone pointing at the bodies.

She looked relieved.

"Do I even want to know?" Laurence asked.

"Sebastian shot some of them, Mel and I fried the rest," Mia stated bluntly. "Quentin destroyed the infrastructure to take out any hidden sigils. Alex let us know whether Quentin had wrecked every spell so we could move on. We cleared a path room by room until we found you, then Basil..." She paused. "What exactly *was* in that box?"

"The ghosts of Vincent's victims," Basil squealed, sounding delighted that he'd been asked. "As many of them as we had time to collect, anyway."

"Huh." Laurence blinked. "Revenge," he added thoughtfully.

"That's all they would've wanted," Basil agreed.

Laurence looked down at the half-wrecked staircase, and began to navigate his way down it carefully. He tested each support strut before he shifted his full weight onto it, and picked a different spot every time one felt like it might give way. The hallway floor was no better, with ragged, cracked floorboards, and pitch-dark holes lurking beneath them.

On one hand, he'd intended to trash this place himself, before the duke could get his hands on it. On the other, it would've be nice if Quen could've at least left the stairs intact so they could get out in one piece.

Laurence reached for his phone, but it wasn't in his pockets, and he cursed under his breath at the loss of yet another one. Maybe it was in Ru's house somewhere, but he wasn't holding out much hope that it had survived stun grenades and flood water.

Beyond the bodies, the doorway to Vincent's throne room was dark, with a dim flicker of candlelight beyond that did little to brighten it.

"C'mon," he sighed. "Let's get the books, then I guess we just follow the trail of destruction to find the right doorway home, yeah?"

"Correct," Angela said.

"Man, I am going to sleep for days," Laurence muttered, and started to tread carefully over the strewn bodies of women whose names he didn't know, and who had probably been stolen out of their lives just to wind up dead at his feet. He wished he could have done something to save them, or that Mom was here to perform a rite for them.

He couldn't, and she wasn't.

"May the Goddess guide you," he said quietly. "May your next life be brighter. May you be born into a better world than the one you left behind."

It was the best he could do, but it was better than nothing, and he continued past them until he reached the throne room.

Then he steeled himself in preparation for the stink, and stepped inside.

THERE WAS MAGIC IN HERE, and it took all of no seconds whatsoever to locate it, because the duke stood by Vincent's empty throne, idly flipping through the pages of a book.

Laurence strode towards him across a room which — either thankfully or regretfully — hadn't been in Quentin's path of destruction, and ignored the gasps or hisses from everyone who followed behind him.

"Where's Mom?" Laurence demanded.

"Still with me," the duke said. "Perfectly safe." He paused with a finger between pages, and raised his head to regard Laurence, then he scanned the rest of the crowd like he was marking off a checklist in his head. "I see you succeeded," he added as he faced Laurence again.

Quentin stepped up alongside Laurence, but he didn't start yelling, and he seemed remarkably steady on his feet, too.

"You've done a lot of damage," the duke mused. "But the place needed it, frankly." He crinkled his nose in disgust as he snapped the book closed, then gestured around himself with it. "I'll take care of this. Clean it out, get rid of whatever is the source of that rancid stench. Probably left carcasses littering the place like an absolute animal." He looked Laurence over, then added, "Hm. You'll want to take care of that, I suspect."

Laurence looked down at himself, but figured the duke wasn't commenting on the state of his bloodied, tattered t-shirt. "Of what?"

"The binding." At Laurence's frown, the duke added, "Your soul?"

Laurence raised his head as the duke echoed what Herne had already said.

Vincent was dead. That should've fixed the problem, but the duke clearly thought it hadn't.

"You're shitting me," Laurence said slowly.

Rufus moved in to stand next to Laurence, on the other side from Quen. "Vincent Harrow is dead," he began, and Laurence was almost relieved that Ru thought the exact same thing as he had.

The duke shrugged. "But a demon has his soul, for the rest of time. If you don't solve—" he pointed at Laurence with the book "—*that*, Laurence will follow him as and when he also dies. You'll want to fix it, and probably fast, judging by the amount of trouble he gets into."

"How?" Quentin took a step forward, but didn't go any further. "Is there a spell? How do we do this?"

"Your guess is as good as mine," the duke said. He actually sounded apologetic, too, like he genuinely didn't know the answer and was sorry about it. "I presume that his little immortality spell was interrupted before it could finish."

"Great." Laurence scanned the piles of books, then stalked around them, searching. It *had* to be here somewhere. Vincent had studied it enough to memorize the spell he wanted, but where could he have put it once he was done with it?

There it is.

The Book of Yew lay discarded on the floor. It hadn't even been locked again.

Laurence hurried across to it and scooped it up. "It's got to be in here somewhere. We find the spell he used, then we can see what it did, and work out how to reverse it..."

"Except that now belongs to me," the duke said calmly.

"Now, hold on," Quentin began.

"Like hell it does," Ru snapped at the same time.

Laurence licked his lips slowly and bit his lower lip, then he closed the book and put it down on the nearest pile.

"You're right," he said quietly. "It does."

"This is *my* library!" Rufus argued. He stalked towards the duke and shoved a finger into his face. "And it's coming home with me!"

The duke smiled right at Ru like he was tolerating a toddler's tantrum.

"A deal was made," he said.

"A deal?" Ru spat the question out. "There's no deal that—"

"Ru," Laurence murmured.

"What?" Rufus whirled on the spot and turned his glare onto Laurence.

Laurence sighed and met Ru's anger with defeat. "That was the deal," he said, his voice low. "He kept Mom safe, and in return he gets Vincent's sanctum and everything in it."

"I'm willing to exclude the living from the deal," the duke said, as though he were granting them a huge favor.

Hell, maybe he *was*. The wording of the bargain hadn't been great, and Laurence had been too terrified of losing his mom at the time to nail it down. They'd been in a hurry, and maybe the duke had taken advantage of that, or maybe he'd just got lucky.

No way does this guy leave anything to luck.

"You knew Vincent would want Ru's library," Laurence said to the duke.

"Of course he would," the duke agreed. "It's what we all do, Mr. Riley. We seek out knowledge, and accumulate it, because knowledge is power. And now you, too, have gained knowledge."

Laurence raised his hand to run through his curls, but caught sight of the drying blood smeared over his fingers just in time, and stopped himself. "Yeah," he agreed bitterly. "I have. Will you bring Mom home, or do we have to come get her?"

"I will return her to you," the duke assured him. "You have my word."

"Okay." Laurence nodded slowly, then he turned his back on the books and made his way back to Quentin. He gazed into Quen's eyes, at the grim determination in them, and took his hand. "Let's go."

"Laurence," Rufus began.

"Let's *go*," Laurence repeated.

He set off out the way he'd come, with Quentin's hand in his, and didn't look back.

55

LAURENCE

Laurence marveled at the sheer thoroughness of the destruction Quentin had wrought on his way through the sanctum. It sure was an innovative way to deal with all the defenses, so long as nobody wanted to use the place after. He wondered how many corridors there were, how many doors out into the world Vincent had planted, and how long he'd been here at the center of his web, reaching out from it to ensnare whatever he wanted.

For now what mattered most was getting out and never coming back, so he kept his thoughts to himself. Nobody else seemed to want a conversation, and that suited him just fine.

They reached the first intact doorway Laurence had seen since leaving the throne room, and Quentin opened it for him. Beyond was a whole other world, with cutesy Halloween decorations, yet another ruined door, and Kim and Estelita sitting cross-legged on the floor. Laurence felt the threshold as he passed through it, and the girls scrambled to their feet to hug him before Kim peeled off to go hug Soraya.

Laurence desperately wanted to go home, but it felt rude to cut and run. Besides, he had a more important question. "Where's Amy?"

There was assorted mumbling and head-shaking, but no answer, so Rufus pushed through the crowd and hurried out through the wrecked door into the night air.

Laurence was about to run after him, but felt a gust of fetid air rush by, and he looked over his shoulder in time to see the doorway to Vincent's sanctum shake itself to pieces. The magic evaporated, leaving nothing more than a regular doorway in its place that led into a deserted lounge.

"If his house is flooded," Jon mused, watching Rufus sprint across the road, "he should not enter it alone. Even a few inches of water can be remarkably dangerous."

"Yeah," Laurence grunted in agreement. "C'mon."

He gave chase, and judging by the herd of elephants behind him, everyone else had come along too. By the time Laurence was across the street and through the wooden gate — though it was such a jolt that nothing happened as he ran over the brass which now sat slightly raised at what used to be the threshold to Ru's sanctum — Rufus had already opened the front door.

"Ru!" Laurence called out. "Wait up!"

Rufus actually waited, though as Laurence caught up to him he saw it might have been for the water flowing out over the front doorstep to slow down.

Laurence winced at it all. "Fuck. Where's it all coming from?"

"The house has been outside of the real world for over twenty years," Ru said quietly. "And in the real world, the earth under it was just... hollow. It's possible the ground shifted over time, even if only slightly."

Laurence nodded slowly. "Then when the house reappears, the foundations don't sit exactly right," he realized. "And your mom put those magic portals on all the water, electricity, waste..." He eyed the water that ran over his sneakers, and added, "Ew."

"A slight misalignment probably broke a sigil," Ru concluded. "Now the pipes are not matching up *and* there is no magical connection between them, so..." He gestured weakly at all the water. "My house is ruined," he sighed.

"If I may," Jon intoned from behind Laurence.

Laurence and Ru both turned to look at him. Jon stood there, on the gravel, with Basil on one side of him and Quentin the other.

"What?" Ru sounded slightly polite, which Laurence put down to Jon having saved his life.

"I am an engineer," Jon said. "Large structures are my area of specialty, but I am also skilled with electrical engineering, plumbing, structural engineering, and so on. I am willing to survey the grounds and buildings to make a full assessment of the damage and then, if you are able to fund the tools and materials, undertake the necessary repairs."

Ru stared at him. "Maybe," he said, sounding cagey.

"But in its current state I would advise that the property be considered structurally unsound," Jon continued.

Laurence winced. "In the meantime, you can stay with us?" he offered. "I mean, we're kinda running out of rooms, but we've got a couple spare still; you'd just have to share a bathroom."

The water was finally slowing down to a trickle, but the inside of the house was utterly dark and uninviting, and Laurence peered into it hoping he wouldn't have to go in.

"I'll think it over," Ru muttered, and waded into the hall.

"Was I unclear regarding the structural integrity?" Jon asked Basil.

"No, hon, you were totally clear," Basil whispered.

"I'll go," Quentin said. He leaned in to kiss Laurence lightly on the cheek, then followed Rufus into the house, and created a small ball of fire in the air to light their way.

Laurence watched them go, then turned his back on the house and spied Alex chatting to Rodger over by the truck, so instead of spending any more time standing in water that was probably full of nasty bacteria, he headed over to them to check if Rodger was okay.

And maybe find out what had possessed him to volunteer for a raid on a warlock's sanctum.

"Hey," he said gently as he approached Rodger and Alex.

They stopped talking, though not in any guilty kind of way, and both offered Laurence wan smiles.

"'Sup?" Rodger asked.

"You had to wait for an ambulance?" Laurence raised his chin. "Everything go okay?"

Rodger shrugged at him. "Seems so. I told them the guy I'd made the call for had got up and run off, and I apologized to them a whole hell of a lot. Now I guess I wait and see whether or not they fine me for wasting their time."

Laurence nodded sympathetically. "Damn. I'm sorry. If they do, let me know, okay? I'm sure Quen will take care of it." He bit the inside of his cheek for a second. "You're okay though, right? You didn't get hurt?"

"Naw." Rodger gave him a wry grin. "I might be dumb enough to jump into an SUV full of stun grenades, but I draw the line at walking into the bad guy's evil lair. You never know when you're gonna need a designated driver to get you home after your weird mystic superhero battles, so..." He shrugged. "Figured I'd tag along, help where I could, and stay out of everyone's way if I couldn't. How about you, boss? You good?" He pointedly looked down at Laurence's bloodied hand and ruined shirt, then up at him with raised eyebrows.

"Oh, yeah." Laurence wiped the hand against his pants to dislodge more of the dried blood. "It's the bad guy's blood, not mine." He glanced at Alex and hesitated, then decided to come clean and answer the question more honestly. "Small problem in that my soul is now just a little bit bound to the bad guy's, and the bad guy gave *his* soul to a demon in exchange for power, so it sounds like if I don't find a way to break the binding I end up with the demon too if anything happens to me, but that's a tomorrow me problem. Today I just wanna go home and sleep for like three weeks."

Rodger's eyes had slowly widened while Laurence was speaking, and then his mouth did the same thing. "Well, if you've got books and you need help researching, hit me up. I'm your guy.

I can get, like, totally into it. Seriously. And I do my best work under pressure, I swear."

Alex snorted. "That doesn't sound healthy."

"Maybe," Rodger agreed. "But whatever works, Boo."

Laurence held his hands up in case they were about to start a fight with each other. "I appreciate it. Thanks. I'll stick a pin in it for now, though, since Quen's dad just, uh…" He winced and glanced over his shoulder toward the house to make sure Ru wasn't right behind him. "Stole Rufus' whole library," he finished as he turned back to Rodger.

"Ohhhh, daaaaamnnnn," Rodger breathed. "That's a lot of books. Can't you just, like, steal them back?"

"I—" Laurence broke off before he could finish insisting it was impossible.

Why couldn't they steal them back? The duke *had* told him this shit went down all the time. Sooner or later he'd be expecting it, right?

Laurence grinned slowly and patted Rodger on the shoulder with his cleaner hand. "Good point. Definitely hanging on to *that* idea," he said. "I'll talk it over with Ru once he's got a home to live in. Thanks. Both of you," he added to Alex.

Alex gave a confused little smile. "What did I do?"

"You came along too, when you didn't have to," Laurence said. "You've known us all of like five days. You didn't have to help us, but you came anyway, so, thank you."

Alex's smile lingered before it began to fade, and they took on a more serious expression. "You saved my life," they said quietly.

Laurence squeezed their shoulder, too. "After you saved mine. Anyway, I just wanted to say thanks. Hopefully we'll get going soon. Though, uh, not in my truck." He winced. "There's probably a warrant out for my arrest now that I've busted out of jail."

"What?" Alex blurted.

"You did *what?*" Rodger gasped.

"Hoo boy, I am so fucked." Laurence laughed nervously, then made his way back towards the house. He stopped just out of reach of the trickle of water spilling out over the doorstep, and hoped Quen and Ru weren't at each other's throats already.

More importantly, he silently prayed that Amy Jenkins was in there, alive and well, because if Vincent had taken the time to go find and kill her, Laurence wasn't sure he'd ever be able to forgive himself.

56

QUENTIN

QUENTIN FOLLOWED RUFUS INTO THE CAVERNOUS HALLWAY. He had debated whether to elevate himself above the water underfoot, but it was barely an inch deep now that most of it was out on the driveway, and fussing over his shoes was far less important than searching for Rufus' mother.

Rufus made his way directly to the wide staircase, so Quentin fell in a few steps behind him, and did his best not to offer styling tips for the outdated decor — a task made far easier by picking out the extent of the damage done by the battle which had occurred.

There were crooked picture frames and shattered glass, bullet holes and scorch marks. If there had been any blood spilled earlier, Quentin presumed that the water must have done away with it, for he saw none so far.

At the top of the stairs, Rufus dove left along a corridor.

Quentin was about to follow when he caught sight of something on the floor, glinting in the firelight he bore with him. He crouched down to peer at it, then recognized it immediately, despite the myriad of cracks across the screen.

Laurence's phone.

He picked it up with care and slipped it into a pocket, then hurried after Rufus, since was supposed to be ensuring that the witch was safe.

"Amy?" Rufus bellowed. "Amy! Are you in here?"

Quentin sprinted in through an open door, and was brought up short by Rufus barely three feet into the bedroom, so he stepped around him and evaluated the area. It was decently sized as bedrooms went, although with more of the outdated furnishings which seemed to be a feature of this house, and a general air of abandonment. It had a double bed, which was messy enough to have been slept in and left unmade, but other than that there were no signs of life.

He reached for the light switch nearby, but it did nothing, and he chided himself for even trying.

"Rufus," he said softly.

"Amy!" Rufus finally moved further into the room and began the rather absurd process of looking behind curtains, or under the bed.

Quentin pursed his lips and stepped forward more cautiously. He swept his gaze across every surface in his search for any kind of clue as to what might have happened in here. The bedding was thrown to one side of the bed, so he looked to the other, and found a doorway near it. An en suite, possibly, or a closet. Regardless, if a person unaccustomed to sleeping here had been rudely awakened by the sound of gunfire outside their room, he doubted very much that they would remain in the bed.

He crossed to the door and turned the handle, then pushed on it gently and brought the light with him.

It was definitely a bathroom, and the shower curtain had been drawn across the bathtub, so Quentin stepped inside and made his way to perch lightly on the edge of the closed loo seat.

"Amy?" He asked softly. "It's quite all right. Vincent Harrow is dead. You're safe."

Quentin tilted his head faintly to listen, and he caught the edge of a rasping breath from the other side of the curtain, which made him let out a small breath in relief. He didn't wish to be the bearer of terrible news, and — far more importantly — he didn't wish for Rufus to have lost his mother, especially not so soon after discovering that she *was* his mother.

"Who are you?" Her voice was tiny, terrified, and cracked.

"My name is Quentin," he murmured. "I'm Laurence's fiancé. Rufus is here."

"I heard," she said quietly.

Quentin frowned softly, but before he could say anything else, Rufus barged into the bathroom and stared at him.

"What're you doing?" Rufus demanded.

Quentin turned to look up at him, and took in the wild, frantic look in his eyes, with which he sympathized entirely. He tilted his head towards the shower curtain. "Amy," he said softly, "I'd like for us to leave here, if that's all right? The house has taken significant damage, and we're concerned that it isn't safe to stay inside."

Rufus stared at him as he stormed past. He used a hand to shield his eyes from the ball of flame, then that same hand reached out and grabbed the shower curtain. He hesitated there, though, before he had pulled the curtain aside. "Amy?" he said, all bluster suddenly gone from his voice. "It's… It's me… I'm…" He grunted. "I don't wanna say personal stuff in front of this asshole. Can you come out?"

"I let you down," Amy said quietly. "I'm sorry."

Rufus turned to glare at Quentin, but Quentin simply crossed his legs and rested his hands together on his knee, then gave Rufus a gentle nod.

"It's fine," Rufus groused as he turned back to face the curtain. "I'm just glad you're safe. But he's right, we can't stay here. Can we go, and then, like… talk about this—" he ground the words out as though having feelings was the single worst thing he had experienced tonight "—somewhere else?"

Quentin heard Amy's soft sigh, and then the curtain moved, pulled aside from within.

The poor woman looked absolutely haggard. Her long, plentiful hair was a frizzy mess. Her pale skin was blotchy and uneven, and she wore only a clean towel wrapped around herself and held in place with one hand. The dark circles under her eyes made it clear that she'd had very little sleep these past few days, and skin damp from spilled tears glimmered in the firelight.

On a good day, Quentin suspected that she was radiant, but today was not a good day.

He rose to his feet and averted his gaze lest she feel unsettled by having a stranger see her in this state.

"Okay," she said quietly.

Quentin listened to the rustle and shift of bodies. Once a small, bare pair of feet appeared in his peripheral vision, he pursed his lips. There was water downstairs, and then a gravel drive. He would carry her if necessary, but she might prefer to walk out of her with her dignity intact, so he murmured, "Do you have shoes? Clothing?"

"Laurence went to try and find something for me to wear," Amy replied. "I don't know if he managed it?"

"No," Rufus muttered.

"But I have shoes," she said.

Quentin nodded a little. "Then let's start with those, and take it from there. We have vehicles outside; you needn't travel far." He hesitated, then added, "But if that is too much, I'm sure we can arrange an alternative."

"We'll see." Amy cleared her throat, then added, "I'm glad he's dead."

Quentin couldn't help but recall the sight of Harrow's naked body straddling Laurence's, with Rufus bleeding to death alongside them, and he was inclined to agree.

IT TOOK VERY little time for Amy to pull her shoes on, then she removed a blanket from the bed and wrapped it around herself, over the towel.

Quentin led the way back down the stairs as Rufus held Amy's hand, and he heard Amy gasp.

"What happened?"

"He invaded with his entire coven, raided an SUV full of grenades, and stormed the castle," Rufus muttered. "Destroyed the sanctum, trashed the wards, wrecked my home, stole my fucking library, then he was a hairsbreadth away from killing me and raping Laurence when the psycho here turned up and saved the day."

Quentin's breath hitched, and his heart began to hammer against his ribs. He almost missed a step, and was only able to catch himself by grabbing quickly at the handrail. "He *what?*"

"Part of the spell," Rufus muttered. "You... got there in time," he added more gently. "I promise."

"It's all so much," Amy said, though her voice was distant.

The ball of fire overhead sputtered and died, blown apart by the wind. Quentin gripped the handrail harder as his mind began to spiral in a catastrophic collection of *what if's*.

What if he had been too late?

What if he hadn't resisted performing the co-location spell so doggedly?

What if Laurence's soul wound up trapped with that monster, instead of in Annwn, when the time came?

"Hey," Rufus yelled in his ear. "You're gonna bring the house down on us, dipshit!"

"Quen?" Laurence called from further away. "It's okay, baby, I'm right here! Everything's okay!"

"I have to go," he breathed faintly. He took in lungfuls of air to try and steady himself enough for what needed to be done, and — once he was sure enough to proceed — he added, "Get in, loser, we're going shopping."

For one second, he was both in the darkness of Rufus' hallway, and the crisp sunlight of the English countryside.

Then he shifted his balance, and left the dark behind.

IT WAS APPROACHING MIDDAY, according to the position of the pale sun overhead. The sky was dusted with thin clouds that grew more grey towards the distant horizon, but Quentin turned his back to that and gazed up at the vast, bloated building he had grown up in.

He lived in a house in San Diego which Laurence considered enormous, yet which was running out of space. Father rattled around in this one with over a hundred rooms to spare, and all of them were as empty as his heart.

Quentin allowed the cool autumn air to permeate his lungs and caress his skin, and he used it to calm himself, to sweep away the chaotic clamor of outcomes which had not taken place.

Laurence was safe.

Harrow was dead.

Quentin shivered a little as he regained his composure. It was, in fact, bloody cold out here, and the sooner he got inside the better, so he strode across gravel to the front doors and banged on them until Thorne let him in.

Her training was impeccable. She didn't so much as flicker at the sight of him there in his undershirt smeared with blood, or allow her gaze to linger on his miraculously-healed arm.

"Myriam," he said as he stepped inside. "Where is she, please?"

"The library," Thorne said.

"Thank you. And Michael?"

"He had to depart little under an hour ago," she advised him.

Quentin nodded and hurried across the Great Hall to the east corridor, then along it to the nearest of the entrances to the library, only to skid to a halt in the doorway at the sight he found there.

Father stood, exactly as he had only minutes ago, book in hand as he idly flicked through it. More and more books popped into existence around him, building up new piles on the floor to join all the other stacks which were already on the floor.

Myriam was sitting on the sofa nearest to Quentin, watching the duke, though she looked up to Quentin as he arrived, and let out a soft gasp.

"Quentin?" Myriam leapt to her feet and hurried to him.

"It's done," Quentin murmured. "Laurence is safe. Harrow is dead." He took her hand and squeezed it, but his gaze was on his father. "Those books belong to Rufus," he added.

"Most used to," Father said without looking up, "but by no means all. Many were Harrow's own collection."

Quentin watched the collection continue to grow. Perhaps Father was using a secondary spell to move books without touching them, but Quentin suspected the far more likely scenario was that his father was using his telekinesis to come into contact with the books and shift them from one location to another, which was far beyond what Quentin would have considered possible if he hadn't seen it with his own eyes.

But he had come here for two things, and he would not leave without them.

He glanced to Myriam as he took a step towards his father, and she offered him a gentle nod as she squeezed his hand, so he returned his attention to the books and continued his approach.

It did not take long to find the one Laurence had picked up in Harrow's sanctum. A relatively small number of the tomes here were as grimy and grotesque, and even fewer were bound in brass. Quentin laid eyes on it, then stopped a foot away and looked to his father.

"I'm taking this one," he said calmly.

Father paused, and raised his head to peer down his nose at Quentin. "Are you, now," he mused.

It didn't sound like a question.

"You should return Rufus' library to him." Quentin reached for the wood-covered book with his gifts and separated it from those around it, then drew it through the air towards himself. He wasn't willing to let it come into contact with his skin, but perhaps if Father could transfer a whole library from one place to another without using his hands, Quentin could at the very least relocate a single book.

"He is welcome to come fetch it himself. Or, at the very least, try." Father snorted softly. "Foolish child couldn't even protect it. He has no right to claim it as his own." He continued to gaze at Quentin, though perhaps for the first time that Quentin could remember, his expression bore something other than disappointment.

Instead, he seemed pensive, and Quentin didn't like that at all.

"I shall pass on the message," Quentin advised.

Then he said the words, and his father was gone.

57

LAURENCE

Time snapped back into place. Quen vanished.

The wind cut out immediately, and Laurence splashed across the hallway to grab at the empty space where Quentin had been. He slipped on the tile floor and caught himself with the handrail, gasping.

Did *Quentin* do that?

It sure felt like he had, and looked it, too. He'd quoted a line from a movie Laurence was sure Quen had never seen, then disappeared into thin air, and...

Laurence swallowed tightly and stared up at Ru and Amy. "He used magic?"

Rufus huffed. "Oh, your unhinged boyfriend nearly kills us all, and your problem is he used magic to *stop* himself from finishing the job?"

Laurence stared at him. Rufus *knew* Quen was terrified of magic. But maybe he didn't grasp exactly how scared of it Quentin was.

No, he knows. He learned that when we came back from Hades.

"We've got to get out of here," Laurence said. He could worry about the rest of it once they were safely outside of this death trap. Ru's home hadn't had any maintenance since Paula and Todd died, and maybe not even since Paula had taken it out of the world and tucked it away in its own little bubble, so the time to absorb the fact that he'd just witnessed Quentin trigger a spell was *not right now*.

He righted himself and tested his footing on the wet floor tiles, then let go of the handrail, and looked at the sheets Amy was wrapped in.

Fuck. He'd tried to get her some clothes, then gone straight from arrest to jail to freedom to almost becoming a warlock's new permanent body before he'd found any.

"Let's get you to the SUV," he added with a nod to her. "Then we can drive you wherever you want to go."

"I don't want to go home," Amy said. She stepped onto the hall floor with care, hanging on to Rufus' hand and using her elbows and armpits to trap the sheet in place. "I don't think I can go home. Not right away."

Laurence totally understood. He'd seen the way Harrow had broken in and taken her, and he wasn't sure he'd want to go back to that place straight away, either. "Yeah, I get it," he assured her. "C'mon. We can all go back to mine, get cleaned up, have something to eat, then rest, okay?"

She nodded to him, and he followed as Ru steered her out of the house and onto the driveway.

Wherever Quen was, Laurence prayed that he wouldn't be gone for long, because the one thing he needed right now way more than sleep or a shower was to be in the arms of the man he loved.

THERE WAS ONLY SO much room in the SUV, even after all the empty crates and boxes got moved into Laurence's truck. Rodger gladly took the wheel, and once Amy and Rufus were comfortably in the back, the rest of the teens piled in around them, and Sebastian took the passenger seat up front. That left Mia, Angela, Jon, and Basil without seats. Alex had offered to turn themself into a boa constrictor so they could free up a seat, but everyone still standing had refused the offer.

Laurence hefted the gate out of the way so that Rodger could drive out, then he closed it again, and headed back to the others.

"If you wanna take the truck—" he began.

Time slowed, and Quentin appeared in front of him, with one hand in Myriam's, and the Book of Yew floating inches from his shoulder.

"Stop trying to make fetch happen," Quentin murmured.

With his last syllable, the world resumed as though nothing had happened.

"Motherfucker," Mia gasped. She'd bounced into a defensive stance faster than Laurence had ever seen her move, and she huffed at Quentin. "Is this what you're going to be like now? Appearing and disappearing without any warning?"

"There was warning," Angela said dryly.

"To be fair, you gotta be able to sense magic to know that," Basil chimed in.

"Bambi!" Myriam rushed to Laurence and drew him into a tight hug. "Goodness, you look dead on your feet."

"Mom," he gasped as she crushed the air out of his lungs. He wrapped his arms around her, and took his eyes off Quen to bury his face against her hair. "Thank the Goddess that you're okay!"

"We have so much to talk about, dear," she murmured to him as she gently swayed him in her arms. "But not right now. You must be exhausted."

"Yeah." Laurence freed his face from her hair, sought out Quen, then drunk in the sight of him: scarred arms on display; his hair wild and unkempt; and the book still hovering near his shoulder.

Laurence blinked, then untangled himself from his mom, and hurried over to hug Quentin tightly instead. He sagged against that slender chest, and into those thin arms, and he breathed, "Thank you."

"It's all I could retrieve," Quentin said apologetically. "Father says that if Rufus wishes to recover the remainder, he is welcome to — ah — try to do so himself."

It wasn't what Laurence had meant to thank him for, but he was too exhausted to explain, so he nodded against Quen's healed shoulder and hung on tight. "Let's go home," he mumbled.

"But not in a truck that'll get us arrested," Mia added from behind him.

Laurence groaned. Bed had seemed within reach, and now it was so far away again.

"It's fine," Basil said. "We've got another option."

"It's true," Jon agreed.

Laurence felt Quen's body tense slightly. He pulled away just enough to lean back and make eye contact, but before he could say anything, Quen spoke instead.

"Get in loser," Quentin said, sounding like he'd had enough of those words for a lifetime, "we're going shopping."

Then Laurence was in his own backyard, with the soft crash of the ocean at his back, and for the weirdest moment he could see Ru's house and his own coexisting in the same space.

Then there was only his own home, and he stared at Quen as — one by one — Myriam, Basil, Jon, Angela, and Mia appeared on the lawn around them until, with a soft sigh, Quentin murmured, "Stop trying to make fetch happen."

Laurence shook his head numbly. Angela had said this spell of the duke's took intense willpower and concentration from one second to the next, and Quentin was using it like he'd been practicing for years. Even more breathtakingly, he seemed almost at ease with it, and was still managing to suspend the Book of Yew in the air at the same time.

Ah, Goddess, not now!

Laurence gritted his teeth as his dick decided this was a great time to wake up, and he grabbed the grimoire so Quen didn't have to hang on to it anymore. "Baby, you're amazing," he breathed. "But if you don't mind, I want to get this somewhere safe, take a shower, and go the fuck to bed."

"Of course," Quentin said quietly. "I quite understand."

Laurence eyed him, but it was clear that Quentin was crushing everything down into a box to keep a lid on, and now wasn't the time to try and open it. He'd heard what Ru said to Quen, knew damn well what had set him off, and Laurence would have lost his shit just as much if he'd found out Quen had been moments from...

He swallowed and turned to the hedge that led to the back door, then hurried around it so that he could get inside and try not to think about how narrowly he'd avoided another assault.

LAURENCE DIDN'T WANT to sully his altar with the book, and he sure didn't want it in his bedroom either, so he wound up taking it up to his den and stuffing it away behind a potted parlor palm. He'd have to find a better place and cleanse his space after, but it would do for now.

That done, he headed back down to his own room and made straight for the bathroom, where he ditched his shirt straight into the trash, and his pants into the laundry basket. He made sure the shower wasn't too hot, stepped in, and rinsed Vincent's blood off his hand and Rufus' from his chest.

The water only ran a little pink between his toes, and Laurence hung his head under the stream while he watched it swirl away down the drain.

His night had been non-stop. A rollercoaster of adrenaline and panic, hunter and hunted, and now he was off it at last his body wanted so desperately to collapse into a quivering heap.

And what about Quen? Laurence didn't even know what he'd been through, but whatever had happened had pushed him so far that he'd used magic, and somehow managed to draw Basil and Jon in, too.

Laurence let his eyes close. He thought briefly he could try to find out whether sleeping while standing up was all it was cracked up to be, but he *really* didn't want any speck of blood left on him before bed, so he forced them open and reached for the shower gel.

His deal with Rufus was through. They'd tracked down the man who murdered Ru's parents, and Laurence had killed him — thanks to timely help from the ghosts of Vincent's own victims. Rufus had been his teacher, but now Ru didn't have a library or even a home, and Laurence wasn't going to ask for lessons from a guy whose entire world had fallen apart.

What he *would* do was help Ru rebuild his life. Maybe even get him out into the real world more. And *definitely* suggest he get therapy. After all, Ru was sitting on all the money his parents had left behind; he might as well put it to good use.

Satisfied that he had enough of a grip that he wasn't about to start crying in the shower, he washed himself thoroughly, then left the cubicle to towel himself off and go brush his teeth.

Finally, he tucked himself up in bed to wait for Quen, but passed out the moment his head hit the pillow.

LAURENCE

Laurence became dimly aware that he was tightly tangled up in a knot of limbs and sheets. He was snug, safe, and extremely reluctant to regain more consciousness than he already had, so he attempted to burrow his head down and pretend he hadn't noticed a thing.

It didn't work. All that happened was an increasing awareness of the soft breathing and comfortingly familiar scent which enveloped him, and Laurence had no alternative but to admit to himself that he was waking up. He let his eyes open slightly, since they seemed so desperate to, and gazed at Quentin in the subdued light of the bedroom.

Goddess, he was beautiful, even before he got all his grooming done. Maybe *because* he was all wild hair and faint stubble right now, which would all be tamed and controlled by the time Quen got dressed.

Quentin's lips twitched faintly, though his eyes remained closed. "Are you staring, Mr. Riley?"

Laurence laughed. "I sure am, Mr. Riley."

Quentin's eyes drifted open, and his fingers traced tiny circles in the small of Laurence's back. "Would you like me to leave you be so that you can rest some more?"

"Nah." Laurence leaned in to kiss him lightly, but as Quentin responded in kind, the kiss deepened between them until Laurence's head reeled and his heart raced. He gasped when he pulled away, and eyed Quen. "Well, okay, I guess that's one way to make sure I don't go back to sleep."

"Mm. I'm afraid that I have another." Quentin's gaze clouded slightly, which meant his other way of keeping Laurence awake wasn't going to be sexy.

"Go on," Laurence prompted him.

"According to Martin, the police arrived in the night to try and arrest you. You weren't here, and he told them as such, but apparently they've had a car outside ever since. Presumably they are waiting for your return."

Laurence jerked back and sat bolt upright even as he tried to untangle his legs from Quentin's. "Oh, shit," he gasped. "Shit!"

He was wide awake now, and his feeling of security was abandoning him in a rush. Goddess, they were expecting him to come home through the front door, not to teleport in via the back yard, and if he didn't show sooner or later they'd go get a search warrant, and if Laurence was still here when they did, Martin would be charged with obstruction, Laurence would get hauled away in handcuffs, and he'd never make bail because he'd already proved he was a flight risk.

Panic crawled up his spine, and he threw his bedsheets off.

"Laurence," Quentin said softly.

"This is bad," Laurence insisted. He stumbled out of bed and onto his feet, and was halfway to the curtains before he realized that if he opened them to check for cops, the cops might also spot him. "Freddy." He snapped his fingers and turned to face Quen. "Freddy said he'd get me a lawyer."

"I'm sure he has it in hand." Quentin eased out of bed and slipped fingers through his hair to push it back from his forehead, then walked around the bed. He approached Laurence, offering his hands, which was when Laurence finally took in that Quentin was wearing pajamas. "Look at me."

Laurence grabbed his hands and did everything he could to shake the sense of imminent doom that permeated his whole body. He drew deep breaths as he gazed into Quen's glasslike eyes, and allowed himself to luxuriate in the feel of Quentin's thumbs rubbing across his knuckles.

"I won't allow them to take you," Quentin stated.

"We can't—" Laurence's protest died under the absolute conviction in Quen's gaze.

"I will not allow them to take you," Quen repeated calmly. "You have had an awful night, after a frankly terrible week, and if they attempt to come in here and arrest you, we shall simply…" He inclined his head. "Be elsewhere until Frederick has dealt with it."

Laurence wanted to protest, but he didn't have the heart, and Quen was *super* hot when he got this way. Even hotter once Laurence realized Quentin was basically saying he'd just teleport them somewhere else and let the cops search an empty house.

He blinked slowly. "You used magic," he breathed.

Quentin's nose crinkled, and he stepped aside. "Basil could not make the spell work for him, and your situation sounded desperate, so…" He sighed. "It had to be done."

Laurence shook his head slowly and followed him, not letting him back off so easily. "And you did it," he said. "Goddess, I'm so proud of you. You have no idea how amazing you are, baby."

"I have *some* idea." Quen's lips twitched. "We have guests," he added. "We should see to their needs, and then speak with Frederick."

Laurence had to admit Quen had a point. The house was overflowing right now, and it couldn't stay this way for long. Mom had to get home and feed Ellie, Jon and Basil would need somewhere better to stay if Ru was going to let Jon help fix his house, and Ru…

Laurence winced faintly.

Ru had to work out where he was going from here, now that his whole life was in tatters, and Laurence had to admit he was worried that this might be where they parted ways.

"Fine," he sighed. "Let's get dressed and go put out the fires."

There was no way everyone he needed to talk to could fit in the living room unless they got really friendly, and since 'really friendly' was not a label Laurence would apply to Quen, Ru, Angela, or Jon, he suggested they take it out to the garden instead. There weren't any complaints, and everyone spread out around or under the parasols. The teens mostly spread across the lawn, the adults occupied chairs, and Martin kept Sebastian and Maria's children entertained indoors with the dogs so that everyone could talk freely.

"Are we gonna light a fire and be emo again?" Soraya asked.

"I mean, if you want?" Laurence leaned forward in his chair and rested his elbows on his knees. "But I thought it was a good idea for everyone to talk about what happened, fill each other in on the gaps, ask questions, and work out what we want to do about it."

Sebastian nodded in agreement. "A debrief is a good idea."

"It's a waste of time," Rufus growled, though he shut up again when Amy squeezed his hand, and Laurence was relieved to see that Ru didn't pull away from her.

"I don't think it is." Laurence watched Ru and tried to find the words for what he wanted to say next. "I feel like everything we've all been through has kind of led to this, like it was... destiny, in some ways."

There was a smattering of protests, especially from the teens.

Laurence raised his hands briefly. "No, hear me out. Ever since my overdose, when I had a whole bunch of visions of my own future, every single one of them came true except the last one. But then that happened too, last night, and..." He sat up slowly, and leaned back in the chair instead, crossing his legs. "I don't know," he mused. "It feels weird. My future is totally unwritten now..." He hesitated, unsure of whether or not to say it, but figured if he was being honest he might as well go all-in. "The last prediction wasn't mine, though. It was Mom's."

Almost everyone turned to look at Myriam, and she rubbed her nose quickly.

"I said that Rufus' goals did not align with Bambi's," Myriam said.

Heads swiveled to Rufus now.

Ru only shrugged. "Prophecy?"

"Tarot reading," Myriam replied.

"Maybe Laurence ends up wanting to move to England and raise little baby assholes or something," Ru concluded.

"Oh, *grandchildren!*" Myriam's eyes lit up with mischief. "There's an idea!"

"No. No, not going there, we're not even married yet, Mom!" Laurence felt the heat rise to his cheeks, and it only worsened when Soraya and Mel pointed at him and whispered to each other. "Anyway, like I was trying to say... I want to take a moment to thank everyone here. Because without all of you, I wouldn't *be* here. I mean, Jon and Basil came all the way from New York at the drop of a hat just to round up some ghosts in case it'd help?" He puffed his cheeks out and shook his head. "Maria and Sebastian uprooted their whole families to come stay here in case some evil asshole they never even knew existed decided to target them? Rodger, Ethan, Aiden, you dropped everything to come over and help out? Like, I can't get over how amazing you all are, and how every single thing that made us cross paths in our lives put us all in the right place, at the right time, to be able to help each other when we needed it most."

"Hey, it's not Thanksgiving *yet*," Ethan laughed.

"But everyone's invited, right?" Mel looked around like she was doing a headcount. "And what about the wedding?"

"Goodness, we don't even have a date," Quentin murmured.

"But of course everyone's invited," Laurence added with a faint smile. "To both." He turned to Ru. "Have you thought about what you want to do with your house?"

"Might as well fix it," Rufus said with another shrug. "Even if I sell it and move somewhere else. I'll stay with Amy until it's structurally sound."

"Makes sense," Laurence agreed. "You taking Jon up on his offer?"

Ru nodded. "Yeah."

"Great. And you guys have figured out how that's gonna work for you?" He turned to Basil and Jon, who were sharing a chair nearby, with Basil perched in Jon's lap and Jon looking like he barely tolerated this arrangement.

"Oh, we'll work it out," Basil said breezily. "I might try and find a job in LA while Jon's down here. Quentin will have to go get our cats soon, before they start eating my books."

Laurence glanced to Quen in time to catch his look of resignation at being voluntold to use magic again, but he didn't protest.

"Amazing." Laurence turned to face Angela. "You *shot* Windsor?"

To her credit, Angela actually winced slightly. "I did not wish for Vincent to get hold of him," she said. "He is too powerful a magical connection to you."

"Uh, okay, well..." Laurence sucked his teeth. "For future reference, he can travel to Otherworld himself if he's delivering a message to Herne."

"Noted." Angela nodded.

"But thanks. Now all I have to do is not get arrested while Freddy sorts out the legal bullshit," Laurence said.

"That could be a while, dear." Myriam pursed her lips. "Michael had to leave shortly before Quentin arrived to collect me this morning. Freddy pushed himself too hard and had a migraine. He may be unavailable for a day or two."

"What *is* this legal bullshit, anyway?" Kim asked.

Laurence drew in a breath and tried to remember when he'd last seen the teens, then — once he had it — decided to start from the top and walk through everything that had happened since Rufus' phone call.

BY THE TIME everyone had had a chance to talk about what they'd done, and filled in all the gaps for each other, the evening had drawn in and the sun began to set over the ocean. Sebastian's wife brought the kids out to watch it go down, and Sebastian and Maria peeled away to go sit with their respective families.

Cops still hadn't invaded his home. Either Freddy had

managed to hire a San Diego lawyer before he'd passed out, or the cops preferred to wait for nightfall to raid the place, but Laurence was way more sanguine about it now. If they came, Quen would deal with it, and Laurence couldn't be bothered to waste time worrying. He *could* check the future, but he also found it weirdly freeing to not know, like the world had finally unlocked itself for him after his overdose, and he wasn't tied to destiny anymore.

No, you're tied to a fucking demon, instead.

That was very much a future Laurence problem. Quentin had taken the Book of Yew from his dad so that Laurence could study it and see if he was able to reverse-engineer the soul binding crap Vincent did to him. Laurence's task was to not die before he worked it out, and since his future finally felt like it was *his* at last, he was growing pretty optimistic about it. And he'd already told Ru that once that problem was fixed, he was happy to aid Ru in the recovery of all his stolen books.

Well, maybe not *all*. Laurence couldn't help but be relieved that the duke now had Ru's anti-telekinesis spell, because knowing that Ru owned it *and* had specifically hidden it away from prying eyes left Laurence weirdly uncomfortable — especially since Ru admitted to crushing on him.

For now, though, the future felt relatively bright, and as Quentin took himself off to retrieve Jon and Basil's cats, as well as return Myriam to the farm, Laurence sat back and watched the sun set, and enjoyed the moment.

QUENTIN

The day after he had found Rufus bleeding from a gash in his stomach while Laurence gutted the warlock who had done it to him, Quentin was finally able to contact Freddy, who furnished him with the contact details of the American lawyer he had hired before he'd overextended himself in his attempt to arm Quentin with as much useful magic as he could.

It was not enough for Quentin to forgive Freddy for all that he had done, but he could at least conceive of a time in the future when — so long as Freddy did not promptly betray them all over again — they might be on more cordial terms.

Whether that would be in time for Freddy to attend the wedding, he could not say.

Quentin had spent much of that day liaising with the lawyer, who seemed quite confident that she could have the warrant for Laurence's arrest quashed without any necessity for Laurence to even appear in court, and since the police car outside their home disappeared that evening, she certainly seemed to be making progress.

It took another two days for her to succeed, by which time Freddy was back on his feet, so Quentin suspected his twin brother had taken rather more direct action. Regardless, it meant that the threat of arrest was over, and Laurence could retrieve his truck from Rufus' driveway at last.

A week later, after Laurence had replaced all of the talismans Harrow had ruined, Windsor materialized in the garden, and Laurence had spent the day spoiling the bird absolutely rotten. Quentin couldn't blame him. He couldn't possibly imagine how traumatic the familiar's loss had been, for either of them.

By the time Thanksgiving arrived, the house was full once more, and Quentin leaned into the noise and the chaos, because it meant that they were alive, for which he was truly grateful. He hadn't understood Thanksgiving before, not really, but now it seemed like a delayed Samhain, and it did everyone the world of good to talk openly about the things — and people — they appreciated the most.

It wasn't until a full month after Harrow's death that the whirlwind finally calmed down, and Quentin had enough quiet to try and process his own feelings at last. He didn't feel ready to speak with Violeta until he had done so, especially as he'd intentionally made sure to be up to his eyeballs on Vicodin during their last appointment, so with the house mostly empty and the Thanksgiving decorations replaced by Christmas ones, he took himself away to sit on the wall at the end of the garden so that he could watch the ocean in peace.

This was a truly stunning part of the world. He had been born almost as far inland as it was possible to get in England, but here he was on the very edge of the ocean, able to reach out and touch it if he so chose. Beneath his feet, a steep and rocky little cliff which water battered at night and day. Further out to sea, on a good day, he could watch dolphins play, or sea lions hunt. In spring and autumn, he even stood a chance of seeing whales on their migration paths, though they were much further out on the horizon; he was more likely to spot the oddly circular patches of clarity their breathing left behind on the surface of the water than the animals themselves. And the scent! There was nothing so invigorating as the tangy, salt breeze, so different from the earthy, frequently manure-laden air of his youth.

He had been so sure that he would not remain long in San Diego.

Now it was his home.

It hadn't truly sunk in until now that he *had* a home. Six years spent bouncing from one city to the next, at first across Europe and then into America, and none of them had been anything more than liminal spaces for him to exist in for a while. He had made barely any friends in that time, lost those he'd thought he once had along the way, and he may well have continued on like that for the rest of his life — presuming that his liver held out.

Instead he had a life. A home. A family.

A fiancé.

A flurry of wings landed to his left, and Quentin dragged himself out of his thoughts to pay attention to Windsor. The bird *looked* all right, but Quentin reached for him all the same, and hefted Windsor into his lap.

Windsor hunkered down in it and cooed happily as Quentin petted his silken feathers.

"How are you?" Quentin murmured, watching Windsor wriggle against his trousers to get comfortable.

Windsor opened his beak and made a flat-pitched purring sound.

Quentin nodded to himself. The poor bird must have had the shock of his life when he'd woken up in Otherworld without any understanding of how it had happened. "Do you wish to talk about it?"

Windsor tipped his head back and forth while he thought it over, then he chattered and clacked his beak, with the occasional caw thrown in for good measure.

Quentin listened, and made small noises at what felt like the most appropriate moments. While Windsor was usually easy enough for him to understand, the familiar seemed to mostly be reassuring himself at the moment, so Quentin gave him the space in which to do so.

After a minute or so, Windsor settled down and gently held Quentin's thumb in his beak, then said, "Laurence."

"Hm?" Quentin raised his head and twisted enough to look

over his shoulder, and — true enough — Laurence had arrived, so Quentin released Windsor, then stood so that he could turn his back on the vista. He jumped off the wall to land lightly on the grass, held out an arm for Windsor to perch on, then crossed the garden to Laurence and met him halfway.

Windsor hopped from Quentin's arm to Laurence's, and Laurence smiled.

"Hey, baby. Sorry I'm late. Traffic." Laurence waited for Windsor to reach his shoulder, then leaned in to kiss Quentin. "What were you doing up there?"

"Oh, we were just watching the ocean," Quentin murmured against Laurence's lips. "And I was appreciating my good fortune."

"Valid. You're a lucky guy." Laurence gave him a sly grin through lowered lashes, then reached around his waist to rest his hands on Quentin's backside. "Almost as lucky as me."

"Almost," Quentin agreed airily.

They laughed together. It came so easily, so agreeably, and Quentin marveled at how he fit so perfectly to this man who was utterly unlike him. There was magic in their differences; the good kind, which healed hearts and joined souls.

Except that Laurence's soul has been bound to a warlock's.

They would fix that. They had to. Quentin would not allow Harrow to drag Laurence down with him into the bed that he had made for himself. Laurence did not belong in it, and if that meant Quentin must apply himself to study for the foreseeable future, so be it. He could not afford to be ruled by his fears.

He'd made a start, and he would push on until Laurence was free.

"You're thinking again," Laurence teased.

"I'll try not to let it become a habit," Quentin said wryly. He began to head for the house, and slipped his arm through Laurence's.

"Sounds fake." Laurence grinned and leaned into him as they walked. "I'm gonna go shower, baby. It's been a *lot* of heavy lifting today, and I'm sweaty. But not in, like, a sexy way."

"You are always sexy," Quentin countered.

"Oh, no, trust me baby, this ain't it." Laurence crinkled his nose as they stepped in to the living room, and he paused to pet the dogs' heads when they sat up. "You wanna join me?"

"Not if you aren't sexy." Quentin sniffed playfully, then petted the dogs himself with a warm smile to Laurence. "Go ahead. I'll feed the girls."

Laurence left him with a light peck on the cheek, and took Windsor away upstairs with him.

Quentin watched him go, then nodded in agreement with Pepper as she wagged her tail. "You're quite right," he murmured. "He *is* wonderful."

HE LED the girls through to the kitchen and fed them by the back door so that they were not under Martin's feet, though the moment the buzzer for the intercom sounded, that was no longer a concern: Martin excused himself from the kitchen to attend to it.

Quentin refilled the girls' water bowls as they ate, washed his hands, and was patting them dry on a hand towel when Martin returned.

"You have a visitor," Martin said. "Your brother. He has agreed to wait in the courtyard."

Quentin arched an eyebrow. "Freddy? Is he alone?"

"My apologies. Your youngest brother," Martin clarified.

Quentin blinked slowly. While he'd thought the idea of Freddy stopping by out of the blue was alarming, he had no idea whatsoever how to think about Nicky doing it.

Nicky is here.

"Good lord," he breathed.

He couldn't come up with anything else to say, and he wasn't sure this wasn't simply Martin's idea of a practical joke, but if Nicky *was* waiting for him...

Quentin bolted into action and all but sprinted for the front door. He wrenched it open and swept out into the white-walled courtyard, which was softly bathed in the washed-out tones of twilight and the warm pathway lights which framed the steps up to the gate.

In the center of it stood a man who Quentin both recognized immediately, and had never seen before. He was tall, solidly built, with familiar sandy-brown hair cut in a neat short back and sides, and he wore dark casual trousers with a wheat-colored polo shirt.

"Nicky." The word fell past Quentin's lips in his shock as he struggled to reconcile this young man with his memories of a thirteen-year-old boy. He slowed as he drew closer, suddenly sharply aware that they hadn't spoken in years, and he searched Nicky's features for any sign that his brother was angry, or upset, or otherwise displeased by Quentin's proximity.

Nicky broke out into a broad, easy smile, and swooped in to wrap his arms around Quentin so tightly that he all but crushed the air out of his lungs. "Icky! Oh my god, look at you! You got old!"

Quentin coughed, partly in alarm at being called *old*, and partly because he could barely bloody breathe, but he returned the hug as firmly as he was able and tried to absorb everything he could about this stranger whom he had loved for thirteen years, and then unceremoniously walked out on. He was easily Freddy's height, with a voice almost as deep, but where Freddy was built like a lock, Nicky had the physique of a winger.

"Good god," Quentin wheezed, and patted Nicky's back to try and get him to ease off a little. "You're made entirely of bricks. What are they feeding you in the RAF?"

Nicky loosened his hold and leaned back, then moved his hands to Quentin's shoulders. "And you're still made of skin and bones," he laughed warmly. "Wow. Six years, eh? Tell me everything, immediately!"

"Everything?" Quentin echoed numbly. He blinked, then added, "Come inside! Have you eaten? Would you like dinner? Are you on leave? What are you doing here? Did Freddy give you the address?"

Nicky laughed again, and gave Quentin's shoulder a friendly punch that was much gentler than it looked like it had any right to be. "Twat," he said fondly. "Freddy said you're getting married!

Married, Icky! I think that means you're the one who has to tell *me* everything first!"

Quentin gazed up at him, thoroughly overwhelmed at how he had no idea who this young man really was, yet holding nothing but a deep, abiding love for him, and he finally managed to let a smile of his own break free.

"That's fair," he chuckled. "Come on, I'll do my utmost to fill you in."

"Gleaming," Nicky said, as though it were some sort of mark of approval.

Quentin turned and headed for the door, and gestured for Nicky to precede him. "After you."

Nicky went ahead and breezed into the house, his head swiveling like a tourist's, and as Quentin followed he almost didn't notice how the faint green glow of Laurence's wards around the doorway flickered and died at Nicky's passing.

Almost.

EPILOGUE

AVALON

Morgan was up a tree when she saw Lyrian approach, so she finished plucking apples and placed them into her basket, then carefully lowered it to the ground with the rope tied around its handle. She tossed the rope down after, to one side so that it wouldn't bruise the fruit, and by the time Lyrian reached the base of Morgan's tree, she was in a much better position to pay attention.

"Morgan," Lyrian said with a bright smile. He was an extraordinarily excitable young man, and it broke Morgan's heart that he'd ever had need of Avalon. "Can I help?"

"I don't doubt it," she said dryly. He hadn't come to the orchard to help her pick apples, though.

There was something in the air. Something she hadn't felt in centuries.

He laughed, and went to go untie the rope from her basket while she carefully lowered herself down the tree trunk.

It wasn't the tallest of trees by any means, but she didn't wish for the inconvenience of a broken leg, and becoming a raven swarm seemed so unnecessary just to travel five feet. By the time her toes touched the earth, Lyrian had coiled the rope over one arm, and held the basket in his hands.

"Thank you," she said as he handed her the apples. "Now, may I be the one to help you, perhaps?"

Lyrian scratched thoughtfully at the front of his robe, then gasped and nodded so quickly that his hair fell into his face and he had to sweep it back with his hand. "Oh, that's right! Emma asked me to give you a message!"

Morgan gazed at him, amused, while she waited for him to deliver it. He would get to it any minute now, she was certain.

"Oh!" He said again, and his cheeks turned red. "Yes. She says there's a man in the village. She's never seen him before, but she doesn't think he's new."

The sense of something in the air grew closer, and Morgan identified it at last.

War.

"Allow me to speculate," she said as her smile faded away. "His speech is not modern."

"That's what Emma said!" And then Lyrian's smile froze in place. "*Can* I help?" he repeated.

"Yes." Morgan passed the basket back to him. "Take these and keep them safe."

Before he could say anything else, she broke apart and took to the mist-laden sky in a hundred winged bodies.

SHE KNEW the form of her own brother so well that it was immediately recognizable at a distance. Everything about him from his armor and tabard to his build and the way he moved was like a long-treasured memory. He was in the center of the village, pontificating as only a Warrior could, and the villagers were arrayed around him in a mixture of polite attention and deep concern that turned to relief when they noticed Morgan's approach.

Morgan drew herself together at the back of the crowd, and walked toward him while her heart raced and her concern slowly grew.

This island was a refuge, a safe haven, and now *he* was here, a danger to them all.

"Arthur," she said as she stopped an arm's length from him. She switched seamlessly to the tongue of their youth, when they had lived in the world as mortals, so that he might understand her. "I thought you to be sleeping."

"Morgan!" Arthur smiled at her, though his eyes were touched with sadness. "Alas, I have awakened."

They both knew what it meant, so Morgan sighed and rested her hand on his chest. "I am sorry."

"It is fate." He rested a gloved hand over hers. "I am needed."

Morgan didn't answer him. Despite their lineage, she had little taste for war, and was never as convinced as he that the world needed it at all. But he had slept at the heart of this island for so long that she had allowed herself to hope he might do it forever.

Her hope had been crushed.

"Where is the Hunter?" Arthur asked her.

Morgan shook her head faintly and centered herself, then withdrew her hand and smiled up at Arthur. "In another world. When the time is right, I will call on him to do what he must."

"And you are certain he will do it?"

Morgan smiled tightly. "He has no choice," she admitted. "He owes me a debt."

Goddess, how she had hoped to never ask he repay it. He could have grown old, died, and moved on, all while believing she had forgotten what he owed her.

Instead, Arthur had returned, which signaled that Britain was in grave peril.

And that meant Bambi was, too.

~ Inheritance **continues in** *Sword of Avalon ~*

ACKNOWLEDGMENTS

Wow. 2023, eh? Phew!

I'm sure *stuff* happened, but mostly for me that stuff revolved around Luna the Wonder Corg. She was diagnosed with degenerative myelopathy fairly early on in the year, and that's not a thing any dog ever recovers from. Much of the year has been dedicated to taking her to her hydrotherapy and physiotherapy sessions, and trying to keep her as active as possible to slow the progression of this disease.

Early in 2024, I got her a wheelchair, which has dramatically improved her quality of life. There's no way of knowing how long she has left, but I'm doing everything I can to keep her comfortable, happy, and mobile. And then, in March, I had another surgery, so I'm sure you can imagine how hectic it's been.

Add to that the deterioration in my eyesight from the cataracts I'm *still* on a waiting list to have treated (and have been since 2019), and it's sure been a time!

Wheel of Fate, therefore, wouldn't have been possible without help and friendship, and my thanks go out to:

- Fofo, without whom I wouldn't have written any of these books. Fofo is the best friend anyone could ask for, and deserves all the best things in life!
- RJ Bayley, the world's greatest narrator (fight me on this), for his incredible patience and kindness while I sail through several deadlines.
- Ed and JuJu Bug, for driving me around when I can't see, and taking care of Luna while I recover from surgery.
- Luna, for being SUCH A GOOD GIRL, YES SHE IS!

- Mum, for helping out with literally everything.
- Turkey, Katie, and Fofo, the beta-reader team of my dreams!
- Katie, for being the best con mum *and* author assistant in the world (fight me on this, too).
- Dute, for the endless streams of both reassurance and science facts!
- Alasdair and Marguerite, for being SUPER COOL EXTRA AWESOME as ever even in the middle of trying to move house.
- Hobo, for being Hobo.
- Everyone in the Discord server!
- And, of course, YOU, for loving this series enough to still be with it! THANK YOU!

Sign up to the newsletter or join the Discord if you haven't already: Fofo and I have a huge *Inheritance* tarot deck project on the way (yes, still, told you it was huge), and you won't want to miss it!

Wheel of Fate was mostly written to music from Teya & Salena. I say 'music', but we all know I mean *Who the Hell is Edgar?* on repeat for six months.

See you in 2025 for Sword of Avalon!

- AK Faulkner, London, April 2024.

ABOUT THE AUTHOR

AK Faulkner is the author of the *Inheritance* series of contemporary fantasy novels, which begins with *Jack of Thorns*. The latest volume, *Wheel of Fate*, was released in 2024.

AK lives just outside of London, England, with a charismatic Corgi and a violent three-legged cat. They don't actually fight crime at all; they *are* the crime.

Join the Discord server:
discoverinheritance.com/discord
Sign up for the *Inheritance* newsletter:
discoverinheritance.com/signup

INHERITANCE

Season One:
Jack of Thorns
Knight of Flames
Lord of Ravens
Reeve of Veils
Page of Tricks
Season Two:
Rites of Winter
Sigils of Spring
Spells of Summer
Runes of Fall
Wheel of Fate

Visit discoverinheritance.com to learn more about the characters and world of Inheritance, and sign up to the newsletter.

Join the Faulknerverse Discord server at discoverinheritance.com/discord.